## OTHER BOOKS BY ROBERT DALEY

FICTION

*Year of the Dragon*
*The Fast One*
*To Kill a Cop*
*Strong Wine Red as Blood*
*A Priest and a Girl*
*Only a Game*
*The Whole Truth*

NONFICTION

*An American Saga*
*Prince of the City*
*Treasure*
*Target Blue*
*A Star in the Family*
*Cars at Speed*
*The World Beneath the City*

TEXT AND PHOTOS

*The Swords of Spain*
*The Cruel Sport*
*The Bizarre World of European Sport*

# ROBERT DALEY

# THE DANGEROUS EDGE

Simon and Schuster
New York

Copyright © 1983 by Riviera productions
All rights reserved
including the right of reproduction
in whole or in part in any form

Published by Simon and Schuster
A Division of Simon & Schuster, Inc.
Simon & Schuster Building
Rockefeller Center
1230 Avenue of the Americas
New York, New York 10020

SIMON AND SCHUSTER and colophon are registered
trademarks of Simon & Schuster, Inc.

Designed by Irving Perkins Associates
Manufactured in the United States of America
10 9 8 7 6 5 4 3 2 1

Library of Congress Cataloging in Publication Data
Daley, Robert.
    The dangerous edge.

    I. Title.
PS3554.A43D3   1983         813'.54         83-579
ISBN 0-671-47057-4

*For*
*Theresa*
*Suzanne*
*Leslie*

*Our interest's on the dangerous edge of things.*
*The honest thief, the tender murderer,*
*The superstitious atheist, demirep*
*That loves and saves her soul in new French books—*
*We watch while these in equilibrium keep*
*The giddy line midway: one step aside,*
*They're classed and done with.*

—ROBERT BROWNING

# PART I

## CHAPTER 1

Lambert, the would-be playwright, the ex–war hero, the expatriate, stepped back to admire his handiwork. Once again it dazzled him. Once again he saw it in terms of drama, one written, produced, directed by and starring himself. His stage setting was this ravaged bank vault and it was perfection. He noted the gaping doors to safes, the piles of wrecked lockboxes, and the refuse on the floor—papers out of the boxes that came up over the insteps of his rubber boots—over all their rubber boots. Costumes and makeup seemed to him equally brilliant. Casting too. The eye doubted nothing. A dozen actors working hard. Bare sweaty torsos. Gloves. Grimy faces.

It was the middle of the third night without sleep and Lambert, being high on triumph, exhaustion and Dexedrine, no longer saw the world clearly. He did know where he was, underneath the Banque de Nice et de la Côte d'Azur, which made him laugh. Just another American making a name for himself on the French Riviera. In his euphoria it seemed to him almost normal to be there. The American

11

century had begun. America having saved the world, owned it. The green passport opened any door, permitted any excess, dominated the European Continent as guns never had, and even bank vaults couldn't stop it.

He glanced around at the characters he had assembled—those he could see, for there were three interconnected strong rooms and he could not see everybody. There were two teams working, six French mobsters brought to Nice from Marseille, and six English-speaking soldiers of fortune who, like himself, had been washed up here when the shooting stopped.

Such casting, in Lambert's opinion, made for great theater. Although some of the actors were identified only by stage names, these were bizarre: St. Jean, Frère Jacques, The Enforcer, Freddie the Jeweler, The Walrus, Henry the Welder. Jean was no saint; he ran stables of hookers from Marseille to Toulon. Freddie was a jeweler and fence, Brother Jacques a loan shark, and The Enforcer just that. Henry, also known as The Torch, was truly a welder by trade, or had been; Lambert understood him to be the foremost hit man and torturer in Marseille, and for weeks had been slightly afraid of him. The Walrus in real life was an ex-wrestler; his mashed face and puffed-up ears proved it. A seventh Frenchman, known as The Pope, watched the bank from an apartment across the street. He played the role of lookout, a walk-on.

The soldier-of-fortune roles had been carefully cast also, though the choice was large. Lambert had chosen only men he knew well, had worked with before and trusted absolutely: two Australians, a Lebanese Arab, a former RAF fighter pilot, and an American Army deserter. The sixth soldier of fortune was Lambert himself, and he had a nickname too: *Le Cerveau*—The Brain.

Curtain going up.

There was no curtain, no audience, no play. Real men had been ravaging the vault all weekend, and the loot was piling up on the tables. Real sweat ran into their eyes and down their backs, for the heat was real too, and it was cooking them. In the close, unventilated vault, body heat alone would have driven the temperature to unsupportable levels, but blowtorches had been operating around the clock too. Safes had become ovens too hot to touch. The air was almost unbreathable. The vault's multiple odors, its stench, its cloying gases, had become oppressive. They were as heavy as horse blankets. One wore them, one could not take them off. Worst was No. 3 strong room, where the communal toilets, employed by twelve men during an entire weekend, were ranged against the massive vault doors: open buckets they had brought in with them plus several silver soup tureens—family heirlooms no doubt—they had discovered in one of the safes. The tureens they had filled up first—"soup's on"—laughing and pissing, as if this compounded the joke of being in the vault in the first place. But the buckets were full now too, and in the superheated air their odor bloomed. The stench of steaming urine, of liquefying feces was now so intense that it had emptied No. 3 of everyone but The Walrus, whose nose was so flat it perhaps no longer worked. Like a prospector working a claim other miners had abandoned, the ex-wrestler went on swinging his pickax into No. 3's safe-deposit boxes. All the other Frenchmen were in No. 1, the soldiers of fortune in No. 2. The two groups had no language in common and did not quite trust each other.

It was The Walrus who now dug into the box containing the pornographic pictures. Behind him ran a table bolted to the floor, and he turned and upended the box. What fell out made no noise—no jewelry, rare coins, or gold bars. Only paper, and paper baffled him. His gloved hand stirred it around and the packet of pictures fell off on to the floor. They were postcard-size, bound with a rubber band, and he bent to pick them up.

Lambert, in the middle strong room, worked a different lode: tall French safes on wheels that lined all the walls, that stood shoulder to shoulder like a regiment of World War I tanks. Lambert's giddiness, his heady contemplation of his "play," came and went. The safes remained there. Every one had to be opened, and he was doing it. He worked beside Roy LeRoy, and it was the hardest work he had ever done. Roy's torch burned circular holes in the doors, after which Lambert used pry bars to force back locking mechanisms that had swelled from the heat and become almost impossible to budge. The sweat ran down Lambert's grimy body and cut white grooves to the skin.

As he worked, he kept an eye on The Walrus through the door. He kept an eye on everyone as best he could. Between spates of euphoria he was as watchful as a museum guard, for this was "his" vault, "his" treasure. It was as if he feared the vandal who might try to desecrate them.

"What have we here?" chortled The Walrus in French, and he shuffled the photos through huge gloved thumbs.

Lambert dropped what he was doing and went in there. He was followed by the American army deserter who went by the alias Roy LeRoy and, after a moment, by the two Australians and the figher pilot. The other Frenchmen remained in No. 1.

"What boobs on this one," giggled The Walrus. "Admirable. Formidable."

"Yeah," said Roy LeRoy, peering over his shoulder, but he did not smile, and he glanced quickly at Lambert.

Lambert took the pictures and examined them.

Scenes lit by flashbulbs. Lots of flesh. Participants in grotesque poses. Jeweled masks and grinning mouths. They were playing to the camera and to each other. In the background stood a row of what could only be called cheerleaders, also masked, also nude.

Scenes from an orgy, Lambert decided. Photos never meant for sale. In most pornography that Lambert had seen, tattooed sailors worked over obvious prostitutes in cheap hotel rooms. But the setting here was somebody's parlor. There were paintings on the walls, and expensive furniture. Also these people were somewhat older. The men looked freshly barbered. You could almost smell the cologne. The women looked as if they had been to the beauty parlor that very day, sitting under dryers. Getting ready. Ready for this.

And they all wore jewelry. Women in necklaces and earrings, and nothing else. Men waving rings, watches and rampant erections. Jewelry like insignias of rank. People willing to shed their clothes and inhibitions, but not their status.

"Prominent local citizens at play," said LeRoy in English.

"Yeah." In better light than here, Lambert decided, it might be possible to recognize faces.

"Those are worth money," added LeRoy.

This idea was about to occur to The Walrus too, and Lambert glanced at him.

"Put them in your pocket," said LeRoy, still in English.

"He said something about me," said The Walrus, and his eyes flicked from Lambert to LeRoy and back again.

"He was admiring your photos," said Lambert. He spoke French because he had a French wife. He was also the only man in the vault whose home base was Nice. He thought of all the others as being more foreign here than himself.

"These I keep," said The Walrus, snatching the photos back. He rammed the packet down into his boot.

"If anybody is keeping those pictures," said LeRoy in English, "we are." He had lifted a sledgehammer off the floor. His muscles had tensed, and he looked eager to swing it. He said to Lambert: "Say the word, and I lay him out."

"He weighs three hundred pounds."

"The hammer don't care how much he weighs."

"Oh, for Christ's sake," said Lambert, "there are five more of them in the other room. Are you going to lay out all five simultaneously?"

The two Australians and the former fighter pilot were poised on the balls of their feet, like men in a barroom. If a drunken quarrel was about to break out they were ready for it. They waited with a kind of glee. After holding all weekend, the coalition was breaking down.

"What did he say?" demanded The Walrus.

Criminals are predators, Lambert realized. He thought this a dramatist's insight, and congratulated himself on it. Every criminal is a free lance. They have no more notion of teamwork than sharks.

"I said something to you," said The Walrus menacingly.

They were incendiary photos and had to be got out of the wrestler's boot. This was clear to Lambert. They must be kept away from Roy LeRoy also, for once outside this vault they would start a conflagration. They would light a trail for the police to follow to Lambert's door. To everybody's door. And he sought the words to prevent this. His French was adequate most times, but when he was tired or rattled it tended to become clumsy.

"He said he wishes to regard again she of the big tits," said Lambert, and he forced a grin that was not successful. Sweat ran down its cracks, so that he both looked and felt like a man crying. "Me too, as a matter of fact."

Mollified, The Walrus handed them over. "How would you like to precipitate yourself on to those boobies there?" he asked, pointing. His ruined face was closer to the photos than Lambert's. "Formidable," he said.

Lambert, after studying the photos, began to disparage them. They were badly lighted, he told The Walrus. They were out of focus. They didn't show much. The women were rather old.

"I was going to give them to Faletta," The Walrus explained. But he began to look doubtful. "He's got a collection."

"My agreement with Faletta was no paper," Lambert added carefully. "Cash, gold bars, unset stones only. We take nothing that can be traced."

It was Lambert who had imposed this restriction. Paper left tracks. Blackmail, he had argued, posed unacceptable risks. Besides, he saw himself as Robin Hood, who did not indulge in it. Faletta, sitting at a table in his bar in Marseille, had merely shrugged. Faletta was a Corsican. Most of French organized crime—the so-called Milieu— was Corsican, and its headquarters was Marseille. Faletta had agreed to provide the financing, the gear and the additional manpower Lambert's scheme required.

"Paper means if it's got writing on it," said The Walrus. "This is dirty pictures. Dirty pictures aren't the same."

"Photos count as paper," Lambert told him. "Faletta will get mad." There were a number of Milieu clans in Marseille. Faletta and his brothers ruled the biggest of them, and had for thirty years.

The Walrus stared lovingly at his photos. He could give them to Faletta or keep them to show cronies. One or several triumphs seemed assured.

"Those are not professional pictures," said Lambert. "Those are amateur pictures. Let us paste them upon the wall." There was a calking tube on the floor. It was there because Lambert in advance had thought of everything, though not this. He grabbed it up. It had been used on the Friday night to seal the seams of the vault doors, as well as all ventilating ducts, so that no escaping smoke or odor or noise could give them away. He pointed it like a gun and squeezed off compound against the wall. Dabs spattered like bullets. Each would hold a photo. "The chances are the people in them are known to the officers of the bank," he said. His voice grew frantic. He began to slap photos on to the dabs. "Let us give the bankers an amusement when they open the vault tomorrow."

The Walrus seemed to like this idea. He did not protest. Instead he started again to giggle, even as Lambert pressed the final photo to the wall. There—the calking tube was empty. As was Lambert.

The Walrus looked proud, like an art collector gazing at his hanging Rembrandts. "It's the first thing they'll see when they come in here," he said in French.

"They'll laugh their heads off," said Roy LeRoy in English. Though he stared covetously at the photos, the sledge was back on the floor against his leg; the crisis was past.

Back in front of the safe he had been opening, Lambert stood blinking. His pry bar and levers hung out of the hole like a dentist's tools protruding from a toothy mouth. He stirred them around. For a moment he could not remember why they were there, or why he was.

In No. 1 Freddie the Jeweler sat at the long center table sorting. He examined each item through a loupe, rejecting more than half as paste, or too hard to fence. Through the door Lambert watched him push pieces contemptuously off on to the floor, where they disappeared into the refuse.

Except for catnaps Freddie had sat at his table all weekend, a small meticulous man who had made his own deal with Faletta: sorting and appraising only. He had worked no blowtorch, swung no hammer. Both groups of men had come to hate him. Lambert too. Despite the stupefying heat he still wore a white shirt, now slightly gray, and a bow tie that had hardly wilted at all.

Forget Freddie, Lambert told himself.

Taking up the walkie-talkie he contacted The Pope. Static was bad and the lookout's reply barely audible. Still no police interest in the bank, The Pope said. A bicycle patrol had just gone by without stopping. The rain, after two days, seemed to be slackening.

Rain. A city built on hills. The bank was in the low part of Nice, only a few blocks back from the Mediterranean. The water would cascade downhill until all of it collected into the final few sewers that emptied into the sea. One of these sewers passed by the bank. It was the sewer they had used to get in here, and their only way out. It would be running high. How high? The Brain had not thought that out in advance either.

The eleven other men in the vault knew nothing about two days of rain. He had not told them.

# CHAPTER 2

Less than two blocks away was a nightclub known as Les Folies. Two empty sightseeing buses marked "Riviera by Night" were parked outside on the Rue Masséna. Rain slid down their sides. Inside the club, hunched over tiny tables, about thirty foreign tourists watched the last of the floor show. A bottle of cheap champagne leaned in a bucket beside each table. The place smelled like the coats of wet dogs.

At the end of the bar sat Commissaire Robert Bellarmine, chief of the Brigade Criminelle, Nice detachment, Sûreté Nationale. He warmed a snifter of Calvados in cupped hands. His fedora was pushed back on his head. He watched the crowd, not the show, and his principal emotion was resentment. He did not like foreigners, resenting their bad taste as much as their money. Although the war had been over more than eight years, France was still on its knees, still dependent on them, and only places like this prospered.

Bellarmine was a tall, sallow man. There were deep creases beside his mouth, which was small, with a black mustache above it. One would guess that he rarely smiled, and that his humor, when it came, would be sardonic. He had been there about twenty minutes, and had watched the end of a trained-dog act, followed by a rather clumsy magician. The dogmaster dated from before the *Anschluss*—only his animals were new—and the clumsy magician was perhaps German, though he claimed to be Dutch. In France the wounds were still open, and an entertainer who admitted he was German could not hope to find work.

Now the spotlight focused on the former pimp who supposedly owned this place, and whose job it was to announce the final act on the bill, which he did in French, English, Italian and German, speaking very fast to get it all in, to the added resentment of Bellarmine. He could save himself the trouble of announcements in French, Bellarmine believed. The French could not afford his prices. And the expense of the dog act and the magician also. Running a nightclub like this was only a different kind of pimping. One pandered to the tastes of foreigners, particularly Americans, who came to see only one thing, the one attraction on view nowhere else in Europe or America this year, the nude dancers. Breasts. They ogled topless French girls, and took it as proof that all Frenchwomen were whores. The girls were not even strippers; they simply danced naked to the waist. There was nothing immoral about it, and it made Bellarmine furious that the foreigners thought there was. He sipped his Calvados carefully, making it last.

"Ladies and gentlemen, I give you the exquisite, the delicious"—there came a fanfare from the musicians, followed by a roll of drums—"Murielle Rettys."

Bellarmine, watching, thought: and out dances Odette, wearing the glamorous name and not much else.

The audience had met Odette earlier. Fully dressed, she had opened

*18*

the show with a song. Later, she had done a Spanish dance with castanets. In between, three other nude dancers had performed. The photos of all four girls could be seen out front, gold stars pasted over their nipples.

Odette whirled out on to the floor. She wore a long flouncy skirt and a kind of filmy shawl that she clasped to her bosom as if feeling the cold. She bowed. When the music started, she straightened up sharply as if harkening to the song of a bird. At once her arms swept back like bat wings, and it was seen that she wore nothing under the shawl. Dropping it behind her, she began to dance.

It made Bellarmine in his dark corner bury his nose in his snifter. The pungent fumes filled his nose, his lungs, his eyes.

"She's quite a dancer." The ex-pimp Jo Lorenzi had materialized beside him at the bar.

Bellarmine lit a Chesterfield. The flame shone on his yellowed fingers. He breathed in smoke.

"Yes, sir, I'm lucky to have her." Lorenzi, a Corsican, was solidly connected to the Marseille Milieu, according to the file on him. Perhaps he owned this place or perhaps he was a front. The police believed the Milieu controlled every night spot on the coast. In France only two businesses were booming, tourism and crime, and sometimes they mixed.

"Not a bad crowd for a rainy night," commented Lorenzi.

Bellarmine peered into his Calvados.

Lorenzi had signaled the barman. To Bellarmine he said: "What are you drinking?"

But Bellarmine went to the door and stepped outside. The rain had stopped. He stood smoking. After a while he flicked the butt into a puddle and went back to the bar.

By then Lorenzi was again in the spotlight. He thanked people for coming. Four languages. He thanked them over and over even as chairs were pushed back and people crowded out past the bar. Bellarmine could hear them climbing into their buses outside. He watched the waiters who had begun piling chairs on top of the tables.

Odette came toward the bar from the dressing room. She wore a red wool dress and a red hat with a single tall feather sticking up out of it, and she carried her cloth coat. Smiling happily, she kissed him on both cheeks.

"I must have been really good tonight, *chéri*. Look at this." In her hand was a fifty-dollar bill. "A tourist gave it to me."

"What did he want in return, if I may ask?"

"He's already gone. He just liked my dancing."

"Your—dancing," said Bellarmine.

"What's that supposed to mean?"

"Let's go." He took his raincoat off the bar stool and went out. Odette followed. Outside he pulled his hat brim down, and they walked along the Rue Masséna. He heard a car go by several streets away. The sidewalk was glistening and wet. Odette held the bill up to the streetlight.

"Fifty dollars American," she said. "More than two weeks' pay."

Police *commissaires* were better paid than nude dancers, but it was a lot of money to Bellarmine too. He said: "Not at the official rate of exchange."

"I like it better when you're amusing, *chéri*. For a moment I thought you were jealous."

Bellarmine was thinking about Americans rich enough to tip Odette fifty dollars—and about Odette who was poor enough to take it. He was thinking about foreigners and their money. He wasn't jealous, he was angry.

There was no sound except their footfalls on the pavement.

"Where are all the *putes?*" Odette asked conversationally.

At this hour there ought to have been a prostitute in every doorway.

"We scooped them all up," Bellarmine said. The black police van—prostitutes called it the salad basket—had come through earlier, preceded by carloads of *flics* in plain clothes. "Most of them, anyway."

Whenever possible, prostitute raids were staged on nights like this, so as not to cost the girls too much business. The Brigade Mondaine depended on the *putes* for bribes. The other brigades, including Bellarmine's, needed them as sources of information. No one wanted them any madder at the police than necessary.

"Then you were out working." Odette sounded disappointed. "I thought you stayed up late to watch me dance."

"I've seen you dance."

His reply annoyed Odette. "I could stand a little support, you know. Being an *artiste* is not so easy." Turning her back on him, she stopped to peer into the darkened window of a dress shop. A single black dress, staked out by pins, occupied the entire window. None of these shops had much stock.

Bellarmine, waiting, thought about the prostitutes. Every one of them belonged to some Milieu *mec*. They were being interrogated now. Tomorrow, after their sanitary inspection, he would talk to some of them himself. *Putes* marched up and down the streets day and night picking up a lot of information which was to them only gossip. In exchange for this gossip, the police allowed them to work. The principal police response to crime was not, had never been, *cherchez la femme*. It was *cherchez la pute*.

"What should I do with my fifty dollars?" Odette had turned from the window.

"Stick it in your bank." Odette's "bank" was her hand douche syringe standing upright on its rubber bulb on a shelf. Inside its nozzle, which was as thick around as a flaccid penis, her tight little roll of savings seemed to her safe.

"You're not in a good mood, are you?"

They had turned off the Rue Masséna into the Place Grimaldi, a square surrounded by big old plane trees. In the center were benches and a play area. On the near edge stood a newspaper kiosk and, next to it, a corrugated-iron *pissoir*. He could hear the water inside still trickling down its walls.

They went upstairs. The building had been there since 1850, and was a walk-up. They lived on the third floor. While Odette pulled out the bed, Bellarmine went to close the shutters. The *pissoir* stood almost directly below the window. Odette's view when she opened the shutters in the morning, or any other time she chose to look out, was of men entering and leaving the *pissoir*, hands busy at their buttons. She sometimes complained about it.

"I want to go to Paris, *chéri*."

Bellarmine had begun to get undressed.

"I want to sing at the Olympia."

The Olympia was the most famous music hall in France. Headliners sang there—Edith Piaf, Maurice Chevalier, a new young star named Yves Montand. The Odettes of this world did not sing there. Odette had a fixed jurisdiction just as he did. Hers was the small clubs of Nice, Juan-les-Pins, St-Tropez.

Odette said: "We could both go. You could get transferred."

He couldn't get transferred. He was a *commissaire*, of which the Sûreté had hundreds. He hung his suit coat and vest in the armoire.

"You could get promoted."

The next rank up was *commissaire principal*. He was thirty-four—too young. He was at the bottom of the advancement table. His *principalat* would come in four to five years. Provided he committed no blunder first, offended no one who could hurt him. The Sûreté was an almost military bureaucracy, sixty-five thousand men.

"Will you at least think about it?"

He went into the kitchen. The apartment had two rooms, main room and kitchen. The toilet was in a closet off the hall, and there was a portable bidet under the kitchen sink. There was no bathroom. One learned to wash at the sink standing up. Once a week one rented a cubicle at the public baths down near the railroad station.

Bellarmine began to brush his teeth. Odette stood in a bathrobe in the doorway watching him gargle. "I have a nice voice."

He looked up at her. "You have nice breasts."

Every day a detective probed beneath the surface of people's imaginings until the hard surface of truth was revealed. Truth was almost always painful. People spent their whole lives ducking it.

Odette waved the fifty-dollar note at him. "How do you explain this? Men like hearing my voice."

"Men like looking at your tits."

"You're a *salaud*, Robert."

Odette was in tears. But it finished the way these arguments always finished: Odette panting and moaning beneath him.

"If I'm going to stay, we should get married."

She had burrowed up against him. He could feel her toes against his shins, her hot breath against his neck.

He did not answer. We are two people who just make the day darker for each other, he thought, and stroked her shoulder. It was past three A.M. and he was desperate for sleep.

# CHAPTER 3

At Lambert's order hammers and torches stopped.

In the vault the sudden silence was like a war zone after a bombardment. It seemed louder than what had gone before. They were all glancing around, as if one could not trust what could not be heard— as if one couldn't trust peace.

They had best leave fast. They would go out under mountaineers' packs, taking only loot, leaving everything else behind to mock the police: their tanks, tools and cables, their remaining food and wine—proof that they had been there. The Brain had planned it this way in advance: mementos of a luxurious weekend at public expense. The *flics* would be livid. As a small boy Lambert had learned that it was a mistake to make authority figures angry, but he would disregard the lesson. He would indulge himself.

The men were tired and the stowing took time, more time than Lambert had allowed. Sweat continued to pour down their bodies. But they were happy. It was almost over now.

The Brain marched Henry the Welder—The Torch—into No. 3 and up to the great vault doors. Henry was holding his breath over the buckets. "I should be used to the smell of shit," he said pleasantly. "When you garrote a guy he almost always lets go into his pants. Stinks just like this." He laughed. "Did I ever tell you about the time—"

"Yeah." Lambert had heard most of the stories Henry was so fond of telling about himself, and believed them. It had amused Henry during the occupation to assassinate Germans—which skill had opened up a whole new career for him afterward.

"Weld the door shut," Lambert told him.

"What for? It's a time lock. It can't open until it's time."

This was the final detail of The Brain's grand plan. "Suppose today it can't open at all?"

The Torch was about forty, of medium height and heavily muscled. His broad flat face had an almost Oriental cast to it. Green eyes spotted with flecks of yellow. Now he grinned, disclosing bad teeth. "I get it. An extra day's start on the *flics*." He pulled his visor down and set to work.

The tunnel entrance was in No. 1, high up on the outside wall. Crouched under their packs, the men waited for Lambert's signal. Though they had not believed in him at the beginning they were all disciples now, and they waited for the word.

With the exception of Freddie the Jeweler, who carried only a satchel of jewels, they were carrying up to a hundred pounds per man. Most of this weight was gold. The boxes had contained hundreds of gold ingots, thousands of gold coins, a dozen or more gold dinner services. The French were gold hoarders, always had been, for only gold was proof against invasion, occupation, inflation, devaluation,

23

war—all the recurring natural disasters of Europe. But even gold wasn't proof against The Brain, who now sent his men up the ladder one by one.

As Lambert waited his turn he decided he wanted to leave some message for the authorities to find. Something to make them madder. He could scrawl it on the wall. A message to the director of the bank? Or a message to the cops? Should it be a signature or a curtain line? He was not sure.

Lambert picked up a blowtorch and ignited it. This flame was his pen, he would burn his words into history, and he waited for them to occur to him.

*"Merci, monsieur le directeur."*

Not good enough.

*"Interesting work in pleasant surroundings."*

A possibility, but he discarded it. Moving to the wall, he adjusted his flame and printed out the words:

"LA COMÉDIE HUMAINE CONTINUE."

He stepped back and studied what he had written. Probably the most famous line he would ever write. It seemed to him both profound and hysterically funny. It would do. He was satisfied. It was a line guaranteed to increase the size of tomorrow's headlines, thereby increasing the pressure on the police to find him and lock him up, but he did not care. He laughed. The police would mobilize every resource. He still did not care.

The last of the men had climbed the ladder and disappeared into the hole. Lambert, imagining himself alone in the vault, prepared to say goodbye to it.

However he was not alone. Unknown to him, The Walrus had decided to leave a signature behind also, and several minutes previously had dropped back into No. 3 strong room to prepare it. While Lambert was composing prose with a blowtorch, The Walrus was systematically and carefully tossing the contents of the latrine buckets and soup tureens on to the paper that littered the floors—peoples' stocks and bonds, their insurance policies and marriage certificates, their love letters, the titles to their houses—showing contempt for all they stood for, after which he was just as carefully wading and stomping through the stew he had made, stirring the gravy, turning it into glue.

Lambert smelled this before he heard it, the acidic perfume, the wafting fecal gusts, and he rushed in there.

The Walrus was enjoying himself. His mashed face wore a beatific grin.

"What are you doing?" demanded Lambert.

"We had to wade in shit to get in here," explained the Walrus. "It's their turn now." He had a soup tureen in each glove and before Lambert could speak he sloshed the contents right and left. His boots plastered it down.

For months it had pleased Lambert to imagine the awed faces of the bank officials and police who would enter this vault after he had left it. He had imagined their admiration for him, their profound respect for the incredible—well—theater of it. And so to see what The Walrus was doing sickened him. He had wanted reverence. He would not get it. Men would step through the vault doors holding their noses. The desecration he had feared had indeed been committed. The museum guard had not been vigilant enough. A mindless vandal had besmirched the only perfect work of art that Lambert had so far conceived—might ever conceive.

Lambert said carefully: "It's your turn on the ladder."

"I haven't finished yet."

"You've done enough. They'll get your idea."

The Walrus conceded. Still grinning hugely, he went forward, while Lambert stood there. He felt stunned, as if from a blow. The Walrus' work, like his own, was irreversible. There was nothing he could do.

In No. 1 strong room he shouldered the final pack, switched off the lights and began to climb.

The tunnel was about twenty feet long, well buttressed, a work of art in itself, safe as a mine. He crawled along it. When he came out into the sewer he was hit by a column of cold air which, however fetid in actual fact, smelled amazingly pure and fresh, and he stepped down into the fast-flowing current and went forward. The sewer here was an oval-shaped culvert only about four feet high. Bent nearly double, and with his pack sometimes scraping the ceiling, and his face only a few inches above the water, he moved along under the Rue Deloye. Crouched like a skier he followed his miner's light. He had two city blocks to go before the culvert got any bigger. The muck swirled past his boots, the frigid wind bathed him, the strain on his thighs was enormous, and he worried like conquistadores leaving Mexico, like conquerors leaving many places probably, about being drowned under the weight of his plunder.

25

Ahead he could perceive the lights of the others; they were not moving, and he guessed before he got there that the Rue Chauvain sewer, the major trunk line, must be in flood.

It was. Roy LeRoy was standing down in it. The flow was up to his crotch, flooding past him. He was clutching a pipe. It was all he could do to hang on.

The men were fanned out on a ledge and Freddie the Jeweler had begun to whimper. "We'll be drowned like rats."

In English Roy called up to Lambert: "We can't wade through it carrying these heavy packs. We'll all go under."

In their exhaustion the men had become panicky. It was not so much fear that paralyzed them, Lambert saw, as the conflict between fear and greed. The only way out, it seemed, was to abandon the loot they had worked so hard for.

But Lambert spoke soothingly in English, then in French. He explained how they would rig a lifeline. Someone had to go back to the bank for a rope. When there were no volunteers, Lambert wriggled out of his pack and went himself. He was listening to his own thunderous applause. It gave him a boundless energy, a feeling of enormous confidence.

When he returned he assigned jobs to the strongest-willed among them. Roy LeRoy carried the lifeline downstream. As the current propelled Roy along, Henry the Torch reeled him out. But LeRoy was fighting to keep his feet, and the others watched the dim, jerking light on his hat.

The Jeweler whimpered: "You're going to leave me here to drown."

The lights from the hats seemed to burn Lambert's cheeks. He was caught in multiple spotlights as if on stage. They were looking for leadership, and he gave it. They would move down the lifeline two men to a pack, he ordered, two trips per man. His own hat jerked light from face to face. "Loop your arms through the armholes," he said. "Hold on to the rope with both hands."

Rigging the lifeline had consumed much too much time. Outside it would soon be dawn. Men and packs started down the sewer. When the Jeweler refused to move, The Walrus slung him over his shoulder and carried him out. Henry the Torch and Lambert shouldered the last pack and followed.

The sewer's flood debouched into the underground Paillon River. It spewed them out. The river, moving at saner speeds, calmly received them. They climbed up on to its banks and threw themselves down

26

on the stones, to lie with chests heaving, only momentarily safe. The Paillon had been roofed over years ago, and here ran under the bus station, under the municipal casino, under the public gardens. Its bed was enormously wide, but the river itself ran down a narrow center channel. The men lay on their backs in total darkness except for the feeble glow thrown off by their hats. Above was the underside of the city. It was about two stories up and the light did not carry that far, but Lambert thought he could hear noises up there. Outside it must be daylight now, or nearly. The leader's job was to lead. He forced his men to their feet. He was as exhausted as they, but could not let it show.

Their vehicles, two vans and a jeep, waited upriver parked just under the edge of the crust. They had driven in as far as they dared. The riverbed was made up principally of round, shifting stones as unstable as the stony beach in front of the city. Now they trudged along, slipping and cursing under their packs, making a good deal of noise. Their eyes were on their feet. Their heads drooped. Lambert, glancing up, could make out vague car shapes ahead, shapes that hardened too quickly as daylight increased behind them. He did not see the *clochard* until it was too late.

The man wore rags. He must have been there since last night— must have crawled in under the crust to sleep. It was their noise that woke him, their exhausted, carelessly loud approach. He had been sleeping against the archway that supported the last of the crust. Rising to his feet, he decided he wished to converse with these men, and he stumbled toward them. He appeared to be only half awake and in a semistupor. Perhaps he was still drunk. He came forward asking for a match to light the half-smoked butt in his hand. Had he known who they were he might have asked for their autographs. All he really wanted was a little companionship.

He had just converted himself from a *clochard* to a witness.

There was a moment of stupefaction during which no one reacted. Then Roy LeRoy, who happened to be closest, slipped out of his pack, grasped the two arm loops in one hand, and swung the pack with great force into the man's upper body.

He said "Ooof" and went over backward without even bending at the waist, then slid and rolled down the embankment into the shallow water. As the derelict's face came up spitting, LeRoy jumped down the embankment into the water and planted his left foot on the man's throat, pinning him to the bottom. Current swirled past both Roy's

27

shins, higher on one than on the other. The *clochard* was visible through planes of water, his features distorted by terror and by eddies.

"He would have told the world about us," said LeRoy to Lambert. His tone was conversational.

"Yes."

"Need a hand?" asked Henry the Torch in French.

"They would have made a big hero out of him," said Roy LeRoy. His pose was awkward.

"Yes."

The man's knees had risen up out of the water. He began to kick.

"Let me give you a hand," said The Torch in French, and he stepped down into the water. Bending, he pushed on the derelict's knees, straightening them out.

The water was fast-moving and very clear. Lambert looked down through it at great staring eyes and twitching feet. Surprise is as immobilizing as fear. Surprise and fear are the same. This crime he had concocted was being lifted up into a wholly new category and he was powerless to stop it.

The other men had crowded around, leaning down from the embankment. The Brain's brain seemed to have stopped working. Decisions raced around inside his head, and stayed there.

Reaching down into the water, LeRoy grasped a scruff of clothing and dragged the corpse up the embankment. "We don't want the cops to find him."

Lambert said: "No."

"They got the guillotine in France," said LeRoy. "Unless you want to end up with your head under your arm."

"No."

Henry the Torch had dropped to his knees. He was strangling the corpse with his hands to make sure. Lambert could not take his eyes off this outrageous scene. It seemed to him that he could not move, could not even speak.

"Get a rock," said The Torch as he worked. "Bash his face in so they don't know who he is."

Lambert found his voice. "No," he said.

"That does it, don't you think?" said The Torch. The *clochard* had been murdered twice, and The Torch stood up looking satisfied.

Discussions began. They were conducted in whispers by the French in French, while the soldiers of fortune gazed off in different directions. St. Jean, the whoremaster, wanted to drag the derelict back into the sewer and stuff him behind a pipe for the rats. The Torch agreed. The soldiers of fortune offered no suggestions. In an hour or two they would be out of the country, never to return. The problem did not concern them.

But Lambert would stay in Nice. It concerned him, therefore, very much. He had begun reasoning again. Sooner or later the corpse would be found, and laid on them, he said. Therefore they would have to drive him out of here and dump him somewhere else. He glanced around, but no one would meet his eyes.

"I'm not driving through Nice with no stiff in the back of the car," said The Torch.

Lambert saw he would have to do it himself. "Load him in the jeep," he said.

"You're crazy," said Roy LeRoy. But there was grudging admiration in his tone which Lambert saw and was pleased by. The role of hero again seemed congenial. He watched LeRoy and The Torch lift their victim into the jeep. They pulled a tarpaulin over it.

Under the crust the light was brightening fast. They were far behind schedule. The first vanload of men and loot drove out, followed five minutes later by the second. Lambert smoked a Lucky Strike all the way down, then climbed into the jeep, engaged both gear levers, and drove upriver. He came out into low slanting sunlight. The jeep lurched and slid. His hips jerked in compensation. Down in the trench of the river he felt like a man driving under the battlements of an enemy fortress. At any moment a sentry might appear on the ramparts and peer down.

About a mile upriver he drove up the dirt exit ramp, bounded across the sidewalk and down into the Avenue Gallieni where he joined traffic heading back the way he had come. This traffic was mostly bicycles, and therefore silent. He drove among groups of men in black trousers, pedaling in ankle clips, probably barmen and concierges moving toward their jobs in the great hotels that faced the Mediterranean. At seven the breakfast calls would start to come down.

As Lambert crossed tram tracks, the corpse behind him shifted position as if alive. The jeep had been stolen by one of the Milieu gang in Marseille several days ago. Lambert had no papers for it. If he were stopped, he thought, he would not need any papers.

At this hour the sun threw enormously long shadows. Fingers of light clawed down side streets. He came to the Place Masséna and crossed it. The street now was the swank Avenue de Verdun, jewelry

29

and antique shops, art galleries, banks. At the Ruhl Hotel he turned on to the Promenade des Anglais. The Mediterranean was on his left, and its early breeze caught the lumpy tarpaulin, making it flap. He could hear the sea too, as it washed repeatedly over the empty stone beaches.

The Promenade being virtually empty of cars, he increased speed, and soon Nice was behind him. Now villas dotted the pale-green hillsides. He began yawning. It's crazy to drive around with this corpse he told himself. I should get rid of it right away. But there was other work to do first.

When he came to the Var River he turned away from the sea, drove ten kilometers due north, then turned up into the hills toward a certain villa. He pulled up to its wrought-iron gates and had to get out to open them. Driving the jeep inside, he parked it beside vans and cars. He went into the villa and into the main room where the others were waiting.

The room was dark. Some of the windows were open but the shutters in front of them remained shut. A breeze blew through, and dim electric lights burned. The twelve other men—The Pope was there too—sat on boxes or on the floor. They had formed a circle and while waiting for Lambert had been drinking champagne. The packs lay in the center of the circle. Lambert came into the room and joined the circle without speaking. Someone handed him a champagne glass.

The Pope proposed a toast, and they all drank.

The borrowed villa was almost empty of furniture. Henry the Torch had found it. During the weeks of digging the tunnel, the Milieu group had camped out here. Lambert's men had lived in a furnished apartment he had procured. Roy LeRoy had lived on his boat, and Lambert had lived at home.

The contents of the packs were dumped out onto the floor. The mood was cordial, and the split into two equal parts took less than twenty minutes. The Jeweler had a scale for weighing the gold, and he had made a rough appraisal of each piece of jewelry, which was accepted without comment by both sides. The cash was easier to deal with. The dollars, pounds, francs, marks, and lire were simply split down the middle: one half to each team. Some haggling then ensued. Lambert's men wanted to sell their share of the jewels. The Pope, speaking for the Marseille group, agreed to buy. He named a figure. He was about fifty and had a Parisian accent. Lambert imagined him a man of some education—a disbarred lawyer perhaps.

In English Roy LeRoy said to Lambert: "Tell him it's worth more."
But Lambert was too tired, and refused. "Pack of crooks," muttered
LeRoy.

Lambert and his men retired to an adjacent room where the money
and gold were further subdivided into six equal shares. Lambert, who
might have demanded more, wanted nothing extra for himself.

"That's a surprise," said one of the Australians.

LeRoy said: "You don't know this man like I know him. He don't
care about money." He slapped Lambert on the back.

They returned to the other room, each man dragging his own
sack. Lambert himself had two, one for currency, one for gold. It was
time to leave. The men from Marseille, looking deliriously happy,
had jumped to their feet. One by one they began embracing Lambert,
Roy LeRoy, the fighter pilot, the Arab, the two Australians. There
was much kissing on both cheeks. As Lambert and his men filed out
into the driveway, the Milieu group stood at the door waving goodbye.

Outside, the soldiers of fortune said their own goodbyes. They
shook hands all around. It was over. They had shared the bank job,
a kind of world championship of adventures. They had shared other
adventures previously, but most likely most would never meet again.

When the other four had piled into one of the vans and driven
away, Lambert and LeRoy still stood on the gravel.

"What will you do?" LeRoy asked.

Lambert was peering under the jeep's tarpaulin. He knew it was
too late now to get the corpse on to a boat. "Take him up into the
hills and dump him into a ravine." After a moment he pointed to the
sack of gold at his feet. "Sell this for me, will you?"

"Sure. Not to worry." LeRoy used his war-surplus PT boat for
smuggling cigarettes from Tangier to the Riviera. He would be in
Tangier by tomorrow, he said, and he heaved the sack onto the floor
of his car beside his own.

Lambert drove the jeep farther up into the mountains. He owned
a two-hundred-year-old stone farmhouse above a village thirty miles
north of Nice. It was quite high up. There were terraces below it that
were all overgrown. It had been in ruins, and he had bought it cheap.
He had put in a bathroom and rebuilt the roof. Perhaps now that he
had money, he would restore the rest of it. The road climbed higher,
passing through a number of old stone villages still huddling behind
walls erected against the dangers of an earlier age. Finally Lambert
could see his own house isolated on its hillside across the valley.

His wife had perhaps spent yesterday, Sunday, in the house. Possibly she was still there. He was conscious of the grotesque burdens in the rear of the jeep, money and death, and he did not wish to meet her. Continuing up past the house, he drove into an orchard hidden from the road and made his way on foot down through a forest of cork oaks toward the rear of his house. Was she there or not? He peered through the bedroom window looking for her. The shutters were closed, but he found a gap. The bed was empty, though unmade. The kitchen was empty too. He found her in the bathroom taking a shower. The small window, though slightly ajar, was otherwise steamed up. He could not see her, but he could hear the water pounding. There was a gas hot-water heater on the wall above the sink, and he could hear it pounding too. It pounded with the same noise the blowtorches had made cutting open the safes.

Water and gas heater stopped almost simultaneously. Then the shower curtain parted, and he waited for her to step out. He waited for a look at the naked body of Jacqueline Lambert, née Bourgelet, aged twenty-eight, his wife.

A leg came out through the curtain first, and he found he was excited. He waited to see the rest of her step out on to the mat.

She did so, and reached for a towel. Water dripped off skin smooth as a seal's. She was tall, big breasted for a Frenchwoman, with a trim, narrow waist and long legs. Her hair was plastered to her skull. She dried it, fluffing it up. The towel moved her breasts around, further arousing Lambert. He was exhausted and still full of drugs, and still in danger also, and his wife's nakedness seemed to him the most erotic thing he had ever seen. As the towel moved between her legs, his arousal only increased. Pulses throbbed in his temples, in his groin. His heart beat still faster. He felt himself switch from Peeping Tom to sexual deviate. The one was harmless, but the second craved violent release from such tension, and was not harmless. He wanted to break in on her. On his own wife. He understood how these things happened. His urge was to throw her on the unmade bed, to rape her. If she resisted, then he would kill her.

Naked and unaware, his wife moved alone in her private world, while her husband's heart pumped and his legs tingled.

She stepped into underpants, then bent to hook on a bra. Lambert's breath slowed, and presently he climbed back up into the forest and hid in the trees. A little later he watched her come out on to the road and stand waiting for the bus. When it came she flagged it down and climbed on board. It had produce and bundles lashed to the roof, and he watched until it reappeared, descending the switchbacks on the other side of the valley. His wife kept a small perfume shop on the Rue Masséna in the center of Nice. It had been her mother's, and he saw that she would open it a little later than usual this morning. It was almost as if, sensing he was nearby, Jacqueline had waited for him.

He drove the jeep across the cobblestone yard and into the shed behind the house. He left the sack of cash in the back beside the corpse. He removed his boots beside the back door and went inside. On the floor of the closet in the hall stood a cardboard box that served as a laundry hamper. He stripped and dropped his filthy clothing in on top of what was there. This reawakened the bank odors, the sewer odors, and he stood over the box sniffing them, smiling, vividly aware of his past three days and nights.

At last he padded naked into the bathroom, which was still steamy and moist from its previous occupant. He stepped into the shower, turned on the water, and as the mud and sweat washed off his body he remembered each detail of the bank job. He was like a businessman taking inventory of his stock. He was like a teen-ager reviewing his first sexual intercourse, the most beautiful act of his life so far— at any rate the most amazing. The water poured down on him. They had broken open the first safes—so far so good. The loot had begun piling up on the tables—the dream ended there. Lambert, exhausted, was coming down off his extended high. The water relaxed his muscles but increased his dismay. Although he had more money now than any playwright, this meant nothing to him. To an artist, only artistic perfection counted, and as depression set in he could see none. Less than half the safe-deposit boxes had been opened, and his play was full of bad jokes as well; pornographic pictures calked to the wall, human excrement tramped into documents on the floor. And the end was rout—a terrified retreat through the sewers, a senseless murder, a corpse still to be got rid of.

Although the world was willing to forgive a great artist all excesses, the failed artist was treated, usually, like a criminal. To society the one was as irresponsible and therefore as contemptible as the other. Lambert's disappointment was immense. This crime would not bring him fame, as he had hoped. He would be considered a common thief. Standing in the shower he began to cry. He cried his heart out. The tears ran down his face.

A little later, stepping out on to the floor, he dried himself off—

33

tears first, then the rest. He fell asleep naked, sprawled diagonally across the big bed.

Outside under the shed with the patience of a horse that has returned from a hanging, the jeep waited.

# CHAPTER 4

Sunlight exploded into dark corners of the city. It pierced the shutters of Bellarmine's bedroom, waking him up. It hung upon his wall like a row of white spears, and he lay there blinking. At the Banque de Nice et de la Côte d'Azur the sun struck the plate-glass window and seemed to shatter into pieces. It rebounded off glittering desktops, off people's eyeglasses, it sent a shaft of illumination down the stairs onto the backs of the three bank officers who waited for the timing mechanism to begin to open the great vault doors. At Villefranche harbor, five miles away, where Roy LeRoy stood on the deck of his PT boat, the sun came up off the water and slapped him in the face. It left his cheek feeling red and hot. It made him turn his head. In the mountains, even Lambert was awakened by it. He had slept an hour. His hysteria had passed. He got up, stared out at the dappled trees, and in his mind began to correct the events of the past weekend as if correcting a play. Presently, having made certain decisions, he began to dress.

Bellarmine shaved at the kitchen sink. He chose to shave in cold water because the gas hot-water heater made too much noise. Odette was still asleep and he wanted to keep her that way.

But she woke up anyway.

"We should get married."

Dressed and ready to go, he stood over the bed. "You like not being married. It's very exciting to you."

True. In a country as solidly bourgeois as France, irregular liaisons were permitted to very few categories of people: to criminals, of course, who had no good name to lose, and to policemen, who had

34

none to lose either; and all entertainers, especially *artistes* such as Odette. On these categories and one or two others the public had been unable to impose its will. All other Frenchmen and Frenchwomen were obliged to be, or at least appear to be, respectable. The world saw France as a permissive place. The world was wrong. The entire nation had adopted the bourgeois morality of a small town.

"Or else I want to go to Paris."

"But you don't have any contacts in Paris. I have to go to work now."

He put his hat on. Though a sunny morning, it was February, and in winter a hatless man did not look or feel dressed. He carried his raincoat—the only coat he owned—over his arm.

"Will you come home for lunch?" Odette said. He usually did. In France everything closed from twelve to two, including police stations.

"I'll have to see."

"Well I won't be here," she shouted.

He tugged down the brim of his hat. Her voice followed him down the hall, shrieking. "I'll be in Paris."

He went out and down the staircase.

At 9 A.M. precisely a series of rumbles could be heard from inside the vault door. It was like gas noises inside a stomach, and it brought a half smile to the face of Jules Monot the bank's *directeur général*. But he erased it quickly—the bank business was no laughing matter to him—and nodded to the assistant managers who flanked him, each of whom inserted a long, flat key into the doors. At a further signal from Monot the keys were given half a turn each, which caused additional interior bolts to retract. This was the high point of Monot's day. In a moment the tabernacle door would open and he would stand once again in the presence of the holy of holies. Monot's religion was money. These moments, each morning's celebration, were sacred to him, and no employee was permitted to deviate from the ritual that he had ordained.

The opening of the vault, the actual act, he reserved for himself. Now he grasped the large handle. Now he turned it to a horizontal position. Now he tugged gently. The two doors weighed five tons each, and each morning glided open at his merest touch.

But today there was no response to Monot's pressure and he tugged harder.

A puzzled frown. He jerked the handle several times, then instructed

35

the two assistant managers to re-engage the locking mechanisms, withdraw their keys, and step back. He wiped his brow. They would start again.

It didn't work; the door remained stuck. Monot couldn't believe it.

On the staircase behind him other assistant managers waited for working capital for the tellers' cages. Behind them Monot perceived customers. On Mondays there were always early birds.

"Please wait upstairs," cried Monot petulantly.

The ritual was ruined. Again and again the flat keys slid into the vault doors and were turned. All three men listened to the satisfying noises. But the vault did not open.

From his own office Monot phoned Fichet-Bauche, the firm that had built and installed the vault before World War I: their vault was stuck, he cried into the phone, send a crew to open it. He instructed his tellers to clear the bank of customers, and to pull the shades down over the plate-glass window. The bank would remain closed until the mechanics had opened the vault.

Bellarmine ate breakfast a block from his flat at the Café Prado at the corner of the Rue Halévy. He sat at a small wrought-iron table with a marble top. He dunked a croissant into his café au lait and munched it and read the *Nice Matin*. The young Queen of England, he saw, was at sea with her husband on her yacht. And there was a new film, dubbed in French of course, starring Marilyn Monroe, who was described as the Rita Hayworth of the Korean War.

Up at the bar, already drinking wine, stood a row of laborers. They would be drunk by noon. And the room was already full of smoke. Off in a corner a few old men were already playing dominoes; Bellarmine could hear the pieces clacking on the marble.

In Pakistan followers of the Aga Khan had paid him his yearly stipend yesterday, his weight—101 kilos—in platinum. Fat old bastard. In Egypt, now being run by General Naguib, the government had begun auctioning off the jewels and art collection left behind by the deposed King Farouk.

An accompanying photo showed Farouk in the street in Monte Carlo—gross, fat, a sexual deviate by all reports. He was followed everywhere by colleagues of Bellarmine's, which was very expensive in police manpower. Nonetheless, someone would probably kill him before long, which would be no loss to anyone.

The stirring croissant moved the saucer slightly, so that it scraped on the marble.

In Moscow secret police chief Beria had fallen, and in Washington the fall of Senator McCarthy seemed to have begun.

French readers were fascinated by foreign people, foreign problems right now—possibly, Bellarmine speculated, because their own seemed to them insoluble. French industry was operating at 50 percent capacity or less. One out of every two Frenchmen earned less than twenty-seven thousand francs per month—less than the minimum wage. The average Frenchman could afford a pair of shoes only every two years. Meanwhile, French taxes were being pumped into the Indochina war, where the generals were promising that the Communist guerrillas, who were killing French boys in hordes, would shortly be suppressed, and in Paris the government was crumbling once again. Since 1945, premiers and governments had changed every few months, not one of them stable or able to get France moving again. France survived because America continued to pump money into the French economy. The figure in today's headline was $11 billion over eight years.

The article concluded with a note that brought a sardonic smile to Bellarmine's mouth—France was better off than Italy, where 324,000 people still lived in caves.

He dug into his pack of Chesterfields—the first of three packs each day—and lit up. Forget the Italians, who to him had never been anything but pitiable. France was not Italy, nor Africa nor India. It was, or at least had been, the most civilized country in the world. He had believed in France. In the war he had risked his life for her, not once but many times. But his devotion seemed misplaced. His country had proved not worth saving. He saw no sign of French pride, saw only people who craved American dollars, and thus the American presence. The French had become entertainers of tourists. Like lapdogs they would sit up and smile upon request. There were more Americans on the streets of Nice every week, every day, many of them so rich they had brought their transport with them, fat, insolent cars that exactly matched their fat, insolent faces, and all over France it was the same.

Bellarmine walked up the Rue Masséna to his bus stop. It was going to be a mild midwinter day. The doors to the shops were open. People were sweeping out their shops. He passed a wineshop, a *charcuterie*. He passed through the wine and cheese aromas they sent out onto the street. He passed a bakery, and the hot breath of the ovens came out the door at him in gusts. He passed a modiste shop—ladies' hats in fantastic colors and shapes—this quarter catered to tourists,

37

and the hats in the windows were so expensive almost no French-woman could afford them. Still, women had to have hats, and he did not know how they managed. Then came a window displaying a single fur coat. Perhaps a tourist would buy it. And receive a discount for paying in dollars.

When he came to Jacqueline Lambert's perfume shop Bellarmine stopped and peered in at her through the glass. She was whisking a feather duster along the shelves. He did not know her name, had never spoken to her. He had simply noticed her a few months ago. She was oblivious of him. He watched the way her body moved. She was about the same age as Odette, but taller. He wondered if her breasts could match Odette's. She had a fine thin nose, and her eyes seemed very alive, very intelligent.

He wondered too if she could match Odette's singing voice. That wouldn't be hard.

He turned away from the glass as his bus came. He jumped up onto the crowded rear platform, showed his police card, and pushed forward to grasp a strap.

Roy LeRoy pointed his PT boat out of the marina called the Darse at Villefranche. The Arab who worked for him sat at the prow facing forward, legs crossed, the breeze in his kinky hair. The sacks from the Banque de Nice were stuffed under the bunk in LeRoy's cabin below, the door was locked and the key was in his pocket. Although he had been awake three full days, he felt clearheaded and alert, and he steered with great care. The harbor channel was narrow, scarcely wider here than the PT boat's beam. The Darse had been built for pleasure boats. They were tied up gunwale to gunwale on both sides of the channel, so that he passed between two rows of prows, and the PT boat, though basically only a monstrous speedboat, dwarfed them all. It was more than sixty feet long, and fifteen feet at the beam. It was powered by three 12-cylinder Packard engines, ran on aviation fuel when he could get it, and could touch fifty knots flat out on a smooth sea.

Right now the boat was inching along. LeRoy's only risk was ramming something and being unable to clear the harbor. The channel followed the curve of the seawall, and he had to be extremely careful. There were people out on some of the decks. Yachtsmen were always friendly, and when they waved to him, LeRoy waved back. To do otherwise was to cause comment. He was not interested this morning in causing comment. Everyone knew his was a smuggler's boat—what else could it be? But he never brought contraband in here. When customs agents came by he invited them on board and poured out whiskey. He sent them away with cartons of Philip Morris. He spoke to them in broken French and they thought him a very droll fellow. If one signaled him now to stop for questioning, he intended to wave and keep going.

When the lighthouse at the end of the seawall at last passed to starboard, LeRoy swung the helm, fired the other two engines and headed straight out into the Mediterranean. The PT boat jumped forward with a lurch that nearly threw the Arab over the side. LeRoy laughed raucously. The sea was still virtually flat. The PT boat broke it into shards. The sun bounced up as if off a million knife blades.

In an hour the PT boat would be well outside the thirty-mile limit patrolled by French customs cutters, and LeRoy would be safe. He was safe already. Cutters were slow. On the Mediterranean on a day like this a PT boat could run away from any vessel ever built.

Swinging the wheel to starboard, he set a course for Tangier, about one thousand sea miles ahead, a free port where any contraband could be bought or sold, no questions asked. It was a dangerous place. It was full of dangerous people working dangerous deals. To LeRoy it was a good place, his kind of town.

The PT boat skimmed across the water. It bounded from swell to swell with a series of slaps that resounded like pistol shots. LeRoy's eyes were squinted nearly shut against the wind.

The mechanics from Fichet-Bauche had worked the same flat keys, had listened with stethoscopes to the interior mechanism. They shook their heads. They said the doors must be stuck.

"I know that," shouted Monot.

They said that the doors were impregnable. If the mechanism had malfunctioned, this could be repaired only from the inside. They requested permission to open a hole in the wall with drills. They would drill a large circle through twelve inches of reinforced concrete. Directeur Général Monot, looking about to cry, fled upstairs and let them do it.

Lambert at the wheel of the jeep steered higher up into the mountains. The road climbed beside a river down in the bottom of a gorge; the mountains rose up in steep slabs to both sides, and Lambert could not see the tops of them. The road was a ledge cut into live rock. Below it the river was noisy and in flood, and the surface of the road was damp wherever the spray came up. Down in the gorge it was dark and cold and there were many tunnels. Inside the tunnels it was dark night, headlights shone on wet rock, and drops of icy water splashed down on Lambert's shoulders and skull. The drops drummed on the tarpaulin that covered the back of the jeep.

The road came out into a high valley with peaks all around. Ahead was the village of St. Martin-Vésubie: rooftops that huddled inside a wall, a jutting church steeple. Lambert was sixty-five kilometers from Nice, with still farther to drive, and he had begun to tire. A café au lait would keep him going, he decided, and he resolved to stop in the village.

At this hour on a Monday morning he had supposed that its streets would be empty; to stop would be safe enough. Instead he found that a market was in progress. There were stalls of produce blocking the entrance to the village, and a gendarme stood at the crossroad directing traffic. He motioned Lambert into a slot between two pickup trucks.

Lambert parked, hesitated a moment, then got out of the jeep. As he stood beside it he studied the contours of the tarpaulin covering the rear compartment. If you knew it was a body, you could tell. Would it attract the gendarme's attention? This is crazy, he told himself. But awareness of his danger was as pleasing as sexual titillation. The gendarme was about ten feet away and seemed to be watching him. If he came over it would mean the guillotine.

There was a tingling sensation in Lambert's hands. It moved up into his forearms. All the hairs were standing up. He felt marvelously alive, and he strolled past the gendarme and away from the jeep.

The streets became narrow, steep and empty. The mountain air was cold and damp. In his excitement he was having trouble catching his breath. He came out on to a three-sided square and walked to the edge of it. He looked down on still another mountain torrent, then gazed out at mountains piled one atop the other. The sun was in his face and it was very bright.

A number of cafés rimmed the square. Lambert sat down outside at an iron table, and a waiter came out and took his order. While waiting, he breathed in great lungfuls of cold, clear air, but his heart kept pumping hard and his excitement level did not diminish.

After finishing his coffee he strolled back the way he had come. The streets were steep, and as he walked uphill the walking pulled at the muscles of his calves.

He came out through mounds of vegetables, through hanging fowls, hanging rabbits. The gendarme was in the same place.

"*Ça va, chef?*" Lambert said to him as he passed—another moment of intense excitement.

"*Ça va,*" answered the harried gendarme, and once Lambert had started the jeep, he halted traffic so Lambert could back it out of its slot. Lambert saluted him in parting, and the gendarme saluted back.

The road out of the village was straight and flat between two rows of great old plane trees. At the end came the bridge over the river and the road narrowed and started up toward the Col St. Martin. The switchbacks began. The pass was sixteen kilometers distant. The road climbed steeply all the way, and the switchbacks never stopped.

When he reached the pass he saw that the road ahead was blocked with snow. It had not been cleared. It led on toward Italy a few kilometers away; in summer the frontier was open. The rest of the year it was snowed in.

Lambert turned off the ignition and got out of the jeep. The sun off the snow was blinding. He stood listening. There were banks of snow on both sides of the road. It was cold up here. His sweater felt thin. He had gloves on and he pulled the scarf tighter around his neck. He listened in all directions but could hear nothing except the wind, and he walked over and peered up the side road that climbed to the new ski station called La Colmiane. The station operated weekends only. It was not a village. There were just a few lifts—not even a restaurant. The road surface coming down was clear except for blots of ice where the sun on the embankments had caused melted snow to run. After a few feet the water had quickly congealed again.

Lambert decided not to continue up to the ski station. There could be a solitary skier up there, or workmen fixing one of the lifts—you never knew. He was not a fool.

Moving to the rear of the jeep he loosened the covering. After peering in under it, he straightened up and listened carefully once again.

Satisfied, he threw back the tarpaulin, which folded with a sudden crackle. The *clochard* lay faceup and Lambert grasped him by his rope belt and hair, lifted him out, and stood him upright beside the jeep. He was stiff, of course, and very light, undernourished for years and years probably. His eyes were open. He looked surprised, or perhaps only offended, and Lambert felt sorry for him.

This was the moment of greatest danger and Lambert prolonged it, stepping back to light a cigarette. He savored the cigarette and the risk together. He studied the derelict and at the same time absolved himself of blame in his murder. Death itself was not new to Lambert. He was not a squeamish man. A few years ago he had marched through fields in which corpses lay on the ground as casually as hay bales, and as numerous. He realized that, under the law, he was guilty of this murder. The law would call it a natural outgrowth of his crime, and therefore willed by him in advance. But he did not accept this verdict. He had willed no such thing. He had simply been unable to stop Roy LeRoy in time. The Torch strangling the guy was meaningless. Lambert understood LeRoy's action perfectly well. It had been forced upon them all, and in a sense Lambert was glad it had happened, as it got them out of a tight spot. He simply rejected any responsibility for it.

Just then he either heard a vehicle grinding up toward the pass or only thought he did. Dancing the *clochard* close to the embankment, he gave a great heave and chucked him over. It was like heaving a golf bag up onto a flatbed truck, except that there was no platform for the *clochard* to land on. Lambert heard him bounce several times, and a cloud of snow rose up, and when he climbed up on top of the embankment, he noted that the corpse had disappeared. He studied the scene carefully. From his feet the wall of mountain plunged almost straight down. A small avalanche had been started. He watched until all the loose snow had stopped tumbling. There—it was over, and nothing showed. Good. The job was done. Lambert jumped down off the embankment, got back into his jeep and started downhill toward Nice.

There was no vehicle coming up to meet him: his moment of terror had been due to imagination only. The road was clear as far as St. Martin-Vésubie, and this time he skirted the village and did not stop. By then he was in a rage. He had begun to contemplate the guillotine, surely the most grotesque method of execution any country had yet devised, and he was furious at his colleagues for having abandoned him to such a threat—to this morning's too-rich emotion. The images that filled his head were overly vivid. One cannot really imagine being gassed or electrocuted or hanged, but one can feel the heavy blade on the nape of one's neck, and one can hear one's head drop into the basket. It wasn't fair that they had left him to risk this all by himself. He believed in his lucky star: nothing bad could happen to him. Nonetheless, his luck could run out someday, if he kept pushing it this way.

Nor was the risk entirely over even now, and as his mood cooled he came to certain other decisions centered principally on an idea, a plan that had come to him—a way of taking out a kind of anti-guillotine insurance policy. It was a good plan, strong on many levels. It required him to commit further deviltry in the bank, and this pleased him. It was even a way to pay off his colleagues for leaving him the corpse. It would put him one up on them.

All this time he was coming down out of the mountains. It took him about ninety minutes. He drove the jeep into the streets of Nice, parked in front of the railroad station, and got out.

There was a suitcase in the back that had shared space with the corpse. Lambert carried it inside the station. Behind him he had left the key in the jeep's ignition. With luck some kid would steal it and abandon it somewhere else—the idea of a twice-stolen jeep made him snicker. He walked the length of the station, exited by the far door and engaged a taxi at the taxi stand. He ordered himself driven to the Ruhl Hotel, and there he was shown to a room on the sixth floor overlooking the Promenade des Anglais and the Mediterranean. He was in it only long enough to admire the view and to get some things out of his suitcase. He was careful to hand around money both entering and leaving the hotel.

He stepped across the Promenade through the traffic, descended the stone staircase to the beach and headed toward the mouth of the Paillon. He was wearing gray slacks, a gray-striped tie, a blue V-necked sweater, and sunglasses. He looked like a prosperous tourist out for a stroll along the beach. He moved carefully over the shifting stones, a duffel bag bunched up under his arm, and when he had walked a little distance, confident that he was alone and unobserved, he sat down, withdrew rubber boots from the duffel bag, and tugged them on over his shoes.

He entered the Paillon from the beach, and took the short brisk walk upstream to where the sewer debouched. He climbed into it. The itinerary now was as familiar to him as city streets. As he had hoped, the water level had dropped way down and barely covered his insteps. He waded along, carrying nothing except the empty duffel bag and a hand flashlight. When he came to the tunnel they had dug, he dived in and crawled along into the vault.

All this time the bank's own safecrackers were working. As the first drill bit pierced the vault wall, Lambert was standing inside No. 3 strong room. The point of the bit came probing and whirring into the

43

room like a dentist's drill inside a too-big cavity, and he moved up close to it. He thrust his pelvis out like a matador defying the point of the horn. To be in that spot at that moment was to risk a goring one more time and it gave him an emotion akin to glee. A shout of triumph rose to his throat, and he barely restrained it in time.

Then he got down to the business he had come for—the insurance policy—the collecting of papers and documents off the floor, the most valuable ones he could find, stuff that, if worse came to worse, he might trade in exchange for his head.

But he went to the pornographic pictures first. He shined his flashlight on them. He wanted them down because they marred his work of art and because, if he could identify the faces, they might be worth whatever price he cared to put on them. The calking compound had still not set. The photos came off the wall leaving the paste behind.

For the rest he filled the duffel bag with whatever looked both choice and unsoiled by The Walrus. The public documents—house titles, canceled checks, marriage certificates—he cast aside. What seemed personal, and especially what seemed secret, went into the duffel bag. He took papers out of each strong room, and in Nos. 1 and 2 did not have to be careful. When the bag was full he climbed back up into the tunnel and waded swiftly down the sewer for the last time. As he came out into the sunlight and on to the stony beach he looked himself over. There were a few mud stains at his knees and on his hands. He brushed his trousers off—what was left would not be noticed—and then bent down and washed his hands in the sea. There was no one in sight except a man walking a dog far down the beach. He removed his rubber boots and built a cairn of stones over them close to the seawall. He was leaving clues all over the place—the boots, a jeep, a corpse—but none, he was confident, could be linked to the bank job, or to the man, The Brain, who had planned it.

Slinging the duffel bag over his shoulder he hiked in shoes over the pebbles and stones toward the Ruhl, and the staircase from the beach up on to the Promenade des Anglais. He was smiling, and felt very good indeed. The duffel bag bumped him in the rump as he walked.

The rape of the Banque de Nice was complete.

# PART
## II

# CHAPTER
## 5

Detectives worked out of the *commissariat* on the Rue Gioffredo. So did the uniformed *flics* who patrolled that part of the city. The two roles were separate. Uniformed men could not be promoted to detective rank, nor detectives broken to uniform. Normally detectives—they were called *inspecteurs* here—came straight from civil life after passing competitive examinations. Uniformed men wore kepis. From their white leather belts hung white leather holsters covered by flaps, each containing the regulation small caliber automatic. They also carried white nightsticks. To detectives they were known as "guardians of the peace" or else, somewhat contemptuously, as "white batons."

The *commissariat*, a five-story walk-up, dated from the middle of the last century. There was a wide marble staircase whose oak banister was supported by wrought-iron risers. The oak had been worn smooth by hands, and the risers were rickety. The marble steps were cracked and stained and, in the center, eroded to sharpness by a hundred years of shoes.

The place smelled like police stations all over the world: the doubtful perfume of a house inhabited solely by men, and never properly cleaned. In the air hung an indefinable essence of cheerlessness and gloom. Nothing was new, cared for or recently painted. This was a place dedicated to sordid events, to momentary violent emotion, to weeks and years of boredom and routine. There was never enough money. The building's telephones had no dials and worked through an archaic switchboard. Detectives could wait all day for a call to go through. In the washrooms there were sinks streaked gray, and hot-water taps from which nothing ran or had ever run.

Bellarmine's office was in the back on the fourth floor. The room was small. A pair of grimy French windows looked out on the court-yard, onto orange tile roofs, people's kitchens, permanent hanging wash. The desk was piled high with files and papers relating to ongoing cases, which were called *affaires*. Two straight chairs, a coat-tree. To one wall was pinned a street plan of Nice, population 250,000, fifth- or sixth-biggest city in France. On another hung several items: a photo that showed Bellarmine shaking hands with government dignitaries after a celebrated arrest he had made in Paris, single-handedly, several years ago, plus some framed press clippings from the same case. The headlines carried the criminal's name, Ange Vinceleoni, known as The Angel of Death, not Bellarmine's. During his career, The Angel had shot down two bank tellers, the driver of a postal truck, a detective, and two gendarmes who had stopped him at a roadblock. He was news, not the man who caught him. Bellarmine was a lowly *inspecteur* then, one of six assigned full time to find The Angel. He should never have gone after him alone.

The Angel, after killing the gendarmes, had holed up somewhere in Paris, according to informants who also said the Milieu considered him a liability and had disavowed him; word had gone out that, although he was not to be given up to the police, he was not to be helped.

The Angel would have to get help somewhere, Bellarmine had reasoned, and after studying his dossier, and also those of criminals he was known to have associated with over the years, he reasoned further that The Angel might try to make contact with a certain prostitute he had once lived with. There seemed to be no one else to whom he could turn.

The prostitute had been in jail for the past four months on a charge of criminal receiving, but The Angel probably didn't know this, and

Bellarmine requested permission to stake out the building in which she had lived.

Permission was denied by the *commissaire* in charge, a man named Sapodin, who was Bellarmine's present chief here in Nice as well. The Sûreté was too short on manpower to indulge such farfetched ideas, he said. Surveillance probably would have to be conducted from the street from a parked car, and the Sûreté was short on cars also. It had none to spare.

The Angel was the most wanted fugitive in France, and therefore, Bellarmine reasoned, would not dare show himself by day. He would come in the night, when Bellarmine was off duty and might, if he wished, be waiting for him.

He went and looked the building over. It was on a poor street in a working-class neighborhood in the 18th Arrondissement. Dating from about 1830 or before, it was five stories high, four or five apartments per floor. It had a single common toilet in the courtyard. Surveillance could be conducted from this toilet, which had a wooden door. There was a crack in the door. From inside one could see out. The Angel, if he came, would have to cross in front of the toilet to reach the stairs.

From nightfall until nearly midnight the toilet—the courtyard too— was always busy as people prepared to go to bed. Meaning that The Angel would not come, if he came, until midnight or later. This would permit Bellarmine a few hours' sleep each evening. The plan was feasible. By seven A.M., when the toilet and courtyard would become busy again, he could leave and go to work.

He decided to conduct the surveillance. He decided to devote a week to it. There was no light inside the toilet; he could not read. There was no bowl to sit down on, just a basin set into the floor with two cleated footrests and a hole in the center. His excitement came and went. Sometimes he thought The Angel would appear any minute, and his heart would thump. Sometimes he was sure he would never come. Sometimes people hammered on the door wanting to get in; he would pull the flush and step out, averting his face. As soon as the toilet was vacant he would lock himself back in it again. It was wintertime and by the middle of each night he stood half frozen. His back got stiff, his knees hurt, his feet were icy cold. He was averaging three or four hours' sleep per day and at headquarters sometimes nodded off over his reports. The week passed, and The Angel did not come.

However, he had been sighted one day in the 5th Arrondissement

47

across the city. Someone answering his description broke into a ground-floor apartment, stole food and a maid's handbag, and escaped on a bicycle.

He's desperate, Bellarmine reasoned, and forced himself to devote a second week to his surveillance.

The Angel came on the ninth day, but not through the courtyard, not past the toilet in which Bellarmine, standing up, shivered and dozed. He broke open a door at the side of the building and went up the service stairs. He went up to the fifth floor and knocked on what had been the prostitute's door, softly at first, then more loudly, and with increasing rage. When he tried to shoulder the door down, he woke the entire floor. People began shouting "Stop, thief!" and then "Police, help, police!" He pulled out both his guns, but instead of using them he ran.

Bellarmine, having leaped out of the toilet, did not know what was happening or even, at first, where the noise was coming from. He had his gun out. It was nearly seven A.M. but still dark. In the courtyard burned a single low-watt bulb.

The Angel came down the main stairs two at a time. As he crossed the courtyard Bellarmine threw a shoulder block into him, but he was a big man coming at speed, and Bellarmine went down, not The Angel. Then The Angel was out on the street where he leaped onto a bicycle. Bellarmine was in the street too, running after him, shouting "Police. Stop that man." He put his gun in his pocket to be able to run faster.

He chased him into the Boulevard Barbès. The buses had begun running. A bus crowded with working people had just pulled away from the curb. It was gaining speed. The Angel was pedaling hard. He was abreast of the back platform and he attempted to transfer from the moving bike to the moving bus.

"Make room," he shouted. "The police are trying to nail me for no license plate on my bike."

He grabbed the handrails and attempted to force his way up onto the already overcrowded platform. But there was no space for him, a detective or someone was chasing him, and he had not boarded at an approved bus stop, and so the ticket taker planted a foot in his stomach and pushed hard. The Angel went flying off the bus into the void. He struck the pavement and lay there half stunned, and then Bellarmine was on top of him, wrestling his hands behind his back and into handcuffs.

Now Bellarmine in his office turned away from the clippings on the wall. He had given due credit to the *commissaire* in charge, Sapodin, and this was in all the news reports. The stakeout in the prostitute's courtyard had been Sapodin's idea, he had told everyone. With the result that Sapodin was now a *divisionnaire* and in charge of the Nice Sûreté detachment. Bellarmine himself had been sent almost immediately to the FBI Academy in Virginia for four months. Sapodin arranged it, a display of fine French cynicism, no doubt, for it kept Bellarmine from elucidating on the affair in any interviews that might have followed with government ministers or the press. Bellarmine's own promotions had come no faster than if he had never made the celebrated arrest.

Well, he thought, he did ask for me when he got the job here.

The top half of Bellarmine's door was frosted glass, somewhat loose in its frame, on which knuckles now knocked.

"*Entrez.*"

It was Commissaire Lussac, the new young chief of the Brigade Mondaine, the vice squad. Lussac, twenty-four, had been appointed to the Sûreté with *commissaire* rank straight out of law school. He had been commissioned, assigned to Nice and handed vice, and begun to learn his job. He had never yet stood for nine nights in a courtyard toilet. He came in bearing an armload of file folders.

"Ah, Lussac, the prostitute specialist." To Bellarmine a law license did not make a man a detective. "And how are operations on the gallantry front?"

"Fourteen folders," said Lussac, and dropped them on the desk.

Most *inspecteurs* and *inspecteurs principal*, lacking sufficient education, would never make *commissaire*. In France, and this included the police, education was esteemed in and of itself, not because it was useful, or could be transformed into something useful, but as if, like a chunk of gold, you could buy something with it right away. Law graduates like Lussac started their police careers as *commissaires*.

Still seated, Bellarmine rested his palm on the dossiers. These were the so-called judicial dossiers on the fourteen whores Lussac's men had arrested the previous night. They were fat dossiers. Each arrest of each girl would be noted. Attached would be handwritten reports of what she had said during each interrogation, and she would have been made to sign each one. Cross-references would relate to any pimps or known hoodlums she may have mentioned or was known to consort with.

49

"Should I bother reading them?" asked Bellarmine in the same mocking tone.

Lussac's resentment showed on his face. The older man both noted this and ignored it.

"There's a girl known as The Stinger—"

Bellarmine cut him off. "Who has a remarkable susceptibility to gonorrhea. Every time the doctors examine her she has a fresh dose."

Lussac, wanting to be liked, offered a smile. "By the time she's thirty she'll be immune to penicillin."

"Single-handedly she'll launch a mutant strain of clap upon the world," said Bellarmine. But he did not smile back. "What about her?"

The Stinger when interrogated had mentioned that a big coup was being planned for Nice.

"A coup?" said Bellarmine sharply. "A postal truck? One of the hotels?" The sacking of the Banque de Nice would not be discovered for another six hours. The idea of it never entered his head.

The Stinger was repeating gossip and had no details, Lussac said. She was very young, only twenty, and easy to talk to. She had her information from her girl friend, an older prostitute who was also being held. Lussac had interrogated this woman too. She was a harder type and had told him nothing.

"I'll talk to them," stated Bellarmine.

"I talked to them myself."

"I'll talk to them," Bellarmine repeated.

It made the younger man quite angry. "When?"

For maximum cooperation he would do it tonight, just before he went home. This seemed soon enough. The girls would imagine themselves about to miss still another night's work. They'd be eager to talk just to get back on the street. But he did not owe Lussac this explanation. He did not owe him any explanation at all. He said, "Leave them in the dryer the rest of the day. That will be all, Lussac."

The young *commissaire* turned and wrenched open Bellarmine's door. He slammed it behind him so hard that the frosted glass rattled in its frame. Behind his desk Bellarmine shrugged.

In the afternoon he headed over to the Palace of Justice to present several routine *affaires* to a *juge d'instruction* named Henri Fayot. But as he walked he mulled over a possible case that was not routine at all, and that was perhaps better off forgotten. He came out into the square in front of the palace. It served as a parking lot for official cars, and some chauffeurs stood in small groups smoking.

He stopped and lit up himself. He bought his Chesterfields on the black market—no one could afford to pay what they cost in the state-controlled tobacco shops—and he was into his second pack of the day. He was trying to decide if he dared ask Fayot for permission to meddle in an affair that did not really concern him. It had to do with the two casinos. Apparently, politicians and lawyers were involved. It was not a good case for a policeman who valued his career. What would Fayot's reaction be? He might refuse to hear anything about it. He might choose to denounce Bellarmine to Sûreté superiors or to the potential subjects of the investigation and this would probably enhance Fayot's career at the same time that it ruined Bellarmine's.

But perhaps instead Fayot would accord him the official sanction he needed, and this might make both of them, ultimately, heroes. Provided of course that, ultimately, he broke the case. An informant had come to him with some startling disclosures. But suppose he succeeded only in stirring up the mud?

The Palace of Justice, which resembled a colonnaded Greek temple, sat atop a high pyramid of steps. He took in another lungful of smoke.

Did he or did he not dare to mention the casino case to Fayot?

It was time for his appointment. He threw the butt into the gutter and crossed the square.

As he entered Fayot's office, he glanced at his watch: 3:14 exactly. A detail. It did not seem to him particularly significant, but the even tenor of his life had about ten minutes more to run. At the Banque de Nice et de la Côte d'Azur the mechanics had at last broken through the vault wall. They were enlarging their hole, which was already the size of a man's head. They had not so much as glanced inside yet, but soon would.

Fayot was one of ten *juges d'instruction* assigned to the Nice courts. He came around the desk fingers foremost. *"Monsieur le Commissaire, ça va?"*

A small, pompous young man. About thirty. Gray suit. Black shoes that gleamed. Bow tie. Pale-blue eyes, broad nose underlined by a black mustache. A solid middle-class background. After law school, three years of magistrates' school, and assigned to Nice. A career as a high government functionary. Not much money but enormous respect. A career that would end, perhaps, with his appointment to a seat on the highest court. No, thought Bellarmine, you can't trust a man like this with secret evidence against politicians.

They shook hands. Or rather, Fayot, having offered his fingertips, quickly withdrew them. He gestured toward two leather armchairs

51

and they sat down and chatted. So far, Fayot was pretending they were equals, which they were not. They sat under a magnificent crystal chandelier. This big, ornate office had been built during a more gracious age: parquet floor, marble fireplace, walnut woodwork, drapes.

It seemed almost the office of a prince, and to Bellarmine this was fitting. These *juges d'instruction* were the princes of the judicial system. They were sometimes called the most powerful men in France. No major investigation—they were called *"instructions"* in French— could be opened or closed except by authority of a *juge d'instruction*. Policemen such as Bellarmine worked directly for whichever *juge* was charged with each case. The *juge* took sworn testimony from witnesses, from the police, from prisoners awaiting trial, who were required, in effect, to give testimony against themselves. He took down hearsay testimony and it was not excluded. Prior arrests and/or convictions became part of the new case record and heavily influenced his decisions. The dossiers of the case he would later hand over to the prosecutor for presentation in court, but all pretrial decisions were his alone. He alone decided whether to indict or not indict suspects, and could base this on very little evidence, almost none; the *instruction* was secret by law throughout. He could order suspects thrown in jail at once, no matter how flimsy the evidence against them, and leave them there awaiting trial sometimes for years. The law gave him much latitude; he was supposed always to listen to the dictates of his conscience. Of course his decisions could be appealed, but the process was long and slow. And he himself, once appointed to the magistrature, could not be removed from office.

Juge Fayot frowned and glanced at his wristwatch, and they got down to business. They began to discuss the case folders Bellarmine had brought with him.

"Anything else?" Fayot asked when they had finished.

Briefly Bellarmine reconsidered his possible casino case. Without warrants, which only a *juge d'instruction* could supply, he could not go forward. But it would be madness to mention it to a man like this. Bellarmine, the man who had collared The Angel of Death bare-handed, did not dare do it.

"No, nothing else," he said.

"Well then—" said Fayot, rising to his feet, hand outstretched.

The phones on Fayot's desk began to ring. There was also a commotion in the hall. Across the city the mechanics had just peered through the hole into the vault, had viewed the devastation inside, and the news had now reached the Palace of Justice.

"We'll take my car," said Fayot to Bellarmine.

They went down the stairs running.


The anteroom of the vault was already crowded with policemen. More kept arriving. The hole was still being enlarged, and the air was white with dust.

Although it was not yet Bellarmine's case, he took it over. Chasing all the uniformed men and most of the others up into the bank proper, he thrust his head and one arm into the vault. The stench that wafted up over his face momentarily stunned him. His flashlight beam swept around, and in a few seconds he withdrew.

When the ragged hole was big enough, he sent the smallest of his detectives slithering through in his underwear, then passed his gun in to him, for the thieves might still be in the vault.

"It's difficult to feel brave with no pants on," the detective muttered from inside. But after a moment he turned and moved forward, and Bellarmine watched hairy legs that leaped carefully from cover to cover. It was like watching the legs of an ostrich. The detective's gun seemed to belong to a different creature entirely.

The vault being empty, the detective began to call out all that he found—the tunnel, the message burned into the wall, the spot-welds.

"Spot-welds?"

Bellarmine ordered hammer and chisel handed in to him, then listened to the muffled ringing blows as the welds were knocked off. "Voilà," called the detective. "Try it now."

And so the vault doors opened at last. The splendid ruins stood revealed, the Taj Mahal of crime scenes. Bellarmine glanced around him. Men stood with mouths agape, as if staring into some fabulous whorehouse. They wanted to get closer, to touch everything. But no one could enter until the experts from judicial identity had completed their work.

The murmur of voices had begun. At Bellarmine's elbow Fayot said: "Look at those safes."

Fayot said: "They certainly left a lot of gear behind."

Fayot said: "Those poor safe-deposit holders."

Fayot said: "Why did they stomp shit into all the papers?"

"To show their contempt for society, perhaps," Bellarmine muttered.

Although Fayot seemed dazzled, Bellarmine was not. He was

53

revolted. From where he stood he could read the message on the wall: "LA COMÉDIE HUMAINE CONTINUE." His eye kept returning to it, rereading it. To the press and the world it would sound, he believed, funny. It would turn the looters into gentlemen and their crime into a prank. Though their message was profoundly arrogant in nature, and profoundly antisocial as well, the world would, most likely, laugh. The newspapers would never print what this room smelled like, not wanting to ruin a good story, nor mourn the anguish of the victims. The world would ignore the truth of the crime—Bellarmine saw it as an attack against private property, against the fabric of society itself—and celebrate it instead as a technical marvel, which it appeared to be, and as a monumental joke, which it was not. The world would applaud the ingenuity of whoever planned it, and the perseverance and audacity of those who had carried it out.

The evil that had been perpetrated here would be completely overlooked, Bellarmine believed. He was having a policeman's reaction. A feeling of helpless rage welled up in his chest.

Technicians from judicial identity arrived. The public prosecutor came, together with many of the important police officials of the city, including Commissaire Divisionnaire Sapodin, fat, bald and sixty, the highest-ranking policeman in the city. He wore his usual Homburg, and in his buttonhole his usual red boutonniere. Most of these men nodded, patted Bellarmine on the back, and quickly left the bank. Only Sapodin seemed to realize how big this case was, or would become. "Keep me informed, Bellarmine," he warned. "Not like The Angel of Death case, eh?"

All this time, Bellarmine kept his eye on the bemused Fayot, for he wanted the case, and Fayot could give it to him or not as he chose.

It was not certain Fayot would assign the case to anyone right away. Perhaps he would prefer to wait a few days, give any political pressures a chance to develop. If so, then the case would surely go to the Brigade Mobile out of Marseille or to the Office for the Repression of Grand Banditisme out of Paris. It would probably go to these units anyway later, as the leads spread out. Bellarmine's only chance was to get in at the start—meaning immediately.

"Brilliant," murmured the *juge d'instruction*. He shook his head with admiration. "This crime is brilliant."

This infuriated Bellarmine, but he forced the reaction down. He wanted this case. He had not had a really big arrest since Ange Vinceleoni; that had been long ago and, it seemed to him now, a fluke.

"Genius is not predictable. They're out in front of you."

"Geniuses are men who change the world," said Bellarmine, voicing an idea out of his childhood. Once childhood had ended a man never again fully trusted such ideas, but he remained in the grip of them always.

"The only one who can deal with genius is another genius," said Fayot.

Bellarmine reached out his hand toward the vault. "Men like this are not geniuses. Please—"

Fayot said; "I've spoken to the prosecutor. He has ordered me to open an *instruction* in this case. And I'm confiding the case to you. I've just signed a *commission rogatoire* in your name. Here—"

The official paper Fayot handed over made Bellarmine legally responsible for the case. It ordered him to "have the courtesy to proceed with an investigation in view of identifying the author or authors of the break-in at the Banque de Nice this date, to determine the circumstances and the motives, to interview all useful witnesses, to proceed with all searches, seizures, confrontations and requisitions useful to the manifestation of the truth."

It was a paper that conferred extremely broad powers on the police officer to whom it was issued. In effect it was an open search warrant, and an open arrest warrant too. It was up to Bellarmine to determine which places he wished to search, including people's domiciles, and which people he wished to arrest, all on his own authority, and if he chose to abuse these powers, the victims would have little recourse against him.

Bellarmine put the *commission rogatoire* in his pocket. The men who had perpetrated this outrage were common criminals and he would catch them. He had the case. He had what he wanted.

Something to live for.

# CHAPTER
## 6

Most shops on the Rue Masséna remained open until 8 P.M. Business was not good and shopkeepers had learned to keep long hours. Jacqueline Lambert's shop was still open, and she was trying to sell flacons of Joy, the most expensive perfume in her stock, to two middle-aged American ladies, her last customers of the day. She was selling hard. Their tour was going on to Rome in the morning. It was now or never. She spoke in ounces and in dollars. She knew the names in English of all the ingredients, and the two women imagined she spoke English fluently, which she did not.

The first words Jacqueline Lambert ever spoke in English were "Choo-choo-choo baby"—a line, or part of a line, from one of the catchiest songs of the day. She was a doctor's daughter, eighteen at the time and attending a dance organized by the American Red Cross in the Palais de la Méditerranée, normally a casino. Nice had been liberated about two months before, fierce combat continued farther north, and the city swarmed with soldiers soon to return to the front, most of them not much older than Jacqueline. It swarmed with prostitutes too, who were carefully screened out of Red Cross dances, as was, in theory, all alcohol—the bar served only soft drinks and tea. The Red Cross's purpose was to introduce clean-cut American boys to "nice" young French girls, to offer them, as it were, alternative entertainment.

Such social subtleties were lost on most of the girls. They were lost on the excited Jacqueline, who wore her hair up on top of her head, making her look older, she hoped. She wore dark-red lipstick, the fashion that year, and rayon stockings that had been mended many times, and her best dress, indeed her only nice dress. She sat beside her girl friend on straight-backed chairs against the wall. About two hundred other girls sat on similar chairs around the perimeter of the room, all wearing their best dresses, their best smiles, while twice that many bareheaded soldiers in olive-drab uniforms milled about the center of the room. One of them approached her. He wore a crew-cut that showed most of his white scalp. His overseas cap was stuffed under one of his epaulets and hung down over his breast like a foulard. He had a smooth, scrubbed, very young face.

"Would you care to dance," he said in English.

Searching for something to say, Jacqueline jumped to her feet. "Choo-choo-choo baby," she said.

She danced with him for an hour, during which time neither spoke a single word to the other.

The next day she began a crash course in English. She borrowed a set of English-language records. They were scratchy and had to be turned over every three minutes. She memorized vocabulary and phrases out of books. The Americans had opened a PX on the Boulevard Victor Hugo. It was said to be loaded with chocolate and with nylons. It was said they were hiring girls as clerks, provided they spoke at least a little English, and she was hoping to qualify for such a job.

Now Jacqueline's two customers told her she had a charming accent in English.

"You flatter me," she answered. She had several sales pitches, and a rather complete vocabulary of perfume terms. But in other areas her English was halting. Flashing her professional smile, she explained about the 20 percent discount for payment with American traveler's checks.

She had made the sale and was wrapping the packages when the bell over the door tinkled. It was activated by pressure on the doormat. Someone had entered the shop and when she looked up to see who was there she gave a start: her husband.

However, she recovered quickly, and handed the packages over. As she made change, her smile was back in place.

Lambert stood silently near the door watching her, the way he had watched her across the counter at the PX the first day she ever saw him. She had been waiting on a rough-looking enlisted man at the time. He had just asked her for a package of rubbers, a word she had never heard before, and while several of his cohorts giggled insanely behind him, he had rephrased his request in various ways, none of them comprehensible to Jacqueline. Working hard to understand him, she kept pointing to various objects. A gallery hung above the shop area, and this was often patrolled by the major or the lieutenant in charge of the PX, who spied down on the girls. She was afraid one was up there now and would fire her for failure to speak English.

Finally under the counter she found what the rough-looking soldier wanted—and when she saw what it was, her face turned to flame. The customer was laughing so hard he could barely stand. They were all laughing—except Lambert, who came forward when they had gone and apologized for them. They were idiots, he told her. It wasn't her fault. But she was so embarrassed she couldn't meet his eyes. He came to see her every day after that. He just stood there and watched her, and at length her embarrassment passed. One day she gave him a wry smile. He was a twenty-one-year-old second lieutenant and he invited her to a Sunday-afternoon tea dance at the château on the Chemin de Fabron that had been taken over to serve as an officers' club. They put a lei of carnations around her neck as she came in the door, and young Lieutenant Lambert told her where he came from—New Jersey, a place she had never heard of. He had spent two years at a university before the Army, he said, and would go back there when the war ended. He was going to learn to write plays and become rich and famous, he told her. They danced for hours and in the intervals he taught her how to smoke.

As the two women prepared to leave her shop, Jacqueline sprayed them with perfume from demonstration bottles provided by the companies. With a smile she showed them out.

After the bell had tinkled again and the door had closed behind them, Jacqueline turned at last to face her husband.

"Well," she said, "I haven't seen you for a while."

"We'll go to dinner," said Lambert. He was grinning. "And then we'll make a night of it."

This confused Jacqueline. She threw a glance back toward the stock room, which was where, five nights a week, she lived. It was where she had expected now to prepare herself dinner, for the dilapidated farmhouse in the mountains was too far to reach except on weekends. The stock room amid the racks of stock contained a narrow bed, a table, a toilet, and, in an alcove, a hot plate and sink.

"I haven't seen you," she said, "in how long?" Sometimes her husband slept with her in the stock room. Sometimes—lately for instance—she didn't see him for days, even weeks at a time.

"We're going out," Lambert said. "We'll have a nice time."

He knew where the keys were kept, and where the light switches were concealed. He began locking up. He flipped all the proper switches, dousing the overhead lights, illuminating the display window. He was pretending Jacqueline was not angry at him. The big, broad grin had never left his face.

"We're celebrating," he said.

"I'm tired, dirty and not in the mood."

Lambert had her by the hand. She followed reluctantly. He led her out onto the Rue Masséna and across the public gardens toward the Promenade des Anglais and the sea.

"If you think I'm going out looking like this, you're crazy."

His excitement mystified her. At the same time she felt herself begin to respond. He had had this effect on her always, beginning with those first tea dances. His enthusiasms were like a child's. He was like a carnival barker, always promising her a ride on the best roller coaster in the world.

They approached the Ruhl Hotel. It faced the Mediterranean, a six-story white palace built around 1900. Concealed lighting illuminated its lavish façade. It seemed to rise up in tiers like a cake, and it wore all the extravagant decorations of Victorian times: frosting around all its double French windows, fine-boned wrought-iron balconies in front of every room, and all of its four corners were rounded off into turrets with conical roofs like medieval forts. They walked in under the porte cochere, passing the one Rolls-Royce and the two Ferraris parked there, passing also the doorman in his elaborate uniform. At their approach the doors were wrenched open by uniformed grooms—small boys only twelve or fourteen years old from the look of them—stationed there around the clock to perform this function.

Jacqueline's heart went out to them—little boys who had already joined the country's work force. Why were they not in school all day and home now doing their lessons? "What are we coming in here for?" she asked.

But Lambert only grinned and led her to the front desk, where clerks in evening clothes flashed bright obsequious smiles and called him by name.

At the concierge's desk he ordered champagne sent up.

"*Oui*, Monsieur Lambert."

Everyone knew his name. Everyone was unctuous. He must have passed this way earlier in the day, Jacqueline thought grimly. He must have distributed considerable money. Where did he get it from?

Farther on waited the elevator, a great wrought-iron cage hanging from thick ropes. There was another groom to operate it. They rose up out of the lobby, which was two stories high, carpeted, crowded. It seemed to Jacqueline to take forever before the next floor descended in front of her eyes and cut off the too-rich view.

59

Disembarking on a high floor, they walked along a corridor: waxed parquet wood dotted by islands of Oriental rugs.

"I don't understand," said Jacqueline, as Lambert pushed open the door to a room. Lambert's joke would have a punch line soon.

"We'll spend a few days here."

"You're mad."

She saw a duffel bag standing upright, and a suitcase that lay open upon a rack. This seemed normal enough; he must have rented this room. But laid out on the bed was a black silk dress, and this was not normal at all. Jacqueline crossed the room and the smile was gone from her face. She stared down at the dress on the counterpane. After a moment, as if to prove it real, her finger touched it.

"Do you recognize it?"

"It was in Zuccarelli's window."

"I saw you admiring it one day. Now it's yours."

"We can't afford it."

"This afternoon I bought it for you. Paid cash, too. If you don't like it, I'll give it to the chambermaid."

Jacqueline again wondered about the money. Mostly she was touched by his generosity, and dazzled by the dress itself.

Lambert said: "Madame Zuccarelli said it would fit you. Any minor adjustments, she'll do for you tomorrow."

"But I don't understand," said Jacqueline. Her hand stroked the dress. "Are we celebrating something?"

"Yes, we are. I'll give you three guesses."

Jacqueline could think of nothing. She shook her head.

"It's simple," said Lambert. "I sold my play."

At first he used to talk about his "play" constantly, and he even worked on it from time to time. With the royalties he would take her to America, he promised. He seemed to have a romantic desire to become famous. In the meantime, to claim to be a playwright afforded him stature in France, and he was aware of this, and went on doing it, even though for the last several years she had not seen him write a line.

"You sold your play?" And then again on a high, incredulous note: "You sold your play?"

Well, it was possible. Tears came to her eyes. Then she was in his arms. "Eddie, I'm so happy for you. Oh, Eddie, Eddie." Was this what it was like to weep tears of joy? She was weeping and laughing at the same time. She had decided to believe that it was true. "This is so marvelous for you. You've waited for it so long. Oh, Eddie, you did it, you did it."

"I always knew it would happen," said Lambert, and he moved about the room preening. "Try on the dress."

Obediently Jacqueline stripped to her slip. "I didn't even know you were still working on it. It's been so long. When did you finish it?" She drew the dress on over her head, then turned so Lambert could button her up the back.

"You haven't seen much of me the last three months. What did you think I was doing?"

She had imagined him in the grip of some fantastic new pipe dream. He was a man who moved from one crazy scheme to the next, most of them at least slightly outside the law. For a while he would have money, then for months or years he would have none. Had she misjudged him all these years?

"You sent your play to America and they took it." Opposite the bed was an antique armoire with mirrored doors. She pirouetted in front of it. "And the dress is lovely. Did you get a telegram, or what? How did you find out that they took it?"

Lambert seemed to take this question as a rebuke. His smile vanished. He said: "You don't believe me."

"Of course I believe you." Did she? Moving close, she embraced him. "No one would joke about a thing like that. It would be like joking about a death in the family."

"The telegram came today." Lambert's smile had come back on. "And when I went to the bank the money was already there."

Jacqueline pretended to shiver with delight. "Let me see it."

"You want to see it?"

Disengaging himself, Lambert reached inside the suitcase and drew out the telegram that, earlier, he had sent to himself. Jacqueline read it, and when she looked across at him her lips were moist and her eyes shining. "Who is this Alexander Levy?"

Lambert had kept in touch with the Broadway news in the Paris edition of the New York *Herald Tribune*. "Only the most important producer on Broadway," he said. When choosing a name to sign to the telegram he had decided on a big one.

There was a knock at the door, and two waiters entered with glasses and champagne. The bottle protruded from a bucket of crushed ice. Lambert made a show of examining the label. "Bollinger's 1947," he said, "very good." After pouring the two flutes full, the waiters withdrew.

61

"To you, Eddie." She had seen the telegram and was holding some of the money. She believed.

"To us."

Both drank. "Are we," she asked, "rich?"

Like a newly successful playwright playing down his achievement, Lambert gave a kind of bashful shrug. "You might say we have some money."

"Enough so we won't have to live in the back of the shop?"

Lambert said expansively: "We can sell the shop."

"Oh, we shouldn't do that," said Jacqueline. "Not yet anyway." She stopped, and tried to pick the correct phrase. In his moment of triumph, she did not want to hurt his feelings. But one of them had to think of the future, and Lambert never did. The next play might take another eight years. "Your next play might not be this successful," she said.

His face fell, became the face of a small boy, so that Jacqueline added hurriedly: "I'm sure it will be just as successful; it's only a precaution."

Lambert became expansive again. How quickly his mood changed. "Would you like to take a bath before dinner? Wait till you see the bathrooms."

There were two sinks, his and hers. There was a huge stall shower with a heavy glass door. The bathtub was longer than Jacqueline was tall. Thick towels hung on heated racks. On the wall hung two terry-cloth bathrobes, floor length. Jacqueline gazed at all this, her face rapturous.

"Undo me," she said, presenting her back. "I can't wait."

Lambert carried the champagne bucket into the bathroom. He refilled the two crystal flutes. Jacqueline lay stretched out in the tub. Her hair, inside a towel, was piled on top of her head, and all of her was underwater up to her ears. They toasted each other and drank.

"Luxury," said Jacqueline, "thy name is a bathtub of one's own."

"I'll buy you one."

"I'm being very selfish," she said when the champagne was half gone. "I should get out so you can have your bath."

"Stay," said Lambert, and she watched him step into the shower stall. Very quickly he disappeared behind the steam. But from time to time he wiped the vapor off, made funny faces at her, or pressed his nose and mouth against the glass.

They finished the champagne on the bed, lying back against the headboard, both wearing their terry-cloth robes. When her glass was empty, Jacqueline set it down on the end table and, leaning over, gave her husband a long kiss.

When the kiss ended, Lambert undid the belt of her robe.

"I've never," she murmured, "made love to a successful playwright before." She had never made love to anyone before, except her husband. The dashing young soldier with the big ambitions had given her nylons, chocolate and cigarettes. Later he had offered her weekends in Paris or Rome—in any fabulous place she might name. But to a girl of Jacqueline's upbringing at that time and that place it was out of the question. And there was no honeymoon until after the wedding.

They dined sumptuously at the Manoir Normand, in those years the best restaurant in Nice. Foie gras, Belon oysters, coq au vin, cheeses, pastries. Waiters hovered around their table throughout; one or another lit every cigarette. Tablecloth and napkins of real linen. Heavy silverware. Crystal that was unbelievably thin, and out of which they drank a 1934 Château Lafite.

"I guess that wine cost a fortune," said Jacqueline afterward in the street.

Lambert translated francs into dollars in his head. "About five dollars a bottle," he said. "We playwrights earn more money than that per word."

She put her arm around his waist. "Excuse me. I forgot for a moment whom I was with." They were both laughing.

"Tomorrow," suggested Lambert, "let's go to Switzerland and go skiing for a week."

"What about my shop?"

"We'll go by in the morning and put a sign in the window."

"What about your locker club?"

This was more complicated. Recently Lambert had rented a capacious cellar in Villefranche and had fitted it out as a locker room. To Jacqueline it represented one of the few satisfying schemes he had ever conceived, for it was not illegal and it brought in regular money, which they needed. Villefranche was the headquarters of the U.S. Sixth Fleet. Each time the fleet came in—and it was in port eight to ten days each month—hundreds of sailors in uniform flocked ashore, and they required a place to change. The Navy would not allow them to keep civilian clothes on board ship, and in uniform, "nice" girls would not date them, and they would also be refused entrance to most Riviera hotels, restaurants and clubs. The solution was to keep their civilian clothes, their liquor, their cigarettes, their packages of nylons in rented lockers in Lambert's club.

"The fleet is due in day after tomorrow," Jacqueline said. Every shopkeeper in Nice knew these dates, for when the fleet was in money was spent.

"I've arranged for Roy LeRoy to open the club for me," replied Lambert. He had done no such thing. The sailors would flock ashore and be unable to get at their things, a notion that did not bother Lambert but might bother Jacqueline. Best to keep it from her.

LeRoy's name brought a grimace to Jacqueline's face. "He frightens me."

"Why?"

"I wish you wouldn't see him."

Lambert only laughed. "You're imagining things. Roy's my best friend."

She knew he had been involved with LeRoy and others in a cigarette-smuggling ring. They had owned a number of boats, bringing American cigarettes in from Tangier. Thousands of dollars were involved on each trip. France was starved for the so-called *blonde* American tobacco. She believed it was Lambert who had organized it all, had bought the boats, had arranged for the waiting trucks that carried the contraband to Paris and other northern cities, had paid the lawyers and furnished the bail money when one of the others got caught. But Lambert had been out of the cigarette business for some time now, or at least so he said.

He took her to the casino in the Palais de la Méditerranée, where she used to go to the Red Cross dances. The gambling rooms were on the second floor. They were crowded. Most men, Jacqueline saw, wore tuxedoes, and many of the women were in evening gowns. It was all very elegant but her husband wore a dark suit and in her new black dress she did not feel out of place. He gave her forty thousand francs and found her a seat at a roulette table. For a while he stood behind her, encouraging her to gamble. He told her she was there to have fun, she must not think of her chips as money. Jacqueline gave him a distracted smile. These few chips in her hand represented almost a month's profit at the perfume shop. She began to play, but so cautiously that Lambert soon lost interest and wandered off. She spied him across the room later playing at the baccarat table. She knew little about gambling, but she could read the signs above the tables, and the limit at his baccarat game was one million francs, a figure that made her shudder.

She went over there just in time to see him lose 300,000 francs on a single hand.

Though appalled, she kept her voice level. She said, "Let's go watch the stage show." He laughed and gave in to her. They went downstairs into the nightclub, drank more champagne, and watched acts similar to those Bellarmine had witnessed in a different club the night before. A magician with a strong accent who was possibly Spanish. A trio of roller skaters who did dangerous tricks at great speed on a small circular platform. Four nude dancers, two with nice faces, all with nice breasts, none very skilled at dancing.

After they had returned to their hotel room, they stood out on the balcony in the night. It was chilly. To the west they could see the dark weight of the Cap d'Antibes pushing out into the sea. To the east bulked the Cap Ferrat, another angular jutting cape. There were lighthouses at the end of both capes. From this distance the beams winked on and off like flashlights. In between was the dark curving bay. It was entirely rimmed by a glittering necklace of lampposts.

Their's had been a troubled marriage. The dashing young soldier had seemed to Jacqueline, after a time, not so dashing anymore. She was a French bourgeois woman of the midcentury, and her values were those of her class and time. She believed in hard work, and in thrift, and in fulfilling her obligations. Whereas Lambert, she soon learned, seemed to love principally excitement—the more romantic the better. He seemed to trust mostly to charm and luck. On occasion he had contracted debts that were difficult for her to pay off. At first, being legally unable to work in France, and with the value of the franc dropping precipitously nearly every day, he had derived income from changing money on the black market. He bought tourists' dollars with francs supplied by "contacts"—it had never been clear to her who his backers were—and was never caught. This was bad enough, but later had come the cigarette-smuggling ring. With the profits he had purchased the farm. He was not caught there either, though others were. When she learned what he was doing, she had been frightened—he would go to jail, and her reputation would be ruined. She had begged him to stop, but he had laughed at her fears. He was out of that business now, she believed.

Standing out on the balcony she contemplated not the night sky or the dark sea but her renewal of faith in her husband. He had completed his play finally, and sold it, and now he would not go to jail after all. Instead they both might go to New York for opening night. She had drunk enough for the idea to make her giddy.

She was also cold. They stepped back into the hotel room, got undressed and crept into the big bed. Lambert switched off the light and they snuggled into each other's arms. A vague but insistent voice told Jacqueline that this was all too good to be true. But she stifled it. Believing herself smug with happiness, she soon fell asleep.

# CHAPTER 7

The buses had stopped running for the night. The bars were dark, the streets empty, but behind drawn shades lights still burned inside the bank.

Facts had begun to collect. Bellarmine knew from the leftover gear how meticulously the job had been planned. It had taken months certainly, which postulated a base in Nice, and patience, and a higher than usual criminal intelligence. He knew from the empty food packages how many meals had been consumed, and therefore that about a dozen men had taken part. He knew at least one had been an expert welder, and there was so much discarded jewelry on the floor that another must have been a jeweler.

These few details constituted a focus, pilings on which an investigation could stand. The gang should have carried everything away with them, Bellarmine thought. Then we would know nothing. Instead, imagining themselves clever and funny, they opt for a joke—and leave us a place to start.

Approximately how much loot they had got away with he knew also, and the sum was staggering. It was the biggest crime of its kind he had ever heard of.

The identity section had trooped upstairs from the vault, having found not one fingerprint nor any other identifying evidence. Bellarmine was using Monot's desk as his command post. The section chief, whose name was Dumas, stood in front of it.

The identity men had boxed the contents of the latrine buckets. They stood behind Dumas holding their boxes as gingerly as explosives. Maybe the lab could determine something useful, Dumas said.

"Blood types, perhaps," he said. "Anything." His men, looking sheepish, walking carefully, followed Dumas out of the bank.

The lab was in Marseille. Dumas phoned later from there. The "specimens" were no good, he reported. Too many men had contributed to each bucket. Everything was all mixed up. Sorry.

Bellarmine had requested the list of safe-deposit owners and Monot had handed it over. There was no list. It was a leatherbound ledger. Every entry was written out by hand. Bellarmine had flipped the big pages, hundreds of them. The wind had bathed his face. By counting the names to a page, and multiplying, he concluded that there were around four thousand active entries in this ledger, and two thousand inactive ones, and they were in no order that he could determine. Detectives would have to check out each name, because whoever planned this job had been in the vault before, meaning that probably he was—is—a box owner. Six thousand names, Bellarmine thought—my God.

The phones had rung all afternoon and into the night. Among those who called was Adjunct Mayor Picpoul. Here it comes, Bellarmine had thought, the political pressure.

Picpoul was the most powerful man in Nice. In municipal elections a candidate for mayor ran not alone but at the head of a slate of about forty men, adjunct mayors and technical counselors. One vote elected the entire slate. The mayor also ran simultaneously for a seat in the National Assembly—normally he was elected to both jobs and thereafter lived in Paris and let the rest of the slate run the city. In Nice at the moment the man who ran the city was Picpoul, and Bellarmine knew this.

He declined to get on the line.

A short time later came a commotion at the front of the bank, and the adjunct mayor swept in followed by an entourage of about ten men. An entourage of this size was a display of raw power, and it shocked Bellarmine. Heavyweight prizefighters perhaps traveled with this big a retinue, but no one else did. It was so unusual and so bizarre as to frighten ordinary men into almost instant servility. Even Bellarmine felt this fear, though he tried to shrug it off. A policeman at a crime scene outranked everybody. Bellarmine should not be afraid of this man, and he went forward and shook his hand.

Picpoul was short and burly with thick gray hair. He wore his coat over his shoulders, like a cape, like a film star. He extended lacquered fingers, like a cardinal or a pope, as if offering his ring to be kissed.

The entourage formed half a halo around him, men who seemed balanced on the balls of their feet, ready to jump in whichever direction Picpoul leaned.

Picpoul said: "I've come to inspect the vaults."

"My apologies, *monsieur le maire.* That won't be possible."

Picpoul frowned, and members of the entourage burst forward. Voices were raised, harsh words uttered. Bellarmine wavered, and a compromise was worked out. The adjunct mayor could peer into the vault but not enter, lest evidence be disturbed. Bellarmine led him down the stairs, the entourage following, and they watched the detectives who were already at work sorting.

The stench was strong. Picpoul sniffed the air a few times. "I'll need a list of boxholders," he asserted. "And a list of boxes broken into."

He had no right to such information and Bellarmine was determined not to give it to him.

"Have papers and documents been stolen?"

This idea had not yet occurred to Bellarmine. "I don't think so."

"How do you know?" Picpoul seemed agitated—more agitated than he should have been. Bellarmine noted this and it puzzled him.

"Instinct."

"Instinct?" shouted Picpoul.

"To stomp shit into them shows no respect for them at all," Bellarmine explained, trying to calm him down.

The entourage parted. The adjunct mayor led everyone up the steps. "I want those lists on my desk by ten A.M. tomorrow."

"*Oui, monsieur,*" said Bellarmine. He did not intend to comply.

But soon afterward Commissaire Divisionnaire Sapodin came to the bank. Sapodin too had an entourage and he waited at the front door while it formed around him. It was smaller than the mayor's— only four men—but still impressive. As he moved into the bank he seemed accompanied by a great rush of air. Bellarmine had to hurry to keep up. "I want a list of boxholders, and a second list of which boxes have been hit."

Bellarmine told him that the only list at present was the thick ledger. The *divisionnaire* put his Homburg down on a desk. In the overhead light his bald pate glistened. It was late at night and the carnation in his buttonhole had wilted. "See that the adjunct mayor gets a copy too." He gave Bellarmine a brief smile. "We don't want City Hall mad at us, do we?"

68

"We work for the Minister of the Interior."

"Picpoul may have the minister's ear, eh? We can't be sure, can we? So see that he gets it."

"*Oui, monsieur.*"

The *divisionnaire* led the way to the front door, where the Homburg went back on his head and he again addressed Bellarmine.

"Need some more men? I'll send you over Lussac and his crew from the Mondaine." It was almost as if, having asked a favor, he was determined to pay it off quickly.

Bellarmine returned to Monot's desk, where he studied the phone messages that had come in. Many names were unknown to him, but he saw that the *étude* of Maître Verini had phoned twice. The lawyer behind every suspicious deal on the coast. But perhaps it meant nothing, he brooded. Perhaps it also means nothing that the adjunct mayor came here in person. He could think of legitimate explanations in both cases. Or it could mean that both men were showing undue interest in this bank. And he began to consider again the possible casino case that he had not dared bring to the attention of Juge Fayot earlier that same afternoon. If there was in fact a case to be made, then Maître Verini was certainly involved, and probably Adjunct Mayor Picpoul too. More importantly, this could be the bank where the evidence was to be found.

But he was distracted by the arrival of Lussac, who, looking surly, sauntered up to his desk. "The *divisionnaire* said you needed help."

A warning bell tinkled inside Bellarmine's head. Be nice to this young man, he told himself. He comes from a good family. He is going straight to the top. Five years from now you'll be working for him.

"I should have saved the sewers for you, Lussac," Bellarmine said. He gave the younger man what was almost a smile. "Your men would feel right at home there."

Lussac's face darkened.

Bellarmine's feet were on Monot's desk, and he lit a Chesterfield. "Put half your men to work inventorying the gear in the vault. The other half can start wiping the shit off the documents on the floor. Have them use the same stroke as when they wipe their ass."

Lussac glared at him.

"Half and half," said Bellarmine. "Don't show any favoritism now."

When Lussac did not move, Bellarmine added: "You wanted to be a policeman, didn't you? Well, that's the type of dirty job *flics* get stuck with all the time. So get to it."

Lussac, making an effort to control his temper, said: "Let's have a truce."

It made Bellarmine feel suddenly churlish. "Sure."

"We're going to be working together, aren't we?" When Bellarmine did not answer, he added: "I released those two whores, The Stinger and the other one."

"Fine." He could always find them again. They were whores. Where could they go? They lived their lives in public. They were as visible as film stars.

"You won't have time to talk to them today."

"Probably not."

"And the truce?"

"Sure," said Bellarmine. "But put your men to work, will you? I'm sorry, but it has to be done."

Except for the white batons who would remain there on guard all night, he was the last to leave the bank. He went out into the night, and the city felt empty. At the Place Masséna he stood under a streetlight. A car came around the top part of the square, and turned off into a side street. When it was gone the city was silent again. He walked halfway up the square and peered across at the Casino Municipal, which had been closed by municipal order some months ago. There was a wooden barricade, plastered with posters, all the way around it. Even the sidewalk cafés at ground level had been put out of business. A lot of people had been hurt, a few enriched. The casino case tantalized him. Nice had always had two casinos in the past. Now it had only the Palais de la Méditerranée overlooking the sea. A syndicate—the money was rumored to be American—had recently bought the Méditerranée. Simultaneously Adjunct Mayor Picpoul had sent city engineers under the Municipal, which stood on pilings over the Paillon River. The engineers had certified these pilings as unsafe, and Picpoul overnight ordered the casino boarded up. Had Picpoul been paid off? Had others? According to Bellarmine's informant, yes. According to this same informant, Maître Verini, whose *étude* had handled all these transactions, had become afraid and had stashed incriminating documents in a vault in one of the banks. But the informant didn't know which one. The Banque de Nice et de la Côte d'Azur, perhaps? It was the most important bank in town, and the closest to Verini's *étude*. It was the logical bank. If so, the documents might at this moment be lying on the floor of the vault amid fifty thousand others. He could bend down and pick them up. Of course he would have to know what they looked like.

Forget the casino case, he cautioned himself. But he continued to stare across at the condemned building. Like any of the habitual gamblers who had patronized it, he could feel emanating from it a magnetic pull, an almost irresistible attraction. The casino seemed to be making him extravagant promises, the same ones it had made to so many other gamblers in the past. With a single roll it could expand his being, change not only his life but his very perception of life. He might nail an adjunct mayor, perhaps the absent mayor himself. He might send political convulsions through France. Such a triumph could make him a different man, liberate him, somehow give him back his purity again.

He turned away from the casino. He discarded its possibilities, tantalizing or not. In the real world a man did not desire to turn back into a choirboy. One took what was handed out, and did not wish for better. He had been handed a devastated bank vault, a case such as most detectives never saw in their whole careers, and that was enough.

He walked toward home. The muscles down the sides of his back felt cast in bronze, and his shoulders ached. Passing Odette's nightclub he peered in through the glass, but the club had closed for the night long ago. He walked on.

When he stepped inside his flat, the place seemed to him as empty as the town. He was at first surprised, then alarmed. The main room was dark, but the shutters had not been closed, and light from the street showed that the bed had not been pulled out of the wall. He felt a spasm of—perhaps it was fear. Had something happened to Odette?

He switched on all the lights. No sign of her. There was a closet at either end of the hall, and two armoires. He rushed about jerking open doors. Odette's clothes were missing. Her toilet articles were gone from the cabinet over the sink. He began to look for a note, but found none. He sat down in a chair to think it over. Where was she? What had happened?

Then he thought of her douche syringe—her bank. Rushing down the hall he threw open the door to the toilet. On the shelf on the wall in its proper place, upright on its rubber bulb, stood the syringe. He felt a momentary elation. If her bank was still here, then she was. Grasping the plastic penis in one hand, he tore off the rubber bulb with the other.

The hollow plastic tube contained no tightly rolled bills. It was empty except for a thin, curled paper. Bellarmine spread it out under the light.

"GONE TO PARIS."

His detective's instinct had led him right to the note, as she had known it would. How well she knew him. He was curiously touched. She had taken her money but left the syringe behind as—As what? As a souvenir of her passage through his life, perhaps. And his through hers. He gave a hollow laugh. No one ever touches anyone else, he thought, and love is a myth.

Returning to the other room, he pulled the bed out of the wall. A little later he crawled into it alone. Unable to sleep, he put his foot out to where her warm leg ought to have been, but that side of the bed was cold. He was used to being lonely. He had been lonely with her there. Loneliness was normal, nothing to get upset about.

# CHAPTER 8

He felt hung over. Finally he had paced most of the night, smoking too many cigarettes. Just before dawn he had come to a different decision. He was going after the politicians and lawyers too, and he stood in the street waiting for the post office to open to make a phone call to his informant.

There was no phone in his flat. He had been waiting for one for months. The French telephone system was one of the most archaic in Europe, especially in the south. Two-year waits were not uncommon. Most Frenchmen, when they wished to telephone, went to the nearest post office, where they waited on line, or to the nearest café, where they were first obliged to buy a drink at the bar.

This morning a gray-faced woman, one of the legions of civil functionaries, took her place behind the telephone desk. Wearing a gray post-office smock, she looked as grim as a prison matron. Bellarmine wished her *"Bonjour,"* but she chose not to reply.

He gave the number he wanted, and waited while the prison matron wrote it down in her ledger. The counter between them was deliberately high so that he could not see what she was doing. In France every functionary sat behind such a counter. Picking up the phone on her desk, she dialed his call.

Two people to make one simple phone call, he thought. What a waste!

"Don't hang up," she ordered into the receiver. With her chin she indicated the row of booths opposite her counter. "Cabin number three."

He stepped into the booth and closed the door. Through the glass he saw that she watched him with a stern eye, as if afraid he might try something. This annoyed him also. The scarcity of telephones, the inefficiency of the telephone system—he was using up too much strong emotion too early in the day. Why should I care, he asked himself. But the answer came back: because France is my country.

The informant, Lasserre, was already on the line. "I told you," he cried, already half terrified, "not to call me here."

Lasserre was chief clerk in Verini's *étude*. He was about fifty, the same age as the *notaire*. The two men had been friends since law school, or before, but Verini had become rich, while Lasserre was still chief clerk. Was this why, after so many years, he had turned informant? People informed for a variety of reasons, most of them very deep and very dark. To probe for their exact motivations was like stepping down into a latrine pit. One became covered with their filth. A man learned not to do it. Informants were often more depraved than the criminals they denounced. One probed deeply enough to substantiate the story they told, and that was all.

"I need to know the number of his lockbox," Bellarmine said. In the night he had convinced himself that he already knew which bank: the Banque de Nice. "If I have to get a warrant to search the *étude*, I'll be forced to reveal your name." Bellarmine realized that he was trying to punish the man by threatening him. Punish him for what?

There was an anguished silence. Then: "But I can't. Don't you see?"

"Calm down," Bellarmine said. He had thought all this out in the night. "Verini must carry a lot of keys."

"I can't steal his keys. I can't do it."

But Bellarmine only pursued him. "Does he give you keys to unlock cabinets? Or leave the bunch of keys on his desk?"

Lasserre had begun breathing hard.

"The key I'm looking for is about six centimeters long, flat. On the

73

head a letter followed by a three-digit number. All I want is the number."

"I don't know."

"Try very, very hard." He hung up.

Leaving the phone booth, he crossed to the counter where the prison matron would count the seconds and tell him how much his call had cost. She worked off stopwatches, one for each booth. He saw her lips move as she calculated. He waited as she did the multiplication in pencil on a scratch pad.

"Three hundred and fifty francs."

Withdrawing his billfold, Bellarmine handed over the three one-hundred-franc notes and the one fifty. The larger notes were pastel pink but tattered; the smaller one had been handled so much it was about to disintegrate, and there was almost no color left. The outlandishly inflated currency of France, he reflected. What used to constitute a week's wages now paid for a local phone call. With each financial transaction, no matter how small, a Frenchman was reminded of his country's humiliation—and contributed to it further. It made Bellarmine want to climb up onto a high place and give a scream of outrage. But the only way to display how he felt was to put people in jail. He would put the sewer gang in jail, and he would put the casino gang in jail as well, and his scream would be heard all over France.

He went to the Café Prado and drank two cafés au lait. The morning papers called the bank break-in "The Crime of the Century." They called it "exquisitely thought out" and doubted the police would ever solve it. We will see, Bellarmine thought grimly. He left the café.

As he passed the perfume shop he noted that it was closed. There was a sign on the door: "On Vacation." He missed seeing the unknown young woman, whose face always brightened his day.

At the bank a tall, husky individual stood just inside the door. Bellarmine reacted to him as if to clues. Late forties. Short crew cut—lots of scalp at the sides. Checkered sports coat. Obese knot in his necktie. The nationality of any man in Europe could be determined by his clothing, by his haircut, and by his jewelry or lack of it. Frenchmen wore two-inch trouser cuffs, and an Italian's suit coat was cut square and stopped short at the top of his buttocks. This man wore heavy wing-tip shoes and argyle socks. On his left hand was an enormous ring. But the clues were too many and without variety.

Bellarmine had the answers—most of them—before the clues ended. Obviously a foreigner. Obviously American. A tourist? Impossible. A *flic* then. What kind of *flic*? And why was he here?

The man's handshake was as hearty as his grin. And his voice was too loud. "Charlie O'Hara."

Bellarmine gave no reaction. He waited.

The man whipped out his badge. "Of the FBI." It was one of those ridiculously tiny FBI badges. "I went to see Commissaire Sapodin and he sent me over to see you."

O'Hara was speaking French, but with a strong American accent. He shook out and proffered a package of French Gauloises cigarettes. Bellarmine, having recognized the brand, refused it. Harsh black tobacco. He was annoyed. The French envied Americans their cigarettes above all things, and to affect a taste for Gauloises seemed to him patronizing.

He led the way back to Monot's desk, where O'Hara abruptly stopped trying to speak French.

"I understand you speak English, Commissaire. In fact, I understand you're a graduate of the FBI Academy. You're one of us."

Bellarmine was not one of them. "I was a foreign observer," he said, and lit one of his Chesterfields. Four months in Virginia had seemed long to him. He had learned how to fire exotic firearms such as did not exist in France, and how to buy information from informants for enormous sums of money such as did not exist in France either.

"I'm attached to the embassy in Paris," O'Hara said, and he grinned, obviously trying to be friendly. "I'm called the legal attaché."

Bellarmine did not grin back.

"Well, yesterday I got a cable from Washington. You'll never guess from whom."

Bellarmine puffed on his cigarette and studied the knot in O'Hara's tie.

"From Mr. Hoover personally," O'Hara said. He was working hard at the friendliness. "He told me to get my ass on down here. I came down on the Blue Train. Got in this morning."

When Bellarmine only sucked in another lungful of smoke, O'Hara's grin faded, and his voice became cold. "I need a list of the safe-deposit holders, and also of the boxes that have been hit."

God, thought Bellarmine, those lists are popular. He said carefully: "What have lock boxes in Nice got to do with Mr. Hoover?"

75

O'Hara said he didn't know, he was just the messenger boy. "My orders are to stay here till I get them."

"Excuse me," said Bellarmine, picking up the phone, and as he dialed the *divisionnaire* he spun his chair around so that O'Hara could not overhear him.

"This FBI *mec* says you sent him over here—"

"Give him what he wants," said Sapodin. "Get copies made. One for the adjunct mayor, one for me, one for him. You never know when we might need a favor from the FBI."

The many faces of Sapodin. To his subordinates, reflected Bellarmine, a martinet. To the press, a dedicated *flic*. But the moment he encountered weight of whatever kind, he desired, like all high police officials, only to be accommodating. People of weight found him the most genial of men.

The mayor, the *divisionnaire*, and the FBI all wanted those lists, and Bellarmine sensed already that there would be others. He swung around to face O'Hara. "There is only one list so far," he told him, and showed the handwritten ledger. "You'll have to wait."

It made O'Hara give a low whistle. "If an American banker kept records like that, they'd put him in jail. Don't you have machines?"

Bellarmine looked at him.

"Jesus," said O'Hara, "no machines."

Bellarmine kept his temper. "Could you find out why Monsieur Hoover interests himself in this thing?"

"I don't see how," said O'Hara blandly. "I mean, I'm here and he's there." He leaned aggressively forward. "So when do I get the lists?"

"Find out why Hoover wants them," said Bellarmine, adding under his breath: or you'll never get them.

He decided to stall everyone, but this proved not easy to do. Rich and important men, most of them Paris-based, all of them worried, began to collect in their Riviera villas, in their grand apartments overlooking the Promenade des Anglais and the sea. Most had no difficulty getting through to Sapodin, who in the face of such wealth and power was even more genial than usual. Several times he sent Bellarmine out of the bank to meet with them.

To leave the bank was in itself an ordeal. The crowd outside was larger, more densely packed and angrier day by day. Bellarmine's picture had been in the *Nice Matin*—the crowd knew who he was and tried to surge upon him. Each time he could feel its mass pushing against the line of white batons. Each time instinctively he glanced

76

behind him at the safety of the bank. These were the other boxholders, the ordinary ones, all four thousand of them it sometimes seemed, people with no access to Sapodin or anyone else. He had been vaguely conscious of their voices through the glass and shades. But out here in the fresh morning air in the street, their noise was attached to contorted faces and shaking fists. It was something he could feel as well as hear.

"My life savings are in that box," a voice shouted.

"Just tell me if my lockbox was hit or not."

He was obliged to push through, saying nothing while people spat at him and newsreel cameras rolled.

"*Espèce de merde.*"

"*Salaud.*"

Reporters pressed close shouting questions that he did not answer. Uniforms surrounded him, wedging him like a heavyweight contender down the aisle and into the car.

The influential men he went to see all held lockboxes at the Banque de Nice. All demanded immediate access to them. This was impossible, given the state of the vault, Bellarmine told them. It was not the possible loss of cash or jewels that concerned them, he saw. All were worried about "personal" papers their boxes had contained that might now be in the hands of the sewer gang. None would tell him what these personal papers might be.

"Are we waiting for the blackmailer's letter?" one shouted. "Is that what comes next?"

What kind of guilty secrets would cause such panic—in some cases outright terror—Bellarmine wondered, even as he attempted to reassure them. There was no evidence that anything but valuables had been stolen, he said. There were tens of thousands of pieces of paper on the floor of the bank and detectives were sorting them now.

This notion, that *flics* on their hands and knees were poring over their secrets, only increased their outrage and their demands. Immediate access—

"*I'll break you for this.*"

When Bellarmine argued that the integrity of the crime scene had to be preserved, nearly all of them in one way or another threatened him.

There was one exception, an eighty-two-year-old industrialist named Marcel Doussac, who had moved into a suite at the Ruhl that was full of flowers.

"My box contained, if I remember correctly, about twenty thousand American dollars and four gold ingots."

"You'll be indemnified."

The old man walked over to the French windows, pushed the curtain aside and peered out. The windows gave onto a balcony, and beyond that was the sea. There was glaring sunlight in the room. He was said to be the richest man in France.

"I have so much money and so little time that if twenty thousand dollars fell out of my pocket I might not bend down to pick it up. It isn't the money, it's some documents."

"Are you going to tell me what kind?" Usually this question set these men raving. Alone among them, Doussac replied calmly. He was worried about bearer's bonds relating to one of his companies.

"Whoever turns up at the next board meeting holding those bonds would take over my company. It wouldn't be the thief who stole them. It would be some Argentine businessman, some Panamanian he sold them to. There would be nothing I could do."

Bellarmine watched him.

"It's the first company I ever started, and it means something to me."

"Give me the box number."

"Thank you," said Doussac.

Back at the bank, Bellarmine went directly down into the vault. Ten detectives were working. Documents were being tossed from the floor into cardboard cartons labeled A to Z.

He found that Doussac's box was indeed among those rifled—his hand moved its broken door back and forth. But it would be a while before anyone knew whether his bearer's bonds, or any other papers, had been stolen. Bellarmine still believed not. This crime did not feel to him like that sort of crime. The Brain seemed too careful a man. But it might be possible to settle the question fairly quickly. Doussac's box was in strong room No. 3. "Clean up this room first," he told his men. If Doussac's bonds were missing, it would mean he had a wholly different category of crime on his hands.

While waiting he carried the ledger around in his briefcase. No copies were made, and he ordered no list of broken boxes made either. He also increased the pressure on his informant in Maître Verini's étude.

The next time Maître Verini telephoned, Bellarmine accepted the call.

Verini's voice was unctuous, confident. It was the voice of the most important *notaire* on the coast, the so-called keeper of the secrets of the Côte d'Azur. It was the voice of a man who was both a lawyer and a power broker, who understood human greed and had become rich off it. It was the voice, according to rumor, of a crook who had brokered corrupt deals for years. He had brokered both sides of this casino business, or so the informant had said. He had arranged the sale of the one casino to a syndicate and the simultaneous condemnation of the other.

Verini told Bellarmine he had a business proposition for him. They had best meet as soon as possible.

Verini's villa was in Cimiez, the most expensive residential quarter in the city. The living room was richly decorated. There must have been a dozen paintings on the walls.

"Can I fix you a whiskey, Monsieur le Commissaire?" Verini peered at Bellarmine through thick glasses. The *notaire* wore an imported tweed sports coat, English by its cut.

Whiskey meant Scotch. Only recently discovered by the French, it was already the drink of choice of those who wished to consider themselves sophisticated and chic.

As the *notaire* prepared the drinks, Bellarmine said bluntly: "What's your proposition?"

Verini's personality seemed to change. An ice cube escaped like a bar of soap onto the floor. He overfilled one of the glasses so that part of its contents, as he lifted it, slopped onto the Oriental rug.

"My proposition—" he said, and began a fanciful tale of English heirs, of a will that might or might not stand up in court, of an investigation that Bellarmine might undertake in London, which would clarify the entire matter. He mentioned an incredible fee. "So can I tell my principals you're interested?"

Bellarmine was satisfied that there were no missing heirs, no missing millions. He waited.

The *notaire* sipped his drink. "That's good whiskey, wouldn't you say? So how's your investigation going down at the bank?"

"About as well as expected." Bellarmine watched Verini's eyes. They were enormous behind the thick glasses, and were darting this way and that.

"I have some clients who have boxes there. No information has come out of the bank at all, as you know. They don't know whether their boxes were hit or not. They don't know whether their possessions are safe or in the hands of the sewer gang. Is that what you call them, the sewer gang? They certainly would like to know." A long clumsy speech.

"The stuff is being sorted."

"Some of them can't bear to wait any longer."

"Why don't you tell me what we're talking about?"

This was followed by a very long pause. Then Verini said: "One of my clients was a bit concerned about some photos he had in his box."

"Photos?"

"Photos." Verini gave what was supposed to be a leer. But it did not come off. Bellarmine had the impression that sweat had popped out on Verini's brow, though it hadn't. Rather there was a powerful, palpable anxiety.

"Pornographic photos, you mean."

"Your men may have found them by now."

"Maybe." He watched Verini for any change in expression, any tic, any clue to what this was all about.

Verini attempted a low chuckle. "My client would probably pay plenty to have those photos back." And he let the bribe offer, if that's what it was, hang in the air.

"I might be able to find out for you." Bellarmine's face betrayed nothing. He sipped from his Scotch. "Why don't you give me the numbers of the boxes you're interested in, and I'll see."

Verini stood up abruptly. "You must be tired, Monsieur le Commissaire. I mustn't keep you any longer." And he plucked the half-consumed drink out of Bellarmine's hand and ushered him toward the door.

*Merde*, Bellarmine thought. I've spooked him. Either that or he's lost his nerve. Bellarmine was being marched across the garden toward the steel door in the hedge.

Verini's unctuous smile matched his voice. "We'll speak again about London in a few weeks. *Bonsoir*, Monsieur le Commissaire."

And the door clanged shut. Bellarmine still had his hat in his hand; he tossed it disgustedly through the window on to the front seat of the black, unmarked Citroën.

The phone rang almost as he came into the bank. It was Lasserre, who had found the key, and he read off a number. The frightened informant also gave Bellarmine the name of a woman, Verini's daughter. "The box is in her name. She lives in Australia."

"Thank you."

"It's finished," cried Lasserre. "It's over. Don't ever call me again."

Bellarmine went down the stairs to the vault. The detectives were about to close down for the night. They were rolling down sleeves, reaching for hats and coats. The floor of No. 3 strong room, he noted, had been cleared of paper. No. 2 was partly cleared. No. 1 was still untouched. In each room the cartons stood in a row. Some were nearly full, and several, the ones the detectives called "slag heaps," were overflowing. The slag-heap cartons held papers and documents that could not be identified.

He checked out the number Lasserre had just given him. Verini's box was in No. 3, close to the entrance to the vault. Its door seemed to have received an unmerciful battering by a pickax or some such tool. It was so deformed it no longer fit the hole to which, by a single hinge, it still hung.

The detectives stood watching him.

"Did anyone come across any pornographic pictures?"

He saw the grins come on, and one of the men rummaged through the nearest slag heap. After a moment's search he handed Bellarmine what at first glance appeared to be a deck of playing cards.

Bellarmine fanned out the deck. The backs of each card were quite graphic, and when flipped fast made a kind of motion picture. This was standard mass-produced pornography. He saw no way it could embarrass Verini or even be linked to him. Snapping the rubber band around the cards, he tossed the packet back on the pile.

"Anything else?"

"Maybe one of the day guys found something," offered the detective. "I think we would have heard, though."

They were anxious to be off, but he held them. He asked about Doussac's bearer's bonds. He gave the name of the company, the only name on the bonds: Établissements Lyonnais.

The L box was dumped out onto the floor, and all the men on their hands and knees searched through the pile. They did not find the bonds.

The detectives waited for permission to go home. The L box, refilled, had been pushed back into its place in the row.

"See you tomorrow," said Bellarmine. He shook hands with each of them and watched them go up the stairs. He heard them go past the guards at the door and out into the night.

He went over to the slag heap, found the packet of photos, and

81

studied them again. No, these could not be what Verini was worried about.

Which meant that the bearer's bonds were missing, Verini's pornographic photos were probably missing, and so, most likely, was evidence relating to the casino scam. Documents had been stolen from the vault after all, documents worth far more in human pain than the missing money and gold. There was a blackmailer out there somewhere, he could count on it, and crimes coming that would surpass in ugliness everything seen so far. He could count on that too.

Who did he advise of this and how soon?

He decided to advise no one. So there were sharks in the water close to the swimmers. So what. To sound the alarm would mean even bigger headlines. It would cause increased pressure on the investigation. To sound the alarm was not in Bellarmine's interest. It would probably bring a higher-ranking officer in here to take over the case. The way to keep the case was to impose an information blackout if he could. To keep those lists away from all the people clamoring for them for as long as possible. For this he needed help, and so, early the next morning, he summoned Directeur Général Monot.

Since the opening of the vault Monot had had nothing to do but contemplate his misery. His real problem, Bellarmine told him now, would be the eventual indemnification of boxholders. Owners would all exaggerate their claims, and this would cost the bank and its insurance companies a fortune. However, Bellarmine had a way to make the boxholders submit honest claims. The bank should keep secret the numbers of the two thousand looted boxes, and the names of their owners, and at the same time make all four thousand owners, not knowing if their boxes had been hit or not, submit sworn inventories of their contents.

"I don't see it," said Monot.

Few owners would dare submit fraudulent claims when maybe their boxes were intact, Bellarmine explained. They would fear being made to open the box. If its contents didn't match the inventory, that was attempted fraud. "Would one risk attempted fraud when perhaps the box was safe all along?" he asked. "I don't think so."

Monot was beaming. "I like it. I like it."

The idea was adopted by the boards of both the bank and its insurance companies that afternoon. All information on the boxes was to be withheld from the public until further notice. The police were asked to enforce this decision and had no choice but to obey. The bank was custodian of the boxes, not the police.

In time the numbers would leak out anyway, Bellarmine knew. He had not even gained himself much breathing room—a few days perhaps. Not nearly enough.

# CHAPTER
# 9

He drove himself and his detectives hard. The red chisels, left behind by the gang in such abundance, proved to be the most popular model in France. No hardware store owner could remember selling more than three at a time. The acetylene tanks could be traced no further than a construction site in Nîmes from which they had been stolen. And sewer-system maps, it seemed, were available at City Hall to anyone who asked for them. No record was kept.

Detectives canvassed residents along the Paillon, but no one had noticed anything unusual down along the riverbank, except for a dog walker who mentioned a *clochard* who often slept against the piling under the crust. He gave his description.

Bellarmine sent his men out to round up *clochards*. "Every time you collect five or six you bring the dog walker in to look at a lineup."

Detectives moved along the beaches, along the riverbanks, through the public gardens, the railroad station, the quays. They shook bums awake all over Nice.

"You, on your feet."

They soon tired of bending down to wake them. They learned to give instead a kick on the sole of the shoe or the side of the leg. They kicked away the rolled-up newspapers or whatever served as pillow.

"You. Wake up."

Many were placed in lineups, and the dog walker, more furious each time, was made to come in to view them. He identified no one, and by now was so angry he probably never would.

"Keep looking," Bellarmine ordered his men.

Tips from the public were received and, no matter how farfetched, were checked out. An old woman fingered her neighbor, a Nazi sympathizer during the war, she said, and just the type the police might be looking for. An anonymous phone call named the restaurant on the port where the gang had dined every night during the preparation of their coup. The owner turned out to be an enormously fat fifty-year-old female. Detectives staked the place out, tailed the woman everywhere she waddled. But after three unproductive days Bellarmine called them in and sent the woman a *convocation*.

This was a blue paper that ordered the recipient to appear at a specified *commissariat* at a specified hour for "a matter that concerns you." The very vagueness, together with the extremely broad powers of the French police, most times struck terror into the recipient's heart. At the *commissariat* on the Rue Gioffredo, Bellarmine made her wait. An hour went by. Two. She sat overflowing her chair, sweating and afraid. She had an overnight case between her feet, for the police could hold her if they wished, even throw her into the women's house of arrest to await trial, and she knew this. By the time she was shown into Bellarmine's office she could hardly talk.

Her story was as he expected. It was true she had allowed people to believe she knew members of the sewer gang. But she didn't. She had bragged about feeding them every night only to increase business, and it had worked. Since the crime, all her tables had been full at every service. No harm done. She attempted a terrified smile.

He lit a cigarette and blew smoke across the desk.

"Wait outside, *s'il vous plaît.*"

He left her on a bench in the corridor the rest of the day. Each time he passed she tried another smile. He ignored it and her, left her alone with her great fear until night fell, when he sent someone to release her.

Informants were picked up and grilled. Bars were raided, and every dubious patron was brought to the *commissariat* for questioning. Prostitutes were rounded up repeatedly until for several days they disappeared from the streets in protest. But apparently there were no echoes of the crime moving through the Nice underworld. Not even a hint of a trail was picked up. Bellarmine himself interrogated the young prostitute known as The Stinger. He reduced her to tears, but she knew nothing. Her girl friend might know more, she said, weeping. But she lived in Marseille and had gone back there, and Bellarmine could not afford a day in Marseille trying to find her. It was a trip he might have to make, but not yet.

The press reveled in the crime, and in each police setback. It was as if press and public did not want this perfect crime solved. The

Brain especially was described in heroic terms and his probable attributes were conjectured. All of which served to increase the pressure on Bellarmine, who was obliged to respond constantly to telephone calls from police commanders, prominent politicians, government ministers. It used up a tremendous amount of time.

The press began to suggest that documents had also been stolen from the vault. Was it for this reason that the names of victimized boxholders had not yet been released?

"Anything in it, Bellarmine?"

Commissaire Divisionnaire Sapodin had summoned him to his office.

"The bank has told me nothing, monsieur."

"The pressure is on, Bellarmine. I had a call from Paris from the minister an hour ago." The *divisionnaire* meant the Minister of the Interior, and his tone was apologetic. "He gave me some box numbers—five or six of them. Boxes that belong to some important people. Wants to know if they were hit or not. I hate to go against the bank's wishes—the men who run the Banque de Nice are big men too. But we work for the Minister, don't we?"

"*Oui, monsieur.*"

"Who do you think The Brain could be?"

"He's from Nice. He has to be."

"Then the underworld here should be talking about him, and they're not. How do you explain that?"

"I can't."

He had sent a series of telegrams to the central archive in Paris for the dossiers of all past Sûreté "clients" who knew banks, who knew Nice, and who otherwise might qualify as The Brain.

Sûreté headquarters was at 11 Rue des Saussaies, a horseshoe-shaped building across the street from the Elysées Palace. It was six stories high and surrounded a central courtyard. The archives, which took up almost the entire top floor, had interior windows that looked down on the black Citroëns and waiting chauffeurs of Sûreté dignitaries. The file drawers rose from floor almost to ceiling. They formed narrow somber alleys. They were staffed by a hundred *inspecteurs-archivistes* whom they seemed to have formed in their own image—narrow somber men in gray smocks.

On file was nearly every adult in the nation, the innocent as well as the guilty, for according to French police thinking the one might well become the other—it was best to know about everyone in advance.

The millions and millions of dossiers were classed in three categories: *Dossiers Individuels* for known criminals; *Dossiers Criminels*—documents relating to their crimes; and *Dossiers Administratifs*—information on every citizen who had ever applied for an identity card, a passport, a fishing license. *Dossiers Individuels* were cross-indexed both phonetically and by nickname—nearly all French criminals had nicknames, the more lurid the better, it seemed. And of course nothing was computerized. The computer did not yet exist. The older *archivistes* carried the details of thousands of crimes and criminals in their heads. Upon receiving Bellarmine's telegrams, they put together a package of dossiers and sent it to Nice on the night mail plane.

Bellarmine studied these dossiers, but they did not satisfy him. Not one of the men depicted, it seemed to him, had enough imagination or stature to fill the role of The Brain.

"We have his dossier on file," said the *divisionnaire* after the daily briefing. "You just haven't dug it out yet."

"He's a local man," said Bellarmine. "A gang of out-of-towners doesn't just walk into this city and knock over something as big as the Banque de Nice."

Sapodin said: "I want that man, Bellarmine. I want The Brain."

"*Oui, patron.*"

"So how are you going to do it?"

The loot from such a crime, as every policeman knew, was more volatile than TNT. It had too much energy to lie still very long. Sooner or later, it would exert so much pressure on the men holding it as to overcome their reluctance to spend it. They would want to show it and themselves off. They would want to display their success. They would want to get spoken about.

"We wait," said Bellarmine, "for the loot to show itself."

"You can't wait too long," said Sapodin. "Pressure's too great. There isn't much time."

The Walrus and St. Jean sat hunched over a marble-topped table on the glass-enclosed terrace of a bar on the Rue Thubaneau in Marseille. It was a cold winter morning. There were electric heaters on the board floor of the terrace all the way around the perimeter. The glass next to their table had misted over, and they had to keep wiping the condensation off to see out. They wore their hats and coats.

A business negotiation was in progress. Across the street three or four prostitutes were already at work, and the negotiation concerned certain of them. Each girl patrolled about fifty meters of sidewalk, each tilted her head at every male who passed by, and from time to time the two men watched them. The low sun slanted in on their profiles and on the empty espresso cups in front of them.

All the girls opposite belonged to St. Jean. One, who today wore a red wig, was known as La Duchesse. She was about thirty and worked the bottom of the street. She came into view only once every several minutes. Despite the six-inch spike heels on which she walked, she had a stately carriage, and a haughty manner to go with it. She wore the latest Paris fashions and looked expensive, which she was not. All the girls on the street charged the same price, whether they worked for St. Jean or another. Free enterprise was not permitted. The Milieu abhorred competition.

The Duchess had worked that sidewalk for the past eleven years. The Walrus wanted to buy her from St. Jean, together with her stretch of sidewalk, or a better one. The whoremaster, who was perfectly willing to sell, was bargaining carefully.

"Why La Duchesse?" he asked. "She's the best girl I have." This was, sadly, not true, though it had been once. The girl's appeal had fallen off. Though she was still beautifully dressed, she was of course less ripe than she had been, and the vacuous expression in her eyes had got worse year by year.

"She appeals to me," said The Walrus. To him she had class, more than any whore in Marseille. Also, he believed she appreciated him. He had taken her upstairs several times, and had paid her, and she had marveled at his great size.

The Duchess's receipts had fallen way off. St. Jean had wondered at first if she was holding back money. For a time he had stationed someone across the street to count the clients she accepted. But the sums checked out. Next he had sent trusted men to sample her favors, undercover agents so to speak. They had auditioned her. She might just as well have been a singer or an actress auditioning for impresarios. The performer had failed the audition. The reports St. Jean got back explained why business was down. She had lost enthusiasm. She simply lay there. She studied her fingernails behind clients' ears. She had become blasé about her work.

He had talked to her. Being a kind of father figure, he had at first exhorted her. When that didn't work, he beat her up, using the flat of his hands so as not to mark the merchandise too much. But her

87

receipts continued to dwindle. Well, it happened to all girls in time. They were like sports heroes. It wasn't their legs that went first, but their love of the game. They lost, literally, their desire, a quality more important by far than experience or expertise. They were no longer winners, and it became the coach's job to pick the best moment to get rid of them—to sell them or trade them if possible. In the case of the Duchess this moment had clearly come.

Ruminations such as this depressed St. Jean. Everyone got old. One suffered with these girls at every stage of their careers. The Walrus would find out. "What do you want to get mixed up with girls for?" St. Jean said to him, and his voice was full of feeling. "They're nothing but trouble."

"I want to be somebody in Marseille," replied The Walrus earnestly. He was not articulate, and was unable to put into words the inchoate ambitions inside him. But within the Milieu the stature of a man depended on running girls. A *mec* was expected to live off their earnings, to sit in cafés all day, and in nightclubs all night, while his girls plied their trade across the street.

"A man who don't have his own *putes*," said The Walrus earnestly, "is a nobody."

"Well," said St. Jean, "La Duchesse is a valuable piece of property. I'd have to get a lot of money for her."

"Then you'll sell?" The Walrus was elated. *"Formidable."*

They began to haggle over money. St. Jean held out for a certain sum, and they soon agreed. It was about four times what the Duchess was worth at this stage of her career, and St. Jean had got rid of the problem she represented at the same time. He was very pleased. The Walrus was pleased also. He was bright enough to know he had paid too much, but then start-up costs were bound to be high in any business. Additional girls would not cost as much.

"I want her to be happy when she comes to work for me," he told St. Jean now. "That means finding a better spot for her. I want to move her up closer to the corner."

St. Jean shook his head. "I'd advise against it. Corners are very expensive."

"I want that corner there." With his sleeve The Walrus rubbed the mist off the glass and pointed across the street.

"That's Françoise's corner."

"Move her down."

"How much?"

"It ought to be included," said The Walrus doggedly.

St. Jean thought it over. "All right," he said. "I'll move Françoise down. She's a pain in the ass anyway."

He used the French expression: Françoise had become a *casse-pieds*. Françoise was young, a star, and difficult to control. She had poor commercial instincts. If she liked a client she stayed upstairs with him too long. She did not like standing under umbrellas and on rainy days would not work at all. She claimed to have eight-day periods—eight days' income gone out of every month. So he would demote Françoise. She deserved it.

The two men shook hands. The deal was made. As they stood up, St. Jean tossed some bills down on to the marble. The Walrus would fetch his money and they would meet again later today.

"Running girls is not easy," St. Jean advised him as they parted, and again his voice became charged with emotion. "They won't give you no respect. You'll see. They'll break your heart."

For his share of the Nice bank job The Walrus had received bank notes, gold ingots and a handful of loose jewels, but only the cash was real to him, and he had distributed it for safe-keeping among safe-deposit boxes in seven different banks in Marseille and neighboring Toulon—The Walrus knew about bank break-ins, and was taking no chances. The gold ingots and loose jewels he kept in a locked strongbox inside a locked suitcase inside a locked closet in his seedy flat in the old quarter of Marseille. He returned there now and withdrew several stones that looked valuable to him. He did not want to part with his cash, even to buy the services of the Duchess. He would sell some of this stuff. He would go to see Freddie the Jeweler. As an afterthought, before leaving his room, he also shoved a four-inch gold ingot into his side pocket.

The Jeweler kept a small store on the Canebière about three blocks up from the Vieux Port. His principal business was the buying and selling of used jewelry, some of it stolen, and a selection was on display in his narrow window.

As the bell over his door tinkled he looked up sharply to see who the new client might be. The sun was behind the man and Freddie could not see his face. He did note that only an inch or two of sunlight showed between the client's massive arms and the door-jambs. Then he saw that it was The Walrus. Freddie was mindlessly, instinctively afraid of the ex-wrestler, and had been since the first time they met.

"What are you coming in here for?" Freddie demanded anxiously. His fear was twofold. He feared the man's great strength, and he feared his stupidity, which could bring the police down on them all. "Somebody might see you. I don't want you coming in here."

The Walrus carried the loose stones clutched inside a sweaty fist in the pocket of his overcoat. A small velvet cloth lay atop Freddie's glass counter. The Walrus pulled out his fist—it was like producing a concealed weapon—and clapped it down on the velvet cloth. The knuckles opened and the moist stones spilled out.

"I need some cash."

Freddie's forefinger stirred the stones while physical truth—his fear—struggled against commercial truth—he had too many unsold stones already. Commerce won, though barely. "I don't think I can take on any more right now," he hazarded. "I mean I can't."

"This stuff is supposed to be liquid. Just like cash." The two men studied the stones.

"Well, it's not. You have to sell it. It takes time." Freddie's voice became a whine. "I can't take them. I just can't." If the ex-wrestler now decided to bring that great ham fist down on the countertop, the glass would shatter and the jewels would go flying. Everything on the shelf underneath would go flying also. Or he might decide to hurl The Jeweler through the front window out into the street.

But The Walrus said only: "What should I do then?" and his voice sounded genuinely meek.

Sensing that the oaf meant him no harm, Freddie arranged his eyeglasses on his ears while he sought a suitable reply.

"You have plenty of cash," he said. The Walrus had decided not to wreck his place, and Freddie could not believe his luck. "Use it. When you run out of cash you can sell this other stuff. It's safer that way anyway. We all should wait about six months until this whole thing dies down."

From his pocket The Walrus withdrew the gold ingot. "What about this?"

Gold was just like money, The Jeweler told him. It could be handed across the counter in any bank in France and they would give him cash, no questions asked.

The Walrus nodded. "Why don't you just give me what this is worth?"

The Jeweler squirmed inside his collar. Rolling the ingot over, he showed where it was stamped with the seal of the Bank of France, and with a serial number. "It could be dangerous to take this to a bank right now."

"Not a bank. You. You give me the money."

Again The Jeweler began to whine. He had no cash to spare, he said. Faletta had divided up the loot according to a system of his own. The clan leader had paid off The Jeweler almost exclusively in jewels, and it would take a long time to sell them. Now The Walrus wanted to stick him with this ingot too. It wasn't fair. The Jeweler was a loyal team member, but the others were all treating him badly.

Somewhere in this speech The Walrus realized The Jeweler was not going to help him. He was not really surprised. The difference between The Jeweler and himself was education, he believed. These educated *mecs* were always too worried about themselves to be true friends. Friendship and education were incompatible with each other. When education came in, loyalty went out.

For The Walrus, this was profound thinking, it gave him the start of a headache, and it moved him to action. His thick fingers scraped up the loose stones into another fist. The fist got rammed into his coat pocket again, and he spun around and stormed out of the jewelry store. The door slammed.

Freddie nearly fainted with relief. He felt like a motorist who just had walked away unscratched from a head-on collision.

About three doors down the street The Walrus paused in front of the principal Marseille branch of the Banque de Nice et de la Côte d'Azur. As he hesitated, his hand patted the bulk of the ingot in his pocket. But the serial numbers worried him. He decided not to risk going into this bank, and he strolled up the Canebière looking for another. The cold sun was on his shoulders and the cold mistral wind blew in his face. Presently he came to another bank, the Crédit Lyonnais. He went in and dropped his ingot on the counter in front of the surprised teller.

"Gimme cash."

At Bellarmine's orders, serial numbers from the ingots out of the Banque de Nice had been printed on circulars and sent to every bank in France. However, the comparing of numbers to lists is a tedious business, and difficult to do in a bank as busy as this one was this afternoon. Besides, Nice was 120 miles away, and the crime that preoccupied the Riviera was of no great import here. The teller merely got on with the paper work involved, and when it was done, he passed The Walrus the money—an inch-thick sheaf of ten-thousand-franc notes, each as large as a hand towel, though worth only about twenty-eight dollars, the largest bank note printed by the French treasury.

That the ingot's serial number matched one on the police circular would not be noticed by bank officers until the next day. Out of embarrassment they would not notify the police until the day after that.

The Walrus left the bank and strolled back the way he had come, moving leisurely through crowds down the boulevard, the wad of money riding his coat pocket on top of the loose jewels. He felt rich, and the weight—gold was heavier than a revolver—was gone from his pants as well.

In the bar that afternoon he again met with St. Jean, and paid him, and the two went out into the street and informed La Duchesse that she had changed hands. The Walrus then made her a short speech. From now on he would take care of her, and as a bonus for the many years of service he knew she would give him, he was improving her turf, moving her up closer to the corner.

Though he expected gratitude, he got none. Instead, the woman displayed a kind of panic. He did not understand why, but in fact she was attached like a cat to a specific place. After eleven years of walking the same stretch of sidewalk the change seemed to her too momentous, a violent upheaval in her life. Though the difference was only about two hundred meters, she became profoundly disturbed. She would miss being able to chat with her girl friends at each turn-around, her habitual clients might no longer be able to find her—she did not want this change.

The Walrus returned to the café where he took the same table next to the window. He ordered a Pernod, which he stirred with a massive finger, and for the rest of the afternoon watched his new acquisition marching up and down the new stretch of sidewalk opposite. He was wearing all new clothes: new camel's-hair overcoat, new felt fedora—it looked tiny on his great head—and black crocodile shoes. As he watched his Duchess, his thick chest swelled with pride. He had made good at last, had become a man of property like other prominent members of the Milieu. He had reached the top of his profession—*le haut du pavé* in Milieu jargon—the top of the sidewalk.

St. Jean meanwhile wondered what to do with the unexpected money in his pocket. To him it was found money, as opposed to Banque de Nice money, which he had had to work for. He was too experienced a man to spend any of the Nice money in an ostentatious manner, for the police might be watching. But The Walrus' payment to him fit into a different category. It was a windfall. It was there to buy something with, though what? Finally he decided on a present for his steady girl friend, who walked a piece of sidewalk on the Rue Longue, and a new pair of crocodile shoes for himself. And he went to ask her what she wanted.

The loan shark known as Frère Jacques was on an extended vacation. He had gone home to Corsica, where he spent most of his time in cafés. He did some bragging. He bought people a lot of drinks. He picked up pretty women and bought them presents. But on the whole he behaved discreetly.

Henry the Torch was behaving discreetly also, or so he believed, for he was operating mostly around Cannes, which, being neither Nice nor Marseille, seemed to him safe. He was carefully investing his money. On the same day that The Walrus bought up, so to speak, the Duchess's contract, Henry the Torch followed a real-estate agent into the lobby of a nearly completed apartment building in Cannes. Although she babbled about its luxurious appointments, pointing out the mirrors, the crystal chandeliers, he only snuffed the air. The lobby reeked of fresh plaster. There was plaster dust on the marble floor, and as they crossed to the elevator they left their footprints in it. It got on Henry's black crocodile shoes. He frowned and, as the elevator climbed, transferred the white film from his shoes to his trousers. Like a dog, he lifted first one leg, then the other.

The elevator was tiny, and it climbed upward too slowly. The middle-aged agent was expensively dressed and coiffed. She wore rings on both hands. She was locked in a tiny cubicle chest to chest with Henry the Torch, which made her study him closely for the first time. Suddenly he did not strike her as a potential buyer. He had the manners of a thug, and a Corsican accent. He was breathing on her, and with each exhalation came a gust of garlic. If he wasn't a potential buyer, then what was he? And what was she doing alone with him in this empty building?

Each Riviera town had a distinctive personality. Menton was full of retired people. Monte Carlo was faded and run-down. Juan-les-Pins was brand-new and full of nightclubs—in summer, people walked barefoot in the streets. Nice was like a dowager empress, heavy and out of style, living on its reputation. It had catered to Queen Victoria and to the Grand Duke of all the Russias, and would like to do so again. Before the war it had catered to rich English tourists, and it was still trying to do so, even though they were no longer there. Because of currency restrictions, the English, rich or not, could no longer come abroad. There was a new foreign colony in Nice and it was American, which was not the same thing, and Nice was still trying to learn its desires.

The most elegant town was Cannes. It was the last place, the agent thought, to appeal to this man whose name she didn't know and who was wearing a leather overcoat. Cannes had a sand beach, one of the few, on which starlets were sometimes photographed in bikinis during the May film festival—bikinis were seen only in France at this time and for the most part only on starlets. Cannes' most elegant street was the Croisette, which ran along the beach. It was lined with palm trees and jewelry shops, and was overhung with luxury hotels. Its flower beds were bursting with color; the plantings were replaced by city gardeners as soon as they faded so that Cannes seemed a city perpetually in bloom. There was also a number of splendid villas along the Croisette, most of them now being torn down, to be replaced by exclusive new apartment buildings like this one, which sold out even before they were completed. Most buyers were people investing in real estate. A few were French—bankers and film stars—but the majority were foreigners. Foreigners had money and they were buying up the Côte d'Azur.

But to the agent, Henry the Torch did not fit into any of these categories.

"What sent you to our agency, monsieur?" she asked nervously, as the elevator continued to rise. But the burly man only grunted something, and as his leather coat brushed against her, she became afraid. She noticed his eyes, which were green, with yellow glints. They were the coldest eyes she had ever seen, dangerous eyes, and they shone out of a flat, almost Oriental face.

When the elevator stopped, he seemed to push open the door by expanding his chest. It was like watching a man burst the buttons of a shirt that was too tight for him. Then, instead of holding the door for her, he simply stepped out into the hall, and the door swung back, nearly knocking her down.

"Plan to live here yourself, do you?" she asked. The hall was dark and in her fear she could not get the key in the lock. "Investing, are you?"

Henry the Torch did not answer.

She pushed the door open and was struck by a burst of sunlight. She pushed against it and stepped into the room. She was thinking purely in physical terms—an empty building, a man in a leather overcoat and crocodile shoes. If she screamed no one would hear. She decided to attempt to stroll to the French windows—from there she could call for help. But the stroll turned into a lunge, and she yanked them open and stepped out on to the balcony five stories above the sea. It was very windy, too windy. If she screamed, no one would even hear her. She peered down on the thrashing palm trees. Out on the Mediterranean there were white caps on the water.

Although its view was the apartment's main selling points, the man in the leather overcoat had not followed her onto the balcony, proving him no buyer. The rapist stood by the door, smelling of leather and garlic, his breath whistling through his deviated septum, blocking her only means of escape.

She took a gulp of fresh air and stepped back into the room, where she gave him her brightest smile and edged toward the door. "Isn't it a beautiful apartment?"

"I'll take it. How much?"

She heard the words, but they made no sense to her. She was almost to the door, and in a quavery voice she continued her sales pitch—note the elegant moldings, the brass door handles, the marble floors.

"I seen enough. I'll take it."

If she could get behind him, she could make a run for it. "Of course it's expensive," she blabbed on. "Of course it's more than you would want to pay."

"You deaf, *ma vieille?*"

"A Hollywood director has bought here." She was totally unnerved. "And one of the Rothschilds, and—"

"You want to unload it or not?"

Her office was three blocks inland from the sea. Only when seated behind her desk, with secretaries and another agent nearby, did she feel safe. She got the forms out.

The burly man in the leather overcoat was seated beside her, and when she glanced into his lap she saw that his big hand caressed a thick roll of ten-thousand-franc notes. "How much for a down payment?" It made her peer in confusion at the forms, as embarrassed as if she had caught him working over his unbuttoned fly.

Then he was gone. She picked up the pile of money he had given her and realized she was sweating. She had sweated even into the shields in her dress, which felt soaked.

She talked it over with the other salesman. They decided Henry must be a peasant farmer who had just inherited money. Not trusting currency, he had wanted, like all French peasants, to place it immediately in real estate.

"But why not a pig farm?" said the other salesman. "Why a luxury apartment on the Croisette?"

"Can you see him up there living next to the Rothschilds?"

Both agents thought it very droll, very droll indeed.

Still wearing his brown leather overcoat and black crocodile shoes, Henry the Torch turned up for the closing several days later and spilled millions of francs out of an attaché case on to the table. They took down his address, date of birth, and other particulars off his identity card—they already had his name and signature—and the sale was concluded.

Within a day or two this transaction was the talk of the real-estate trade everywhere along the coast.

Henry's other preoccupation was his teeth, and he went to the most expensive prosthetic dentist in Marseille. He wanted all his teeth capped. "Make me a smile like a choirboy, *toubib*," he said.

Having concluded his examination, the dentist straightened up from the chair.

*Toubib* was the rude word for doctor. The dentist hated being called *toubib*. He said: "I can do it, of course. But that sort of work is very expensive." He was irritated, and he gazed not into Henry's face but at the black crocodile shoes that pointed toward the ceiling. Only gangsters wear crocodile shoes, he thought.

"Name the figure, *toubib*."

The dentist was surprised, but he named a sum.

Although he had expected to see the patient flinch, this didn't happen. "You got it."

"Perhaps we should discuss the fee a bit more first," the dentist said. Payment with a patient like this was always a problem. "Suppose we say half down and half when the job is completed."

"Half down," repeated Henry, and he dug into his pants pocket. His hand came up clutching a gold ingot. "How about I pay with this?"

The dentist handled the ingot. He knew gold. "Do you have any more of these?" he asked. This ingot could go straight into his safe-deposit box, and from there into people's teeth, tax-free.

"Maybe."

"I'll accept this as down payment." Two ingots were worth more to the dentist than the price he had named. "And a second one when you leave here."

"Smiling like a choirboy."

"Right," said the dentist, and smiled like a choirboy himself.

Henry the Torch lay back and opened his mouth, exposing his decayed molars, and blew a wash of sour breath into the dentist's face.

In Tangier harbor Arab dockers had loaded Roy LeRoy's PT boat with four hundred cases of tax-free American cigarettes, all its hold could take, a hundred cases each of the four most popular brands, Chesterfields, Lucky Strikes, Camels and Philip Morris. Roy had purchased this cargo at a legal warehouse on the quay, handing across fifteen thousand dollars in cash, seven and a half cents per pack. When his buyers came aboard from fishing boats off St. Raphael tomorrow night he would double his money. He would count their cash out of an envelope by the light from his binnacle and only then permit them to begin tossing cases down into their boats.

The price had fallen lately. Just after the war it used to be triple that. American cigarettes, which were heavily taxed in Europe—in France they cost close to fifty cents per pack in the government-controlled tobacco shops—were beginning to be manufactured now in Belgium or such place, and in addition the Milieu in the last two years had gone into the trade in a big way. In a few more months, Roy believed, maybe a year, American cigarettes would be a glut on the market. This was why he had gone back to work so soon. He meant to cash in while he still could.

The business had changed many times since Lambert had come up with the idea in 1948. Their first boat was a twelve meter yacht which Lambert had rented in Antibes from a financially strapped English lord named Derby-Haig. The Limey's money was blocked in England. Roy always referred to him as Lord Derby-Hat. Lambert rented the boat for only one month, for they had intended to make only one trip. Lord Derby-Hat had been very worried about his yacht, but Lambert assured him they were only going on a cruise to Greece with their wives. They returned the yacht a month later, no problems, having made a profit of $12,500. Immediately they went looking for bigger, faster boats, and for a crew they could trust to sail them.

That first load had been delivered off Genoa, to men working for some Italian count Lambert knew from somewhere. All these European noblemen were now broke and scrambling for a living. They had circled around in the dark three miles offshore trying to find the boats that had come out to meet them. This was when Lambert had decided they would need radios and radiomen too.

At their peak they had had twelve men and four boats. The Italian count had remained their best customer, and they had restricted their sales to Italy for years. Lambert had wanted to stay away from France because he lived there, and because he was afraid of the French police, whereas the Italian customs service, La Finanza, was a joke.

They began to service France only later, once they had the PT boats. It seemed safe enough. At fifty knots per hour a man was not afraid of anybody. They had picked up the PT boats at an auction in Gibraltar in 1950, forty thousand dollars each, outbidding the Turkish Navy, as it happened, which had them laughing for a week. That was one of the funny things that happened. There were many others.

It was not all profit. When they were still using Fairmiles, one of them broke down off Alicante, Spain, and had to put in for repairs. The Spaniards confiscated the boat and threw everybody in jail—the English captain, whose name was Thompson, and the same two Australians who had helped with the Banque de Nice job. Lambert had hired Spanish lawyers, had bribed everybody, until finally the men were released on bail. They had never gone back for trial, so that the boat and its cargo were lost, and the bail money too. Much the same thing happened in Italy a year or two later. About then the Milieu entered the cigarette trade in a big way. Milieu thugs came forward to "buy out" the independents. There were some killings. Most of the independents sold their boats for whatever they could get. Lambert merely walked away from his, saying that the business wasn't fun anymore. Thompson took one PT boat and LeRoy the other. But Thompson's soon broke down, and he sold it and got married to a girl from Nice. LeRoy didn't know what he was doing now. Making babies, probably.

That left Roy LeRoy, still defying the Milieu, still making good money out of cigarettes, though he knew with prices dropping he would have to find something else soon, and now as he conned his great speedboat slowly out of Tangier harbor he resolved to visit Lambert in Nice as soon as he got his cargo off-loaded. Maybe Lambert had ideas about what to do next.

A man dressed like an Arab fisherman stood on the seawall watching him go. He was an undercover French customs agent watching for just such shipments as this one. LeRoy knew him. French customs had been trying to catch him with a shipment for years, but he was too slick for them, or maybe just too fast. For as long as his boat had all three engines running he had nothing to worry about. To LeRoy the undercover agent was a joke, and he gave him a big wave. The man did not wave back.

After watching the PT boat clear the harbor, the agent walked back along the seawall and out of the port and up the street to the post office where he sent a cable to Marseille. The agent had no illusions. He had been performing this function ever since the cigarette trade started, seldom to much effect. Tomorrow customs cutters might be sent out to search for LeRoy's PT boat, which would be approaching the French coast by then. Whether they would find it or not was another story. A PT boat, being made of wood, could not be picked up on World War II radarscopes, and the French coastline was long. LeRoy would approach it in the dark, and probably get through.

The only way to stop these shipments was to search for the boats by air by daylight and track them in. But even this was difficult, almost impossible—the sea was so big, and a PT boat so small. Unless it trailed a wake—at top speed a PT boat's 4,000 horsepower churned up a wake two to four miles long—you had little hope of finding it, and experienced contraband runners like LeRoy did not leave wakes. As soon as they got within two hundred miles of the coast, they throttled way down, and the great wakes together with the hope they represented quickly vanished back into the sea.

By the time the agent had sent his cable and left the post office, LeRoy had begun his run across the Mediterranean. All three engines were booming, and the Arab beside him was hanging on. LeRoy himself wore a ferocious grin. It amused him to think of cutters leaving shore in the night to intercept him. They hadn't laid a search-light on him yet, and he doubted they ever would.

In the morning Jacqueline Lambert looked out into the hall and the shoes outside the hotel room doors had been waxed and buffed all the length of the corridor. Every morning it was the same, but to see them still amazed her. She brought their own shoes inside.

They were in the Palace Hotel in Zermatt, having come there by train via Milan.

European trains since the war were always extremely crowded. The bombers had destroyed much of the rolling stock, and with money so

99

short it could be replaced only bit by bit. For the masses there was no other means of transportation. In third class, passengers often had to sit astride their suitcases in the corridors. She and Lambert had done it during their honeymoon trip to Paris in 1946. They were very poor. Lambert had used up his separation pay during the courtship and he had no job. He was not permitted to hold one.

And so now Jacqueline was unprepared for the luxury of the first-class tickets Lambert had bought. There were only six places in each compartment. Theirs was not even full, and it had fresh antimacassars on all the headrests. The train moved through the dark coastal tunnels and came out into all the sunny Riviera towns. Flowers bloomed on all the platforms, and the stationmasters in their blue uniforms all looked smart. On the Italian side it was all much poorer.

After Genoa the train ran north toward Turin and Milan. They were out of the rugged coastal mountains, and the fields were brown and bare in the sun.

At Milan they spent the night in a first-class hotel, and the next morning went sightseeing: the cathedral, the *Last Supper,* the narrow streets of the old part of the city, the smart shops. Italy was famous for leather goods, and Lambert bought her a new handbag, shoes and gloves.

They took the train through the Simplon Tunnel into Switzerland, and at Brig changed to the narrow-gauge railway up to Zermatt. It was dusk when they got down from the train. It was very cold. A row of porters waited outside the station. They were from the various hotels and met every train. There was a different hotel name on every cap. The porter from the Palace took their bags and they followed him to the horse-drawn sled that would carry them to the hotel, for there were no cars or taxis in the town. In the last of the daylight they could see their breath rising above their heads, and they climbed into the sled and pulled a rug over their laps. The porter mounted beside the coachman, and they were off, the sled runners grating over the hard snow. Clouds had come down, and they could not see the high surrounding peaks. A few tentative flakes began to fall, and then it was snowing hard.

They went into the hotel. In a gigantic fireplace, logs blazed. Behind the desk stood a clerk in a cutaway coat. He took Lambert's green American passport and Jacqueline's blue French one. A second clerk, dressed the same, showed them to their room. Lambert had specified a view of the famous Matterhorn, but when they peered out through the curtains they could see only swirling snow.

The dining room was crowded with young people in ski clothes and was loud with the babble of many languages. There was a fireplace in the dining room too in which more logs blazed. They dined on hearty Swiss food. There was dark, chewy bread and Swiss red wine that was heavy and full-bodied and made them both giggly.

By morning the storm had blown itself out. There were fresh sled tracks through the streets, and blots of snow on the crowns of the lampposts. Smoke rose from the chimneys, and the streets were blue. When they went outside, the village itself was still in gloom. People hurried toward the lifts like laborers on their way to work, their skis slung like tools over their shoulders. Lambert took her into shops and they outfitted themselves from skis to boots to matching knitted ski hats. Their hats had red pompons on them. Jacqueline had only to lift something off a pile, or examine its price, and Lambert bought it for her. Both were laughing before they had finished, and she had never felt so precious to him.

When they came out the sun had tinged the peaks all around, and a cloud broke in two so that the great Matterhorn at last stood revealed, towering above them all, a gigantic brown spearhead to which snow clung like cake icing. It stunned them both. It was far higher, far more gorgeous than they had expected, and isolated from all others. It was like a manifestation of God. It was absolutely awesome. Several seconds passed before either could even speak. "Look at that," she breathed, and Lambert answered: "I know," and they embraced each other and stared at what both believed must be the most grandiose mountain in all of creation.

Lambert hired a ski instructor, a big, blunt man called Hans. He was about forty and totally humorless, but by the end of the second day he had them trying the lower slopes on their own.

Each morning she watched her husband call down for breakfast, and for all the French- and English-language newspapers available. The papers reached Zermatt one day late. Lambert read them religiously nonetheless, sometimes with great amusement.

Often he laughed out loud.

"This fellow they call The Brain must be a helluva guy," he said with what sounded like admiration. This upset her, though she tried not to let it show. She did not want him admiring criminals. It was as if she feared that, finding mere admiration insufficient, he might seek to join them. He already had too many predilections in that direction, it seemed to her. Of course all that was before he had sold his play. She was convinced now that he had sold it.

She refused to read any newspaper accounts herself. They sat at their little table in the sunlight pouring in the French windows and drank their breakfast coffee, and Jacqueline watched her husband smiling and chuckling over his newspapers, and eventually she got used to it. She told herself she was being unreasonable and a shrew. They were on a second honeymoon after all, let him do what he wanted.

And she allowed herself to feel languorous and content, often remembering scenes from their first honeymoon, like the time they shared a bag of cherries in the streets of Paris or the time they were unable to go into a certain museum because the tickets cost too much.

Often she remembered their courtship too. It had lasted a long time, for soon his leave ended, and he went back into combat, and she didn't see him again for four months. It was during this period that he won his medals and became a hero, while she went on working in the PX. He was in the hospital the American Army had taken over, the St. Roch on the Rue Pastorelli, when she found him again. He had been shot through the left buttock and was very embarrassed about it. She was one of a group of girls of good family the Red Cross sent to visit the wounded. The bullet had left a gaping exit wound. He was there a long time on his side with drains in him. She was studying English and he was studying French, and by the time they could dance together again they could also talk to each other—half in French, half in English and she learned of his hopes for the future, of the plays he wanted to write, and she fell in love.

Now in Switzerland, Lambert too felt content, and not yet restless. The papers were a joy to him. The Walrus' work was never mentioned—this was a pleasant surprise. Instead the press distributed only—one could call it nothing else—praise. The Brain was a genius. The crime was "The Heist of the Century." How gratifying.

In addition, it was written that the police had no clues and the crime would probably never be solved. This was gratifying also, and Lambert believed it.

The day came when they carried their skis to the Gornergrat cog railway and rode up to eleven thousand feet, from which point "down" looked very far down indeed. There was a restaurant. To give themselves courage, the condemned couple ate a last meal, lunching outdoors on a terrace in full sunlight, surrounded by snow and air. They drank a bottle of wine, and then began the long, gentle run down to the village. Each time one of them fell it would send the other into gales of laughter.

Once they stood resting, poles planted, and Jacqueline gazed at the mountains all around. She glanced at her husband, who was breathing deeply beside her, leaning on his poles, and she thought: It is not his money he is spending on me, but his triumph. He is a success at last and he has come back to me for the second time. The sensation of being precious to him seemed to expand inside her with each new cold breath she drew into her lungs.

"Why don't we move to Switzerland?" said Lambert suddenly. He was not looking at her, but across at the Matterhorn. They could do it if they wished, he said. They were rich enough to go anywhere they chose.

"Or Italy," he offered expansively. "You like Italy. We could move." Either place would be safer for him than France.

"I'll race you to the bottom," said Jacqueline and pushed off.

As she plunged downhill, she thought that he was offering to fulfill any whim that might have entered her head. If she so wished they would move even to a new country. But she had no whims left. They had all been satisfied. With his success her husband had become a different man, strong, forceful, incredibly generous. To her, now, Nice seemed quite grand enough.

As for Lambert, his mood had changed before he reached the bottom of the run. He had wanted his wife's approval, and had worked this past week to get it. He hadn't had it in many years. Now he had it again, with the result that he had become bored. Skiing bored him. Switzerland bored him. He was tired of being alone with his wife. He was anxious to get back to Nice, where the action was. He wanted to sniff around the detectives. He wanted to get close enough to laugh at them.

Besides, a new idea had come to him—a way to invest his recently acquired capital. It was a scheme that would require help. He needed to get in touch with Roy LeRoy.

Going down from Zermatt, they changed trains in Brig again, and in Milan checked into the same extravagant hotel as before, and when they went upstairs to their room after dinner, Lambert was carrying a new batch of newspapers to read. They were a day later than the ones he had seen that morning in Switzerland. He sat up in bed turning pages, and Jacqueline left him and lay in a hot bath and fantasized contentedly about the future.

"When we get home, I think I'll buy a car," her husband said to her when she came out. Unknown to her, increased mobility was vital to his new scheme. Besides, he could afford a car now.

Jacqueline looked at him in amazement.

"With a car we can live on the farm and drive down to Nice every day. We can really fix up the farm."

"There's a two-year wait to buy a car," she said.

"Not if you pay in dollars."

It was true. With dollars you got immediate delivery and a big discount as well. She would have to get used to thinking in terms of dollars. America really was the promised land, the richest and most generous place the world had ever known. For an American every dream was possible.

Climbing into bed, she reached out and pushed the papers off his lap onto the floor.

"My papers!"

She turned off the light and rolled onto him. "Your wife," she said.

"Maybe I'll have a baby," she whispered a little later. "Maybe he'll grow up to be a famous playwright like his father."

Lambert gave a pleased laugh. "Maybe he will."

The next day they returned to Nice, where Jacqueline expected that the honeymoon would continue. Instead Lambert mysteriously departed. He did not say where he was going or when he would come back. He just went.

He flew to Madrid in an Air France Viscount, and from there to Tangier, but Jacqueline didn't know this. In Tangier he missed Roy LeRoy, who had already sailed, which was a nuisance, but he found the Moroccan contacts his new scheme required—men in dark suits whom he met in the backs of tearooms—and he forged an agreement in principle with them. He then flew to Algiers and set up a similar scheme there.

Jacqueline could do nothing but wonder what dark business he might be up to, and wait with increasing agitation for his return. Each morning she opened her shop at 9 A.M., and each evening at 8 P.M. she closed it. All day she stood in it, and except for occasional customers she was alone. At night she slept alone in the narrow bed in the stock room, and she waited.

She refused to admit to herself that the second honeymoon was over, having lasted not even as long as the first.

# CHAPTER 10

At the Nice railroad station, accompanied by Lussac, Bellarmine boarded the train for Marseille, where he intended to find and interrogate the prostitute Denise Lasablière. According to her colleague, the girl known as The Stinger, Denise had recognized someone named Jeannot in the street in Nice several nights before the break-in, and had surmised that a coup was being planned. As a lead it sounded no better than it had two weeks ago. The difference was that by now he had no better ones left. In every other direction was a blank wall. Meanwhile, The Walrus' gold ingot had turned up in Marseille, the bank there was permanently staked out in case the same man came back with another one, and Marseille police officials were clamoring for the investigation, saying it ought to be turned over to them. Bellarmine had to keep showing activity lest the *division-naire* or someone, acceding to these demands, take it away from him.

"How will you handle her?" asked Lussac. He had sat in on The Stinger's interrogation, and had been amazed at how gently Bellarmine treated whores. This whore, anyway. He had made her cry, but had then been nice to her, with the result that she had talked freely— much more freely than she had talked to Lussac.

Lussac now had been watching Bellarmine closely for days, had begun to feel admiration for him, and as a result their relationship seemed to him improved. "Will you treat her as gently as The Stinger, or what?"

"I don't know yet," said Bellarmine curtly. He was no more immune to hero worship than the next man, a weakness in himself that he despised. He stared out of the train window.

On one side was the beach and the aluminum sea. The other side was easier on the eyes: scrub fields that reached upward toward carnation farms, toward hills studded with villas, and beyond that toward the Maritime Alps, which were so high there was snow on them. But the railroad tracks, where there were beaches, stayed close to the beach. Often they ran over a beach or through it, wasting the most valuable beachfront property in the world. It was incredible that this could have happened. The explanation was that the railroad predated the bathing suit. It had been built at a time when beaches were used only to beach fishing boats, when no one, male or female, dared show himself in public half undressed.

Bellarmine's first job would be to find this Denise Lasablière. He would meet with Commissaire Devereux, chief of the Marseille Mondaine, a man he did not know, and would ask to see her file. Devereux would be hostile, of course, for Bellarmine was invading his territory—what could be more normal? That's why Lussac was along. Perhaps Devereux would agree to cooperate with a colleague in vice.

The train ran through the Riviera towns: through Cagnes, where Renoir had painted; through Antibes; through Golfe Juan, where Napoleon had landed on his return from Elba. After Cannes the mountains came right down to the sea, and the train plunged through a succession of tunnels.

The hostility of Commissaire Devereux was a given. One coped with it as one could. The police world, no different from the larger world outside it, contained scores of factions all squabbling among themselves. It was often said that *flics* stuck together everywhere, at all times and at whatever cost. To prove this, one pointed to their conduct whenever a policeman was murdered. Did they not join hands like brothers at a funeral? Indeed they did. Such events brought out the best in them, and for as long as the emotion lasted they behaved like the tight-knit family that outsiders believed them to be. Unfortunately it did not last very long. It could almost be said that *flics* lived from funeral to funeral, that their funerals made them glad. The orgy of emotion was as much a high as alcohol or drugs. They lived for a time on a lofty plain of honor, devotion and brotherhood. They gave and received only love, and with single-minded passion they hunted the murderer down.

And then it ended and more usual emotions returned. Like politicians they fought over jurisdiction, over protocol. Like actors they fought for credit, for a headline. Given the chance to make a major arrest, to break an important case, they were willing, figuratively speaking, to destroy each other.

As *commissaires*, Bellarmine and Lussac rode first-class, a rare taste of luxury for policemen. Their compartment contained only six places, and was otherwise unoccupied. The seat cushions were plump, and they rested their heads against crisp linen antimacassars. At Sûreté headquarters in Marseille, such luxury would be absent, and as Bellarmine watched the scenery he wondered what his reception there would be. Between the tunnels he looked down on small, empty beaches entirely rimmed with towering red porphyry rocks. The tunnels were full of coal smoke from the locomotives, and in the longer ones the compartment filled up with the odor of burning coal, and the coal dust seeped in under the window, and their clothes and hair and nostrils became impregnated with it. Then at last they were in Marseille, and they got down from the train and walked out through the station.

The Sûreté headquarters building had been built just behind the palace of the bishops of Marseille. It was known therefore as the Bishopric. It stood as an enclave inside Milieu territory. The streets radiating out from it were lined with Milieu-run cabarets and bars, and were heavily frequented by prostitutes.

Bellarmine and Lussac showed their police cards at the door and were directed to Devereux's small office in the second floor rear. It was much like Bellarmine's in Nice. Scarred desk piled high with folders. Two wooden chairs. Tall windows that looked down on the courtyard—on the inevitable black Citroëns, the inevitable groups of chauffeurs smoking.

"How goes it?" said Bellarmine.

They exchanged the perfunctory ritual handshake.

"Enchanted," said Devereux, but he asked at once to see their order of mission—not a good omen—and although he agreed to produce the dossier on Denise Lasablière, he did not move to do so. Instead he remained seated, smoking, cigarette pinched in the corner of his lips.

He was about fifty. Shiny gray suit. Graying hair. Gray mustache stained yellow by nicotine. "What's it about, if I may ask?"

"Something we're working on." Bellarmine was vague for two reasons—because he did not want anyone meddling in his case and also because, in common with other policemen elsewhere, he did not trust men who worked vice.

"Something she was mixed up with in Nice?" suggested Devereux.

"Something like that." It produced a long silence. Surely Devereux knew Bellarmine had the bank case. The entire Sûreté knew. But he didn't know what other cases he might be working on. Perhaps Denise was involved in one of those.

Devereux got up and left the room. When he came back he dropped a fresh dossier on the desk. Bellarmine and Lussac, bending over, thumbed through it. There was her photo. There were various arrest forms, surveillance reports and signed *procès-verbaux*. There were a great many men mentioned, including some named Jean, but no one known as Jeannot, its diminutive.

Bellarmine studied the prostitute's photo. To Devereux, he said: "Where could we find her?"

"Rue Longue."

"Anything special we should know about her?"

Devereux only shrugged.

"You're not being too helpful."

"How can I be helpful when I don't know what you're looking for?"

Bellarmine thought about it. "She may have been associated with a man known as Jeannot."

"You've got her associates there in the dossier."

"No Jeannot, though."

"I'll have her brought in. You can ask her."

Bellarmine shook his head. "I'd rather go ask her myself. I'll borrow this photo, if I may."

Again a shrug by Devereux. He concentrated on straightening the pile of dossiers on his desk, and as they left the room, he called out after them: "Bring it back when you're finished."

Bellarmine and Lussac went out of the building. A few minutes later they walked into the Rue Longue. They passed a number of cafés with glass up around the terraces. They came to a brasserie that looked empty. They went in and took a table against the glass. The waiter came over.

"Black coffee," said Lussac.

"Calvados," said Bellarmine. They sat and peered out at the street through the glass at pedestrians who moved up and down on both sides. Cars went by. There were prostitutes on both sides also, but they were not so easy to pick out. Like deer in a forest, they had adopted protective coloration, they hid in the fauna.

"Do you see her?" asked Bellarmine.

"No. I hope I recognize her. I only saw her once for about five minutes. She had a wig on and was outrageously made up."

"The American Navy was in that week," Bellarmine commented. "That was why she was working Nice in the first place. That must be the way they want their French whores to look." The notion annoyed him. Even our whores, he reflected, genuflect to American money.

108

It was necessary to study the candidates for a considerable period before deciding even whether they were *putes* or not. A woman strolling along was not a *pute* until you had seen her walk back and forth several times.

"She may be upstairs with a client," conceded Lussac. "Or not be working today. Maybe she's having her period."

They kept watching. A woman peering into a shop window, if she moved on and was not seen again, was not a prostitute at all.

"And she may not resemble this photo very much," said Bellarmine, glancing down at it. "That's what I'm worried about."

One by one prostitutes working within range of the café were identified as such, studied, and discarded.

"We better order some food," said Bellarmine.

They lunched on broiled chicken, French fries and a green salad, and drank a carafe of fresh fruity Beaujolais from the previous year's harvest. All the while they watched the street, but they did not see Denise. They finished lunch with tiny cups of strong black coffee.

"There's one," said Bellarmine. It was a girl they had not noted before. She was working the other side, and they studied her. She was wearing a mink coat and hat. They watched her walk up to the corner, turn and come back. From time to time she peered into shop windows. She went up the street and they lost sight of her, and then they saw her coming back.

"I think that's Denise," said Lussac, and Bellarmine agreed. She seemed to match the photo. She was elegantly coiffed, every hair in place. She must have just come from the hairdresser. Her beige mink coat looked new and must have cost plenty.

"Business must be good," said Lussac. "I mean, she wasn't wearing mink in Nice."

Bellarmine stood up. "Wait for me here," he said and went out.

He crossed the street and walked up to the prostitute. Up close he thought she was definitely Denise. As he approached, he played the role of client—he eyed her up and down. It made her tilt her head to one side, but she did not speak. He came abreast of her and stopped.

"How much?"

"Four thousand francs."

"That's a lot."

She shrugged and walked away from him. He had insulted her. She was no longer interested. He had to hurry to keep up. She was striding, playing the game all women played, even prostitutes. The put-off was the come-on. He was amused, and found it hard to repress a smile. Resistance—apparent resistance—was what closed the sale. It never failed. "Okay, let's go," he said to the back of her head.

She did not answer, or even look at him, but her stride took on direction. It became determined—the pace of a woman on her way to work.

She turned into a building. He read the plaque on the wall: "Hôtel de Tourisme—Reception One Flight Up." There was no lobby. He followed her up steep stairs. At the top was the hotel desk. Behind it lounged a bald, skinny individual reading a newspaper. He plucked a key off the board behind his head and handed it, together with a towel, to Denise.

"You pay him for the room," Denise said. "Fifteen hundred francs."

She waited while Bellarmine fished out the money. He followed her down a narrow hall and into a small, dingy room where she closed and locked the rickety wooden door. She took off her mink and hung it on a wooden hanger behind the door. The mink hat went on a peg. Her movements were businesslike, efficient. She fluffed up her hair. She might have been a female executive about to sit down at her desk.

The room contained a big brass bed, a single wooden chair, a lopsided armoire, a sink, a bidet. The mattress under the counterpane was as lumpy as terrain that had been shelled. A lot of wars have been fought on that bed, thought Bellarmine.

When he turned back to Denise he saw that she had unbuttoned her dress down the back. It had fallen forward off her shoulders, exposing a bare midriff, a tight lacy bra. Her hand was outstretched. "Four thousand francs," she said.

Most whores had empty eyes. This one did not. Bellarmine reached into his pocket and withdrew his billfold. Denise's hand waited confidently for money. Instead the billfold broke open only as far as Bellarmine's police card.

"*Merde*," said Denise, and her hand dropped.

"Sorry," said Bellarmine.

The whore stood there, undecided what to do next.

"Nice coat," said Bellarmine. "New, is it?"

He had walked to the door, where he stroked the fur, being careful at the same time to note the label.

"Do I get undressed, or what?" To the whore this was perhaps an interrogation. Or perhaps it was something else.

"Oh, yes, please do."

Either way she was out four thousand francs. With a theatrical sigh, she stepped out of her dress and hung it like her coat behind the door.

She had a nice body, he saw. She stepped out of her half-slip.

"I thought I knew all you *mecs*," she muttered. "You must be new here."

The lace panties underneath matched the lace bra. She wore a garter belt and what looked to Bellarmine like American nylons. When she turned to hang up the slip he saw that the seams were absolutely straight up the backs of her legs, and he nodded appreciatively. She had nice legs.

He loved watching women get undressed.

She had sat down on the straight chair. Her fingers worked at the garter snaps and one of the nylons sagged halfway down her thigh. She eyed him speculatively. "Are you just going to watch, or what?"

"I want to ask you a few questions."

This stopped her. She tugged the stocking up and snapped the garters back on.

"You have a very nice body," he told her, "please don't cover it up." He draped his coat over the bedstead and untied his tie. "You were in Nice a couple of weeks ago. One day you happened to meet a group of your men friends from Marseille. You remarked on it, I believe."

For a second she sat as if frozen. Then she resumed peeling her stockings off. "You're the *flic* Madeleine mentioned." Madeleine, Bellarmine remembered, was The Stinger.

Denise continued to undress. When she had finished, she stood up and walked toward him.

"Who were the men?"

"It was dark out. I thought I recognized a *mec*, but I wasn't sure."

If The Stinger had warned her, then she had had weeks to prepare a story. Bellarmine was disappointed. It was unlikely he would get anything useful out of her now. She stood waiting for him beside the bed.

"Who's Jeannot?" he asked.

"A *mec* I used to know." She pulled the counterpane down, turned back the covers, and lay down. A bolster ran across the top of the bed with two pillows lying on it. She reclined on one of them against the brass headstand. Her ankles were crossed. Then she shifted position, crossing her knees. Every time her legs parted it distracted him.

"Tell me about Jeannot."

111

She gave a name, Jeannot Courteline. It meant nothing to Bellarmine and was surely a false trail. He was wasting his time here, except that she was nice to look at.

"He used to be my husband."

"Your real husband?"

"What we call 'husband' in the profession."

"I see. Go on."

"We broke up."

"Where is this Jeannot now?"

"I don't know. I think he left Marseille."

"And you have a grudge against him?"

"He put a new girl in my spot and turned me over to somebody else." An ordinary woman, naked, was more than vulnerable. She was totally on the defensive. But this one was not. Bellarmine studied her.

"Listen, if you could put that *mec* in jail you'd be doing me a favor." She shifted her legs again.

When interrogating whores one learned to strip them first, hoping to strip them psychologically as well as physically, but they were extraordinary creatures, and often it did not work.

Denise tapped the pillow beside her. She had become confident. "Come to bed."

When Bellarmine did not answer, she sat up and reached for her stockings.

"No, no," he murmured, "don't get dressed just yet."

The psychological battle continued. He kept her naked and, he hoped, dominated; at the same time she used her nakedness to arouse him—distract him at least. A woman naked was not disarmed at all. She still had all her weapons. She bristled with them. They were ready on an instant's notice to go into action. And they were weapons, Bellarmine reflected, that tended to dominate the male in any man. There were reflexes over which one had no control. It had to do with one's perception of what was beautiful, useful. It had to do with loneliness. He had not had a woman since Odette. Not very long, and yet—

It amazed Bellarmine that a woman—a whore—could still do this to him at his age.

"How long since you've seen this Jeannot?"

"A while. He used to talk about knocking over banks all the time. You should look for him. I could give you some places you might look. And if you find him, I hope you beat the shit out of him. What else did Madeleine tell you?"

"Madeleine? Madeleine who?"

She sat up, reaching for him. One breast swayed outward, and then the other. Reaching out, she grasped him by the belt buckle and drew him toward the bed. "You're cute," she murmured. "And we're here, we have the time. We shouldn't waste it."

"Who was this Jeannot with?"

"When?"

"In Nice the night you saw him."

"He was with some other *mecs.* I didn't know any of them."

"Why don't you try to describe them to me."

All this time Lussac sat at the window in the brasserie. He watched the street. He stared down at the dregs in his coffee cup. At last he saw Bellarmine coming toward him, crossing the street carefully, wading through traffic. Bellarmine came into the room and sat down at the table. He pushed his hat back on his head.

"You were up there long enough," said Lussac. He grinned.

"You can wipe that leer off your face, Lussac."

Bellarmine signaled the waiter and ordered another coffee. "I suspect I've been listening to fairy tales," he said, "but we have to check them out."

They went back to the Bishopric where he sent Lussac up to talk to Devereux, one vice *flic* to another. Perhaps Devereux would offer up some information. Lussac was to check out this Jeannot Courteline. He was also to request photos of every Milieu name in Denise's dossier.

While waiting Bellarmine decided to use the time to patrol the corridors of the Bishopric, looking into the offices of colleagues from the past, and of dignitaries who might be of use to him in the future. To get ahead in a huge politically structured organization such as the Sûreté, one needed to shake a lot of hands, inquire after the health of a great number of wives and children.

To his surprise he was treated as a celebrity. Men came out of their offices to talk to him, to slap him on the back and ask about his case. They told him about the one ingot that had turned up. They were watching the bank in question in case another did. Almost all of them offered help—any help he might need, just ask. These were the same men who were working behind his back to take the case away from him. He was the pride of the Sûreté, they told him. He was the envy of the Sûreté too. He had the biggest case in the country, and was faltering, and these men, behind their cherry smiles, were squeezing informants, haunting Milieu haunts, trying to pick up the trail that seemed now to have led to Marseille.

It was 4 P.M. before Bellarmine and Lussac were out in the street again.

"Jeannot Courteline has been a guest of the penitentiary administration these last five years, so she didn't see him in Nice any time recently."

Bellarmine said nothing. They were walking fast.

"Where are we going?"

"To see about a fur coat."

The name on the label had been *Fourrures Dufy*. They found the shop about four blocks up the Canebière—a small, immaculate place sandwiched between a bank and a jewelry store; it had two mink coats and a leopard on display in the front window. Bellarmine stopped to study them for a moment. Although he had never understood the power that jewelry held over women, he thought he understood the allure of furs. Furs, it seemed to him, had many of the same qualities as women themselves. Furs were something to pet, they felt good to the hand. Furs had life. They were smooth and sleek and warm, and related to a woman as a man did, offering protection from cold and storms. They enveloped her like the arms of a lover. And finally they had psychological appeal: they surrounded her like money, like armor plate. Inside her fur she was untouchable.

Bellarmine stepped into the shop and, when the owner came forth, identified himself. "I want to ask about a coat. Do you have those photos, Lussac?"

Lussac showed the photo of Denise Lasablière. "Did you sell a mink coat to this woman?"

The owner recognized the face. His eyes darted from the photo to Bellarmine and back to the photo. "I can't be blamed for selling a coat to such a woman," he said. He licked his lips. "There's no law against selling her a coat just because of what she is."

"What is she?"

"It was clear what she is. One does not have to know a woman intimately to see that."

"Was she alone?"

The owner took a deep breath. He looked from Bellarmine to Lussac. "There was a man with her."

"Can you describe this man?"

"A gentleman. A lawyer or doctor I would have thought. About fifty years old. Frankly, it surprised me that such a man would buy such a coat for such a woman."

"Do you have a record of the sale?"

The owner consulted a ledger. Bellarmine watched as his forefinger drew a line under the name. "Here's her name right here. Denise Lasablière." He looked up beaming. "Do I have it right? Is that the name you're looking for?"

"Do you have the man's name?"

"No. Should I have?"

"What was the date of the sale?"

The owner read the date out of the ledger. Bellarmine nodded, showing no emotion. But he was very pleased. It was shortly after the break-in. Give the gang half a day to return to Marseille, and another few days to sleep off the binge, after which the *mec* goes out and buys his girl friend a mink coat. Why does he buy her a mink? Because he has just proved himself a super provider. He wants every *mec* on the street to see the proof. He wants all the other whores to see it. We are in the presence here, Bellarmine reflected, of that most irresistible of human desires: the desire to strut.

"Would you recognize the man again if you saw him?"

"I think so. They were here about an hour picking out the coat."

"Commissaire Lussac, please show this gentleman your other photographs."

The furrier identified the photo of a convicted pimp named Jean Jacques Montenegro. "Was I right about him being a doctor or lawyer?"

"Did she call him Jeannot, by any chance?"

"I'm afraid I don't remember."

Lussac then wrote out a *procès-verbal* and the furrier signed it. It went into Bellarmine's briefcase alongside the collection of lies Denise Lasablière had signed sitting naked on the side of the bed. They went out of the shop into the street.

"Maybe it's something," muttered Bellarmine. "And maybe it's not." The sidewalks were crowded. They walked along in silence until they came to a café. Bellarmine led the way inside and they stood at the zinc bar. Lussac drank another black coffee. Bellarmine sipped another Calvados, smoked a cigarette, and did not speak.

"What next?" asked Lussac at last.

Bellarmine could ask them at the Bishopric to put a twenty-four-

115

hour tail on this Jean Jacques Montenegro, who might be Jeannot, but it was too soon and too big a risk. The risk was twofold. If Montenegro felt the wind on his neck before Bellarmine was ready to make arrests, then he would evaporate. So would the entire gang, and he would have nothing. The second risk was perhaps even more acute—if he asked for help, he risked having Marseille take over his case.

Of course he could arrest Denise Lasablière. She had signed a false *procès-verbal*, and that was perjury. Or he could drop her for criminal receiving—the coat. It might stand up. According to law an arrest gave him the right to grill her for forty-eight hours straight before she was allowed to contact a lawyer. He could have teams of detectives relaying each other, hammering at her. After two straight days and nights she might crack. She might cough up the whole case.

Or she might not. Whores were tough. They were strange people. And if she did not crack, then—again—the gang would be warned too soon.

"We go back to Nice," he told Lussac.

"There's nothing else we can do, is there?" said Lussac.

Bellarmine drained his Calvados, paid for both drinks, and they went out of the bar. Tomorrow he would telegraph Paris for the dossier on this Jean Jacques Montenegro, and for the dossiers also of all known associates. He would study these. Perhaps the next move would be indicated from something in them. Apart from that he could only wait. Wait for the money to show—so far he had only one gold ingot and one mink coat. Wait for the blackmailer to show. Wait for someone to make a major mistake. Perhaps the mistake had been made already, in which case he was only waiting for it to turn up. He was tired and discouraged, but this was normal. A detective spent his entire professional life seesawing between the two poles of human existence, between light and darkness, seeing and blindness, between hope on one side, despair on the other.

# CHAPTER
## 11

Lambert and his wife entered the Welcome Hotel in Villefranche-sur-Mer and went through into the dining room. The hotel had a faded prewar elegance—white tablecloths, glittering glasses, dull, heavy silver. The waiters wore tuxedoes. But the tuxedoes were shiny, and there were more waiters than patrons. At one of the few occupied tables Roy LeRoy sat alone. He was small, with long, somewhat oily blond hair. He smiled and started to rise as Lambert approached, his two gold incisors gleaming in the light. But when he saw Jacqueline he sat down again, and his face went grim.

"I brought my wife," said Lambert, amused.

"So I see."

"She wanted to come."

"Sure," said Roy LeRoy. "Great."

"How do you do?" said Jacqueline in English. Lambert saw that she was making an effort to be polite. The antipathy she felt for LeRoy, and he for her, was so obvious it was comical.

A waiter had come forward to take Jacqueline's coat. She was wearing a fur jacket.

"Who gave you that?" said LeRoy.

The jacket was rabbit, and some years old. "Édouard, he give it to me," said Jacqueline, with a glance at her husband. Lambert waited for the joke he sensed was coming. He liked Roy's sharp wit.

"To keep you warm or to keep you quiet?" said Roy LeRoy.

Lambert burst out in a loud guffaw.

Jacqueline turned to her husband. "What do he say?"

She had understood perfectly well, Lambert believed. "He said it's a nice jacket."

Turning back to LeRoy, Jacqueline gave a brittle smile. "Thank you very much."

The Lamberts sat down, and the maître d'hôtel, who had approached the table, handed out menus.

Lambert peered over the top of his menu at LeRoy. "You don't look happy."

LeRoy's menu closed with a snap. "Tonight is important," he said.

Lambert grinned at him. "She wanted to come."

"So I see."

Jacqueline only stared stonily at her menu, so that LeRoy's gaze shifted from Lambert to the top of her head. "We got things to talk about, for Chrissake." Since it was not clear to LeRoy how much English she understood, he considered it dangerous to say anything at all, and Lambert saw this.

"I got to know a few things," said LeRoy. His arms waved in frustration.

When Lambert began to laugh, Jacqueline, without looking up, said in French: "What's so funny?"

"You two together," said Lambert.

"You have a droll sense of humor."

"Would you like to see my new car?" said Lambert to LeRoy.

"Excuse us, lady," said LeRoy, rising from his chair, and he strode out of the dining room.

Lambert put his menu down, and his napkin on top of it. He pushed himself back from the table and stood up. "I'll be back in a minute, *chérie*."

"Oh, take your time," said Jacqueline. "Take all the time in the world. Don't mind me."

Lambert found LeRoy fuming, standing outside the front door in the night.

The hotel was tall and narrow. It overlooked the water. When the American Navy was anchored in the Rade out front, its thirty rooms were taken by the wives of officers following the fleet. But tonight the Rade was empty and so largely was the hotel.

On the quay in front of the door was parked Lambert's new Studebaker.

Lambert put his hand on it. "What do you think of her?" he asked.

"Your wife or your car?"

"Jacqueline's okay." There was a squirrel tail tied to the car aerial, and Lambert tugged on it.

"She gives me a pain in the ass," said LeRoy.

Lambert laughed again. "Is this where you live?" he asked. He

118

glanced up at the hotel. The rows of balconies rose above him in the night.

"When I'm in town. What about the deal?"

From the hotel the quay curved around the waterfront, and there were a number of restaurants with tables and chairs out front on the quay.

"I like this car," Lambert said, patting it.

It had a front deck out over the engine, and a back deck over the trunk. There was plenty of chrome. In design it was the most futuristic of all American models, and for this reason, presumably, it had not proved particularly popular.

"I've seen the ads for it in *The Saturday Evening Post*," said Roy LeRoy. "You can't tell if it's coming or going."

"You get *The Saturday Evening Post?*"

"What's wrong with that? Is the deal on or off?"

"I can't picture you reading *The Saturday Evening Post.*"

"It keeps me in touch with the States. I haven't been back since I shipped out in 1942."

"I'll bet you like to read the love stories," said Lambert.

"I read them once in a while."

"You really do?" Lambert found this humorous. "I don't believe it. You really read those trashy love stories?"

"Sure," said LeRoy defensively. "Why not?"

"Jesus," said Lambert. "The big smuggler reads all the love stories in *The Saturday Evening Post*. If I told anybody they wouldn't believe it."

"If you're such a hot writer, how come the *Post* don't publish your stuff?"

"They wouldn't be interested in me," said Lambert. "I'm a serious writer. Besides, I write plays."

"Bullshit," scoffed LeRoy. "Did you ever finish one?"

"You sound like my wife," said Lambert.

"Your wife. When I saw you had your wife with you I couldn't believe my eyes."

"She climbed into the car," said Lambert. "I couldn't get her out." He began to laugh again. "You know why she came tonight? Because she's worried about me. She thinks I keep bad company." He gave LeRoy a friendly sock in the arm.

"She's right." LeRoy's expression did not change. "What about the deal?"

Lambert again gazed up at the hotel. "You got bunks on that boat. So why do you live here?"

"Because the bed here don't go up and down and side to side all the time."

"I thought you were used to that by now."

"Let me explain something to you. A man don't ever get used to that."

"It's a pretty luxurious hotel for an international criminal like you."

"Was luxurious," LeRoy scoffed. "The bathtub takes an hour to drain. Nothing's been painted or repaired since before the war. And the slick French toilet paper—I got to bring my own toilet paper in from Tangier. What about the deal? Is it on or off?"

Lambert felt great affection for LeRoy, whom he had first met in combat outside Salerno in 1943. "We'll talk about it later," he said, still teasing him. "It's rude leaving my wife alone at the table this long. Let's go back inside."

"Just tell me if you got a source or not."

"My new car really handles beautifully," said Lambert. "In a week I've put about three thousand miles on that Studebaker. I've been to Lyon, to Metz. Metz looked good for a while, but it fell through and I had to go all the way to Luxembourg. Yeah, I got a source."

Roy LeRoy at last smiled. He clapped Lambert on the back. "Good man," he said.

The two went back into the hotel. As they re-entered the dining room and approached the table, Jacqueline gave them a brilliant, false smile. "Did you get it all settled?" she said in French. "Whatever it is I'm not supposed to know about."

The two men sat down at the table. "What's she saying?" muttered LeRoy.

Lambert, studying his menu, ignored the question.

"The maître d'hôtel," said Jacqueline to her husband, "offered to see me home. He thought I had been abandoned, you see." She began to giggle, but when LeRoy looked at her distastefully, she choked the giggle off.

"Let's order," said Lambert, frowning. This was done and dinner at length was served.

Afterward all three went outside and stood beside Lambert's Studebaker in the night.

"Maybe you wonder where the money come from to buy this car," said Jacqueline in English to Roy LeRoy. "My husband sell his play, that is where."

LeRoy grinned at Lambert. "You're a tricky bastard, aren't you?"

"It's not a play you'd like," Lambert said to him. "It wouldn't fit in *The Saturday Evening Post.*"

He opened the door for his wife, and she slid into the front seat. He slammed the door and walked around the back of the car. LeRoy followed.

"I'll pick you up here in the morning about eight," Lambert said over his shoulder. "We'll drive down the coast. Scout out a good beach to work from."

"And after that?"

Lambert grasped the door handle. "I take off for the north to settle the arrangements."

"How long will it take you?"

"A week, two maybe."

He opened his own door, and slid in behind the wheel. LeRoy stuck his head through the open window. "Good night, Mrs. Lambert," he said to her. Jacqueline did not answer.

She remained silent as Lambert steered the Studebaker up the steep, winding hill to the Basse Corniche. The mountains here seemed to rise straight up out of the sea. The port and the old town were at sea level. The Corniche road was on a shelf cut into the rock about a third of the way up the mountain. Above it shone the lights of a few villas. Below, as Lambert steered toward Nice, was the sea.

It was Jacqueline who broke the heavy silence. "That man terrifies me."

"You're wrong about Roy," said Lambert confidently. "Roy's harmless. And he's a good guy." Because Jacqueline's agitation struck him as funny, he gave a low chuckle. "Anyway, you knew I was going to have dinner with him. You didn't have to come along."

"You know very well why I came along."

"Oh?" said Lambert, teasing her. "Why was that?"

Jacqueline did not know what to say. To protect him from LeRoy, to protect him from himself—any answer she might give was the wrong one.

"I never see you," she burst out, "or know what you're up to." Her voice trailed off. "I worry about what you—what you might be doing."

Instead of explaining himself, or relieving her mind, Lambert said only: "I've been very busy the last few days."

Again there was a heavy silence. They came around the headland, where the road turned inland between villas and dropped down toward Nice. It came out at the port, and followed the city street around it.

The port was part marina. On one side individual quays jutted out like concrete fingers. Pleasure boats were moored to them in rows. On the other, moored sideways to the quay, was one of the liners that ferried people and cars to Corsica and back.

Jacqueline said: "You're smuggling cigarettes with him, aren't you?"

"I'm out of that business."

"I don't think I believe you." But from the tone of her voice it was clear she wished to believe.

"Why do you think we've had so little money these last few years?"

"That's true."

"Jacqueline, have I ever lied to you?"

When she did not answer, he continued: "There is very little profit in cigarettes these days. Roy's still in it. Roy's a deserter. He can't go back. He's got to do something. And one guy with one boat can still make a living, I guess."

This explanation sounded logical to Jacqueline. For a moment she had a renewal of faith in her husband. But it did not last. "If it's not cigarettes, then you're into something else," she muttered.

Lambert said coldly: "Jacqueline, don't nag."

So once again she was faced with a wife's awful choice. The wife who nagged drove her husband away. But to keep silent was merely to endure, and the long-suffering wife, she well knew, was equally repugnant to a man.

At the end of the Port de Nice the street turned the corner around the World War I monument, dropped down to beach level and became the Promenade des Anglais. Lambert turned down the Rue Halévy, came into the Rue Masséna, and parked in front of the perfume shop. He got out, locked the car on his side, then came around and opened the door for Jacqueline. She stood on the sidewalk while he locked the passenger door. The Studebaker was the only parked car on the street, and would remain there overnight. To Frenchmen a car was such a precious possession that most owners kept them locked up in garages when not in use.

"I thought we were going to start living up at the farm," said Jacqueline as they crossed the sidewalk. "I thought we weren't going to have to sleep in the back of the shop anymore." It was impossible to keep the accusatory tone out of her voice.

"Jacqueline," said Lambert, "it will take a little time."

She opened the locks in the glass shop door, and they went into the darkness inside. She locked the door behind them. The third lock was at the base of the door, and she had to get down on one knee to turn the key. She walked behind the counter into the corridor leading to the stock room. Lambert followed.

In the stock room she began to get undressed. She arranged her dress carefully on a hanger that hung from one of the high shelves. Sitting on the narrow bed, she removed her shoes.

"You never talk about your play," she said.

"What is there to say?"

"Don't you have any revisions to do?"

"No."

"They just took it? Just like that?" She was trying to pretend that this sounded logical to her.

Lambert lit a cigarette. "That's right."

"When do I get to read it?"

"You know you don't read English very well."

"I'd like to read it," she said. "Will you go to New York for opening night?"

"I haven't decided yet."

"When can I read it?"

"I'll write a letter to New York and ask them to send me a copy."

"You must have a carbon."

"It's pretty illegible."

Jacqueline peeled her nylons off. They were still almost her only luxury, and she concentrated, being careful not to snag them.

Lambert took a drag on his cigarette.

"When does it open?"

"Not till next fall. Maybe not till the following spring."

"You must be awfully anxious. Aren't you anxious to know how it's received?"

"Yes," said Lambert. "Look, why don't I wait down in the shop until you're ready for bed. There isn't enough space in this stock room for two people to turn around."

"I know."

"Don't sound so goddamn angry at me."

But she wasn't angry, she was terrified, though she did not really know why. There was something terribly wrong, she thought, but she had no hard evidence of any kind.

Lambert went down the corridor and stood at the doorway in the dark. He peered out at his Studebaker and at the otherwise empty street. He liked the lines of the car. Two pedestrians went by. One gave a start to see his figure framed in darkness inside. He smoked steadily, giving Jacqueline a good long time to get into bed. When the cigarette had been smoked down to the butt, he pinched off the coal, field-stripped the butt army fashion.

For some time longer he watched the empty street. He wasn't anxious to rejoin his wife. In a town this size in America, he reflected, there'd be cars going by here in both directions. But he'd seen only two cars. It wasn't even late—not even midnight yet.

When he went back to the stock room Jacqueline was in bed, face turned toward the wall. He brushed his teeth, urinated into the toilet, and got into the pajamas that hung behind the door. When he got into bed he could tell his wife was still awake. To forestall conversation he began to stroke her back, her arm. He began to want to make love to her. He reached around for her breast, trying to find the nipple, but she kept her forearm over it, and when he tried to unbend her arm he found that it was clenched hard.

"Okay," he said, and lay back with his hands behind his head, staring at the dark ceiling. After a moment he said: "I have to go away tomorrow."

There was no response from his wife.

"I'll be gone a few days, a week maybe. I don't know for sure."

There was still no response.

"I have some business to do in the north." Women were curious creatures. She was sure to turn over to ask what sort of business, and he waited confidently. He still felt like making love. But she neither moved nor spoke.

After a while he fell asleep.

In the morning he felt her crawl over him to get out of the bed, and soon he smelled the coffee perking on the hot plate. He sat up in bed, and she handed him a cup of coffee. She stood in the most distant corner and sipped from her own cup, her gaze turned in every direction except at him.

By the time Lambert had dressed and was ready to leave, Jacqueline was down in the store. The lights were on, the door open, and she was sweeping out. Lambert was carrying an overnight bag, and he attempted to kiss his wife on the lips as he departed, but she offered only her cheek.

Lambert gave her a big smile, to which she did not respond. "So long for a few days."

"I'll see you when I see you," she said coldly.

124

He went out and got into his car. He waved to her as he pulled away from the curb. She stood, broom in hand, filled with despair, and did not wave back.

That day Lambert and LeRoy drove west along the coast and the squirrel tail streamed straight out from the aerial. From Nice to Cannes the country was heavily populated and they did not stop. But past Cannes the villages and beaches, the villas perched on cliffs overlooking the sea, all were isolated one from the other, and they turned into nearly every cove and inlet. Where there were café terraces with a view onto any real estate they were interested in, they stopped, ordered coffee and discussed the pros and cons. By afternoon, although Lambert continued with coffee, LeRoy had switched to Cognac. Their last stop was Cavalaire, about twenty kilometers past St-Tropez. There was a grove of trees close enough to the beach to hear the waves breaking, and they parked the Studebaker and walked forward.

"You'll like this," said Lambert to LeRoy. "I've saved the best for last."

The beach at Cavalaire faces east, not south. LeRoy saw at once how sheltered it was, and was pleased. They crouched on the sand and he spread out a marine chart. The wind was blowing and it took all four hands to hold the chart in place.

"It should be easy to find," said LeRoy, and he pointed to the two headlands. According to the chart, a lighthouse stood on each. They refolded the chart and stood up, peering about for these lighthouses, but they could not see them.

"Anyway, they're there," said LeRoy. "All I have to do is aim the boat between them."

At the end of the beach stood a restaurant-hotel, and they walked toward it. As expected, being winter, they found it closed, and they stepped up on to the terrace. The shutters were closed, but they found a place where they could see inside. The chairs were stacked on top of the tables in the dining room. They stepped back out to the terrace. It was littered with dead leaves, which the wind blew noisily against the low stone walls. Beside the terrace was a concrete dock that extended out into the sea. LeRoy went down the steps and walked to the end of it, where he peered down into the water.

"Looks deep enough," he called. He was nodding his head vigorously up and down. A PT boat drew five feet.

Lambert stood on the terrace and watched him.

"I like the dock," he called.

He came back up on to the terrace. "The dock is the best thing," he said. "We have to have one."

"I know," said Lambert.

"It isn't cigarettes this time."

Caseloads of cigarettes were usually transferred in deep water from the deck of the PT boat down into the bottoms of the five or six open fishing boats that came out to meet it. The fishing boats nuzzled against the big hull like piglets at the tits of a sow, and the cases, which were light enough, were tossed down to them, usually fifty cases into each fishing boat. There had never been much need for mooring facilities in order to get contraband cigarettes ashore.

But this time the crates would be far too heavy to manhandle at sea. A mooring of some kind had become essential, and the grinning LeRoy was satisfied that Lambert had found it.

They drove into the village of Cavalaire, where they sat down in a café. This time Lambert ordered a bottle of champagne. When it was empty, LeRoy ordered another, and they went on congratulating each other and making plans. At last the sun was going down. The clouds overhead had turned purple, and the sky at the horizon had become a gigantic bleeding wound.

"I'll drive you back," said Lambert.

"Will you sleep in Nice?" asked LeRoy when they were on the road.

Lambert did not want to face Jacqueline again so soon. "I better get on the road right away," he replied. "I've got about a thousand miles to drive, for Christ sake. I'll do a couple of hundred tonight and stop somewhere."

LeRoy nodded, satisfied. "Good."

On a night when no word had come from her husband for more than a week, Jacqueline closed her shop early and caught a bus up to the farm. The trip took nearly two hours, and she was the last passenger but one to get down from the bus. She was carrying a sack of food and a change of clothes, and she went into the house, put her packages down and built a fire in the hearth. She stood in front of the fire in her cloth coat rubbing her hands together, watching the flames, waiting to feel the heat come out into the room. Presently she hung her coat up, put on a heavy wool cardigan in its place, and began to make herself dinner. She whisked eggs in a bowl, poured them into a skillet, and added chunks of cheese and tomato. While her omelet cooked she washed half a dozen lettuce leaves, tore them into pieces over a salad bowl, and poured on oil and vinegar. She broke a loaf of bread in half, put one half away for breakfast and cut the other into pieces and dropped them into a basket. She opened a bottle of local wine. For about an hour she lingered over her solitary dinner. Then, with a sigh, she rose from her chair and began searching her own house.

She had thought it all out carefully in advance. She was determined to ransack it systematically. Her mood would be cold-blooded throughout, and she would find what she would find. It was no good imagining possible reactions beforehand. She would decide on her future conduct when she held the evidence—whatever it turned out to be—in her hands. She would permit no show of emotion, neither before—she hesitated to think it through even this far—or after.

And so she began. But her hand, the one that began pulling out drawers, was, she noted, trembling. So much for controlling emotion. And as she proceeded, she realized she was consumed by fear, the quality of which astonished her. She was as much afraid that Lambert might return and catch her in the act as she was of what she might find. But he would not return unexpectedly she told herself. There were already tears in her eyes as she yanked open another drawer. He was probably a thousand miles away, and involved in God knew what.

Like all such searches, there was something hysterical about this one. She did not know exactly what she was looking for—an end to her doubts about her husband, an end to her anguish. These goals were mutually incompatible and she realized this. She was like a jealous wife looking for traces of lipstick on her husband's clothes. Any physical evidence she might find would only convict him. The best she could hope for was to find nothing, but then all her doubts would remain. Her anguish would be undiminished.

She had begun in the least likely room, the bedroom they shared, as if to put off any result at all as long as possible. Since the bedroom was not his alone, he could have felt no security there, certainly not the kind needed for a hiding place. The bedroom was her nest, rather than his, and seemed to her out of the question. She searched it thoroughly.

There was not much in it apart from the bed, an armoire, and a dresser that contained four drawers, two each. They owned pitifully little in the way of worldly goods, and as she worked, she tried not to blame this on her husband's fancy dreams. In her own drawers were

127

underwear and nightgowns, some folded blouses, three sweaters, some scarves. She was still a very young woman but had many regrets already, and the principal one was clothes. By the time she could afford nice clothes, she would be too old and ugly to want to wear them.

She was immediately ashamed. Her husband owned even fewer clothes than she did. Of course the difference was that he didn't care. She dumped his things onto the bed. Three woolen plaid shirts such as Americans liked, plus two dress shirts, one white and one tan, plus four ties neatly folded.

As she worked, she envied the ordinary jealousy that drove most wives to make a search like this. To find evidence of no more than adultery seemed to her a result greatly to be desired. It would be so simple. A girl friend seemed something she could fight. What she dreaded finding was so much worse, and there was no way she could fight it, no way at all.

Turning to the tall old armoire that served as the room's only closet, she opened the door on his side. A gray suit bought just after the war. A tweed sports jacket. The ski outfit they had bought in Switzerland such a short time ago—the sight of it brought fresh tears to her eyes. Next to it hung his army greatcoat, khaki in color and coarse as a horse blanket, which he still wore for tramping in the woods in winter. And there, pushed all the way to the end of the rod, hung the dress uniform he used to wear to the tea dances in the château that had been turned into an officers' club—to review his wardrobe was like reviewing her life with him. There were ribbons, faded now, over the breast pocket, and on each epaulet a first lieutenant's silver bar. She closed both armoire doors. The piece was lopsided and the doors hung slightly askew. She had to lock them to keep them closed.

She searched the kitchen, the bathroom, then the shed. Nothing. She plunged into the main room. Insofar as her husband's life was focused at all, its focus was here, and she went to his desk and began to go through his papers. She could wait no longer to know. She had postponed searching this room too long already. Her answer was here if it was anywhere. His desk was a peasant's trestle table about three hundred years old. The top was two inches thick, and littered with papers that instinctively she wanted to tidy. As she went through them, she did so. She read as best she could every paper that might be pertinent—the telegram, signed "Alexander Levy," accepting the play, a letter from his father, who was an automobile dealer in Camden, New Jersey, and had plenty of money. She had met her father-in-law only once, about three years previously. He had toured Europe with Lambert's stepmother, and had spent two days in Nice. She remembered him as a tall, heavy man who drank too much and talked too loud. His letter, which must have arrived in the last few days, did not mention his son's success. But perhaps Lambert had not yet written him the good news. Lambert had a brother somewhere too, but he seemed to have cut himself off from his family. And from his American past. Whenever people asked him why he didn't go home he always said: "And do what? Go back to Camden and sell cars?"

Beside the table was a two-drawer filing cabinet. Digging through it, she found the thick folder in which the play had been taking shape for most of the last eight years. She found five versions of the first act, all clearly marked and dated, for at first he had worked on it more or less regularly. There were many sketches, notes, parts of scenes. She found no carbon copy of a completed play, but this did not necessarily prove anything. Nothing else that she read referred to the play at all. But neither was there any reference to other dealings by Lambert, which, if they existed, would be dreadful in nature. She supposed she should be happy with such a result.

Though she had discovered nothing of significance, the search had exhausted her. She sat down in one of the chairs and stared into the great stone fireplace—it was so big there were stone benches inside it to sit on. But the fire had long since gone out, and the room was cold—she hadn't even noticed. She had found nothing to explain Lambert's recent behavior, perhaps to justify it. His own explanation—the play—was still the most likely one. She sat in the chair feeling drained and told herself she believed all he had said to her, the play existed and had been sold, and she herself had nothing to fear. She had told herself for years that one day her wild young husband would come down to earth. Now she told herself he had surely done so.

She got up, turned out all the lights, went into the other room and went to bed. She set the alarm for 6 A.M.—she planned to be out on the road in time to flag down the first bus. She must not be late at the shop, lest she miss a customer, a possible sale. She must think of ways to make the shop more attractive, so that more people would come in; they would tend to buy more too. Another way to increase turnover would be to stay open from noon to two, when all other shops on the street—in all of France—were closed for lunch. As she lay in the dark, her shop came to seem to her the only stability in her life. It filled her whole mind. She clung to it as if to the vision of a loved one, a parent, or child. She felt utterly dependent upon it. She saw nothing else she could count on.

# CHAPTER 12

The FBI agent Charlie O'Hara, having driven the consulate's black Cadillac out on to the airport tarmac, watched the Pan American Clipper completing its turn out over the sea. Aboard would be a congressman named Saul Avery, who, disembarking, would spy this Cadillac and make straight for it, accepting it as his right. He would recognize Charlie O'Hara and be surprised, but only slightly.

After more than two weeks O'Hara was still in Nice, where he did not want to be, ordered to hang about the fringe of a case that did not appear to relate in any way to him or to the Bureau, and no one was telling him why. He had received certain instructions with regard to Congressman Avery and these baffled him also. As a result he wished only to get back to Paris, to his wife, to his daughter, to his apartment, to his two dogs, and to routine liaison duties that he understood. Congressman Avery was no doubt here as part of still another congressional junket. There had been a great many. What was so special this time?

Congress these days was busy giving billions away to almost every nation on the globe—there were still only about seventy of them, though new ones were forming. Most of it went to Western Europe, where major cities and national economies were still in ruins. The money was being spread thickly, like too much butter over burned toast. To oversee such expenditures the congressional junket had had to be invented—congressmen would not only oversee the money, they would ride it. Usually in groups, they climbed aboard one of the new transatlantic land planes. With their four propellers, these planes were very fast, 250 miles per hour average speed, and most times they could cross the ocean without refueling en route. They had ushered in the era of the American tourist and of the congressional junket simultaneously. On nearly every crossing, it seemed, there was a junket. Most congressmen—not all—were careful, once the plane had set down in a European capital, at least to find and shake hands with some important foreign dignitary. Aides would then send a photograph of the handshake back to the congressman's hometown newspaper. But it was a rare congressman who had actually come over to work. Usually the ceremonial handshake was the end of it. In France you could buy pornographic novels in English (never in French) in green covers in any book shop, and there were topless dancers in the nightclubs as well. In Amsterdam you could look over all the prostitutes with no risk—they sat in floor-to-ceiling windows one flight up from the street, and you could take your pick; some were dressed in leather and you could watch them swishing whips across their laps. In Copenhagen there were sex shops featuring dildos and salves, and racks of nudist magazines whose photos had not been airbrushed.

The United States Congress could not believe its eyes. Europe seemed a fleshpot, and was wide open. Of course some ordinary tourists were dazzled too, but they lacked a congressman's advantages. Young tourists could not afford most such pleasures, and older ones usually traveled as couples. Congressmen, on the other hand, tended to travel only with each other.

They had other tendencies in common. They tended to demand free lodging at U.S. embassies or consulates wherever they happened to land, and foreign service officers, who were riding a gravy train themselves and who feared being recalled, were usually delighted to accord it. Other amenities, such as embassy cars with drivers, were demanded, and were accorded also.

For a long time, congressmen thought they could do as they liked in Europe, as if nothing would ever get back home. It was clear that the local police had orders to leave big-spending tourists alone, and important ones strictly alone, and it seemed to congressmen that they were not being watched by anyone. This was false. They were watched very closely indeed by the very men who "volunteered" most times to drive them around in one of the embassy cars, the embassy's so-called legal attaché, the local FBI agent, and this was by direct order of Mr. Hoover in Washington. In fact the most popular embassies merited, in Hoover's view, more than one FBI agent for this purpose. Paris, for instance, had four. Of course the most prominent congressmen would be handled by O'Hara personally. He would meet them with an embassy Cadillac at Orly Airport when they came in—or at Le Havre if they came by ship—repeating this function in the opposite direction when they left. Immediately afterward his reports went directly to Mr. Hoover, and into Hoover's so-called "black file," a cabinet in his office to which only Hoover himself and his deputy, Clyde Tolson, had access. Such reports were neither more nor less than accounts of how individual congressmen spent their days—and nights—in Paris. They were written in prose as obtuse and bureaucratic as O'Hara could make them, masterpieces of understatement, with only a rare hint of humor, such as this line by O'Hara on Congressman Avery: "Subject left premises with female, aged about 30, whose dress showed her legs up to her heart." No congressman had ever seen these files, but after a time all Washington knew they were there, and this explained in part Hoover's amazing power, and even more amazing longevity, as director of the FBI.

Since arriving in Nice on the Tuesday after the break-in, O'Hara had camped out in a guest room up under the eaves of the large and elegant villa on the Rue du Congrès that served as the American Consulate.

For more than two weeks he had gone to the bank every day and learned nothing and accomplished nothing. He had interviewed the director general, a man named Monot. He had attempted to cozy up to the cop who had the case, this Commissaire Bellarmine. Finally the police had finished up and moved out of the bank, and he still had nothing. He had been unable to get hold of those lists, and had so advised Washington. He had no police powers here, and no informants. The Bureau could only expect so much of him. When Washington refused to let him go back to Paris, he had phoned his wife, waiting more than an hour for the connection. He did not know why he was being kept in Nice, he told her. The big crowds outside the bank were gone. The bank itself had reopened for business. Having demanded inventories from every single box owner, it was waiting for the last of these to come in, after which the numbers of the looted boxes would be revealed and owners would be invited to appear and claim their property. It all had nothing whatever to do with the FBI, O'Hara told his wife. How were his dogs, he asked.

Every day he had waited, and fretted. He had stolled up and down the Promenade with all the other tourists, and the winter sun off the water half blinded him. He had visited the Masséna Museum, which had a nice collection of medieval armor. Charlie O'Hara would never have made it as a warrior in those days, he told himself. Couldn't fit into the clothing. Time had passed very slowly.

Last night had come the cable about Congressman Avery, and this morning here he was sitting in a black Cadillac on the airport tarmac awaiting the arrival of a Lockheed Constellation from New York via the Azores, Lisbon and Barcelona, an eighteen-hour flight. He watched the plane taxi up to Nice's small new terminal. He watched about forty-five people deplane. They looked haggard, all except Congressman Avery, who was among the last to come down the steps. Recognizing the Cadillac, he walked straight for it.

Seeing that a French customs officer in blue uniform and kepi moved to intercept Avery, O'Hara jumped out of the car and showed his FBI badge. In his execrable French he identified both himself and the congressman, and the customs officer nodded and walked away.

"Charlie O'Hara, isn't it?" said Avery. He looked surprised. "What are you doing here?"

"I was here on vacation, Congressman," lied O'Hara, as per his instructions from the Bureau. "Heard you were coming, and volunteered to fetch you."

Avery was a big man in his late forties. He had a receding hairline, but the rest of it was thick. He was a man who leaned forward when he moved, exuding power. Now he slung his hand luggage into the back seat and climbed in beside O'Hara. A white consulate pennant flew from the front fender, and it blew in the wind as they drove off.

"Where to, Congressman? The consulate?"

"I'm staying at the Ruhl this time, Charlie."

There were palm trees and banks of flowers along both sides of the road all the way into Nice. The French are big on flowers, O'Hara thought. Why not, they grow here all year around. The French are big on useless products of all kinds, he thought: perfume, wine, high fashion. The French had their priorities screwed up. Always had had.

"A little vacation, Congressman?" O'Hara was fishing, but Avery only looked out the window and did not answer.

"I'd be happy to drive you around while you're here."

"I thought you were on vacation."

"I'm tired of my vacation," said O'Hara.

"Why don't you pick up a girl or something?" snorted Avery.

O'Hara decided he better not push this. But he needed to know why Avery was here, and this meant tailing him. The only trouble was that the man, having just got off an eighteen-hour flight, might sleep for two days.

"A plane ride like that, you got to sleep it off like a binge, I guess," O'Hara said.

"I had a berth coming across," said Avery. "Slept most of the way."

Subjects always disclosed—without realizing it—far more than they imagined. Avery had probably wanted only to brag: he was rich enough to pay for a berth, or important enough to get one free. Either way, he wanted O'Hara to feel—what? His power? His wealth? Envy? Instead he had provided a probable timetable of his movements.

O'Hara, who knew a good deal about this man, conceded the power, but saw nothing to envy. At first he had served as his guide to Paris night life. Avery's tastes had been obvious. He had expected O'Hara to serve him almost as a pimp. Later, each time Avery would turn up in Paris O'Hara had assigned him to one of the younger men, though being careful to sign the reports to Hoover himself. On one occasion O'Hara had been obliged to direct Avery to a doctor who spoke English. The congressman had extended his stay in Paris to accommodate a series of penicillin shots. He wasn't even embarrassed about it, merely shrugged his big shoulders. He had big appetites, he said, giving a huge grin. And an even bigger ego, O'Hara thought.

He figured he had an hour before Avery came out of the hotel. He bought himself dark glasses and a black beret, hired a black Peugeot taxicab and sat in it, parked, half a block past the hotel, on the opposite side of the Promenade. He watched the Ruhl's front entrance, through the screen of palm trees and flowers that separated the two lanes of traffic.

When Avery came out he had changed clothes. The big man now wore tan slacks, a brown tweed jacket and a brown knit tie. His tailoring hid his slight paunch. Crossing the street to a line of taxis, he got into one, and O'Hara tapped his own driver on the shoulder and motioned him to follow.

The trail led down the Avenue de la Victoire and under the railroad tracks. There the steep hills that surround the city began abruptly, and the street climbed in a series of switchbacks. Soon they were above the orange tile rooftops of the city, and the hills were green. There were cork oaks and parasol pines clinging to the steep slopes, with villas dotted here and there. The road descended into valleys, then climbed again, and on each downhill section O'Hara's driver turned off his ignition and coasted, conserving gasoline. The other driver was probably doing the same. French gasoline was the most expensive in Europe, about four times the price back home. Still, it always surprised O'Hara to ride with Frenchmen and realize they were coasting.

He had taken the trouble to study a map of the city, and realized that they were probably heading for the outlying village of St. Pancrace. He made the driver stay a good distance back. There was almost no traffic, and Avery's car could often be seen climbing switchbacks ahead. Finally they climbed up on to the plateau on which the village was set, trailing the other taxi by about three hundred yards, and then it turned through gateposts into a driveway. O'Hara ordered his chauffeur to drive on past. The gateposts, though he searched carefully as they went by, carried no nameplate. No house could be seen from the main road. Avery's taxicab had disappeared.

"To whom belongs this house?" asked O'Hara in French.

"But you do not know this, monsieur?"

"I wish to ascertain the name of its proprietor."

"But, monsieur, as everyone knows, it is the villa of Monsieur Picpoul, the most important man in Nice."

"Stop here. Turn the engine off."

He got out and walked back and peered through Picpoul's bushes but could see little. Avery's taxi was there. The driver stood beside it smoking. Picpoul and Avery were inside the house or behind it. What was this meeting about? he wondered. Other meetings would follow, he sensed, and if this were back in the States he would be ready for them. He would tap Picpoul's phone for one thing, which could be done from the road, and he glanced up at the wires over his head— he knew how to read telephones wires. Also he would send men in there in the night—two to search for and photograph any documents, and a third to plant a few bugs. He would do the same to Avery's suite at the Ruhl. But this was not the States. He was alone here, and if he got caught the courts might not be complaisant.

The only alternative was to go to the French cops—to Bellarmine—for help. Which was to O'Hara out of the question. An American congressman was none of their business.

Frustrated and impatient, he waited for Avery's taxi to reappear. When it did, he followed it back down the hills. On the Promenade des Anglais he ordered his driver to park at a discreet distance from the entrance to the Ruhl.

He watched Avery get out of his own taxi and peer up the street.

The congressman was peering in O'Hara's direction, though surely he was too far away for Avery to see his face. O'Hara tugged the beret farther down over his dark glasses. A moment later he wanted to scrunch down behind the seat, but did not do so. Avery was walking right toward him.

O'Hara got out of the cab and met him halfway.

"Just coming to see if you needed anything, Congressman," he said. He had been unable in the few seconds left to him to think up a more elaborate lie.

"Let me give you a word of advice, Charlie," said Avery. "Stop following me around."

# CHAPTER 13

The gendarmes assigned to Le Chaudan, thirty kilometers north of Nice, lived in a solidly built four-story barracks-type building, with stucco walls and an orange tile roof. Bellarmine parked the black police Citroën in front and got out and looked the building over. A dog lay in the doorway. Some children were playing off to the side. One of the upstairs windows was open and he watched a woman shaking out a mop. When it was built, sometime between the two world wars, the building's walls had been painted pastel pink. It had not been painted since, and the color had faded to the faintest pale-pink wash, an unusual color, nonetheless, for what was essentially a police station. Seven gendarmes, together with their families, lived there in small separate apartments. Only a small portion of the ground floor, Bellarmine knew, was set aside for police operations. Behind the dozing dog there would be a lobby with one or another gendarme on permanent duty behind a high desk. Several offices would give off this, and in the basement there would be two or three holding cells with wooden doors. The detachment was under the command of— he took his notebook out of his briefcase and checked the name once more—a man named Eugène Duclos, fifty-four, whose rank was maréchal des logis-chef—the equivalent of sergeant.

Le Chaudan was little more than a crossroads on the main route from Nice to Grenoble and the Alps, and so Duclos' principal responsibility would be traffic control. But there were also about a dozen nearby villages on both sides of the Var River—you could see some of them huddled on tops of hills—and he was charged with the police supervision of them as well. However, it was probable that nothing ever happened in any of them. Probably Duclos had never arrested a major criminal—or had a good fright—in his life.

Bellarmine went inside and up to the desk.

"Bellarmine from the S.N."

"Yes, sir," said the young gendarme. Though he only stood up in his place, he seemed to have snapped to attention, and his face had taken on an anxious smile.

Duclos must have been pacing his office waiting for him. He sprang immediately out into view, and they shook hands. "Monsieur le Commissaire," he said, and almost bowed. His manner, Bellarmine noted, was nervous, his hand was moist, and his eyes were evasive.

The gendarme behind the desk had sat down and buried his head in some papers; he did not look up. A second gendarme, who had come out behind Duclos, had not so much as come forward for the ritual handshake. Good, thought Bellarmine, for he was in a foul mood. Let them sweat. All of them. These gendarmes here were possibly in trouble, and they knew it.

"Do you want to go straight to the villa?" inquired Duclos.

"If it wouldn't be too much trouble, *chef*."

They went outside and got into one of the Renault Juvaquatres assigned to the gendarmerie. There was a blue police light on the roof. The second gendarme got behind the wheel. Bellarmine sat in the front beside him, and Duclos got into the back. They started out.

The villa, at the outskirts of the village of Aspremont, was about seven kilometers away, but the roads were narrow and steep, and the Juvaquatre, one of the cheapest vehicles manufactured in France, lacked power.

"Not much of a car for chasing anybody," muttered Bellarmine.

"Our cars are not fast," conceded Duclos, and he flashed an apologetic grin.

Motorcycle gendarmes rode fast bikes, mostly BSA's made in England, and chased traffic violators. Apart from that, gendarmes mostly chased nobody. They needed transportation from one village

137

to another and this had best be cheap. There was neither need nor budget for fast cars.

The Juvaquatre entered the driveway and crunched to a stop on the gravel in front of the villa. The three men got out. There was no one around, and they could see no nearby houses. The villa was new. Orange tile roof. Stucco walls painted a pale lime green. Nice chimney. The garden was full of geraniums in bloom, and there were olive trees on the hillside behind the house. Bellarmine tried the door, but it was locked.

"I sent a man to fetch the plumber," explained Duclos apologetically. "They should be here in a few minutes."

Presently a second Juvaquatre rolled into the driveway. A rough-looking man in a leather jacket got out from the passenger side. The gendarme who was driving also got out, but he stayed close to his vehicle, as if unwilling to come within range of Bellarmine's presumed rage.

Bellarmine produced his *commission rogatoire* and waved it at the plumber. "I have a warrant to search this villa. Do you want to see it?"

"What for?" demanded the plumber. "You're the police. To you a man is guilty until proved innocent. It goes without saying."

Bellarmine eyed him. "Nobody said you were guilty, friend. Yet."

"And one wonders why we become Communists."

He unlocked the door and they stepped directly into the main room. Little light filtered through the closed shutters. The floor was marble. There were no rugs, and only a few pieces of furniture, all of them covered by dust sheets: a sofa, two armchairs. People, Bellarmine saw, had sat on the furniture without removing the sheets. There were some boxes that might have served as chairs, and two standing ashtrays, both nearly full of ashes and butts. A can on the floor had been used as an ashtray also. Bellarmine sniffed the air, which was full of the odor of cold smoke.

He began to move through rooms, and the plumber followed him. So did Duclos, but the two other gendarmes had remained outside. Upstairs there were some beds. Bare mattresses. Bare bolsters at their heads. Opening a closet, he noted folded blankets on a shelf.

"How long since anybody's lived in this place?"

"Last summer," answered the plumber.

They went back downstairs. The villa belonged to a concert pianist presently on tour in America. He used it as a summer vacation place.

138

The rest of the year he paid the plumber to look after it. Or at least that was the story Duclos had recounted over the phone.

"And you lent it to a 'friend' for a party?"

"Sure. A party. I wasn't there. You can't lay anything on me, pal."

Withdrawing a manila envelope from his briefcase, Bellarmine poured into it the contents of the three ashtrays. The plumber watched him do it.

"You don't mind?" Bellarmine asked.

"What you do means nothing to me."

"Good." He stared into the envelope. "Judging from all these butts it was a big party."

"How would I know?"

"And your friend is a fag, I see."

"Fag?"

"Take a look," said Bellarmine, offering a glance into the envelope. "Not a trace of lipstick on any of these butts. Most of which are cigar butts, by the way. An all-male party. Your friend must be the queen of queens. You didn't know that about him, I guess?"

"I don't have to answer no questions from you."

"Maybe you'd like to explain yourself to the *juge d'instruction* instead."

He sealed the envelope. The lab in Marseille might be able to make something out of its contents. There had been cigar butts found in the vault, and perhaps these matched. He led the way into the kitchen. An open bottle of wine, about an inch left in the bottom, stood in the sink. Since empties of the same brand had been found in the vault also, Bellarmine decided to take it with him. He looked for glasses, but there were none in sight. Somebody must have washed them and put them back into cabinets. It might be worthwhile to send fingerprint technicians in here. Unfortunately, fingerprints exposed to the air did not last long. He stuck the top of his index finger into the top of the bottle and carried it out the back door toward the cars. The plumber followed one pace behind.

"You want a receipt for this bottle? I'll give you a receipt for the cigar butts too, if you like. Just say the word."

"You know where you can shove your receipts."

As he stood the bottle on the hood of one of the Juvaquatres, and slid his finger free, the garage doors caught his eyes. The garage was set under the house, and he walked over and peered through its windows.

139

"Let's have a look in there."

"It's empty. You can see that through the glass."

"You know something? You begin to give me a pain in the ass."

After a brief hesitation the plumber decided he had best open the garage. Bellarmine went in. In the back was a workbench. On it stood a lantern-type flashlight, similar to those left behind in the vault, and Bellarmine, recognizing it, was so overcome by excitement that he feared it must be visible on his face. The emotion was intense, a rush of heat to the brain, to the cheeks, to the ears; and it was totally unexpected. He picked the flashlight up, turned it, and noted that the bottom was caked with mud. Except for his hands and eyes he tried to keep his body absolutely still, so as to give away nothing.

He even put the flashlight back down, but he did not immediately turn around, waiting until he felt calm enough to do so. He had experienced the equivalent of a surge of power down an electric line, and it had shaken him.

Leaving the flashlight, he stepped back out into the sunlight. "As far as I'm concerned, the search is completed," he told the plumber. "The pianist heard reports that somebody was using his villa. He asked us to investigate, and we've done it. No big deal. You can go lock up."

This speech gave the plumber confidence, as it was designed to do. "Fascist police," the man snarled. "You and your fascist search warrants."

"Lock up," Bellarmine told him. "And the gendarme will drive you home."

While the plumber was locking the front door Bellarmine ducked back into the garage and grabbed the flashlight. Crossing to the Juvaquatre, he stood it on the floor on the passenger side and slammed the door on it.

The plumber came around the building. "Now lock the garage," Bellarmine told him. "Shall I tell the pianist you won't be lending out his villa anymore?"

He watched impassively as the plumber, still muttering, climbed into the second car beside the gendarme and was driven away.

When the sound of wheels on gravel could no longer be heard, Bellarmine turned to Duclos.

"All right," he said in an icy-cold voice, "tell me the whole story."

"*Oui*, Monsieur le Commissaire," said Duclos humbly, and got out his notebook, as did Bellarmine. As the story unfolded, Duclos produced names, addresses, license plate numbers and other such details, and Bellarmine wrote them down.

About ten days before the break-in at the Banque de Nice, the plumber's wife, riding by this villa on a bus, had noticed that the upstairs shutters—the bedroom shutters—were open. This meant someone was using the bedroom, and she thought she knew who. Since the pianist, who had the only other key, was on tour, it had to be her husband. The open bedroom shutters meant to her that her husband was in that bedroom at this very moment with another woman. She reacted as any French housewife might. In a jealous rage she telephoned the gendarmerie at Le Chaudan, gave a false name, and reported that burglars must have broken into the villa. They were perhaps still there. Hurry.

Duclos and two other gendarmes had piled into a Juvaquatre and rushed to the villa as fast as the vehicle would roll—not very fast. There is little enough drama in French villages, even those so close to a big city, and the three officers were excited. They did not expect to interrupt a buglary in progress—the car was too slow and burglaries normally lasted only a few minutes. But even a looted villa would be an exciting change from routine.

However, as they approached the villa they noted that two cars were parked in the driveway, and that four men were seated out on the front stoop. The four men certainly seemed startled to see them. When interrogated, they told a somewhat fishy-sounding story about a party to be held at the villa. They were waiting for a fifth man to come with the key.

Duclos had had no experience with big-city hoodlums. All he knew was that these men were not village types. They had Corsican accents. They did not belong here.

He glanced at his two men, but they only looked disappointed that there had been no burglary. Then he remembered his training: a gendarme, once an investigation has been opened, must ask every question, pursue every lead, write down every detail. To a gendarme, correct procedure took precedence over imagination. A gendarme must be rigid, systematic and exact.

And so, although no crime had been committed and none seemed intended, he asked the four men to produce their identity cards. Three of them did so; he copied off their names, addresses and other details. The fourth man protested that he had left his identity card in another suit, and his wallet with it, and although this was technically an administrative infraction punishable by a fine, Duclos decided not to press the matter. He had a right to ask any French citizen to show his identity card at any time, and for any reason or none, and it never occurred to him that to do so, elsewhere in the world, might have been considered an invasion of privacy or a violation of civil rights. It did occur to him that these men seemed now a trifle too uneasy, their eyes shifted a bit too much, their answers had become slightly too vague.

He decided to wait for the fifth man to show up with the key.

The other two gendarmes meanwhile had circled the house. They had noted down the license numbers, models and makes of the two cars, and in the rear had discovered the garage, and had peered in at a third car. They took down its make, model and license number also, after which they returned to the front of the villa. The four men still sat on the stoop, though they had now become fidgety and silent. The three gendarmes stood on the gravel waiting.

After about twenty minutes a small black Renault turned into the driveway. They saw its nose, and the startled reaction of its driver, but it was not there long enough for the driver's face to be seen clearly, or its plate number read. On perceiving the parked Juvaquatre and the three uniformed gendarmes standing nearby, the driver had jammed on his brakes, thrown his vehicle into reverse, and had shot backward into the road. His tires spun, firing gravel uphill like bullets. Then he was gone.

To Duclos this altered the entire tenor of the affair, and he demanded the name of the fifth man, who was to bring the key, and his address. At this, the apparent leader of the group—his name was already in Duclos' notebook—drew the gendarme aside. The reason for their strange behavior, he explained, was that the "party" was going to be, well, an orgy. He knew that Duclos, a man of the world, would understand.

But Duclos was not a man of the world. He was a village gendarme, and before that he had grown up in a village in the Jura, near Switzerland, that was not very different from Le Chaudan. Impropriety of whatever kind offended him.

He demanded the name of the fifth man.

He was given the name of the plumber, and he noted it down. This done, he ordered the four men to their feet: they would all drive to the plumber's house, to see if he corroborated this story.

The plumber lived in an apartment over a store in Aspremont

142

village. Duclos knocked on the door, and the jealous wife opened it. She seemed frightened at the sight of his uniform, and Duclos tried to calm her by explaining why he was there. He had received a call from a woman about a possible burglary, and had gone to the villa in question and found only these four men.

At this, to his astonishment, the woman burst into tears.

Duclos was becoming more and more confused. He glanced down at the names written in his notebook. They meant nothing to him, and he was no longer certain, now that he had got used to their Corsican accents, that these men were such rough types as he had at first supposed. Nor was it his job to impose his own provincial morality on the conduct of others. If they wanted to have an orgy it was no business of his.

"With your permission, madame," he announced, "we will wait here until your husband returns."

The plumber came in about ten minutes later, and although he manifested surprise to find his kitchen full of gendarmes, Duclos thought his manner not convincing. However, he did confirm having loaned the villa to his friends, and he produced the key and handed it to them.

Duclos, now feeling slightly embarrassed, thanked everyone and left the apartment.

He talked it over with his two men on the drive back to the gendarmerie. All three agreed that the orgy story sounded false, and that the men themselves seemed suspicious.

But the thing bothered him. It stayed in his mind.

Then came the morning when the story broke that the Banque de Nice et de la Côte d'Azur had been sacked. The *Nice Matin* and the Paris papers were spread over the counter in the gendarmerie with all seven gendarmes bent over them, and all marveled at what had occurred. It was Duclos who voiced what all seven were thinking: "Do you suppose those *cocos* at the villa were involved in this?"

Later that afternoon he received a telegram signed by Bellarmine— the same telegram that had gone to every *commissariat* and gendarmerie for miles around. It asked for immediate reports on any suspicious events or observations in recent weeks.

Duclos reached for his telephone at once, but then had second thoughts. This was a big-city crime and he was only a village gendarme. He did not wish to make a fool of himself. Before phoning Nice he had best make sure of what he had.

So he got out his notebook and sent requests to the central archive in Paris for information on the plumber, and on the four men from the villa—he had four names copied down off identity cards, and a fifth belonging to the man who had left his identity card at home. Duclos also sent a second request to the auto registration service of the Bouches du Rhône department for information on owner-ship of the three cars—all three plate numbers were from the Marseille area.

The information Duclos had sent for dribbled in during the next few days. The plumber had once been detained in connection with a truck hijacking, but had been released. The group's spokesman, Gaston Baptiste Angelucci, had a previous conviction for living off the earn-ings of prostitution. At present he exploited, and possibly owned, a nightclub in Marseille. A third man, Claude Yves Rovette, now thirty-nine years old, had been convicted at the age of twenty-three of the armed robbery of a postal truck. No convictions since. The fourth man had no previous record, and the fifth, the one with no identity card, proved not to exist at all.

Duclos was chortling as he read this information. He had discov-ered what in police terminology was referred to as an "association of malefactors." He believed he was about to solve the bank job, the so-called Heist of the Century, single-handedly, and he waited for infor-mation to come in on the auto registrations. The gray Peugeot in the garage traced back to a grocer in Arles, a man who had not been present at the villa, and who had no previous known association with criminals. The two cars in the driveway traced back to third parties also. One of the owners was previously unknown to the law, which was a disappointment, but the other had once done a five-year stretch for manslaughter, which was promising.

By now Duclos was being pulled in two directions at once. He realized that he ought to bring his information to the attention of the Sûreté in Nice immediately. However, he also wanted to proceed further with the investigation. It was his investigation. He had brought it this far, and did not want to let it go. With just a few more details he might break the case wide open, serve it up to the Sûreté, as the saying goes, already cooked—what a coup for the Gendarmerie Nationale.

What a coup for Eugène Duclos.

He sent his six gendarmes into the bars and hotels and all the villages surrounding Le Chaudan. He put on civilian clothes and went down into the coastal cities and spoke with contacts there. But he had no search or arrest warrants. He had neither the personnel nor the vehicles to set up tails. He could not go to Marseille to pick up the trail there. He could not even get back inside the suspect villa and look around.

He personally rang the bell of every neighboring villa and interrogated all the inhabitants, and he filled many pages of his notebook. All this took more than two weeks, and the only information he came up with was either vague or inconclusive or both. The villa had been inhabited by strange men off and on for months. They came and went at odd hours. They kept to themselves.

It shocked Duclos to discover that so much time had passed, and that he had developed no new leads at all. He began to feel the first faint twinges of panic. The Gendarmerie Nationale is a branch of the Army. Gendarmes have no legal status as judiciary—that is, investigating—police. They police only towns and villages having a population under ten thousand. They are never supposed to operate in civilian clothes. Investigations of a serious nature were supposed always to pass immediately into the jurisdiction of the Sûreté.

By the time Duclos finally phoned Bellarmine with what he had, he was in trouble and he knew it.

Now, standing on the gravel, Bellarmine closed his notebook with a snap. "And you waited three weeks before informing us."

"*Oui, monsieur.*" Duclos hung his head. Summary discipline was about the best he could hope for. An official reprimand. Le Chaudan was nothing much. Nonetheless, his wife liked it there and his married children lived nearby. There were places he could be sent that were much less pleasant. An official reprimand would no doubt go inside his dossier, and whenever anyone opened it from now on, that was the first thing he'd see. His career seemed ruined.

"The military mind," muttered Bellarmine, "God preserve us from the military mind."

Duclos did not reply. He was, Bellarmine saw, suitably penitent, suitably crushed. There was no need to say more.

They drove back to the gendarmerie, where as Bellarmine was about to get into his car, an idea came to him. In his briefcase he still carried photos of all known associates of the prostitute Denise Lasablière, and he spread them out on the hood.

"Come here, Duclos."

Duclos hurried forward. He looked anxious to be of service—any service at all.

"The *mec* who had no identity card—do you recognize him among these photos?"

"That one, monsieur."

"You're sure?"

"*Oui, monsieur.*"

Bellarmine read the name off the back of the photo: the mink-coat giver, Jean Jacques Montenegro. Who, surely, was also Jeannot. Got you, Bellarmine thought.

"Is it important?" asked Duclos anxiously. He meant: had he in part redeemed himself? He must have thought the answer was yes, for a tentative grin came onto his face.

Bellarmine stared at him until the grin vanished. "You'll be hearing from us," he said and got into his car and drove away.

Back at the *commissariat* in Nice he prepared his package of evidence, the butts, the bottle, the flashlight, and called for a detective to take it to Marseille to the lab on the next train. Next he set up a schedule of men to tail the plumber around the clock. They were to find out whom he met with, and especially whom he telephoned. If he went into a post office this meant, probably, long distance, and they were to get the number from the telephone attendant afterward. If he went into a café, this would mean a local call from a phone on the end of the bar, or a booth downstairs outside the toilets, and they were to try to get close enough to eavesdrop.

And lastly Bellarmine went to ask the *divisionnaire* to sign a wiretap order on the plumber's business phone. The man had no phone at home.

But Sapodin was busy giving instructions to his secretary, and Bellarmine, standing beside the desk, had to wait until she had gone out.

"What is it, Bellarmine? I'm in a rush, as you can see." The *divisionnaire* was about to leave.

"We may have a lead, *patron*." He pushed the wiretap request across the desk.

Sapodin tightened the knot in his tie and buttoned his sleeves. In between he glanced at the request Bellarmine had typed out. "They've stepped into our web, eh, Bellarmine?"

Bellarmine expected him to ask for details, but he did not do so.

"The police service is like a gigantic spider, eh, Bellarmine? We have our webs out in all directions. Sooner or later every criminal steps in one, and then we have him."

"We may have discovered the gang's hideout while digging the tunnel," Bellarmine explained.

"But is it the only one, Bellarmine? That's what we have to find out."

The boss's prerogative, Bellarmine reflected. To deflate. To heckle. To withhold praise. To withhold even the reaction he had most expected: surprise.

Having put on his suit coat, a red carnation serving as boutonniere, Sapodin bent to initial the request.

"Would you like me to brief you on it?"

"Haven't got time now, Bellarmine." His Homburg went onto his bald head. He was coming around the desk on his way out the door. One couldn't even hold his attention. He handed over the wiretap request. "Keep me informed," he said, shook hands, and was gone.

Bellarmine stayed late in his office, waiting for the lab report from Marseille. The phone rang much earlier than he expected, for good news travels like lightning. People are willing to drop everything to impart it. His heart began to race as soon as he realized Marseille was on the line.

Tests of the ashes and butts, and of the wine bottle, he was told, had proved inconclusive.

"And the flashlight?" said Bellarmine impatiently. Marseille hadn't phoned to tell him about failure. He knew good news was coming.

"We took samples of the pudding out of the tunnel, as you know," said the technician. "Well, what do you think the pudding matches? The mud on the bottom of your flashlight, that's what. The match is perfect."

# CHAPTER
## 14

Gray sky over Nice. Bellarmine at the edge of the Promenade stood looking out at the oily gray sea. He wore his light-colored raincoat and his gray fedora with the brim pulled down. He stood smoking, breathing. He watched the sea as if it offered answers, as if the future were out there like a ship and would, if only he were patient, slowly materialize out of the distant haze.

He had drunk his café au lait, dunked and eaten his croissant, read his *Nice Matin*. That ritual was over, and in a few minutes he would go to his office and begin another. A man moved from ritual to ritual, performing mostly by rote, and it was only during the times in between that he was fully alive. But they were rare.

The dossiers he had sent for would be on his desk. Eight names. Eight men connected to that villa. Eight straws, one supposed, introduced into the sewer gang. And one of them—with luck—The Brain. Today the case would leap ahead. Or it would not.

There was no wind, no sign of waves or whitecaps on the sea. The water swelled regularly six feet up the beach, where it lay for a moment without edges, smooth. Then it seemed to drain down through the stones as if down into the center of the earth. The stones reappeared wet and black, as if permanently stained.

Gulls wheeled and screeched overhead. He went on watching the sea. It was different every day, and yet every day the same.

He recrossed the Promenade through the rush-hour traffic. Hordes of bicycles and motor scooters. A few cars. He walked down the Rue Halévy and into the Rue Masséna, where he would get his bus. People hurried along the narrow sidewalks. The clouds seemed to hover even lower over the streets, and the electric lights were on inside the shops.

Lights were on in the perfume shop too, and this stopped him. He peered in through the glass. Her vacation was over. He watched the unknown young woman arranging merchandise on the high shelves. She wore spike heels and, today, nylons. Usually she wore cotton stockings. Her arms pulled her blouse tight across her breasts. He went in and immediately felt uncomfortable. He felt like a monk who did not know how to behave outside the cloister.

She came toward him smiling. Although he gave a faint smile back, he felt he was committing a kind of adultery, was being unfaithful to his calling, unfaithful to the investigation.

"Monsieur?"

The smile was not for him but for the potential sale, and he had entered without having decided what to say. Now, having glanced rapidly around, he muttered the first idiotic thing that came into his head. "I, er, need a comb." Why a comb? He was not a vain man.

He combed his hair once a day. The rest of the time he used his fingers. He had several combs and did not need another.

"Of course," she said. What could be more normal? She pulled out a shallow drawer: combs reposing on black velvet, more different types than he had ever imagined. Black, green, red, long, short. He was mildly astonished.

"Just a—" he said "—a pocket comb."

She picked one up and handed it to him. He hefted it like a weapon, examined it on both sides, studied it like a piece of evidence at a crime scene.

"Fine," he said, and dropped it in his pocket. Immediately he found himself at a loss for words. It was ending too fast. He should have handled several combs, strung this out a bit.

"That will be three hundred francs, monsieur."

"As much as that?"

"*Oui, monsieur.*"

This was not the line he wished the conversation to follow, and even as he fished money out of his pocket he sought another one. She was watching him almost with amusement, as if she knew she had unsettled him. Probably she unsettled a good many male customers, and enjoyed doing so.

Her face was deeply tanned, and her nose had begun to peel. "You've been away," he told her. But the remark sounded more personal than he had intended.

"*Oui, monsieur.*"

Her hair was longer too. Smiles were hard for him, but he tried one. "The mountains or the sea?"

Now she became unsettled too. Her left hand brushed at her hair, and he saw with disappointment that she wore a wedding ring.

"The mountains, monsieur."

A ring proved little. She might be divorced, or a widow—widows her age were common in France these days. It had not been a good time to be a bride. She could be estranged, or not married at all— women in shops often wore rings as a means of keeping customers like himself at a distance.

"Switzerland, was it?"

"*Oui, monsieur.*"

His questioning sounded to him, and perhaps to her too, like an interrogation. Perhaps he should explain. "I live in the neighborhood," he said.

"But of course."

"I noticed the sign you put in your window," he said, explaining too much.

She handed him change from a five-hundred-franc note. "Will there be anything else, monsieur?"

The women he habitually dealt with were without options. Whores. Shoplifters. One approached them without ceremony. This woman was of a different category and he was annoyed at his performance. He was not used to the procedures of courtship.

"No," he said. "Nothing else." But he was unwilling to leave her on this note. He said: "I'm in a bit of a hurry now, mademoiselle." Mademoiselle or madame? He waited for her to correct him, though not too long. "But I might stop in later to talk to you about perfume. A gift for someone."

For a moment she regarded him. "But of course, monsieur." With another smile, she showed him out. It was the same smile as before and told him nothing. *"Merci, monsieur, au revoir,"* she said cheerily, and closed the door on him.

Having made his arrangements in the north, Lambert had driven his Studebaker back down to the coast where he had gone directly to the farm. His wife did not yet know he was back.

It was cold up there in the mountains, and he lit a fire in the hearth. He wanted a big one, and he worked hard on it, bringing wood in from outside. When at last he had it blazing he went to fetch the sack of documents stolen from the bank. He had hidden the duffel bag under the floorboards in an unreconstructed portion of the house. He had to move a stack of lumber to one side to get the boards up and the bag out. Dragging it close to the fire, he spilled about half its contents into a pile beside the room's one easy chair, then sat down to see what he had that was worth saving. He had stuffed hundreds of papers into that duffel bag. Reading them was not a job he looked forward to. He thought it would be drudgery, and he was not good at drudgery. His genius, he believed, lay in soaring flights of the imagination, in conceiving grand schemes. His cigarette business had been one example. The Heist of the Century another. He liked to compare himself to an architect, able to visualize unbuilt skyscrapers, to a Michelangelo, able to see David in a block of stone.

But to his surprise the documents transported him into another world—into many other worlds. He started by reading wills. It was like looking in people's windows. Wills were among the most private

150

of all documents. They were full of emotion, sometimes exposing smoldering family feuds. In one, a relative was mentioned by name and then disinherited. In another a brother was awarded an object described as worthless.

How to sock people even after death, thought Lambert.

The bizarre objects people had collected, and that these wills would dispose of, amazed Lambert: a Gutenberg Bible; a set of African tom-toms; two rows of Burgundy vines to be divided among three children; a painting by Leonardo da Vinci—imagine someone who owned a Leonardo. This notion so interested Lambert that he read on and discovered that the painting's authenticity rested on a letter by the great French painter Ingres dated 1860, which was attached to the will. Ingres had owned the painting himself at one time.

Still another will described itself as secret; it began by revoking the public will, which all the relatives knew about, thereby shifting the wealth of it instead between a "faithful" secretary, together with her son, and a "beloved" servant together with her daughter.

Lambert imagined clandestine love affairs that had lasted decades. The testator, besides being quite a man, was apparently trying to acknowledge after death what he had been unwilling to acknowledge while alive. He was ninety-two years old and perhaps no longer *compos mentis*. This was indeed his "last" will.

Holding all these wills in his lap, Lambert decided to fit the stories they told into the framework of a play. He would work it all out the next time he was in the mood. After that the writing was just a question of time.

Between his feet he had placed an empty wine carton to hold whatever he would save. He did not expect to save much. One could not easily hide an object as bulky as a duffel bag stuffed full of materials as perishable as these documents. The quantity had to be winnowed way down. He was looking only for an insurance policy for himself. He should keep a few choice pieces only, he believed. They should take up no more space than two or three insurance policies lying in a drawer. They should be as easy to hide as Edgar Allan Poe's purloined letter—a story he had been made to read in high school.

The wills in his lap he tossed one by one into the fire, including the will of the ninety-two-year-old man. The mistresses and illegitimate children were out of luck. The secret testament burned. The public one, wherever it was, stood.

When he came to Ingres' letter he hesitated. It raised the value of the Leonardo by hundreds of thousands of dollars, but this was not his affair. The letter was no doubt valuable in itself, though not to him. It was written on heavy parchment paper and scaled easily into the fireplace. Ingres' paintings had never pleased him anyway.

He became adept at identifying documents by the quality, thickness and color of the legal paper on which they were written—divorce decrees, for instance. All were signed contracts, of course, and most, between the lines, were full of hatred—the hated husband forced to pay; the hated wife guaranteed to receive. Hatred was certainly unattractive to read about. Lambert himself hated nobody. He felt himself on top of the world. He hated only hatred, and in addition he saw no way these documents, these payment schedules, could serve as insurance for himself, so he burned up every decree, canceled all alimony. He remarried everyone.

There were packets of letters—most bound together with ribbons. One packet was from a young man at the front to his mother. The first letter was dated October 10, 1914. The old ink had faded, and the old handwriting style was difficult to decipher. There were about fifty letters in all. Many pages had been mutilated by the censor's razor blade. The last was written in August 1918, on the son's twenty-third birthday, an account of a celebration in an *estaminet*. To Lambert it sounded like a boring party. Apparently the boy had been killed the next day, for at the bottom of the packet was a letter from an officer describing his "glorious death" in an attack.

Lambert gazed thoughtfully at the fire. The mother must still be alive if these letters were being kept, an old lady of eighty or so. The letters looked like she read them a lot. But he had made his decision. Having retied the ribbon, he tossed the packet in on top of the logs and watched it flare up.

Most of the other packets were love letters. Very private of course. Some were salacious, amusingly so. But Lambert's principal reaction, reading them, was contempt for the lovers' writing style. Most people couldn't write at all. These letters had perhaps been meaningful to their recipients—why else confide them to a safe-deposit box—but to Lambert they quickly became boring. The authors being inept, the editor gave them their rejection slips. Into the fire with them.

Acknowledgments of debts passed through Lambert's hands. Feeling magnanimous, he decided to give all debtors a fresh start. One by one he canceled their debts. He canceled them by incineration.

By then he had begun to separate out documents apparently relating to numbered Swiss bank accounts. He studied these for a while. It was against the law for a Frenchman to hold such an account, he believed. Nonetheless, penalties, if caught, would not be severe. The owners would be obliged to pay taxes on their Swiss holdings, plus a small fine. There was a better way to punish such wrongdoers, Lambert believed. All were tax evaders or worse. They were parasites on society and ought to be severely hurt, and he decided to dispense justice himself. He tossed all but one of the certificates toward the flames, and when they fell in disarray he reached for the poker and pushed them close to the blazing logs, thinking: let's see anybody withdraw his Swiss funds now.

He then studied the surviving certificate. On it he had recognized the name Picpoul—the adjunct mayor's name. The illegal account was in the name of Marie Thérèse Picpoul, perhaps the man's wife or daughter. If so, it might be worth saving; it went into the wine carton between Lambert's shoes.

He realized a little better now what he was looking for: important names. One could not hold a nonentity hostage—nobody cared. For nobodies, nobody would pay ransom. However, Lambert was hampered in his search for celebrated people because he had not paid much attention to the French political or entertainment scenes; there must be celebrities of the French business world too, but their names, if he came across them, would unfortunately mean nothing to him. Nor did he understand the various financial documents that passed through his hands, packets of bearer's bonds, for instance. There were no names of individuals on them. The notion that substantial companies might be based on such insubstantial bits of paper was to him inconceivable. For his purposes such bonds were useless. He was not going to be encumbered with them and he watched the flames rise up.

Realizing at length that he was hungry, Lambert went into the kitchen. It was past two o'clock in the afternoon. He had brought with him a crusty fresh *baguette* and a cold beef tongue that lay on its side on a dish. He cut himself several slices. He cut the long, thin loaf in half, then sliced one of the halves down the side. On it he laid slices of tongue. He painted both halves with mustard, then clapped them together. He had some beer sitting outside the back door—there was no refrigerator in the house; the outdoors was the refrigerator—and he brought in a bottle, pulled the cap off it, and took his sandwich and beer into the living room. He also carried with him that morning's *Nice Matin*. Sitting on the floor in front of the fire, he turned the pages rapidly from the last page forward to the front. He was looking only for an article on the investigation, but there was none today, a cheering sign, and he was chewing contentedly on his sandwich when he came to the article on Congressman Avery. Page three was the celebrity page—gossip columns and photos of visiting film stars usually. An American congressman was a change of pace for them, and they had got his name, Lambert supposed, where they got all their names—the hotel concierges received a regular fee for tipping off the paper about guests. The headline called Avery "Nice's adopted son." In the interview he told how much he enjoyed his many vacations on the Côte d'Azur. There were three photos, and Lambert studied them. He had scarcely heard of Avery, but the face was somehow familiar to him. Two of the photos showed Avery in sports clothes in his suite at the Ruhl, and the third, from a wire service, showed him shaking hands with President Eisenhower.

As the recognition became clear to him, Lambert nearly choked on his sandwich. Lunging for the duffel bag, he dumped out everything. On his knees, he rummaged through the pile until the packet of pornographic photos fell clear. He grabbed them up, fanned them out, ogled them. He carried them over to the window, where the light was strongest. His heart was pounding, but his excitement wasn't sexual. Twelve different people had attended the orgy, he decided. Six females, of course. He wasn't studying the females. What did he care who these women were, or why they had permitted themselves to be employed in such poses? He had eyes only for the males—the masked faces, the unmasked erections so prominently displayed—and he was able to identify two men. One was Avery. The other was Picpoul. The backs of the photos bore notations, he saw, perhaps a code of some kind.

There was something else he had noted a while ago—something he had glanced at and put aside. More rummaging through the pile. Here it was—he grabbed it up in both hands and tore the rubber band off. There were two documents. The first, as near as he could tell, concerned the sale of the Casino de la Méditerranée to the Charter Financial Company Ltd. of Luxembourg. This document had caught Lambert's eye earlier. He had not read the one to which it was attached, but he did so now, and it set his heart pounding a second time. It appeared to be the articles of incorporation of this Charter Financial Company, and it listed corporate officers and holders of outstanding stock. The president and chief executive officer of Charter Financial was Saul Avery, who owned 51 percent. Which meant that Avery owned the Casino de la Méditerranée. Another of the major stockholders (20 percent of outstanding shares) was Fernand Picpoul.

And none of this had ever been made public.

Lambert had read the newspaper articles about the sale of the one casino and the condemnation of the other. Juicy articles. Speculation and innuendo mostly. Gossip—and Lambert loved gossip. At the time, the *Nice Matin* appeared to have started an investigation of sorts, but it had hurriedly pulled back.

Lambert's brain was buzzing, yet he sat quietly in his chair munching his sandwich, drinking his beer and grinning into the flames. When the sandwich was gone he rose and stretched, then began to gather up all the unexamined documents, armloads at a time. There was no need to search further, and he carried them to the fireplace and threw everything in. He had the best insurance policy he could have hoped for. It was financial in nature and sexual in nature at the same time. One or the other was at the heart of all successful blackmail, and he had both. He had the principal elected official of one the biggest cities in France, and a loudmouthed congressman who, he now remembered, liked to tell off presidents. The few bits of paper in his hands could make more noise than a howitzer. A scandal was his to launch, if he wished, and he had never felt so powerful in his life, not even when standing in the vault.

In his desk he found a manila envelope that would take the photos and documents, then began to wander through the house searching for a proper hiding place. He wanted to leave the envelope almost out in the open. The most accessible possible spot, provided it was not totally obvious, would be the safest, and he moved from room to room looking for what he needed.

When the envelope was hidden to his satisfaction, he opened another beer. He deserved it. If the cops ever searched this place, an unlikely possibility, they would not find what they were looking for. He sat down with his beer in front of the fire. The day's work was over.

# CHAPTER
## 15

Bellarmine knew at the end of an hour that not one of the eight dossiers on his desk represented The Brain. Several were thick with *procès-verbaux*—you could guess at the *ampleur* of a malefactor's career from thickness alone. Or you could flip the pages, and the colors flashing past would convey the same information, for arrest warrants were red, *convocations* blue, and so on, and some of these dossiers were as multicolored as Christmas lights. In addition to crimes committed, they told also which bars a subject frequented, who his friends were, his routines, for the French police kept extremely close tabs on habitual offenders. They worked hard at it, raiding bars and nightclubs owned by criminal types, or known to be popular with them, every few weeks. They threw cordons around them, rushed in and stood every man present against the wall, the innocent as well as the potentially guilty. Each was made to show his identity card, to empty his pockets for scrutiny, to prove that he had a means of livelihood, and to tell what he was doing there. Legitimate patrons usually had no difficulty in proving their legitimacy, and were released, but individuals of questionable repute were always interrogated, sometimes at great length, and often taken down to the *commissariat* and detained. Every resulting *procès-verbal* went into the man's judicial dossier, and remained there. These dossiers also came to contain reports from informants, raw and unchecked data mostly, each of which began with the notation: "The following information is from a person worthy of faith."

Bellarmine felt intensely disappointed. If he didn't have The Brain, then who did he have? What did he have? Were all eight men members of the sewer gang? Or only some? Or maybe none? He was like a personnel director considering candidates for a job. Which of the eight matched the job description?

He studied the eight names. Except for the plumber, all were

156

unknown to him. Not one was a major Milieu figure, and four of them had no previous record. It didn't make sense.

Montenegro, Jean Jacques. Profession: *commerçant*.

Angelucci, Gaston Baptiste. Profession: *commerçant*.

Rovette, Claude Yves. Profession: *entrepreneur*.

Chiaramonte, Prosper Georges. Profession: *entrepreneur*.

These were the four men at the villa, Corsicans all. *Commerçant* meant shopkeeper and *entrepreneur* meant builder. The two *commerçants* were convicted pimps. And pimps normally were idlers living off women, not tunnel diggers. The mink-coat giver, Montenegro, in addition was fifty years old, which did not seem the ideal age. Bellarmine saw that one of his nicknames was St. Jean. Great name for a whoremaster.

The two so-called builders seemed more suitable. Rovette, thirty-nine, had been convicted of armed robbery sixteen years ago—once a stickup man always a stickup man, in Bellarmine's view. Only three forces were strong enough to effect reform: sickness, old age and the guillotine. But this did not make him guilty of helping loot the Banque de Nice. Not in court. Chiaramonte, from his photo, was a tough guy also, and an even better age, twenty-seven. No arrests, no convictions. Which meant only that he had not yet been caught.

Next came the three car owners, none present at the villa.

Custines, Charles Édouard. Profession: *commerçant en fruits et légumes*.

Roquemaure, Émile Guillaume. Profession: *électricien*.

Cocciolo, Toussain Luc. Profession: *entrepreneur*.

Custines and his wife kept a grocery store at Arles, 92 kilometers northwest of Marseille and 270 from Nice. Roquemaure still lived in Toulon, which was part of the Marseille orbit. Neither man had been born in Corsica. Neither had a Corsican name. But the Milieu would accept a man with a Corsican mother. It would sometimes accept a man with no Corsican blood at all. Bellarmine pondered all this. Neither man had a judicial dossier, even though both were forty years old, which was strange, if they were involved. Had their careers in crime just begun? At forty? Had they begun with a job of the magnitude of the Banque de Nice?

Cocciolo, the third car owner, was more the type. Corsican-born. Five years for manslaughter. Two arrests for assault. And he was another who sometimes worked in the building trades when not in jail. A strong-arm guy. An enforcer. Probably not too bright.

Well, none of these people were geniuses. If they had been, they wouldn't have chosen that villa to hide out in, and Bellarmine would not have their dossiers on his desk. He, himself, if planning to break into the Banque de Nice, would have worked out of an apartment in the heart of the city, for in cities the coming and going of strangers are ignored. The last place you pick is a villa in the country, where someone is sure to notice. And if gendarmes turn up in your driveway two weeks before the crime, and take down your names and the license numbers of your cars, you call the job off.

Did they think the gendarmes were not going to remember them?

He doubted that The Brain, whoever he might be, even knew about the gendarmes' visit to that villa.

How can criminals be so stupid?

The answer was: they were always stupid. Without their stupidity the police would have no success at all, for the criminals had, after all, the entire population of the country into which to disappear.

At least three of the five Corsicans, by their dossiers, were allied with the Faletta Milieu clan, said to be the most powerful in Marseille. Could Faletta be The Brain? A fleeting thought—Bellarmine quickly discarded it. Faletta was in his sixties, too old for sewers. But his name raised new problems for Bellarmine. The case now definitely led back to Marseille, the most corrupt city in France. It was said that Faletta exerted more political power there than the mayor. Politicians, judges and policemen were said to be on his payroll.

Bellarmine went downstairs to Sapodin's office. The *divisionnaire* had been in Paris for the last several days—according to the rumor that had swept the building, he was about to be promoted to adjunct director. If true, this would make him the third most powerful man in the Sûreté. Now, perhaps only temporarily, he was back.

Bellarmine was shown in. Bald head shining, wearing a new gray suit, and a yellow boutonniere today, Sapodin came around the desk and shook hands. He seemed in an exuberant mood, and to Bellarmine's policeman's mind this proved he had got the new job, and would soon move out of Bellarmine's life. Whether he had got it or not he enjoyed enormous power at the moment, the rumor alone assured that, and this was power Bellarmine wished to tap.

"What put you on to this villa?"

Sapodin had interrupted Bellarmine's briefing. His exuberance was entirely gone. He looked thoughtful. The *divisionnaire* saw that the case was about to break, and this was what Bellarmine was counting on. It was perhaps time for him to intervene in person.

"Some gendarmes stumbled on the villa—by accident, of course."

"Not an accident, Bellarmine." Sapodin gave a snort of derision. "The malefactors stepped into our web."

Bellarmine offered him a Chesterfield, and both men lit up.

Sapodin studied his cigarette. "Are these from the black market, Bellarmine? You must tell me who your dealer is. Mine seems to have gone out of business."

"You won't be needing a dealer here much longer."

Sapodin smiled. "That's true."

They stood smoking.

Bellarmine picked grains of tobacco off his tongue. He was waiting for Sapodin to offer to help, but this did not happen.

"If that's all, Bellarmine, I'm rather busy right now. Keep me informed."

"*Patron*, I think it's time you came on the case personally," Bellarmine interrupted. "You should go to Marseille and—"

"I'm too busy for that, Bellarmine. At a later date, perhaps."

"If I go there alone, Marseille will take the case away from us." He stopped. It wouldn't do to mention his other great fear, that the Bishopric was so corrupt that it would be impossible to maintain security there. "It's your case, *patron*." It wasn't Sapodin's case, but his own. "I don't want to see you lose it." One always supposed superiors would see through such lies, but they never did. "If you went to Marseille, you would still control the case. Of course I'd be happy to go with you to do the fieldwork." He stopped, waiting for Sapodin's reaction.

"Eight men implicated, eh, Bellarmine?" the *divisionnaire* said at last.

The office was full of smoke. Both men were puffing. The *divisionnaire* in addition had begun to pace.

"I can't spare much time, Bellarmine. We'll drive to Marseille tomorrow. I'll set up a special brigade and put you in charge as my deputy. On your way out tell my chauffeur he's to have my car ready first thing in the morning."

"*Merci, patron*," said Bellarmine.

Lambert at the house phones asked to be put through to Congressman Avery. He had come all the way down from the farm to get a look at him.

The congressman took so long to answer that Lambert was about to hang up. In reality the delay was less than ten seconds, but time is only a relative concept, not an absolute. Different segments have different weight. The seconds needed to cross a hotel room can seem an eternity.

"Hello?"

Avery's voice was guarded. He knew what all celebrities knew, to put energy—cordiality—into his voice was to invite an invasion of privacy. A smile across a restaurant was the same. The fellow might take it as an invitation to sit down at your table. He was a man used to warding people off even with his greeting.

"Congressman Avery," said Lambert, "one of your constituents calling. Great piece on you today in the paper. I'm downstairs, and I want to shake your hand."

Avery being from New Orleans, Lambert had attempted a southern drawl.

"Well now, isn't that nice," came the false reply. "But—" He was in a meeting, he said. He was too busy to come down.

Probably Lambert was expected to accept the rebuff and hang up, but he didn't. "Congressman, I'm scheduled to address the Rotary when I get back home." Lambert hesitated, and his brief silence implied a threat. "Two thousand members." Another silence. Another threat. "Sure would like to tell 'em I met you here, looking after our interests wherever in the world you might happen to be."

This is all so easy, Lambert told himself.

"I don't mind waitin'," Lambert said into the silence. "I want to shake the hand of a man who's done so much for the state and people of Louisiana."

"Well now," Avery said. And probably licked his lips. Could this caller hurt him in any way? Best to capitulate and go down and shake his hand. Avery believed in the admiration of his public. His handshake was valuable to them. Lambert's request was normal. It was only his insistence that might be strange. Avery capitulated.

"Sure would like to meet a man from back home," he said smoothly.

"I'll wait in the bar," said Lambert and hung up.

About ten minutes later Avery appeared, framed in the doorway to the bar, peering into dimness.

Lambert went over and wrung his hand. "Congressman, to meet you is sure a proud day."

Avery, though hesitating, allowed himself to be swept toward the bar. "I don't have much time."

As they ordered, Lambert stripped him of his clothes, saw him as he had appeared in those photos, and he wondered if women, standing in bars, ever measured men this way, ever stripped away the impeccable tailoring and visualized the undignified rutting male underneath. A woman naked is merely naked. A man in that condition looks foolish.

"Where exactly did you say you were from?" inquired Avery carefully.

"Only about five or six blocks away from your house, congressman." Lambert had no idea even where Avery's district lay, much less where he lived.

Avery seemed to be watching him shrewdly. "And you're here as a tourist?"

"Mixing a little business with my pleasure—same as yourself, eh, Congressman?" That will shake him up, thought Lambert.

Avery frowned into his drink.

"You know something, Congressman?" said Lambert. "You sure do look a lot like your pictures."

"What's that supposed to mean?" But Avery had stiffened.

"Some people don't resemble their pictures too much," Lambert said coolly. "But you do." A slight pause. Then: "Exactly." How nervous is he? Lambert wondered. He must be expecting the blackmail pitch right now, Lambert thought.

Having accomplished his purpose, having insured the insurance, he glanced at his wristwatch as if in surprise. "My stars, Congressman, I didn't realize how late it has become. Have to run. Sure do appreciate this drink with you." Leaving Avery to pay the check, Lambert strode out of the bar and out of the hotel. His Studebaker was parked outside, and he got into it.

As he pulled away from the curb, he replayed the interview in his mind and was satisfied. Avery would remember this meeting, and if ever it became necessary to use the insurance policy, the congressman would be under no doubt that he had it.

# CHAPTER
## 16

In Marseille Sapodin bustled through the Bishopric, bald pate shining, showing all his big teeth. He had developed a booming laugh in the last several days. It rang down every corridor. He was treated with great deference—rumor had reached there too.

Bellarmine only trailed behind him, and kept silent. By the evening of the second day all negotiations had been completed. A new brigade was put together totaling forty-two detectives, men borrowed in almost equal proportions from Nice, Lyon and Paris. Sapodin, while in residence, always referred to the new group as the Brigade Sapodin; as soon as he was gone, the detectives began calling it the Bank Brigade. Two supervising *commissaires* were appointed to assist Bellarmine: young Lussac, from Nice; and Devereux, chief of the Marseille Mondaine.

"I've talked to him, Bellarmine," Sapodin said. "You can trust him. And you need someone on your team who knows Marseille." This was the only reference either of them made to the Milieu's alleged penetration of the Bishopric.

"Satisfied, Bellarmine?" asked the *divisionnaire*. A car was waiting downstairs to take him to the train.

"*Oui, monsieur.*"

"The Brain's the one we want."

"*Oui, monsieur.*"

"Anything else?"

"*Non, monsieur.*"

"Well then, I'm off to Paris. Keep me informed."

And once again he was gone. Bellarmine set to work. Five detectives and one car went to Arles. Their job: to learn all about the grocer, his wife, his one employee, his friends. The grocer had had nothing to do with the crime, and neither had his car, but the detectives, living in a cheap Arles hotel, would tail him for weeks.

Surveillance of the electrician in Toulon was assigned to a team of ten men, for he had eight employees. He and his employees were

162

innocent also. In like manner, teams were set up to tail each of the five Marseille suspects, and to pick up and monitor the telephone intercepts twice a day.

There was a detective staked out in the Crédit Lyonnais bank where he waited for a possible second ingot to turn up. He was incorporated into the new brigade.

And so Bellarmine's entire strength was deployed.

In Marseille the surveillances took place mostly in bars, often in the bar that served Faletta as headquarters, and it soon became clear that all five Marseille suspects were members of the Faletta clan.

Bellarmine went around to Faletta's bar. It was a *bar-tabac* on the Rue de Récollettes. The *tabac* counter was by the door, almost blocking it. A middle-aged couple worked hard dispensing cigarettes, newspapers, postage stamps. There was a steady stream of customers milling about in front of them.

Then came a zinc bar. The two barmen worked in shirt sleeves, serving up apéritifs, coffees. They did not appear to wipe off the bar too often. A new Italian espresso machine, one of the first Bellarmine had seen, had been installed behind the bar. The place reeked of coffee.

Bellarmine was accompanied by a detective named Nicot. They took stools, pushed their hats back, and lit up smokes. When the barman came over both ordered Calvados. This done, Bellarmine at last allowed himself, as if casually, to glance around.

"We're in luck," murmured Nicot.

At a table in the back a card game was in progress. Four players. A fifth man, Faletta himself, sat kibitzing. The players were the two pimps, Montenegro and Angelucci, and the two "builders," Rovette and Chiaramonte. All four had been at the villa.

Bellarmine directed his attention to the pimps. Manicured hands. Loud suits. Silk handkerchiefs dangling like flags from their breast pockets. After a few seconds he dismissed them, and his eyes shifted to the other two. Rovette, the ex-stickup man, was dressed all in leather. He had dirty fingernails. The fourth man, Chiaramonte, was the virgin, Bellarmine remembered. Though much younger, he seemed entirely at ease with the others. A sharp dresser. Brilliant white teeth. Loud laugh. He could be anything, Bellarmine thought: pimp, loan shark, enforcer. Probably began as a common stickup man, then progressed step by step to his current rank—whatever it was—in the hierarchy. Obviously he didn't work. Obviously he had "respect." Obviously too he had been out in the city seven or eight years by now

163

and the police did not even have a dossier on him yet. How did we miss him? Bellarmine asked himself.

And the fifth man, Faletta himself. White hair. Kept a cane between his knees. False upper teeth that he moved sometimes with his tongue as he watched the card game.

"The fire's out in that guy," said Nicot.

"One would say so."

"He doesn't have to get mixed up in a thing like this. He can sit around all day with his hand out accepting tribute."

To Bellarmine this sounded accurate. Faletta may know about the job, he thought. He may even have financed it. But he is not The Brain.

Then who was?

Bellarmine sipped his Calvados.

A man came into the bar. Small. Wore glasses. After hesitating briefly, he approached the card table. He seemed anxious, almost timid, as if unsure of his welcome, but the four players were glad to see him. They embraced him. Like true Corsicans, they kissed him on both cheeks. The newcomer looked very pleased.

At the bar Bellarmine muttered out of the side of his mouth: "Who's he?"

"No idea."

Faletta called one of the barmen into the back. Bellarmine watched orders being taken. The card game had stopped. There was some loud laughing, some playful socks on the arm.

Bellarmine, who had to get back to the Bishopric, dropped money on the bar. "Tail him," he said to the detective. "Find out who he is, where he goes."

By morning he had the new dossier on his desk. A civil dossier only, unfortunately. No previous record. Gilbert Roger Vargelin, a jeweler. The jeweler who had been in the vault, perhaps?

Vargelin had just acquired a twenty-four-hour tail.

"For you."

In the Bishopric, Bellarmine's phone had rung. Lussac handed it over.

The voice on the line spoke guardedly, almost in a whisper. It did not identify itself. If certain arrangements were made, the caller would give Bellarmine the name of the man he was looking for. He would give up The Brain.

"Fine," replied Bellarmine. By now all Marseille knew the investigation had moved here, and there had been many such calls lately.

Each one, momentarily at least, elated him—the case might be about to break wide open. Each one, so far, had only wasted enormous amounts of detective man-hours. His voice showed none of the emotion he was feeling. "Come to the Bishopric. I'll arrange for you to be brought to my office."

The caller refused. He would wait for him in one hour's time at the Notre Dame Basilica on the heights above the city. When Bellarmine protested that he was too busy, the caller repeated his original message and hung up.

Bellarmine contemplated sending Lussac or Devereux or one of the others. He really was very busy. But an hour later he stood in the wind at the wall looking down at the city. Why? He couldn't explain it. He was still very excited. This was how cases of this kind got solved. He felt certain that he was about to meet a man who really could give him The Brain.

The view from up here was quite splendid. One could see not only the city but also much of the coast and all of the offshore islands. The harbor was clotted with ship traffic. There were ships standing offshore waiting their turn to come in.

There were tourists behind him entering and leaving the basilica, and about twenty feet farther along the wall stood a man with a bicycle. Him? Bellarmine asked himself. Ankle clips. Peaked cap pulled down to his eyes. About thirty-five years old. But when the man mounted and peddled away, Bellarmine glanced impatiently at his watch. The caller was ten minutes late.

A few seconds later the same bicycle glided to a stop beside him.

"I can give you The Brain."

Bellarmine's head swung sharply around.

The identity of The Brain was worth ten million francs, the cyclist said. He himself was what you might call a broker. He was there to arrange terms. The terms were ten million francs.

Bellarmine attempted to engage him in conversation. He had men moving into place to follow the contact away from this meeting, and was stalling for time. The unmarked police cars were parked alongside the cars of tourists in the parking lot on the ramp below the basilica. They needed time to get back to them.

The cyclist had remounted his bike.

"Wait," called Bellarmine. The cyclist was peddling away, standing up on the pedals, the bike gaining speed. "How do I get in touch with you?"

"You don't," said the cyclist over his shoulder, "I call you."

A single unmarked car started down the steep, winding hill after the bike. But it couldn't keep up. It was like following the cyclists down out of the Alps in the Tour de France. The bike was faster. It sliced through the apex of every turn, and never slowed down. At the bottom it crossed over behind the port and plunged into the narrow, twisting streets of the old town, and there was no following it in there.

"You lost him?" said Bellarmine back in the Bishopric.

"I'm sorry, *patron*."

Bellarmine turned away. He was annoyed and disappointed, but it wasn't the detective's fault.

The caller phoned late that same afternoon: "Are arrangements satisfactory?"

"You're asking a lot of money," said Bellarmine. He had bitten off most of his fingernails waiting for this call. "We have to have another meeting."

The cyclist agreed. They would meet the following morning in the crypt of the St. Victor Basilica off Avenue de la Corse, about three blocks from the Vieux Port—evidently he was a man who felt comfortable in churches.

The cyclist came into the crypt dressed as before, from cap to bicycle clips.

The crypt was full of tourists listening to a guide. "I've got to have a few details," said Bellarmine tersely.

"If you don't want the information, forget it."

"Now wait—"

"Otherwise ten million francs."

"I'll have to see."

There were five possible exits from the basilica. He had detectives on bicycles covering all five. The caller was tailed back to his place of business, a bicycle repair shop on the Rue du Panier. His name was Antoine Quereyson, a bicycle mechanic by trade. He had no judicial dossier, and his civil dossier contained few facts beyond his age (thirty-nine), his place of birth (the Mediterranean town of Bandol), and the names of his parents, both now dead. Nonetheless, and for no reason he could determine, Bellarmine felt certain that he was not a fake, that he had something, and he waited impatiently for the next call.

When it came, Bellarmine told him he could not make the decision personally on so much money. His superiors would have to meet and evaluate the caller. If they were satisfied, they would hand over the money. For some minutes Bellarmine purred, he wheedled. The

166

caller would have to come to the Bishopric. Then he could have the money. Finally Quereyson agreed.

The next morning he was shown into Bellarmine's office. His hair was slicked down, his cap was in his hand, and he was wearing what looked like his Sunday suit. Bellarmine introduced Devereux as chief of the Marseille Sûreté, and Lussac as the Sûreté's chief accountant. The cyclist, believing himself in the presence of heavyweight dignitaries, took a deep breath. He was much abashed.

"Now, Monsieur Quereyson—" Bellarmine began.

At the sound of his own name, the cyclist blanched.

They kept him an hour. Because they believed—or at least Bellarmine believed—that he could lead them to The Brain they did not at first browbeat him too much.

He had no information himself, he said. The man who did was a relative in close contact with Milieu elements in Marseille.

"What's his name," said Lussac.

"His name," demanded Devereux.

Quereyson would give no name. The relative was risking his life already. So was Quereyson himself. The police had no right to ask for it.

"Who are you dealing for?" snarled Devereux. When he got no reply, he turned to Bellarmine: "Put me alone with him, and in ten minutes he'll tell us his life story."

An expression of fear came onto Quereyson's face, and he turned to Bellarmine. "I come in here like a good citizen, to help the police, and—"

"You came in here like a stool pigeon to fill your pockets at public expense," snarled Devereux.

This was true, of course. The rarest bird a policeman ever saw, Bellarmine reflected, was the honest citizen who gave the police information purely in defense of the public good. The motives of informants were almost always despicable. Informants were despicable. They all wanted something. Yet without them, the police could not function at all.

If the police wanted cooperation, Quereyson said, then they had to pay. Ten million. It wasn't much money for such a big case. He would have to give up his business and leave Marseille afterward, or risk being killed. So would his—his relative. It would be expensive. They had a right to be paid for their information.

"How do we know this information is accurate?" demanded Lussac.

"Or worth ten million," said Bellarmine.

"Ten minutes with him," said Devereux. "Ten."

They had reduced Quereyson almost to tears.

"If you're looking for The Brain in Marseille," he blurted, "you'll never find him. Without my information you'll never find him."

"Tell us more," said Bellarmine coolly.

"I don't know any more," shouted Quereyson.

The three detectives studied him in silence: a cowed figure on a chair.

"We'll give you five million, not ten," Bellarmine said after a time. "Half when we meet the informant and half when—if—his information checks out." He would have to square this with Sapodin, who would surely approve. Quereyson could be paid out of the so-called "black cash register" used for paying informants.

Quereyson nodded agreement and got up from the chair. After a moment he was smiling, and wanted to shake hands all around.

"Now get out of here. My offer holds until midnight tonight."

Was this the proper way to deal with this individual? Bellarmine hoped so. Would he have reacted better to kinder treatment—or to rougher treatment? There was no way Bellarmine could know. One never knew. Each informant was unique. Each had to be manipulated just so, seasoned just so. Detectives each time were like chefs dealing with some new and exotic dish—the recipe for preparing it had not yet been written.

Quereyson, as he came down the steps out of the Bishopric, was walking in a jaunty manner, and the sunlight illuminated the smile on his face. He believed that he had engaged in a battle of wills with the police, and had won. He was stronger than they were. The money would be forthcoming, and in his mind he was already beginning to spend it. Five million was not ten, but to him it was still an enormous sum, more than he had really dared hope for.

But it happened that a man named Besse, a rising young Milieu star, was at that very moment being led by a detective up the Bishopric steps in handcuffs, to be questioned in connection with a series of unsolved stickups. In actual fact the detective had nothing on Besse, and would release him four hours later. He had arrested him only because he ran into him. The French police harassed hoodlums whenever they felt like it, whenever they were bored. It kept the *flics* busy and the criminals off balance. They questioned them until that got boring in its turn, made them sign *procès-verbaux*, and let them go.

Quereyson recognized Besse, and immediately his jaunty walk left him, and his smile disappeared. His eyes dropped to the pavement, and he attempted to slink by unnoticed. There were a number of legitimate reasons why he might have been inside the Bishopric, whether to report a theft or to pick up a new identity card. If Quereyson had only smiled and waved, then Besse, who was focused on his own problems at the time, would have accepted this as normal. It was Quereyson's furtive manner that caught his attention. The *mec* looked guilty. The *mec*, he decided, had been in there singing.

As soon as he was released, Besse took the news to the clan boss, Faletta, who verified it via a policeman on his payroll who worked in the Bishopric.

Quereyson had been locked in an office most of the morning with this Commissaire Bellarmine from Nice.

Faletta sent Besse to the house of Henry the Welder, also known as Henry the Torch, who came down to the car carrying a brown leather satchel. He threw this in the trunk and ordered Besse to get behind the wheel.

"What's up?" Besse said. "Where are we going?"

"Rue du Panier," The Torch told him.

"Then what?"

But the other's flat, almost Oriental face was closed, and he did not answer.

At the entrance to the Rue du Panier, he ordered Besse to stop, and he got out and walked down the street and into the bicycle repair shop. Quereyson, who was working on a bike, came over and shook hands. "*Ça va?*" he said.

"*Ça va,*" said Henry. "Faletta sent me to get you."

"Now?"

"He wants to see you."

Quereyson looked back at the bike he had been working on. It stood upside down on its seat and handlebars. "I'm almost finished."

"Finish it later."

Quereyson was suspicious, though not very. "He's got a job for me?"

Henry the Torch nodded. "He said there's money in it."

Quereyson thought about it. "Okay. Give me a minute to close up the shop."

There were bikes for sale in racks out in front on the sidewalk, and Quereyson wheeled them one by one inside. He saw that the other man was getting impatient. He locked the front door, then pulled down the iron curtain over the door. It came down like a window shade, covering the whole front of the store. By the time he had locked it, The Torch was at the curb signaling to the black Citroën at the head of the street. It pulled to a stop in front of the shop. When Quereyson saw who was driving it he became afraid.

"Get in," ordered Henry the Torch. He pulled open the front door and pushed Quereyson toward it. The bicycle mechanic's knees had become so stiff he could hardly fold them into the car.

The Torch got in the back, and the car headed immediately out of the city by the Boulevard de Dunkerque. Quereyson began to protest, but when he felt the muzzle of a revolver against the nape of his neck, his voice cracked and he began to wheeze. Besse drove out beyond the Marseille airport at Marignane. A series of low stone hills appeared. The car began to climb through the barren empty hills.

"Turn to the right here," instructed The Torch.

Besse steered off onto a dirt road. The car was still climbing. In the front seat Quereyson had begun to tremble. They bounded along. There were empty meadows to both sides. The grass was sparse and the fields were full of outcroppings of gray rock. Henry could feel Quereyson's neck trembling against the muzzle of the gun.

"Stop here," he ordered.

They had reached an abandoned quarry. The hill had been cut away as if to form a small amphitheater. The semicircle of cliffs was about seventy-five feet high and the floor of the quarry was flat. It must have been abandoned before the war because two scraggly parasol pines had had time to grow up out of the stony floor.

Henry the Torch went around to the trunk and got out his satchel. Quereyson still sat in the car. Besse stood beside his door watching Henry and wondering what was going to happen.

"Over here," The Torch said to Quereyson. He waved his gun. He seemed to wave him out of the car. The bicycle mechanic followed on wooden legs.

The Torch led the way to the nearest of the two trees. He was carrying the satchel in one hand and a pair of handcuffs in the other. The gun was in his belt. He paid no attention to Quereyson. But the mechanic followed.

"What's the—" said Quereyson, but he choked on the half-completed sentence, and began to cough. When the coughing ended he said: "—the matter?"

"Stand with your back against that tree. Now put your hands behind you."

Henry snapped the handcuffs on. The mechanic's arms were handcuffed behind him around the tree.

There was a wind blowing. "It's cold up here," said Quereyson. He was trying to put on a show of bravery. "You're not going to leave me up here, are you? Because it's pretty cold out."

Henry had knelt to open his satchel. It contained a blowtorch, which he took out and set up. He had a striker with which he lit the flame. He moved slowly and deliberately. He was a man who took great care of his tools. He adjusted the flame. "We want to know who you've been talking to," he said while he worked. He spoke over his shoulder, as if making idle conversation. "And we want to know what you've been telling them."

Quereyson, terrified, tried to bluff it out. "Nobody. Nothing. I don't understand."

Henry came toward him with the blowtorch. His brow was furrowed with thought. He was a conscientious workman and he was thinking it out. There were many ways of proceeding with an interrogation of this kind. One could start with the subject's hands. The knees were good. People would talk to protect their knees. But today he was in a hurry. He felt the time pressure. He didn't want to spend too much time on this. Faletta was waiting for him. He had to get back to the city as fast as possible with whatever Quereyson's answers would be. He decided he would direct the flame toward Quereyson's crotch. He did so. He heated the buttons and the man began screaming.

"You better tell me what I want to know," he said.

Quereyson began speaking rapidly. He babbled. The cloth began to smoke. The torch came closer and closer. The heat mounted. "Take it away, I'll talk, I'll talk," he screamed.

"Talk first, and then I'll take it away," answered Henry the Torch.

Quereyson admitted he had been to see Bellarmine at the Bishopric. He himself was no squealer, he explained. He was only the broker. The squealer was his brother-in-law, Faletta's barman. His brother-in-law had put him up to it. His brother-in-law was responsible. His brother-in-law ought to be here lashed to this tree, not him. He kept screaming. That's all there was to it. No one had told Bellarmine anything yet. Not about the men from Marseille. Not about the men from Nice either, the Englishmen.

"Is that all?" demanded The Welder.

"That's all. That's all. I swear—"

"You cunt," said The Welder, and brought his flame to within four inches of Quereyson's fly. The cloth caught fire, and then the flesh behind it. The bicycle mechanic fainted and sagged against the tree, slipping slowly down the rough bark toward the ground. Henry shifted his target. He considered himself not a cruel man. He would never hurt anyone who didn't deserve it. He was a welder by trade and this was just a job that had to be done. He had done it as quickly and expeditiously as possible, causing relatively little pain. He played his blowtorch back and forth. He turned Quereyson's face black. He burned off his hair, and the tips of all ten fingers. "I wouldn't want you to be cold," he said, as he worked. He burned up the clothing almost completely. What was left hung in charred tatters on the charred corpse.

When he was finished he poked around until he found Quereyson's billfold. He took the money out, then focused the flame of the blowtorch and incinerated it. He reduced it to dust. There, the job was done.

Shutting down the torch, he removed the hot handcuffs carefully so as not to burn himself. He put the torch back into its satchel, then strode back to the car. Besse, he saw, leaned against the other tree. There was a pile of vomit beside his shoes. He too now approached the car. Henry tossed his handcuffs into the satchel, zipped it shut and lifted it into the trunk. The trunk lid slammed down.

"Let's go," he said.

Besse swallowed hard. "Where to?"

"Back to Marseille. We got another job to do. I'll direct you."

The barman's body was found by a police bicycle patrol on the Quai des Belges at three o'clock the following morning. He had been shot five times, but was still alive. He was rushed to Notre Dame Hospital. He was conscious and a detective tried to interrogate him, but he could not answer questions because his tongue had been cut out. He died later during surgery. The police made no immediate connection between the barman's murder and the Banque de Nice case. There was no reason why they should. Bellarmine was called, and stared down at the corpse—it lay naked on a slab. It had been cleaned up and he counted the bullet holes and did not know what to think. Beside him stood the chief of the Marseille Criminelle, who was satisfied that this was an ordinary mob-related *règlement de comptes*—a settling of accounts. In succeeding days Marseille detectives canvassed regular informants, but no one knew why the barman had been killed—he had crossed Faletta in some way. And, of course, no one knew who had done it.

Such crimes were considered virtually unsolvable, and Bellarmine knew this. Normally the police didn't even try very hard. Let them kill each other. Who cared?

At the Bishopric he kept waiting for Quereyson's phone call, but it did not come, and presently he sent a detective to the bicycle repair shop. It was closed, the detective reported. There was a sign on the door: "Annual Vacation." Quereyson became just another lead that had not panned out. Presumably he had had no real information. He had attempted to extort money from the police, had got cold feet, and had left town. Such things happened often enough. After a while Bellarmine got over his disappointment.

The body that had been Quereyson was not found for nine days. It could not be identified, and at first no one connected it to the tongueless barman. The corpses had turned up, after all, nine days and forty kilometers apart. The police at Aix-en-Provence put Quereyson's murder down as a *règlement de comptes* also—the blowtorch was not that uncommon a Milieu tool in cases of this kind. They made the usual notifications—the Bishopric was notified, but not Bellarmine's special brigade—after which the case went into the files.

Bellarmine heard about it by accident—such a grotesque execution made for hallway jokes—several days later, and drove immediately to Aix to look over the corpse's personal effects. These amounted to a twisted piece of metal that had once been a bicycle clip and some half-melted keys. He took the keys back to Marseille and went to the Rue du Panier. The iron curtain was still down in front of Quereyson's shop, held by three locks. Bellarmine took the least ruined of the keys on the ring, broke off the deformed tip, and tried to insert the shaft into each of the three locks. It fit the middle one, though without opening it of course, being only half a key. Although this would not have proved anything in a court of law, it was enough to convince Bellarmine that the charred corpse had been Quereyson. "What a death," he muttered. "You poor bastard."

By nightfall, having sent detectives out, he knew that Quereyson and the barman had been brothers-in-law.

Jesus, he thought, this is getting really bad.

They probably killed that missing derelict in Nice too, he thought, guessing closer than he knew. And there was blackmail coming, which would guarantee still more corpses. The newspapers, meanwhile, whenever they chose to mention the case at all, still called it

The Heist of the Century, meaning the laugh of the century. Every headline was designed only to titillate.

LA COMÉDIE HUMAINE CONTINUE.

We should tell the press what we're up against, he thought. Wipe that smirk off the face of the world.

But once again, and for the same reasons as last time, it was not in his interest to sound the alarm.

# CHAPTER
## 17

In Toulon one day a stranger got into the electrician's car and drove away. When this was reported to Bellarmine by telephone, he cried out: "Find out who he is. Forget the electrician. Tail the car." But more than a week passed before the same stranger came back. This time he made three quick, squealing turns in a row and shook the tail—an act highly suspicious in itself and vastly encouraging to detectives who had been sitting surveillance for so long on an empty car. When he brought it back that night, they tailed him to the Toulon train station on foot. He bought a ticket to Marseille, and a detective boarded at the other end of the same carriage. By the next day they had him identified.

Baldasaro, Eugène Henri. Profession: welder.

To read only this much, and to heft the thick dossier, made Bellarmine's heart quicken. Convicted of armed robbery of a postal truck 1945. Five years at Les Baumettes. Questioned in raid on Bar Cintra, Marseille, 6/12/50. Questioned in raid on Bar Prado 8/19/52. Questioned in double Milieu slaying 1/4/53. Questioned in raid on Bar Neuvième, 12/3/53. His photo showed a big burly man. A flat, almost Oriental face. Bellarmine kept turning pages. Detained twice last year on suspicion of assault. Both victims savagely beaten. But both were Milieu men, and the cases had not been pursued. By his record the thirty-eight-year-old Corsican was obviously not The Brain. But he was the type of criminal whom one would expect to be involved in a crime like this, and he was perhaps the man who had welded shut the bank vault doors.

Bellarmine called most of his Toulon men back to Marseille, shifting them off the electrician and on to Baldasaro. But The Welder had no phone and proved not easy to tail. He moved up and down the coast each day in borrowed cars, sometimes driving as far as Nice. The owners of these cars now acquired their own tails. Baldasaro, meanwhile, met unidentified persons on street corners in distant cities, and with them went into buildings that were sometimes still under construction. Everybody then came out again, shook hands, and Baldasaro drove away. Detectives could not figure out what he was doing, but when they moved up close, they learned he was looking to invest money in apartments, and had already purchased two, including a luxury apartment in Cannes that the real-estate trade there was still talking about. He saw a certain dentist three times a week and seemed to be having a new mouth made. He went into banks where he might hold safe-deposit boxes, but it was difficult to check this because of the stringent banking laws. In any case, he was spending a great deal of money, and where did he get it all? Bellarmine was elated. So were his detectives.

Only one detail did not fit. Sometimes The Welder was driven about by a young woman in a very small car, and the detectives took down her description and license number.

She was Marie Francine Cignoli, twenty, a student at the University of Marseille, and the daughter of a prominent Marseille attorney. Bellarmine put a round-the-clock tail on her. Since she also had no phone, it was impossible to know her plans in advance. One day she stopped at a street corner and picked up the suspect, who was carrying an attaché case. Both had been tailed to the meeting place, and as the girl's car started north out of the city, both tail cars went with it.

But by Montélimar the tail cars were nearly out of gas, and the four detectives had very little money. They decided to pool all their funds, and one car continued the tail. The other returned to Marseille.

About four hours later Bellarmine received a call from north of Lyon. The suspects had stopped for a meal, and the detectives were worried. Having just filled up with gas, they were down to their final five thousand francs. The suspects were probably en route to Paris, or even beyond. Should they continue the tail or not?

Bellarmine, holding the receiver, was left to speculate and decide. Baldasaro and Marie Francine carried no luggage. What was the purpose of this journey? Eventually the two detectives would be stranded out on the road. Was anything to be gained by letting this happen?

Again Bellarmine turned the pages of Baldasaro's dossier. Armed robbery. Vicious assaults. His nicknames were Henry the Welder and Henry the Torch. Possibly a contract hit man. What was he doing with a young girl, a university student, a lawyer's daughter? What was she doing with such a man? It was at the least a careless act. Was she going to go through life as careless as this?

The detectives were already more than three hundred miles from home, and there was no way to get them money.

"Come on back," he told them.

The couple returned to Marseille two days later. The tail was resumed, and Marie Francine spent the afternoon in the men's department at the Galeries Lafayette shopping. When she visited Baldasaro's flat that night she carried an armload of gifts.

Where was The Brain, and why was there still no sign of him?

Bellarmine was looking for a gang of about a dozen men, but by now more than twice that many were being tailed, plus a number of whores. Whores were a special problem, because their contacts were so numerous. One watched for frequent customers, for contacts that might be social rather than commercial. Only about fifteen phones were being tapped, but most were public phones in places that suspects frequented, particularly bars, and such phones were in constant use. The taps were recorded by stylus on wax cylinders that stood now in rows on shelves in Bellarmine's office, and a full day's conversation took a full day to listen to. In some cases conversations had to be transcribed, a long job, for the typewriters were sticky and detectives tended to have spatulate fingers.

Bellarmine's web had become gigantic, and was still being stretched. It got thinner and thinner. He needed more men, but was afraid to ask for them, for a bigger squad might be thought to demand a higher-ranking man to command it.

He lived in a room in a dingy hotel off the Vieux Port. He was in it only between midnight and dawn. He had trouble sleeping. The whistles from the ships kept him awake, or nightmares woke him. Exhausted, he would sometimes get dressed and go out. He would walk along the quay in the dark, chain-smoking. He would stop to watch cargo being lifted by cranes, or ships being moored. He still had no hard evidence, no witnesses to put in the box. He would stand in the light of a lamppost, as if for warmth, and smoke and watch the dockers work. Where was The Brain? Along the quay there were cafés that stayed open all night. He would go in and drink a Calvados and brood, then go back to bed and lie in the dark still unable to sleep. What had he forgotten? What might he do that he had not done? How soon before his detectives got too close and everybody started running in different directions—to Corsica, mostly. It would be virtually impossible to root them out of there. The island was too small, its villages too isolated, everybody knew everyone and no surveillance would work.

He requested more men. It brought Sapodin down from Paris.

"What's this, Bellarmine? What's this?"

"The men are exhausted, *patron*. They need time off."

"And what do you have to show for it? A single mud-caked flashlight. Do you realize how much this affair has cost already?" Sapodin, temporarily occupying a big office in the Bishopric, banged his hand down on the desk. "The minister's getting impatient, Bellarmine."

"If you like I'll arrest everybody. Do you order me to do that?"

It put Sapodin on the defensive. Bellarmine could indeed arrest all thirty or so subjects. By law he could hold them forty-eight hours incommunicado and without charges. But unless a *juge d'instruction* agreed to indict, he then had to release them.

"I leave the case entirely in your hands. As I told the minister, I'm too busy to take an active part myself, but I assured him you were a competent man. I reminded him of how you and I together nailed The Angel of Death. Don't let me down, Bellarmine."

"*Oui, patron.*"

But he did not get the extra men.

The night was half gone and very dark. There was no moon. Lambert on the dock never saw the approaching PT boat, and because the sea itself was making so much noise, he never heard it either, though he had been straining to. Suddenly its sharp edges emerged from the darkness, the prow gliding up on him like an inquisitive shark.

Jockeying the engines, Roy LeRoy held it away from the dock while his Arab crewman tossed Lambert the lines. They flew toward him thick as snakes, heavy as tree branches. One that he did not see in time struck him hard enough to numb his arm. He made them fast, pulling the boat in against the fenders.

The engines stopped, and LeRoy came up out of the cockpit. The boat was rasping against the fenders. Timing its rise, LeRoy leaped on to the dock beside Lambert.

"You're late."

"It's going to be hard loading with the sea like this."

"I was getting pretty worried."

"It's rough out there. I had to throttle way back."

Lambert had been waiting two hours. So had the men in the truck.

"Well," he said, "it's a nice dark night, anyway."

"Yeah. Where's the truck?"

Beside the dock loomed the dark hotel with all its shutters closed. Its terrace was a receptacle for dead leaves all swirling about. To the other side was the beach, a big one. It ended at the village of Cavalaire, whose few points of light winked in the distance. The truck was parked at the back of the beach in a grove of parasol pines that, in summer, served as a camping ground. The coastal road was farther back still. From time to time a pair of headlights could be seen moving along it. Lambert had been watching the headlights for two hours, but none had swerved off the road into the grove. So far.

The two truckers were asleep in the cab. To wake them up, Lambert rapped on the glass.

"Nerves of steel," commented LeRoy. "Where did you find such yo-yos?" He went around to the back, untied the canvas and shone a flashlight under it.

"Good," he said, and left the canvas flapping. "Let's move fast. This isn't cigarettes this time. The risk is about ten times as great."

"The profits too."

"Sure."

"You're going to be the richest PT boat driver in the Mediterranean," said Lambert, teasing him. "What are you going to do with it all?"

LeRoy stepped toward the cab. "Tell them to pull the truck closer to the dock."

The truck bounded across the bumpy ground. Then it started backward across the sand. Lambert and LeRoy hurried after it. It backed up to the dock.

The truckers began handing out the crates. They were heavy. Lambert and LeRoy stacked them up out on the dock. The PT boat was moving up and down, sometimes even with the dock, sometimes higher. Both men realized that getting the crates aboard was going to be a problem.

178

At last the truck was empty. The stacks of crates on the dock were as high as Lambert's head. The truckers stood on the sand beside the truck and demanded to be paid.

"Not until we get the crates aboard," said LeRoy to Lambert. "Tell them that."

Lambert spoke to them in French, then turned back to LeRoy. "They say they're leaving. You were two hours late. They've been here too long already. They say it's too dangerous."

"Tell them you won't pay them unless they help us load."

"They say the deal was dockside only."

"And was it?"

"Yeah, I guess so."

"Pay them" said LeRoy disgustedly.

"My fault."

Lambert got up into the cab with the driver. Only the dash lights were on. He began counting out dollars, according to his agreement with the seller, the dealer he had found in Luxembourg. He got rid of all his big bills from the Banque de Nice and was glad to see the last of them. Bills that big were always risky to pass.

As soon as he had jumped down to the ground, the engine came on. He and LeRoy listened to the empty truck crossing the sand and then the camping ground. They heard it bump on to the coastal road. Having got that far, being empty, it was at last safe, as innocent as any other vehicle on that road at that time, and they saw its lights come on and turn toward Marseille. They watched until the truck's lights vanished around a bend.

It was safe, but they weren't. The evidence against them was piled on the dock, and they began heaving it aboard the PT boat: crates of M-1 rifles, bazookas, grenades. Arms for Arab customers. Arms to feed the growing revolt against French rule in North Africa. Arms for terrorists. Arms to kill French troops, French settlers.

"Cigarettes are easier to load than hardware," said LeRoy. He stood on the lurching deck and Lambert swung the crates one by one into his arms. The Arab then carried each crate below.

"Will the boat take all this stuff and still float?" said Lambert. Both men were sweating, breathing hard.

"Of course. It used to carry torpedoes, for Chrissake."

As they resumed loading, a box fell to the deck and split open. Grenades rolled about like fruit. LeRoy and the Arab stooped to toss them back into the broken box.

179

It would be daylight in an hour. This was becoming more dangerous with each passing minute, but Lambert, watching them collect the loose grenades, said nothing.

"If I step on one I'll break my fuckin' ankle," apologized LeRoy.

"Take your time," said Lambert. "Plenty of time."

Finally the dock was clear. The last of the crates was stowed below, and the PT boat looked harmless enough—for a PT boat. The sky was beginning to brighten. A carload of *flics* could turn into the pine grove at any moment. Or a customs cutter could come by. The thing to do was for both men to take off, Lambert by land, LeRoy by sea, as fast as possible. Instead, they stood on the dock smoking cigarettes out of cupped palms.

"This is a good spot," said LeRoy conversationally.

"Yeah." If he's in no hurry to leave, then I'm not, thought Lambert.

"We can use it again next time." They stood there smoking, trying to outdo each other in bravado.

"I landed here August 15, 1944," said Lambert. "I was in the Seventh Army. General Patch. The invasion of southern France. When I looked behind me I could see a thousand ships."

"I was out of it by then. In business for myself."

"The big holiday here is not Bastille Day. It's August 15. They have fireworks and all. I come here some years."

Now that there was nothing to do but contemplate the increasing danger, Lambert was aware of the way his ears tingled, and, once again, the backs of his hands. It was a familiar sensation to him on this beach. It brought back memories that seemed to him now to have been pleasant. It was pleasant in itself. I can stand here just as long as he can, he thought. Danger was a delight. Danger was like whores—not only a forbidden pleasure, but one no man would admit he was hooked on.

"This beach is four kilometers long. Did you know that?"

"No, I didn't."

Lambert, watching the dawn come, felt very much alive. He had felt great wading ashore here nine and a half years ago, and he felt great now. "This is my beach," he told LeRoy. "That's why I picked it." He had a right to be here now in the last hour of the night, or any other time he chose. If he felt he owned this beach—owned part of France—it was because he had liberated the place. That the arms in the PT boat's hold would kill Frenchmen was not important. The arms would help liberate another people as he had helped liberate France. The French had no right to protest. Liberty came first.

180

It was getting very light very fast, and still LeRoy made no move to shove off. The stalemate made Lambert grin, and he held his ground.

"I'll be back in a couple of weeks with your money," said LeRoy. "I'm sorry I couldn't help out tonight, but I haven't had a chance to sell the gold yet."

"Sure," said Lambert.

"Line up another shipment of hardware. These customers will take all we can get."

Lambert nodded, still grinning. He wasn't going to budge until LeRoy did. Already it was light enough to distinguish items on the adjacent restaurant terrace, the dead swirling leaves. At his feet the PT boat was still heaving up and down. The Arab was standing down in the cockpit looking worried. He glanced toward the east. So did LeRoy, but not Lambert.

LeRoy flicked his butt into the water. At any moment the edge of the sun would pop up. "Well, I'm off," he said, and jumped down into the cockpit. The engines began to come on. As he cast off the lines, Lambert was delighted with himself, as if he had outlasted a rival in a match of some kind. He remained standing on the dock as LeRoy backed away. It seemed important to outlast him to the end, and he stayed there until the PT boat had come about, until all three engines had come on full and the stern had buried itself in the trough.

His Studebaker was parked in deep shadow against the wall of the restaurant. He got in and moved slowly off across the hard sand, and then the camping ground. When he came to the coastal road he looked back for the PT boat, but it was already out of sight. He turned toward Nice.

He was suddenly dead tired. He decided he would drive up to the farm to sleep. Tonight when he woke up, perhaps he would go see his wife.

Bellarmine went back to Nice for the day because the missing derelict—or, rather, someone who might be the derelict—had been found. He met the detective who had the case in the morgue at the Hospital St. Roch.

"A skier found him," said the detective. "He's coming down from the ski station at La Colmiane on skis and the road is icy, and he slides off the road and crashes down into this ravine. It's a deep ravine. He's lucky he wasn't killed. What stops his fall is the corpse.

It's wedged against a tree with its hand sticking out, and he shakes hands with it and stops himself."

They went into the room. The corpse was lying on a stone table with a shroud over it.

"The gendarmes from St. Martin-Vésubie dug him out," said the detective. "No bullet holes or knife marks. The skull was intact and there wasn't a mark on the body. No identification either. They called me."

"Where are his effects?"

"On the ledge there."

They were in a cardboard carton. Bellarmine stirred them around. "Rags," he said.

"Right. I remembered the *clochard* we were looking for before you went to Marseille. I phoned you right away."

"What about the autopsy?"

"That fits too. His lungs were full of water. Cause of death was, he drowned. I mean, La Colmiane is two thousand meters up in the mountains so he didn't drown up there. Somebody drove him up and pitched him into the ravine. Whoever killed him, I guess. Figured he wouldn't be found until spring."

"The water in his lungs—salt or fresh?"

"Fresh."

"Water from the Paillon," said Bellarmine.

"Maybe. The lab boys say they can't tell. They would resist doing all the tests anyway. Who wants to work that hard on a derelict?"

"Can the dog walker identify him?"

"We didn't ask him."

The detective drew the shroud down off the face. "You see why. The body was frozen stiff and in perfect shape, except for the face."

Bellarmine looked down at it. Small animals had been at work. The nose was gone and the lower lip. The result was not pretty to see.

The detective re-covered the corpse. "The fingerprint check came up negative. We don't have him. Maybe he was a foreigner. Italian or Spanish. Or Arab. A gypsy. We don't even know how long he was dead, because he was frozen."

"Show the effects to the dog walker. Who knows? And canvass the houses all along the road. I know it's a long time ago, but maybe someone saw something."

He went back to the *commissariat* on the Rue Gioffredo. To his surprise Sapodin was there.

They met in the hall and he signaled Bellarmine to follow him into his old office.

"Just got in from Paris," he said as he hung his overcoat in the armoire. His Homburg went in on the shelf, and he closed the armoire doors. "I've come on a matter of gravest importance. May I ask why you are here and not in Marseille?"

Bellarmine began to speak of the derelict found drowned at two thousand meters altitude, bringing to three the murders already connected to this case, the others being—

But he was interrupted many times. The phone kept ringing. Into it Sapodin muttered cryptic phrases. A secretary bustled in and out with papers that he scanned and sometimes initialed. Once he asked Bellarmine to leave the office while he took a particular call.

"What are you proposing, Bellarmine?"

"I'm sick of the newspapers making a joke out of this case. Also we need to do something to cause some movement. I propose that we make these murders public."

"What murders?"

So he hadn't heard a thing. "The derelict, the barman, the bicycle mechanic."

With his hands behind his bald head the *divisionnaire* sat back and stared at Bellarmine. He wore a monogrammed shirt, but his pudgy arms were too short for it, or the sleeves were too long. They were held up by elastic garters around his biceps.

"Are those men central to the Banque de Nice case, Bellarmine?"

"Not exactly, no."

"Is there any way an outsider can connect them to the case? The minister, the public prosecutor, important politicians, the press?"

"*Non, monsieur.*"

"Then I forbid you categorically even to mention them." For a moment his jaws worked, but no sound came out. "Something far more grave has happened. I am going to take you into my confidence, Bellarmine."

"*Oui, monsieur.*"

"You'll be reading about it in the papers soon enough, I expect. Can't stop something like this from leaking out."

Again Sapodin hesitated. To start him talking again, the mystified Bellarmine said: "*Oui, monsieur?*"

"The men who sacked the Banque de Nice appear to have made off with a great many important papers, Bellarmine. We're only beginning to know the scope of it." The bank, Sapodin explained, being under great pressure itself, had permitted certain prominent box owners access to what remained of their holdings. Several of them had reported documents missing.

So the secret at last was out.

"You don't seem too surprised, Bellarmine."

"I'm flabbergasted, *patron*," he lied.

The bank was pretending to make a search for the missing documents, Sapodin explained. In the meantime it had sworn the victimized box owners to secrecy.

"No question about it, Bellarmine. The stuff is gone. But we haven't heard from the blackmailer yet. Any idea why?"

"This is all a surprise to me, *patron*."

Sapodin said: "There's a lot of pressure coming down—all on me, unfortunately." He glanced up and flashed what was supposed to be a confident smile. "Not that I can't handle it, of course." He looked harried. There was a wet sheen on his bald pate. With a handkerchief he patted it dry.

Bellarmine said: "And the future of the Brigade—the Brigade Sapodin?"

"There are those who would like to take my investigation away from me, Bellarmine. For the time being I'm holding them off. But you don't have much more time. That's why I say forget these three cadavers." A wave of the hand dismissed them. "They'd just make new headlines, cause additional pressure. Who are they, anyway? No one cares about any of them. Those documents, though, that's another story. So find them for me, Bellarmine. Find me the documents and The Brain and you'll have done your job. And quickly, eh? I don't know how much longer I can protect you down there. Going back to Marseille tonight, are you?"

Bellarmine, who had hoped for at least one day off, was not going to get it. "*Oui, monsieur.*"

Sapodin came around the desk to shake hands. "Keep me informed," he said.

He went up to his flat and smoked and stared at the walls. There was a gas-burning space heater that vented into what had once been a fireplace. It was seldom used. Riviera winters are relatively mild and gas was very expensive. Better to be a bit cold. Now he turned it on, hoping it would take a month's chill, a month's vacancy out of the walls. He turned it up as far as it would go. In an empty room and empty world at least for a few minutes he would be warm. He had done all he could in Marseille, and the investigation was stagnant again, and he knew he did not want to go back there. There were trains to Marseille every ninety minutes or so. He would have to catch one of them eventually, a prospect he dreaded.

For a while he thought about Sapodin. He had known him for years and knew nothing about him. He had a wife Bellarmine had never seen. He owned an apartment on the Rue Gounod that Bellarmine had never been in. He wore Homburg hats and carnations in his buttonholes and elastic garters to hold up his sleeves. It wasn't much to know about someone. Did he know more about anyone else? Or anyone else about him? To touch another human soul was impossible. The closest he ever came was when he clapped handcuffs on someone. Love was an illusion, the only true emotion was despair.

He went downstairs and out onto the street. When he came to Jacqueline Lambert's perfume shop he stared in at her through the window. After hesitating a moment he went inside.

She came forward with a smile, but it was the same one as last time. She doesn't remember me, he thought. His first need became to justify his presence. "I've been in here before," he said. "I live in the neighborhood."

"Of course, monsieur, I recognized you at once." But her smile did not change. "I haven't seen you in a while, though."

"It was right after your vacation."

"As long ago as that?"

"I've been out of town."

There was a pause. This is going to be hard, he told himself. It was not clear to him what he wanted from this young woman, but it was more than small talk, more than one of her sales pitches for perfume. He intended to invite her for an apéritif at the café on the corner—she would be closing soon—but couldn't just come out with it or she would say no. There had to be preliminaries, though he wasn't good at them. A different illusion had taken hold of him. It was as though his contact with the human race had lapsed. If he could share a drink with her in a bar he could renew it. His outlook would become less pessimistic. He would find it easier to get on that train for Marseille. Easier to breathe.

So he told her he wished to buy perfume for someone, but didn't know which kind.

"Then you must describe her for me, what she is like, her age, her skin. Is she light or dark."

These details, it seemed, determined which perfume a woman

ought to wear, but Bellarmine had no one in mind. There was not a woman in France he could give perfume to, he thought, and felt more dispirited than ever. So he began to describe Odette. It made him feel, for a moment, like a husband attached to the vision of a dead wife.

No customers came into the shop, fortunately; this gave him plenty of time. He had removed his fedora, laid it down on a glass countertop. She plucked demonstration bottles down off shelves. She sprayed perfume on her forearms, the backs of her hands, and held them up to his nose. He snuffed the varying scents of her; saw the blond hairs on her arms magnified a hundred times. As an experience it was perhaps only commercial to her. It was entirely sensual to him, or perhaps only romantic. Toward the end, risking all, he took her hand and pressed it almost to his lips, saying as matter-of-factly as possible: "Let me smell that one again, if you please."

She did not yank her hand away, which proved no more, probably, than her eagerness to make the sale. There—it was done—he held her hand, the one wearing the ring, under his nose. He was within her orbit. He had invaded her personal space, and she did not protest.

She glanced at the clock above the door.

"I'm sorry," he said. "You want to close."

She showed him the same practiced smile. "Oh, no. Not at all."

"I'll take that one, then." It was time to terminate one transaction and attempt another. Yet for a moment longer he stalled. "What did you say it was called?"

She gave him the name. "Shall I gift wrap it for you?"

"That won't be necessary. But—" He hesitated. "As long as you're closing, perhaps I can offer you an apéritif? The café on the corner is nice at this hour."

"I'm sorry, I have a rendezvous." She said this hastily, like a woman who had received many such propositions over the years. By now her response was both quick and automatic. No.

"Surely you can spare five minutes."

The sale she had worked so hard for stood on the glass between them and both eyed it. Bellarmine, who had his billfold out, had not yet handed across any money. A hostage could be as small, as insignificant as that tiny box. Her glance went from the box to his face.

"Don't even think it," he said. "I'm buying the perfume even if you won't have an apéritif with me. But—will you?"

It made her laugh. She took his money and counted out change.

186

"You haven't said no definitely. Yet. Do I have a chance?"

She had begun wrapping the package. Her expression had turned into a smirk, as if she were pleased with herself, or with him, and her eyes rose.

"It's not an entanglement," he promised. "I'm leaving town again later tonight."

When she still did not answer he said: "It's just that—there's been a death." This was true. The derelict could perhaps serve for something. "I'm a bit desperate for someone to talk to." Also true.

She handed him the package. "It will take me a moment to lock up the shop," she said.

He took her not to the corner café but to the Ruhl bar. It was close enough, and the most chic place he could think of, though of course it would be very expensive. They sat down and the barman came over to the table. He expected her to order Scotch whiskey—he would not have resented it—but when she asked for a vermouth-cassis he was very pleased.

"And for me a Calvados."

"You don't speak with an accent from here," she told him when they were alone again.

"Neither do you."

French, being a formal language, imposed formal conventions. It did not permit immediate intimacy. It did not permit the asking of direct questions. They could not simply interview each other. One waited for whatever the other person wished to volunteer.

She was born in Annecy in Savoie, she told him. He said he knew the lake there, and the high Alps just beyond. Her father was a doctor who moved his practice to Nice in 1940 to get his family out of the war zone. He was mobilized just before France surrendered. He bought his wife the perfume shop to tide her over, then went away, and they never saw him again. The Boches moved him from one camp to another until he died. The perfume business was not great during the war and there was not much food either, but she and her mother had survived. The shop was still in her mother's name. Her mother was ill and lived in Vence because the altitude was good for her lungs.

"And you, monsieur?" she said.

He was from Paris, he told her, 17th Arrondissement.

"I don't know Paris very well."

"You sound wistful."

"Sure. Nice is very beautiful, but not the whole world."

He was in the university when mobilized, he said. He sat in a fort on the Maginot Line for eight months during the *drôle de guerre*, the so-called phony war, and then the Germans just rolled over them. In a week the entire French Army was destroyed. A few units, what was left of his own among them, escaped to England from Dunkerque. It was in England, and even for a time in the United States, that he was trained as a tank commander.

"The United States? You've been there? Have you been to New York?"

"*Oui, mademoiselle.*"

"I know some Americans," she said, her voice sounding almost wistful. It made him wonder how many she had known, and how well. "But I've never been there."

On August 25, 1944, he had led a column of tanks into Paris, and the tears had streamed down his face, because he believed no man had ever been this happy before, and he knew he would never be this happy again.

"I drove my tank down streets I had played in as a boy."

There must have been more emotion in his voice than he had imagined, for she seemed much moved.

"I never again found anything to believe in as much as that," he told her.

Both sipped their drinks. Their eyes met over their glasses, and both sent out tentative smiles.

"You really did need to talk, didn't you?"

"Yes."

"The person who died—was he very close to you?"

"No." He saw again the derelict with the half-eaten face. "He was just an old man I wanted to talk to—because of something I'm working on. Nobody cared about him when he was alive and nobody cares about him dead. One can't even know how he died. There is no one to ask."

"A life like that is quite sad."

"Yes, it is."

"And tonight you go out of town again."

"To Marseille." He felt much better about it. He thought he could face Marseille now.

"How long will you be working there?"

"Indefinitely."

He invited her to have dinner with him, and she hesitated a moment, then declined. He decided to accept this decision. It was best not to press too much on such short acquaintance. He glanced at his watch. In that case, he said, he probably ought to catch the next train, and there was one soon. Could he first escort her home to wherever she lived?

She declined this offer too. "But I'll walk with you to the station if you like."

They strolled together down the Rue Alphonse Karr chatting amicably. He did not take her arm, nor she his. There were shop windows along the street, but she did not stop to peer into them. She seemed more interested in him and their conversation than in whatever goods might be on display, and he felt both pleased and flattered.

He still had not asked her name, nor offered his own, and she had not asked for it. The French language permitted this to happen, or perhaps compelled it. She called him *"monsieur."* He called her *"mademoiselle."* In English the equivalent would have sounded stilted. In French it did not, and was sufficient. They had just met. These things took time. For either of them even to request the other's name was to shift their relationship on to a plane the other was perhaps not ready for.

They were together an hour and a half. He never told her he was a policeman and this was deliberate—most people feared or hated policemen, and were hostile to them on sight, and when she asked about his work, he said he was a government functionary. Technically this was accurate. Policemen were so described in the laws under which they operated. In English he might have called himself a civil servant.

She did not tell him she was married, and he did not ask. When he had called her *"mademoiselle"* several times and she did not correct him, he assumed almost with joy that she was not. He might ask her about that wedding band next time—he was determined there would be a next time—but not tonight.

At the crowded station she shook hands with him. A slim hand but a firm grip. "Thank you," she said. "I guess I needed to talk too."

She waited while he walked past the control on to the quay. When he looked back, she waved.

Bellarmine boarded his train and went through to the dining car. By the time the train reached Cannes he was being served grilled sole with new potatoes and a crisp green salad and a half bottle of rosé de Provence. He peered out the window and sipped his wine. Sometimes he could see a town or a beach going by. Sometimes he saw only his own reflection. He felt full of confidence about the case. He was no longer concealing guilty knowledge about the missing documents, and this was a relief. He had been ordered not to mention the murders. The pressure was perhaps greater than ever, but it was all coming down on Sapodin, not on himself. The case would break soon. All it demanded of him was a little more patience.

Jacqueline dined alone also. She had entered one of the restaurants favored by commercial travelers across from the station. It was not her neighborhood, and she was confident she would meet no one who knew her. She ordered only a *salade niçoise* and half a carafe of house red, but afterward, feeling still hungry, she asked for some goat cheese with which she ate half the basket of bread. For a time she was sorry she had not accepted Bellarmine's dinner invitation. But no, it was better this way; she still had a husband, after all.

She had not seen Lambert in weeks, nor heard from him, and before that he had been around several times with Roy LeRoy, who was to her a frightening figure. She did not believe Lambert was writing another play, and she wondered about the first one.

She had almost wished, an hour ago, that he would happen by and see her in the company of another man. It might have shaken him. But this did not occur, and the hour and a half had passed innocently enough.

She wondered what it would be like being married to Bellarmine. She certainly had no marriage now. Bellarmine had seemed to her one of the few truthful men she had ever met. Whatever he was feeling showed on his face, including his loneliness. She believed him one who would never lie to her.

Neither of them had been very honest with the other, but Bellarmine in the dining car entertained similar thoughts. She had seemed to him a woman incapable of deception. He imagined her forthright, dependable, compassionate. She would be worthy of whatever trust a man placed in her.

He had somehow perceived her great loyalty. He had not perceived her unhappiness at all.

# CHAPTER
## 18

At the start of the sixth week a man walked into the Crédit Lyonnais on the Canebière and pushed a gold ingot across the counter under the grille.

"Gimme cash."

The teller turned the ingot over and saw the stamp of the Banque de France and the serial number. It made him immediately nervous. The police circular was scotch-taped to the counter in front of him, but his glasses seemed to have fogged over, making it impossible to read. He fiddled with them, and tried to match the numbers. They matched.

Almost instantly the teller began to tremble. He cast a frantic glance toward the rear of the bank, but the detective seated there was engrossed in *L'Equipe*, the sporting newspaper.

The customer was drumming impatient fingers on the countertop; having caught the eye of an assistant manager, the teller began rapidly blinking. He was trying to send messages with his eyelashes. To his relief he saw the assistant manager speak sharply to the detective, who then jumped up and groped wildly for his gun.

The teller saw no more for he dropped to the floor behind his cage.

The customer was The Walrus, as all would soon know, and he might have escaped if he had simply and promptly sprinted out of the bank. Instead one of his great ham fists shot through the grille and attempted to grab back his ingot. He was not leaving without it, a delay that would have fatal consequences.

Waving his revolver, carefully oiled each night for just this occasion, the detective leaped forward screaming: "*Halte*, in the name of the law."

The Walrus raced for the front door. Behind him the detective pulled the trigger three times.

All three shots went awry. Two went into the ceiling. A middle-aged woman was just entering the bank. The third bullet caught her in the right eye, and she went down. People were screaming. There was a general rush for the door. The Walrus, who had advanced quite

191

far into the bank, in effect had to wait in line to get out. The detective's fourth and fifth shots went wild also, but The Walrus did not know this. Imagining that shots were coming from all over the bank, that he had been caught in an ambush, he raised his hands and slowly turned around.

And so the investigation added still another new name, Jean-Luc Macchiarola, thirty-five, formerly a professional wrestler. No previous criminal record.

Devereux and Lussac began to interrogate him, while Bellarmine was faced with a decision on what move to make next. A woman had been killed. The sidewalk in front of the bank swarmed with reporters. Obviously the police were on the trail of the sewer gang at last. France being a free country, there was no way news like this could be kept out of the next morning's newspapers, or off the radio that night, meaning that, although he still had nothing hard on any of the other suspects, he had best arrest them all anyway, all thirty or more, lest they begin to vanish. It had to be done as fast and as close to simultaneously as possible.

It meant calling in all his detectives and setting up arrest teams, while requesting platoons of white batons and gendarmes as backup. It was a big organizational job and obviously could not be completed in time for detectives to go in before 9 P.M. that night; therefore they could not by law go in until dawn tomorrow. Anything else constituted a violation of domicile. But because of the delay some of the flats, when the doors were broken down, would be empty.

He remembered to perform one other important job—to notify Sapodin in Paris.

Detectives had come back from searching The Walrus' flat. They had broken through his various locks, and they carried with them into the Bishopric a satchel heavy with gold bars and uncut stones, which seemed to prove that The Walrus had actually been in the vault. He was more than just a courier or fence; he was part of the first team. To Bellarmine this was a great relief.

The Walrus' interrogation had already started when Bellarmine went up to see him. He was in a room on the top floor under the rafters, a whitewashed box almost devoid of furniture, whose principal virtue was that a prisoner's screams did not carry from there as far as the street.

Present were Commissaires Devereux and Lussac, plus a uniformed officer with a submachine gun who leaned against the door, blocking it.

A bicycle wheel lay on its side on the floor. There was no tire on it. The Walrus knelt on the sharp rim with his arms outstretched in a cross. In each hand he gripped a *Bottin*—the two-inch-thick, hard-covered Paris directory. He was dripping with sweat. His clothes were soaked with it. There were lumps like tubers on his forehead, his cheekbones, his head.

"Anything?" Bellarmine asked Lussac.

"Not yet."

"Answer me, you piece of shit," shouted Devereux, who carried a walking stick.

Nothing happened, except that the prisoner's arms began to flag. "Raise them, I said," shouted Devereux, giving him sword thrusts in the kidneys with the stick.

Lussac seemed to be enjoying himself. The toe of his sharp-pointed shoe hovered near the bicycle rim. Like the tongue of a snake darting out, it stepped on the wheel, making it wobble. Each wobble, Bellarmine knew, sent the pain shooting from the prisoner's kneecaps up into the roots of his hair.

The Walrus' eyes, Bellarmine saw, were fixed not on Devereux but on Lussac's pointed shoe. Thrusts from the cane only made him grunt; kicks at the wheel brought forth moans of agony.

Devereux too was soaked and dripping. "I'm tired of talking to you nicely," he said. He gave the wheel a violent kick, and again The Walrus moaned.

"Let me know if you get anything," Bellarmine said. Swallowing his revulsion, he hurried back downstairs.

# CHAPTER 19

The black Traction Avants full of detectives, the vans of uniformed police armed with machine guns, rolled out of the dimly lit courtyard and into the dark empty streets. Bellarmine in the lead car rode beside the chauffeur, with three burly detectives in the back seat. Dawn had not yet broken. They rolled down empty boulevards. The streetlights illuminated scraps of paper that blew along the sidewalks in the night breeze.

As if under attack, the convoy began to break apart. One by one the cars, sometimes followed by vans, sought out side streets. They disappeared from view. Bellarmine's car, unaccompanied, turned into the students' quarter of the city.

Marie Francine Cignoli lived on the top floor of a building on the Rue de Turenne, where she had a room, not an apartment. A former maid's room no doubt, with no running water and no heat. There would be a small electric heater standing on the floor to warm it from time to time, and a single toilet at the end of the hall to serve every room on the floor. Poor stupid kid, Bellarmine thought. Though he had never met her, or even seen her, he knew all about her. He felt as if he were her father, for he was about to discipline her severely. She came from a good home. Why did she have to move out of it? Why did she have to move here? What perverted need for excitement made her get mixed up with a mobster like The Welder?

"We go up the service stairs," Bellarmine muttered. "All of you come with me." Five policemen to arrest a single twenty-year-old girl. She would be more than intimidated—she would be terrorized. Which was the way he wanted it.

The room was on the sixth floor. At the time the building was erected, before 1900, servants were happy enough to have just a roof. They did not demand elevators or running water. Quarters under the eaves seemed to them palatial. Bellarmine and his men climbed the six flights of steps. They walked down the dark hall, shoes ringing on bare boards. They shone flashlights on the doors.

"Here it is, *patron*."

"All of you draw your guns," Bellarmine said. He wanted her to see lots of guns. "Keep your fingers outside the trigger guard."

He banged the door with the side of his fist.

"Open in the name of the law."

He could hear movement up and down the hall. In a moment heads would stick out. Voices would grumble about being awakened. Of course their mood would change once they realized what was happening. The transformation from disgruntled sleeper to goggle-eyed spectator would be instantaneous.

The very young sleep deeply, and Bellarmine banged again. Presently he heard her moving inside.

"What is it? Coming." She had a clear, musical voice.

194

The door opened a crack. He saw only a slice of her face, still slack from sleep, and he shouldered into the door, almost knocking her down. She fell back as the door flew open.

She was wearing a transparent nightgown. The detectives ogled her.

"Put something on," Bellarmine ordered. He turned to one of the detectives: "You, close the door."

The girl glanced stupefied from one grim-faced policeman to another.

Modesty, evidently a stronger emotion than fear, then overcame her, and she grabbed the counterpane off the narrow bed. It enveloped her like a shawl.

She began to sputter. "But—but—what—"

Bellarmine drew the *commission rogatoire* out of his raincoat pocket. He held it out to her. "I have a warrant to search this place. You are ordered to assist in the search, and you are forbidden to hide anything that might obstruct or delay the administration of justice." The room reeked of the odor of sleep. The girl, he saw, was trying and failing to comprehend. She had lain wrapped in the heat of her bed, in the enveloping cocoon of dreams, and had awakened to reality before she was ready for it. Reality was incomprehensible words, whose message was nonetheless clear. Warrant. Police. She was in terrible trouble.

Bellarmine saw this on her face. She was small, pretty, and very young, and his heart went out to her. "Do you have here any objects, arms, stolen goods relating to the break-in of the Banque de Nice et de la Côte d'Azur, or to one Eugène Henri Baldasaro, also known as Henry the Torch, wanted in connection with that crime?"

The girl shook her head. Even as he watched, her face screwed up like a person squinting into the sun. She understood now what they were there for, and she began silently weeping.

With a jerk of his head, Bellarmine started his detectives on their search of the room. There was not much to search: a chest of drawers, a small armoire, three suitcases piled one on top of the other. They went through her clothes, through her cosmetics, through her cheap jewelry, her laundry. They flipped through the pages of her books.

A detective handed one to Bellarmine. "Her diary, *patron.*"

The girl still sat on the bed, tears rolling down her cheeks, while Bellarmine read her diary. He paged back through it until he came to her account of the trip north with The Torch—an account three impassioned pages long.

They had spent the night in a hotel at Orléans. It was their first complete sexual experience together, and possibly the girl's first with anyone—it was difficult to tell from the wording. The next morning they had driven on, skirting Paris, crossing the Belgian frontier at Armentières. The man had become tense as they neared the border, but once safely across he began to giggle almost hysterically. Marie Francine had demanded an explanation, but he had refused to give one, still giggling. They had driven on to Brussels, where Marie Francine pulled to a stop in front of the Banque de Bruxelles. There The Torch had gone inside carrying his attaché case. He came out half an hour later, and the attaché case seemed much lighter. The couple had spent the rest of the day like tourists, seeing the sights of Brussels, and then had checked into another hotel, where apparently they spent half the night making love. This time Marie Francine's account was poetic rather than graphic. She had been transported into another world. She had never known such bliss. It was during the lovemaking that The Torch explained his giggling after crossing the border—his attaché case had held about sixty pounds of gold ingots out of the Banque de Nice. Yes, he had been part of the sewer gang.

Marie Francine's only reaction to this news, judging from the diary, seemed to be pride that her beloved would trust her with such precious information. In her girlish hand she promised never under any circumstances to divulge what he had told her.

But she just had. And for this one line, written in her own hand, she would go to jail.

"Nothing," said one of the detectives. He had turned away from the last suitcase.

Bellarmine put the diary in his pocket. "You're under arrest, mademoiselle. Put your clothes on. We're taking you in."

The girl wiped her eyes. "Can I telephone my father?" Her voice was low, almost a whisper. "There's a phone in the bar on the corner—"

"No, you can't."

"Please let me telephone Papa. Papa's a lawyer and—"

"No calls. We'll wait for you outside. Pack a small bag. You won't be coming back."

At the Bishopric he left her in his office together with the three arresting detectives, to whom he had given instructions. They were to continue to question her, but gently. She was not to be hurt.

When he left the office he stood in the hall a moment. Through the door he could hear the girl sobbing. He went downstairs. None of the other cars was back yet, but he had begun to feel confident about this morning's operation. The reporters, later, would be keeping score. The more names on his scorecard and theirs, the better.

In the courtyard he got into the same black car beside the driver.

"Let's go arrest that jeweler, shall we?"

The sky was brighter now, beginning to be blue. The cafés on the boulevard were opening. As they drove along he could see in through the glass. Waiters in shirt sleeves were mopping the floors, readying the chairs and tables.

The jeweler, Vargelin, lived in a luxury building on the Boulevard Massenet. Out front waited two detectives. A third detective was already on post outside the jeweler's front door, they said. There were uniformed men in the lobby, on the roof, and in the courtyard guarding the servants' entrance.

"Let's go in," said Bellarmine. Upstairs he banged on the jeweler's door.

"Open in the name of the law."

Waiting, he felt an eagerness that was rarely there when arresting hardened mobsters, and this was one of the two reasons he had chosen to arrest the jeweler himself. Mobsters were never surprised to be arrested. When he displayed his police card, their expressions never changed. When he snapped the cuffs on, they showed no emotion. It was not very satisfying.

Whereas men like this jeweler usually blubbered, begged, tore their hair—overwhelmed too late by the shame, remorse and guilt they should have felt at the beginning. And this was a pleasure to watch. Each arrest was the end of a morality play after all, and in lieu of applause or as a kind of applause, a detective was willing to accept and in fact needed the tears and grief of his prisoner. The detective was a solitary figure. His work was frustrating. He needed such reactions as proof that he had struck a blow for society.

The jeweler who opened the door wore a bathrobe tied at the waist, and one slipper, and he carried the other in his hand. As the four detectives pushed him back into the apartment, he burst into tears. His wife, frightened by the commotion, came out of the bedroom, followed shortly afterward by a teen-age boy, and they were witness to what was probably the ultimate disgrace that could befall a husband and father. It came not after conviction and sentence, but right now, as the detectives began ransacking the apartment, violating even cushions on the sofa. The woman and the boy looked to their protector to protect them from such outrage, and saw that he could do nothing. He had failed them.

"Get dressed. Pack a small suitcase. You won't be coming back."

Bellarmine had no sympathy for him, and no qualms about disgracing him in front of his family. To him, men like the jeweler were almost the worst criminals of all. Thieves, usually of low intelligence, at least knew they were thieves; there was a certain honesty about them. Whereas fences pretended to live as honest men, compounding larceny with hypocrisy.

The jeweler attempted to control himself. His blubbering stopped, and he wiped his eyes with his sleeve. "May I know the charge?"

A detective had come out of the bedroom carrying a cigar box. Bellarmine walked over and peered down into the box, which was half full of unset jewels.

"There's your charge."

"I'm a jeweler. I have a right to have jewels."

"Say bye-bye. Make it quick."

# CHAPTER 20

Sapodin arrived from Paris together with two other high Sûreté commanders, and went into conference with senior Bishopric officials. It was two hours before Bellarmine even knew he was there.

By then the mood on the second floor was one of gloom. The success of the day's operation, and of the investigation itself, was in doubt.

Sapodin demanded a briefing, and Bellarmine, pacing and smoking, gave him good news first. Solid evidence against The Walrus. But the prisoner was resisting interrogation, twenty straight hours so far.

A solid case also against Baldasaro. They had Marie Francine's diary, and would have additional evidence when the bank in Brussels handed over the gold ingots stashed there. However, at dawn this morning detectives had broken into Baldasaro's flat finding it empty. He must have slipped out during the night. There were still detectives on post at the building. Perhaps he would come home later in the day.

"Not a chance," said Sapodin. "Have you been listening to the radio bulletins?"

Bellarmine had not. He had been rushing from room to room supervising, and sometimes taking part in, the various interrogations.

"And the afternoon papers will plaster the story all over page one," said Sapodin. "What do you expect? You've arrested thirty-eight people, for God's sake. And implicated only two. Two members of the sewer gang out of maybe a dozen."

"It's not quite that bad," said Bellarmine. He puffed on his cigarette.

The two pimps, Jean Jacques Montenegro and Gaston Baptiste Angelucci, were both in custody. Both had been at the villa in Aspremont, and in addition, St. Jean right after the crime had given his girl friend, a prostitute, a mink coat.

"That sounds to me like less than solid proof," said Sapodin.

Bellarmine lit another Chesterfield. "At the moment we can hold them only for pimping."

"Pimping?"

"It's an arrest. It will stand up."

Montenegro, he explained, when questioned by detectives, had presented a pocketful of pay vouchers proving he was gainfully employed. Angelucci, unable to produce pay vouchers, claimed that he lived off winnings from the national lottery. "So we've got them," Bellarmine said. "The pay vouchers are sure to prove fraudulent, and as for winning the lottery, Angelucci won't be able to prove he ever did."

"The public is expecting better news than the arrests of two pimps. What else?"

Montenegro's girl friend, the prostitute Denise Lasablière, was in custody. Bills bearing serial numbers from the Banque de Nice were found in her room. So they had her solid for criminal receiving.

"How much money are you talking about?"

"About a hundred thousand francs."

"Have you thought how that will sound in the press? They stole more than a billion, and you've recovered one hundred thousand."

"We don't know how much is in the bank in Belgium," said Bellarmine, who had known in advance what Sapodin's reaction would be.

Despite himself he had grown more defensive—and angrier with his detectives—hour by hour.

He was trying to conceal these and other emotions from his superior. "What's this about a dentist?"

Bellarmine had ordered the arrests of all frequent contacts of his suspects. This included the dentist that The Welder, Baldasaro, had been visiting three times a week. The dentist's office had been searched, and a single gold ingot found. "We don't know yet whether the dentist is a regular fence, or what. We may find more ingots there."

"The public wants us to catch the men who looted the bank," said Sapodin, "not their dentist."

The scorecard was not that bad, Bellarmine kept telling himself. Sapodin was exaggerating. Or else he had made such exorbitant claims before leaving Paris that he feared now looking a fool. He had scheduled a press conference for later that day. If the news he brought with him was good, then he was a hero. If not, it was Bellarmine who would suffer.

"We have the jeweler," Bellarmine said. "I'm sure he was the one in the vault."

"You don't have *the* jeweler, Bellarmine. You have *a* jeweler. He came into Faletta's bar and shook hands all around. That's all you have."

"He's guilty all right," snorted Bellarmine. "I'm the one who arrested him. I'm the one who saw the guilt in his face, heard it in his voice."

"The court is not going to be impressed by what you saw in his face or heard in his voice. This is France, not a police state."

"There was a box of unset stones hidden in his apartment."

Sapodin thought this over. "Has he admitted anything yet?"

"Not yet," said Bellarmine, "but we could lean on him a little."

Immediately he regretted his words. He was virtually asking for permission to torture a man. Devereux would enjoy it, and if the jeweler cracked, Bellarmine would enjoy it too. That made him no better than Devereux.

"I'd advise against it," said Sapodin thoughtfully. "It's okay anytime to knock Milieu *mecs* around. And it's okay to knock around someone like this jeweler if he's guilty. But if he's innocent, you're buying yourself trouble."

"We have jewelry experts coming in from Nice. They may be able to identify the jewels."

"If they do, then anything goes as far as the jeweler is concerned. Mind you, I'm not condoning brutality of any kind."

200

Of course not, thought Bellarmine. Neither will I as I walk out of the room and leave him to Devereux.

Sapodin shook his head gloomily. "Thirty-eight prisoners, and this is all you've been able to turn up. Not a sign of The Brain either. What about those documents?"

"We've ransacked every place we've hit."

"And that young girl you arrested. People like that are trouble, Bellarmine."

"The girl has confessed, *patron*."

"Wait till you have to deal with her father," said Sapodin. "He's very well connected, Bellarmine. In your place I would not have been so quick to arrest that girl. And the grocer from Arles?"

The grocer, brought into Marseille in irons, had proved so indignant that he had shaken the faith of the men interrogating him, and they had begun again at the beginning. Did he not own a gray Peugeot with the license plates—

"My Peugeot is black," snapped the grocer, and he had pulled out his registration to prove it.

"Somebody must have made up fraudulent plates using his number," explained Bellarmine.

"You should have checked that out at the beginning."

True. He should have. He kept his face blank.

"Five detectives for six weeks—my God."

"I'm about to let him go," said Bellarmine.

"Are you crazy? You hold him the full forty-eight hours, and when you let him go tomorrow you cite an insufficiency of proof."

Sapodin looked thoughtful: "At least twelve men hit that bank. The only one you can actually put in the vault is Baldasaro, and he got away from you. Where's the rest of the loot, Bellarmine? Where's The Brain? Where are the documents? You haven't turned up a trace of those documents."

The legal forty-eight-hour *garde à vue* had about forty hours to run. Detectives would relay each other, hammering at prisoners, keeping them awake, wearing them down. Maybe one or more would crack. Of course, Milieu types rarely cracked, rarely talked.

"I go before the press in three hours, Bellarmine. I hope you'll have more for me by then. I saw the minister this morning. I told him I had perfect confidence in you. He wasn't so sure. For the time being I convinced him."

That afternoon two wholesale jewelers from Nice, partners, sat down at a table in Bellarmine's office. One withdrew magnified photos of jewels from a briefcase. The second reached into the cigar box—Vargelin's cigar box—that lay open on the table. Precious stones sifted like sand through his fingers.

Bellarmine sucked at his Chesterfield. He picked grains of tobacco off his tongue.

"Here's one," the second jeweler said. "Maybe." He had a loupe clenched in the socket of his left eye, and he brought the jewel to within an inch of the lens. After a moment he started to laugh. "This is my stone," he said. "Stolen out of my lockbox in Nice."

"Here's a photo of it," said the other man. It was a big photo, about twenty centimeters by twenty-five.

Bellarmine brought Vargelin up to the room under the eaves in which Devereux and Lussac already waited. The projectors were set up and burning. They focused a brilliant spotlight onto the rear wall, turning the entire wall as bright as an operating room. The bicycle wheel lay on its side on the floor close to Lussac's glossy shoes.

Freddie the Jeweler, who recognized a torture chamber when he saw it, glanced nervously from face to face.

"Is there anything you want to tell me before I leave you here with these two gentlemen?" inquired Bellarmine. Devereux's shirt sleeves were rolled up, displaying hairy forearms. He looked like any honest workman about to take up honest tools. Lussac's face bore a vacant grin, an expression Bellarmine had never seen on him before, an anticipatory glow. With the toe of one shoe, he started the wheel spinning. He likes it, Bellarmine thought.

The crooked jeweler said: "I have"—he swallowed hard—"nothing to tell you."

"Well then—" Bellarmine nodded. "See you later." And he hurried down the hall, not waiting to hear the noises that in a moment would be coming through the walls.

Later Devereux came into Bellarmine's office. He was still in shirt sleeves. There were wet circles under his arms, and drops of sweat on his forehead. He raised and lowered his elbows like a man flying. "Hot work," he said. With a handkerchief he mopped his brow. "Well, our jeweler has confessed to being in the vault himself."

"Did he sign the *procès-verbal?*"

"Of course."

Bellarmine nodded. "Good." He offered Devereux a Chesterfield and lit up himself. They sat opposite each other smoking.

"He apologized to me for it. Rather profusely, I might add. Said he was sorry. By then I bet he was."

"I was pretty sure he was the one," said Bellarmine. He did not want to hear the physical details. Was he squeamish about the jeweler's pain or only about his own part in it? He ought to feel only elation. A confession that could be announced to the press. An enhanced scorecard. "Of course he'll probably repudiate the confession in court."

This was true, but for the moment irrelevant.

"What else did he admit?"

Although a signed confession could be torn up at any time, any collateral information that had spilled forth with it was not physical and could not be. Once revealed it stayed revealed. It could not be called back.

With his tongue Devereux rolled the cigarette into the corner of his stained mustache. "He said no papers were taken from the bank. He said absolutely not. I believed him."

"You believed him?"

Devereux nodded. "He's not very good at pain."

"I see."

"Five minutes on the wheel and he confessed to being in the vault himself. But he refused to squeal on any of the others. Said he was more afraid of the Milieu than of me, can you imagine? Said they'd kill him if he squealed. He begged me to understand. I told him I didn't understand and to get back on the wheel. He started crying. That's when he asked if I wanted to hear about The Brain. Would I forget the Milieu in exchange for The Brain."

Devereux seemed perplexed. To him it didn't track.

"The Brain is not a Milieu *mec*. And he's a foreigner. He spoke with an accent. The jeweler thinks he's from Nice. Thinks he was American."

"American?" cried Bellarmine incredulously.

"My reaction exactly."

"With Milieu *mecs* working for him?"

"I know. There were about half a dozen English and Americans."

It was infuriating. Bellarmine stood up and began pacing.

"He said the foreign *mecs* worked out of an apartment on the Rue Rossini. He was there once. About halfway along the street."

An American. Rue Rossini.

"I guess that's all he knew. I questioned him another hour. Sore hands is all I got out of it." Devereux contemplated his hands. Then he yawned. "Questioning people is hard work, you know that?"

"I can imagine."

203

"I thought I better stop. I still have twenty or more prisoners to question." Devereux again studied his hands.

They were the hands of a sadist in a damp shirt, and the gratitude Bellarmine felt confused him. Was not gratitude a form of love? Was it possible to hate sadism but love the sadist because he practiced his perversion efficiently and simplified one's life? Bellarmine shook his head as if to clear it. These thoughts were too complex. He did not want to think them now. He wanted to rush off to Nice, and he sent Devereux back upstairs.

His mind was racing. He had believed from the beginning that The Brain must live in Nice. And if the *mec* spoke French fluently, even with an accent, that meant he had lived there a long time, which in turn meant he must have applied for a *carte de séjour*, because that was the law. Which put the Sûreté in possession of his photograph. Bellarmine could order detectives to comb the files for photos of every likely suspect. There couldn't be that many.

"I told you Devereux had qualities," said Sapodin enthusiastically when Bellarmine had told him. The great man beamed. "Bravo, Bellarmine."

He had given the *divisionnaire* one of the best of all gifts—confidence to carry off this afternoon's press conference—the arrest of The Brain was imminent. Bellarmine was really much better at reading people's weaknesses than their strengths—most detectives were—and this was a weakness in itself, one that came like the gun and handcuffs with the profession. But this afternoon Sapodin would be photographed with thirty microphones in front of him, and tomorrow's headlines would call him France's Number One *flic*. That's why he was beaming, and it was all to Bellarmine's advantage.

"I want you to go to Nice at once, Bellarmine. I'll wrap it up here and join you there in the morning."

Detectives carrying photos went through the Rue Rossini from both ends. They localized the apartment easily enough—a furnished flat currently unrented. Neighbors said it had been inhabited by several men—all foreigners—for about three months, ending around the time of the break-in, maybe the day after, no one was sure. It was on the third floor—two rooms, kitchen, bathroom. Certain inhabitants of the building hesitated over the photo of Lambert. They "thought" he might have visited the apartment. The landlord hesitated over Lambert's photo also. Handwriting on the lease, which he was asked to produce, seemed to resemble Lambert's. Unfortunately, testimony by handwriting experts was opinion only and always sounded feeble in court.

Bellarmine hated to have to move on information that was perhaps only autosuggestion.

He visited the address given on Lambert's *carte de séjour*—a dilapidated farm in the mountains. There was no one about. In the village they had not seen him in months. A check with the *Police des Frontières* turned up an exit card—he had crossed into Italy the day after the break-in was discovered. Bellarmine's heart sank, for his suspect—the date was perfect—seemed to have fled the country. But a further check produced a reentry card two weeks later—Lambert was back.

He sent men checking all the agencies; the tax people showed Lambert buying an expensive American car in dollars, tax exempt, the day after his return, and this was encouraging also. Where did he get the money? His dossier showed that he had never applied for a work permit even though, as the spouse of a Frenchwoman he had been entitled to one after three years residency. Which meant he had never held a legal job. So how had he lived all these years? As a prime suspect, Lambert fitted the precise profile Bellarmine was looking for.

In Villefranche Lambert sat outside a café on the quay. It was 8 A.M. He was watching the great horseshoe-shaped rade and the American battle cruiser that had just glided into it. The gray hulk had materialized out of the gray mist rising off the water. Its indistinct lines had hardened. Without seeming to move, it loomed sharper, larger. It became finally enormous as it neared its permanent buoys. It was the U.S.S. *Salem*, flagship of the Mediterranean fleet, and at last it was motionless, so low in the water that it looked not so much massive as heavy, like a block of gray steel. It looked as if its smokestacks had been driven through the hull into the floor of the Mediterranean. Lambert always enjoyed watching the cruiser moor. He loved the power it represented, power he himself was a part of—the power of the mightiest nation on earth.

He had arrived at Villefranche early, and had aired out and swept out his locker club. Its door stood open a few feet away, waiting for the onslaught of young sailors. They would want his advice on every subject from buses to girls. He thought of himself as the only American ambassador these young men would meet while in France.

He sipped his café au lait and waited. Already launches were being

205

swung out over the side. In a few minutes the liberty parties would be coming ashore. The ambassador would have to go to work.

Behind him the bar owner came out of the café. There were no other customers and he knew Lambert well, so he sat down at his table. He had a newspaper which he opened out.

"Did you see this?"

It was one of the Paris papers: *France-Soir.* Lambert had bought and read the *Nice Matin* earlier. He flashed the bar owner a smile. "I tip my hat to those *flics,*" he said.

"They've got more than thirty people still locked up in Marseille," commented the owner.

Yes, thought Lambert, and I never heard of almost all of them. The police had most of the case wrong. There were sixteen mug shots on the front page, of which Lambert recognized only four.

"They don't have The Brain yet, I see."

"He's one of these *mecs.*" The owner rapped the paper with his knuckles. "That much is evident. It does not dispute itself."

"Your French Mafia is as bad as our American Mafia," commented Lambert cheerfully. The biggest picture was of Sapodin at his press conference; underneath came four rows of mug shots. In the top row were The Walrus, Freddie the Jeweler, St. Jean and The Pope. To Lambert's surprise the Pope, despite his good accent and good manners, turned out to be a pimp named Gaston Baptiste Angelucci—not at all the disbarred lawyer Lambert had supposed him to to be.

Well, none of them knew Lambert's name, and Milieu guys never talked anyway. He had nothing to worry about.

Two men sat down at a table on the other side of the terrace and the owner went over to them. Lambert watched carefully as they gave their order. One was dressed in a worn gray suit, and could possibly be a cop, but the other was unshaven, wore rough clothes and appeared to be a fisherman. Turning away from them, Lambert gazed out at the cruiser, symbol of his country's invulnerability, and his own. Out there sailors were probably already at the gunsights, checking out distant bedroom windows all around the Rade. The gunsights were powerful telescopes and brought French bedrooms into extremely close focus. The notion brought a smile to Lambert's face.

Twenty feet away Bellarmine watched him. "You're sure this is the *mec?*" he said to the fisherman, who was a detective.

"I'm no more sure than you are, *patron.*"

206

Across the terrace Bellarmine tried to "feel" his suspect's guilt or innocence. It was like trying to feel something through gloves.

So for a time he too studied the cruiser anchored in the Rade. He was as outraged by it as by Lambert's tax free car. He was particularly outraged to have to sit under its guns, under its telescopes—he too knew about the gunsights.

Sailors were clambering down the ladders, leaping aboard the launches. In about ten minutes the foreign uniforms, meeting no resistance, would swarm ashore. His country would be invaded still again. In its weakness it would put up no defense, an old story for France.

And it wasn't just here.

At this moment other units of the U.S. fleet were anchoring off every Riviera town. The invasion was real, not fantasy, and he knew this. It would take place along the entire coast. For forty miles the barmen would be polishing their bars, the merchants polishing their smiles. The prostitutes would clog every street. How could his country regularly demean itself like this? France was not sovereign, and if in their disdain foreigners like Lambert chose to scoff at her laws, this might have been foreseen.

Ignoring the two men across the terrace, Lambert watched the cruiser. Its launches were now about halfway to shore. Another few minutes and the sailors would be climbing up on the quai, chattering with excitement, anxious to be at their lockers and to get to Nice. He would be busy. His café au lait was growing cold now, and he drained it and put money down on the marble table.

When he stood up, he was conscious of the medieval castle that loomed over the town, a great stone fortress that had commanded this harbor for centuries. It was no longer impregnable. The U.S.S. *Salem* could blow it off its perch with a single salvo. The same was true of every castle in Europe. The power is in our hands now, he thought.

His friend, the bar owner, having served the other two men, came over.

"Got to go to work," Lambert told him. But he did not immediately move off.

Bellarmine stood up too. The aftermath of the war prolongs itself intolerably, he thought, and the Banque de Nice can be seen as a logical act. France is still a defeated country. Our policemen ride bicycles, or they ride the train. Most times our investigators don't have enough cars, enough two-way radios. So why not loot the biggest bank on the coast? Most arrogant of all, why not hang around afterwards, under the protection of the guns of that cruiser there, laughing at our feeble attempts to solve the crime?

To arrest an American was an act of great risk. Paris did not like it. His sense of outrage had not diminished. As if waiting for him, Lambert still stood beside the table, and he went over to him.

"Monsieur Lambert?"

"That's me," said Lambert and he flashed a genial smile.

He was tall and thin with a crew haircut, and like most Americans he looked boyish and much younger than his age, which, Bellarmine knew, was thirty-one. He did not look like a master criminal.

Bellarmine said in English: "The human comedy continues," and waited for a reaction.

"Who are you?" said Lambert, and he blinked.

Bellarmine decided he was sure. "Monsieur Lambert, you are under arrest for the crime of qualified theft in connection with the break-in of the Banque de Nice et de la Côte d'Azur."

Lambert's smile vanished slowly. Too slowly to suit the policeman. The man was either a consummate actor, or innocent, and if he was not The Brain, then the risks to Bellarmine's career had just passed beyond all imagining.

"Are you crazy? I'm an American citizen." Bellarmine could not know that Lambert was prepared for him, was again playing a role.

The fisherman had come forward with handcuffs, but Bellarmine shook him off, no longer at all certain. For the moment he would handle Lambert gently. He said in English: "You please will come with me now. I have a car over there under the trees."

Lambert said: "Give me a moment to lock my club."

The "fisherman" accompanied Lambert into the club while Bellarmine paid for the undrunk police coffees.

They bundled Lambert into the police Citroën parked on the square, and it was driven off. The bar owner stupefied, watched this. His wife had come out onto the terrace and stood beside him. "They said he is The Brain." He took his apron off and handed it to her. "I must go to Nice. His wife must be informed." He ran into the back room where he kept his motor scooter. He wheeled it out through the café, skirting the tables, kicked the starter, and mounted it. "I'll be back as soon as I can," he said, and sped away.

Jacqueline Lambert's reaction was to close up her shop and to rush through the streets to the *commissariat* on the Rue Gioffredo where, after identifying herself, she demanded information on her husband. News that she was there was relayed to Bellarmine, who was upstairs and who had already begun interrogating the prisoner. He sent down an order that was brief and direct:

"Arrest her too."

He would get to Mme. Lambert when he could. The woman must know something of her husband's activities. He would see how she stood up under interrogation. In the meantime she could sit in a cell.

He had forty-eight hours in which to crack one Lambert or the other.

# PART
## III

## CHAPTER
## 21

Jacqueline was placed on a bench on an upstairs corridor. A uniformed *flic* guarded her. The corridor ran the length of the building with a window only at the far end. She sat in gloom and was startled every time an office door opened, expelling a sudden shaft of light. She studied the floor, not the future. Terra-cotta tiles, some of them loose, rang to the heels of detectives who entered and left offices. Detectives in shirt sleeves, most of whom stared. She did not meet their eyes. She noted the guns on their hips as they came abreast of her, and the handcuffs dangling down their backs when they had gone by. She felt many emotions: frustration, rage, bitterness against her husband, fear. But chief among them was humiliation. What was she doing here on this bench?

Her guard stood opposite, shoulders against the wall, a submachine gun under his arm. He was about twenty-two. The bill of his kepi was level with his eyebrows. He had the smooth red cheeks of a boy, and could not keep his eyes off Jacqueline, though he tried. His eyes were like small animals—constantly squirming out of his grasp. She was aware of this, and was irritated by it. She was in no mood to be ogled.

"Would you mind not pointing that thing at me."

It made the boy blush, but he adjusted the strap until the barrel, like his eyes, again pointed at the floor. However, almost immediately, both began rising. Realizing it, he blushed again.

"Do you know how long I'm going to be held here?"

"*Non, madame.*" He had his palm on the muzzle, as if trying to force it down or at least keep it from rising farther.

"Can you find out for me?" She gave him a smile.

"I'll try, madame."

"Don't talk to the prisoner." It was Sapodin, who had come out of one of the offices.

The guard had snapped to attention. "Sorry, monsieur."

Sapodin appraised her. She did not know his name, nor any of their names. He was not like the guard. She saw no sexual interest in his appraisal, and so stared back at him, a seedy little man, bald, old. She tried and failed to stare him down.

"May I ask why I am being held?"

He said only: "My apologies, madame," and with a bow continued down the hall.

A little later a young detective came and sat down beside her on the bench. This was Lussac.

"We have a few forms to fill out, madame." His accent sounded well educated. He sat as close as if they were honeymooners waiting for a train.

She hitched herself away from him. "Do I have the right to a lawyer?"

"Not yet, I'm afraid."

Her husband would need a lawyer. She knew none. How would she find one? How would she pay him?

"Now, these forms. Have you ever been arrested before?"

"You have to be a criminal to get arrested."

Lussac only studied her a moment, but his regard chilled her.

"Am I under arrest?"

Lussac gave a slight nod.

"What for?"

"I've got to fill out this form."

"But what did I do?" He had her identity card clipped to his board and worked off that. She kept demanding to know the charge, but Lussac only asked more questions. Her high heels were balanced on the floor. She stared down at them and mumbled answers.

But by the time he stood up and departed, Jacqueline had recovered somewhat. She gazed across at the young *flic*. "Have you been a policeman long?"

"Almost a year, madame."

She gave him another smile, trying to find an ally somewhere, and was using the only leverage at her disposal. "Are you married?"

He glanced nervously up and down the hall before replying. "*Non, madame.*"

"You can talk to me. I won't tell anyone. What's the procedure around here?"

"Procedure?"

She could see he liked being forced to talk to her. Nonetheless, he kept glancing furtively up and down the hall.

"What will happen to me?"

"I don't know, madame."

Suddenly Sapodin was there snarling at the young man: "I thought I gave you explicit orders."

He ordered the young *flic* replaced by an older one. The detective who was with him rushed to obey, and Sapodin stood over Jacqueline until the new guard appeared. Gray mustache. Shiny uniform. No smile.

"Is there a ladies' room?" Despite herself there was a frightened quaver in her voice.

Sapodin gave a jerk of his head toward the door at the dark end of the corridor. "Take her to the bathroom," he ordered the new guard.

Snatching up her purse, Jacqueline strode down the hall. With three men watching her, one of them only two paces behind, she locked herself in the toilet. She had got away from them, if only for a moment. But her triumph was brief. She was in a small, square cubicle. It was not a ladies' room. It was a stand-up toilet; there was no bowl. One was supposed to squat over the hole in the floor. From the cistern high up on the wall hung a rusty chain. She peered down at the hole, brim full, clotted with sodden toilet paper. Toilets of this type were standard in bars and courtyard privies all over France. This one had been used by generations of *flics*, and had contributed its share of humor to police lore. The *divisionnaire* before Sapodin was among those who, squatting with his pants down, had been dismayed to watch his pistol fall off his belt and slide into the hole. However much he tried, he had been unable to retrieve it and had been forced to summon help. That the same thing had happened to a number of

213

detectives over the years was immediately forgotten, and the joke about the *divisionnaire's* gun had delighted hilarious police banquets ever since.

Jacqueline saw that the door was flimsy and its top half was of corrugated glass. Since there was a window in the cubicle high up behind her, she feared she was visible in silhouette in the hall. Her guards would certainly be able to hear everything. She did not want to use this toilet, but had no choice. Having finished, she grasped the chain, but before pulling it got ready to open the door. When she pulled, the water gushed down in a flood. It flooded out toward her shoes, representing still another of the humiliations to which she was being subjected, but she leaped into the hall and slammed the door on it. She smoothed her skirt and attempted to recover her dignity. But the new guard was waiting. Sapodin and the other detective were still waiting also.

"In here," Sapodin ordered curtly.

He directed her into a small windowless room containing no furniture except a bench like the one in the hall.

"You," Sapodin said to the uniformed *flic*, "you guard her from the hall. The prisoner is inside the room, and you're outside. Understand?"

He closed the door on her, but she wrenched it open again, feeling already the claustrophobia of being imprisoned, fighting for a final moment of freedom.

"When do I eat?"

Sapodin eyed her coldly. "I'll send you a waiter," he said, jerking his head toward the uniformed *flic*, who grasped Jacqueline by the upper arm, propelled her back into the room, and closed the door. "Lock it," she heard Sapodin say.

The lock turned.

She had no way of knowing how long she would be locked inside this room. Nor would she know where to turn for help when the door opened again. Help for her husband, for herself. She had no relatives on the Côte d'Azur except her mother, whose health was fragile, no powerful friends. Mme. Zuccarelli, who owned the dress shop across from the perfumery, had rich clients, and might know a lawyer. M. Guerin, who owned the luggage shop next door, had good connections. She could count on the solidarity of the merchants on her street, she believed. They all patronized each other's shops. They all gave each other 10 percent discounts. She could go to them for help. There was no one else.

A single bulb hung from a wire in the center of the tiny room. Brightness, about twenty-five watts. It was stuck with dead flies. She glanced all about her. The walls seemed to be closing in on her and she began to imagine trying to escape. She could ask to use the toilet again, and once in the hall make a run for it. Down the stairs and out into the street. But they would catch her with no difficulty. She had never before been so conscious of a woman's physical inferiority to a man's, which was where, she believed, all a woman's other inferiorities came from. Women were people who could be outrun and overpowered by the least of them. She glanced down at her spike heels. And how could she be expected to run in shoes like this?

She heard the key turn. Her door opened. Sapodin had sent a waiter after all, and he came into the room. Black trousers, white jacket, black shoes splayed and cracked.

"From the café across the street, madame."

She was so frightened she was sure she could not eat. Nonetheless, she ordered a liter of Evian water—by now she had a raging thirst— and a pâté sandwich.

The door was slammed and locked again before she even realized she might have questioned the waiter, perhaps learned something. She might have enlisted his sympathy, sent him out with a message to someone, though to whom? A cry for help that no one would hear.

The waiter made his way out through the *commissariat* entrance through a mass of reporters. News that The Brain had been captured had swept through the city—through the world. Five white batons, arms locked together, blocked the doorway.

Presently the waiter recrossed the street from his café, shouldered through the mob while carrying his tray above his head, and was passed inside by the police guard. Upstairs Jacqueline heard the key turning once more.

The waiter came in and placed the bottle, the glass and the sandwich on its plate on the bench beside Jacqueline. Under the plate he slipped the cash-register chit. He performed exactly as if working a table on the café terrace.

"Let me pay you now," Jacqueline said, opening her purse.

"If you wish, madame."

Jacqueline tipped him. "Are they saying how long I'll be held?"

"The *patron* said no talking," warned the guard, who stood in the doorway.

"*Oui, monsieur l'agent,*" said the waiter to the guard, and shrugged. It wasn't his fault this woman was locked up in here.

215

"*Merci, madame,*" he said, pocketing the tip. He went out and the door was locked behind him.

Despite her immense fear Jacqueline devoured the sandwich and drank half the bottle of Evian. She was still very hungry, and wished she had ordered a more substantial meal. She had no idea when she would be allowed to eat again.

As the waiter came out of the building, his tray under his arm, he was again besieged by the pressmen. Who was the food for? he was asked. A woman prisoner, he told them. Did he know who she was? No, he did not.

"A *pute?*" they demanded.

The waiter thought this over. "No," he said. "The wife of someone, surely. The tip she gave me was very correct."

He could tell them nothing more, though he wished to. He saw their interest in him die, along with their questions, and no one pursued him across the street back into the café. He was disappointed. No one had even asked his name, which now would not appear in tomorrow's newspapers.

Hungry, bewildered, frightened, Jacqueline sat on the bench in the small room. She knew the worst was still to come. They had done well to leave her alone this long. She was in a state of anxiety so acute that there was no resistance left in her. She was resigned to whatever they chose to make her do, to do with her. It was like being resigned to the greatest of the unknowns, to the greatest fear of all. It was like being resigned to death.

Lambert had affected a posture of confidence. Smoking a cigar, he stood with arms folded, rump on the edge of the desk. He grinned into the white light of the projectors. Behind it stood shadowy forms, detectives. Seven at the moment, he believed; he could barely see them. Most were smoking nervously, and he watched the coals glow on and off in the dark, like fireflies on a summer night.

"What did you do with the gold?"

"Where are the documents?"

His grin was fixed, but the cigar moved from one corner of his mouth to the other.

He pretended he did not speak French. "Huh?" he said. "What?"

Apparently this idea had never occurred to them. They had a consultation, and Lambert, watching, was amused. Then Bellarmine stepped forward waving his dossier. "You have a French wife," he said in English. "You must speak French. Don't joke me, please."

216

"I wouldn't joke you, pal." Lambert inside was laughing. "I do know a few words. Bedroom French. Like, *baise-moi, chérie.* It means fuck me, baby. It's something you usually utter in a passionate tone of voice."

"I know what it means," snarled Bellarmine.

"I'm an American citizen," said Lambert, grinning. "I demand to see the American Consul."

Nice was not strong in police interpreters, apparently. They brought in a couple of cops who must have bragged about their ability to speak English. Lambert answered them in double-talk, in pig Latin, in slang. He made them scratch their heads and whisper to each other. He could barely keep from laughing out loud. They went away disgraced, and the questioning resumed in French. He had them at a tremendous disadvantage, and knew it.

He became hungry and asked for food.

"Later," they told him in French.

Still grinning, he began to concentrate on hunger. Hunger was pain of course, but he didn't mind it. It made the senses more acute, heightened all sensation. It made him alert for any trap they might set him. Now comes the hard part, he told himself. I can outlast all of them. It's a very exciting day. I'm enjoying every minute of it. I'm beating them. All I have to do is hang on.

The interrogation continued. Lambert understood the French well enough, he merely tuned it out, like a sermon in church. The projectors did not bother him either. They baked the grin onto his face, which was all to the good. The grin, he well knew, infuriated the detectives. So did his cigars, which increased his confidence and sapped theirs.

"A false arrest like this could really kill tourism in France," he advised them. "Or the American Navy might move the fleet somewhere else. Italy, Albania. Some such place. Then where would France be?" He gave a brilliant grin all around.

"You're The Brain," shouted the fat, bald, older man who must have been the boss.

"I'm an American playwright. I demand to see the American Consul."

Outside the interrogation room Sapodin muttered to Bellarmine: "The *garde à vue* is not going to work." The match flare showed Bellarmine his yellowed fingers. He lit up.

"He has contempt for our methods, contempt for us, contempt for France."

217

Bellarmine thought this too, and it infuriated him.

They went into Sapodin's office. He said: "Perhaps the wife—

"Not yet, *patron*." When at last he confronted the woman, Bellarmine wanted her distraught, ready to babble.

None of the witnesses or suspects who had viewed Lambert through the one-way window had identified him, not the two elderly women from the building on the Rue Rossini where the gang, or part of the gang, had lived during the digging of the tunnel, not the first group of Milieu prisoners either, not even Freddie the Jeweler, who by now was denying his own confession.

Requests for information on Lambert had been sent to other law-enforcement agencies. But the Sûreté's Paris archives had had nothing on him except a civil dossier—his request for a *carte de séjour*—and the Surveillance du Territoire had had nothing at all. Interpol reported no international warrants outstanding. Only customs even knew his name—a file card was found showing he had once been questioned by *douaniers* aboard the PT boat of a suspected cigarette smuggler named Roy LeRoy in Villefranche harbor.

"Our men probably went aboard to pick up their payoff," muttered Sapodin. "Lambert just happened to be there." There was no other entry on the file card, beyond the one date. It was not charged that Lambert was part of any smuggling conspiracy himself.

"Customs has tolerated the cigarette trade for years," said Bellarmine. "It's a national disgrace."

"Would you rather," said Sapodin, "smoke Gauloises?"

Just then a crew-cut head peered around the doorjamb, and a cheerful voice called out in English: "Anybody home?"

It was the FBI agent, Charlie O'Hara, who came in and shook hands with both of them. "I just received another cable from Washington," he explained. "You'll never guess from whom."

"Mr. Hoover," said Bellarmine.

"You're learning," said O'Hara, and looked around the room beaming. No one beamed back. "I gather he talked to your Minister of the Interior earlier today. I'm supposed to find out everything about the case."

He looked into the baleful stares of Sapodin and Bellarmine.

"So who is this guy inside, and what have you got on him?"

"I work a trade with you," Bellarmine told him in English after a pause. "You find out for me all about this Lambert, and I tell you about the case."

O'Hara's meaty paw shot out, engulfing Bellarmine's hand a second

218

time. "It's a deal." He shook hands again with Sapodin also. The *divisionnaire*, grimacing with distaste, promptly left the room.

"One other name I give you also," said Bellarmine. His English sounded stilted to him. "Roy LeRoy." He added the document numbers that customs had given him.

O'Hara, jotting them down in his notebook, nodded. "Anything else?"

Bellarmine wanted information he did not expect the FBI agent to give him, but there was no harm asking for it. "And why you are here, if you can find out. Why Mr. Hoover care about this crime. He does not have enough crimes in America?"

O'Hara went back to the consulate, which was connected by telex via the Paris embassy with Washington, and tapped out onto the wire the names, dates and numbers Bellarmine had given him. Bellarmine's final question—Why was Hoover interested?—troubled O'Hara too, but it was not one that could be sent into the FBI building by telex for everyone to see. He would seem to be challenging the director's authority. The Bureau thrived on gossip, and he did not need talk of this nature circulating about him while he was four thousand miles away and unable to defend himself. But after much thought he decided he could risk a phone call to Washington to a highly placed friend he believed he could trust. The friend, an assistant director, called him back an hour later. Hoover was acting at the behest of Congressman Avery. Apparently Avery had important business interests in the town, and owned a safe-deposit box in the Banque de Nice. His box had been one of those looted. No, said the assistant director, the Bureau had no idea what Avery's box had contained. Here O'Hara heard a chuckle in his earpiece. It cut through the transatlantic static.

"That's what Hoover wants you to find out."

"Then why doesn't someone tell me so?"

"You know the games they play around here."

After hanging up, O'Hara thought about it. Obviously Avery must have lost papers that were vitally important to him, and if he cared enough to put the FBI on the case, then to O'Hara's naturally suspicious and always cynical police mind—Hoover's too—they must have to do with something illegal. Something for which he could go to jail, or be blackmailed.

And I tail him right to Picpoul's villa, thought O'Hara, meaning that the adjunct mayor of Nice is probably involved with him.

Hoover wanted fast inside information with which he could soothe an important congressman, and thereby count on him for future favors.

To Hoover it was one thing to have Congress in his debt. It was quite another to have an important congressman by the balls. Hoover liked to have them by the balls.

O'Hara would like to have Avery by the balls himself, he decided. And if he could get him, he was not sure he would tell Hoover.

O'Hara waited at the consulate until the machine began to pound out the information he had requested, and when it stopped, he tore off the sheets and hurried back to the *commissariat*.

Bellarmine, waiting at the landing, led O'Hara into an office.

"Bad news for you, friend," said O'Hara. "I'm afraid you've got a war hero on your hands." He emptied the envelope onto the desk.

There were two bravery citations and Bellarmine picked them out and read them first. Both referred to action in the Maritime Alps in September 1944. Both were so larded with the heroic phraseology peculiar to literature of that kind that they only hinted at the drama of the actions they pretended to describe. With reckless disregard . . . selfless devotion to duty . . . in the highest tradition . .

Because he had been in combat himself and because he knew the type of country involved, Bellarmine believed he understood what had happened.

"Were you in the war?" he said to O'Hara.

"I was back home chasing spies."

The liberation of Nice and the Côte d'Azur had trapped many German units in the southwest corner of France. They were trying to escape through the Maritime Alps across the frontier into northern Italy, which they still held; the Americans were trying to seal them off. The few roads through the mountains were usually down at the bottom of deep gorges. The roads followed the contours of rivers, and at a bend in the road in a gorge beside the river Tinée the Germans had built a blockhouse and left behind a few men with antitank weapons as a rear guard, who blew up the first tank to nose around the bend. It retreated, burning, just far enough to block the road, making it impossible to bring fire onto the blockhouse, or to approach it closely enough to knock it out. Lambert and some of his men scaled the cliff. It must have taken about two hours. It must have been hot work. From on top, with ropes tied around his ankles, he dropped down the cliff headfirst—or rather hands first, clutching a

220

grenade in each fist, about two hundred feet down in the gorge, until he dangled in front of the slits in the blockhouse. Bellarmine, reading, wondered why, with all that blood inside his head, he hadn't passed out. He had pitched both grenades into the blockhouse and, after they had exploded, was lowered to the floor of the valley where he signaled the advance to continue. For this he was awarded the Silver Star.

Bellarmine turned to the second citation. Near Gap some weeks later, when his unit was held up by a German pillbox. Lieutenant Lambert led three men around behind it and destroyed it with hand grenades and rifle fire. Two of his men were killed outright, the third wounded. Bellarmine could imagine the sudden frantic rush across open ground, the explosions, the screams of agony. Lambert himself was wounded also in what the citation described as the upper left leg. Carrying the wounded man on his back, he had staggered to the rear to an aid station, and there had passed out from loss of blood. He was awarded the Distinguished Service Cross.

"Is that a very high medal?" Bellarmine asked O'Hara.

"There's only one higher," said the FBI agent. "Furthermore, he got it fighting here in France—fighting for you people. He was awarded a number of other decorations too, you'll note. Some French ones too. The Croix de Guerre, I see."

For Bellarmine it was the worst possible news. One becomes a hero in seconds, he reflected. An act of villainy takes much longer usually. Sapodin came in and read the citations in his turn, after which he glanced sharply at his subordinate.

"No previous criminal record?" said Bellarmine to O'Hara.

"No."

The agent, grinning, socked him on the arm. "We got a deal, you and me, right?"

Bellarmine was stirring through the pages that had come out of the envelope. "What about Roy LeRoy?"

"No such person. Not that corresponds with the numbers you gave me, anyway."

"Well," said Bellarmine, "that sounds hopeful."

"We can arrest him for false papers," said the grim Sapodin. "If we can find him. The press will love it."

"You're going to have to give out Lambert's name sooner or later," O'Hara said. He was all business now. "So what do you have on him?"

Bellarmine's eyes shifted to Sapodin. So little, he thought, that

221

neither of us wants to tell you. "Were you able to find out what is Hoover's interest in this?"

"No, I wasn't," lied O'Hara smoothly. "Do we have a deal or don't we? Do you give me some facts or not?"

With a sinking feeling in his chest, Bellarmine began to explain to the FBI man. Lambert was linked to the gang by the Rue Rossini hideout. Witnesses could put him there, he said, though they couldn't—Bellarmine too had begun to lie. LeRoy's PT boat had probably been used to get the loot out of France, he said. He wondered if it had been used to get some of the "Englishmen" out also. So far no one but himself knew about the "English" aspect of the case.

"You're guessing," guessed O'Hara.

"We have evidence," insisted Bellarmine, who was still scanning the telex pages. But he saw nothing more there he could use.

"That's all you got on him?" asked O'Hara incredulously. " A war hero? A man who saved France? You got problems, friend." He stood up. "I better take a look at him," he said with the firmness of a patriot. "Make sure you're not beating the shit out of him."

Such was the weakness of their position that the two French policemen led the patriot upstairs and let him watch the interrogation until such time as the cigar-smoking Lambert began trying to talk to him.

"You there with the crew cut," Lambert said, trying to peer behind the projectors, "you an American? You from the consulate?"

No one answered.

Bellarmine and O'Hara went downstairs together as far as the front door, where they parted. O'Hara was ready to help the investigation in any way he could, he said. But he expected to be kept informed of developments. He was confident that Lambert's rights under French law would be fully respected, he said. He would look in on him from time to time to make sure. His big, powerful grin flashed on and then off again. He meant what he said.

Bellarmine went back upstairs and into the office being used by Sapodin, who began banging his fist on the desk.

"We will be obliged to let the prisoner go," he said. "We have no case. We cannot even hold him for the forty-eight hours."

Bellarmine said: "We haven't tried everything yet."

The two men looked at each other. "The wife?" inquired Sapodin.

"The wife."

# CHAPTER
## 22

He sent a detective to fetch Mme. Lambert. Today's long wait would have intimidated the woman, he believed, an intimidation that was now to continue by other means. He swept his desk clean and was seated behind his name plate, R. BELLARMINE, COMMISSAIRE DE POLICE, when she was led in the door.

It was difficult to know which of them was more surprised.

The uniformed guard, submachine gun under his arm, glanced from one to the other. There was a sudden tension in the room, and he did not know what it was. "That will be all," Bellarmine told him, and he went out.

Left alone Bellarmine and Jacqueline remained silent. Both were trying to reconcile this moment with the memory of the evening they had spent together—that interrogation as opposed to this one.

She was wearing the same dress. Navy blue. Wool. It hugged her figure in front, and at the waist and hips. She stood on high heels, and carried her purse in front in her two hands. "I thought you were some kind of clerk," she muttered.

Her hair was dark brown, very thick, shoulder length. He supposed she had combed it five minutes ago, before permitting herself to be led here, wanting to look her best for whatever happened next.

"You did not tell me you were married," he reminded her.

She ignored his reproach—women usually did, he thought—and instead got angry. "It wasn't me you were interested in that night, but my husband. How stupid of me to imagine otherwise."

"On the contrary."

"You must have thought you were losing your charm. I didn't let slip anything damaging about my husband."

He felt in his pocket for his package of cigarettes.

"I must have been quite a disappointment to you."

He lit up.

223

"I'm sure you used approved police techniques. Is it considered police corruption if you wind up in bed with a woman after you get information out of her? Or is that just one of the bonuses detectives are eligible for?"

Bellarmine, trying to keep his voice flat and even, said: "I never heard of your husband before a couple of days ago."

"I don't believe you."

She was shoving his emotions around like furniture. He puffed on his cigarette and studied her, and for a time neither spoke.

Could any man, he asked himself, dig that tunnel over so many months, and loot the Banque de Nice of so much, without the knowledge of his wife? Without at least alerting the suspicions of his wife? Jacqueline, therefore, was either an active collaborator, or an accessory. Either way, she would go to jail.

But during recent weeks she had been the subject of all the romantic fantasies he had had time for, and he was having trouble abandoning these fantasies even now.

"It's true," he murmured, and ground out the half-smoked cigarette in the ashtray. He did not meet her eyes. "I learned about your husband only by accident, and only hours ago."

"You make me laugh." But she was not laughing, and from the way her chest heaved, had difficulty even breathing.

He reminded himself of her status, and his own. She did not need to know how or when her husband had become linked to the Banque de Nice. On the other hand, he did not want her believing that he himself was capable of feigning interest in her just to further his case.

"I was sincere with you that night," he told her.

He paused, and they regarded each other.

Romantic illusion dies hard. "Let me explain something to you," he said with unnecessary harshness. "Your husband will go to jail as the mastermind of the bank break-in. For your part in it, you will go to jail also."

It was as if he had slapped her. "But what did I do?" From one instant to the next, defiance was gone, and he saw she was close to tears.

"Three months at least it took to dig that tunnel," he said, "so my experts tell me." His voice rose in irritation. "You mean to pretend that for three months you had no suspicion of what your husband was doing?"

"No," she said in a small voice.

"You didn't notice that he wasn't coming home nights?"

"No."

"And when he showed up finally you didn't notice mud all over his clothes?"

She shook her head.

"Who laundered his clothes all those months? Tell me that."

Jacqueline had sat down. Twisting the pocketbook handle in her fingers, she mumbled: "I don't know."

He tried a milder voice. "Who normally does the laundry?"

"You see, I work all day, and he doesn't. He takes it to the *laverie* on the Rue—" She stopped.

Bellarmine's pencil hovered over his notebook. "On the Rue what?"

"I don't know which one he goes to."

"He bought a new car a few weeks ago. Do you know how much American cars cost in France?"

"He sold his play."

Bellarmine stood up and walked to the window, where he looked out over the courtyard. Dusk was leaching the color out of the day, out of the south of France. The orange tile rooftops were going gray.

Turning back to Jacqueline, he said: "You went to Switzerland on vacation."

"Yes."

"You left the day after the break-in was discovered."

"How do you know what day it was?"

"Because I went looking for you that day."

It was an admission that temporarily silenced both of them.

"Oh."

But he could see he had shaken her. The timing of the "sale" of the play was perhaps a coincidence, but she was no longer sure. Assuming she had ever been sure.

Again Bellarmine's pencil was poised above his notebook. "Who did he sell it to? How much did he get for it?"

"I don't know."

"Are you his wife or aren't you?"

"We don't talk about money."

"You don't talk about money or laundry or new cars, and when he doesn't come home for several weeks that seems normal to you also. What do you talk about?" This is not a good marriage, he told himself. That much is clear. Hardly a marriage at all. But he was ashamed of the jolt of pleasure that accompanied this thought.

"He showed me a telegram from the producer."

"What was the producer's name?"

225

"I don't remember."

"You're not cooperating."

She raised her eyes to him, and this time they were brimming. "The name meant nothing to me. How should I remember?"

He went on harassing her. "But you believed him?"

"Yes. No. I don't know."

"Your husband's going to jail, madame. And you with him from the sound of things."

Jacqueline wiped her eyes.

Bellarmine stood up. "Come with me," he said, and herded her by the arm out into the corridor.

"Are you taking me to jail?"

There was so much despair in her question that he was shaken, and wished to comfort her, but could not do so. To him the anxiety of a suspect was not an emotion but a tool, and he was now engaged in manipulating it, like a dentist's drill inside her mouth. He must keep her as intimidated as possible for as long as possible. Although he wished to take her in his arms, he must crack her wide open, until such time as she made admissions that would convict her husband.

"We are going to search your store. You are not going to jail yet only because the law says you must be present during the search."

A motorcycle policeman with his light flashing led the black Citroën out of the courtyard. A second motorcycle followed. The cortege nosed out on to the sidewalk where the crowd of reporters massed tightly around it. It was now nearly dark. Cameras were pressed up against the windows. As flashbulbs exploded, Jacqueline cowered into the collar of her coat, she pressed her purse against her face. Bellarmine felt her shoulder against his and did nothing.

The shops were still open along both sides of the Rue Masséna. The motorcycle *flics* remained astride their machines as the Citroën's doors opened and everyone got out. In the doorways of nearby shops people stood gaping, and a voice called out: "Is there anything you want us to do for you, madame?"

But Jacqueline, busy with her keys, did not answer. Her hand was shaking, Bellarmine noted. Keys would not fit into locks. Locks would not turn. But at last the glass door swung open, the four detectives crowded inside with her, and Jacqueline bent to relock the door.

"You're not going to wreck my store?"

"We'll try not to, madame," Bellarmine told her. He had liked it better calling her mademoiselle. The new word still disturbed him.

It took more than two hours. Detectives examined the cistern

226

above the toilet, the underside of the hot plate. They tapped all of the walls looking for hollow spaces. Certain loose floor tiles rang hollow. They dug each of them up, but underneath found only crumbling cement.

"There's nothing of his here," said Jacqueline. She glared at Bellarmine. She was winning the round, and it made her defiant. "Slippers, some toilet articles, pajamas—" She pointed to them. Lambert's pajamas were red and hung behind the toilet door. To Bellarmine it was as if Jacqueline had thrown them in his face.

They began to go through cartons of stock, some of them still factory sealed. They approached the narrow bed, and kneaded the mattress with fingertips and knuckles.

"Shall we cut it open, *patron?*"

The bed was as narrow as an army cot. Bellarmine turned to Jacqueline. "You both sleep on that?"

When she nodded, he thought: But not too often, I expect.

It reaffirmed his picture of her shaky marriage, and at the same time made a jumble of his emotions. On the one hand it pleased him—if Lambert went to jail she might divorce him. On the other hand, if husband and wife were not close, then where was he to get the evidence to help his case?

Another thought then came to him. If she were innocent of all wrongdoing, she would hate him for having believed otherwise, and for the suffering he had caused her so far today.

"Leave the mattress alone," he ordered.

"Thank you," she said in a sarcastic tone.

They moved down to the front of the shop. The street was dark now; few pedestrians passed by outside. Individual boxes of perfume and other stock were stacked on shelves, in cabinets. Again the detectives hefted, examined each one. As they moved out toward the display window Jacqueline worked behind them, putting each item back in its correct place.

When the search was finished, she permitted herself a bitter smile. "Nothing," she said, "as I told you."

Bellarmine gave her a slight bow. "For your sake, madame, I am quite glad."

The other three detectives, again wearing hats and coats, waited for instructions. "Wait for us outside," Bellarmine told them.

"Are you going to take me to jail now?" inquired Jacqueline when they were alone.

"Why don't you admit how scared you are?"

227

"Do you ever think what it's like for the people you put in jail? Or do you just put them there and forget about it?"

"Are you hungry?" growled Bellarmine.

"Hungry?" Her resistance to him and to the day's ordeal seemed all at once to break down. "It depends on what kind of food one gets in jail."

"Come on," he said, opening the glass door. "We'll go to a restaurant."

But she hung back. "You're suggesting we go out on a date, is that it? And then after the date, instead of taking me home, you take me to jail."

"I don't know yet what I'm going to do with you."

"You mean if I'm nice to you, maybe I don't have to go to jail. I guess I better be nice to you."

For a moment they stared at each other in silence. Then Bellarmine reached for her.

"I'll buy you a meal," he muttered, grabbed her arm, and pulled her out the door.

The motorcycle policemen had been dismissed earlier. Once inside the Citroën, Bellarmine ordered the detective at the wheel to drive up into the hills to the Auberge du Père Bensa in the village of St. Pancrace. The drive took about twenty minutes. "It's a nice restaurant," Bellarmine said at one point. A little later he added: "It's got one star in the *Guide Michelin*." Still later he said: "Monsieur Picpoul lives up here somewhere."

Otherwise the ride was silent.

They got out of the car in the small parking lot under the trees under the stars. The restaurant was brightly lighted, and there was a terrace with metal chairs and tables out front. Bellarmine wished they could sit outside and sip an apéritif. It would feel civilized, would calm them all down. But up here the nights were still too cold for that. They went inside and waited to be seated.

The maître d'hôtel came up clutching his menus. "Table for five?" he said.

"You men sit apart, if you don't mind," Bellarmine said to the detectives. "Two tables," he told the maître d'hôtel.

At the table he sat down heavily. The detectives were given one on the opposite side of the room, and began reading menus, talking animatedly to each other. They had no emotional ties to this case or this woman. They had no headful of vague yearnings to contend with, no ache deep in the gut either and, from the look of them, no suspicion that he did. To them she was just another prisoner.

"A candlelight dinner for two," Jacqueline said. "How romantic."

"Jacqueline"—Bellarmine folded his menu with a snap—"I wish you'd try to make this as easy as possible for both of us."

"Please call me Madame Lambert."

"Would you like an apéritif, or shall I just order a bottle of wine?"

"By all means order a bottle of wine. Or two bottles. Even three. Let's get drunk. You can put them on your expense account."

When the first course was brought to the table, Bellarmine saw that Jacqueline, though she had had only a sandwich all day, did not touch her food. He knew that by rights she should go from here to the women's house of arrest. She should spend tomorrow night there too. He should hold her in strict custody for the full forty-eight hours.

It was also true that he could not bear to see her suffering like this.

"Do you have money?" he asked her.

"Money? Are you going to make me pay for my own dinner"—she looked down at her plate—"that I'm not even eating?"

He had a certain latitude. The law was not inflexible. He could perhaps allow her to spend the night in a hotel. He could put a guard on the door. He would have to square it with Sapodin, and with the *juge d'instruction* also. They would criticize him.

"I could arrange for you to spend the night in a hotel instead of— in the other place. But you'd have to pay the hotel yourself."

Nodding her head vigorously, she began to laugh. "Oh, yes, I have enough money for a hotel." It seemed to him she was very close to hysteria.

"All right then. You'll go to a hotel."

Her eyes again filled with tears. She was laughing and crying both. Then the laughter stopped, and she gazed down at her plate. "Let's eat," she said. And after that she ate quite well.

Later, when he asked which hotel she had chosen, she named a small one on the Rue Masséna opposite her shop. He thought he knew why—she wanted the entire street to know she had not spent the night in jail.

When the Citroën had pulled up in front of this hotel, Bellarmine sent one of his detectives inside to select a room, remaining behind with her in the car. "I'm not going to run," she said with annoyance. "Can I get some things out of my shop?"

He permitted this. He walked her across the street and waited while she packed a small bag.

The same detective went into the hotel with her. He would sit outside in the hall until Bellarmine could send uniformed men to relieve him. But Jacqueline, after signing in, came out again to the car. Bellarmine rolled down his window.

"Thank you," she said, and gave him a wry smile.

His heart seemed to go rushing out of him, as if he were sixteen years old. It went out through the window and into her possession. But if she realized any of this she gave no sign. Turning on her heel, she re-entered the hotel, and he only watched her go.

At the *commissariat* Bellarmine looked into the interrogation room, called a detective—it was Lussac—out into the hall, and asked to be briefed.

"Briefed?" Lussac said. "There's nothing to brief you about. Nothing's happened."

"There'll be men relaying you throughout the night," Bellarmine told him. "Keep at him."

Tomorrow might be better, he thought. Lack of sleep is cumulative. By the end of thirty-six hours or so, if he's guilty he will want to tell us about it. And he went home to bed.

In the morning he took Jacqueline to breakfast at the Café Prado at the corner of the Rue de France and the Rue Halévy. They sat inside at a marble-topped table. It was early. The chairs were still up on most of the tables, and the doors were open to the cool morning air. The waiter in shirt sleeves had been mopping the floor when they came in. Now he was behind the bar working the espresso machine. They heard the hiss as he steam-heated the milk for their café au lait. Then he came over bearing his tray. He put the saucers down, one to either side of Bellarmine's folded newspaper. He added the basket of croissants and went away.

Bellarmine watched Jacqueline stir her coffee. "Croissant?" He held out the basket. She reached across the folded *Nice Matin* and took one. He was conscious of the paper—of Lambert's name in the headlines—standing like a wall between them. It was a barrier that, for the moment, neither could cross.

"I'm sorry," Jacqueline said. "I'm not very talkative in the morning."

"Would you like to read the paper?"

"No."

"There are some pictures."

"I don't want to see them."

"I looked in on your husband earlier."

She looked up from her coffee. "How is he?"

"Cheerful."

"He's always cheerful," she said. "He thinks life is a lark."

Bellarmine said carefully: "If he's guilty he has dishonored you. You don't owe him anything."

Her eyes did not come up. "If he's guilty."

"Your husband speaks excellent French," Bellarmine said after a moment. He had decided to settle the question of Lambert's French. "I'm surprised."

Jacqueline shrugged. "He's married to a walking dictionary, isn't he?" Her eyes met his and she said defiantly, "He takes his dictionary to bed with him every night."

For Bellarmine it made a too-vivid picture.

*"Baise-moi, chérie. It means fuck me, baby."*

Annoyed, he drained his cup. "We will now search your farm. The car is waiting."

During the ride Bellarmine sat in front beside the chauffeur, and did not speak except to give directions. In the back seat Jacqueline sat shoulder to shoulder between two detectives.

The car pulled to a stop on the cobbles in the front yard, and they got out. It was a bright sunny day. Bellarmine noted that it was cold up here, compared to down in the town. There was a chill in the wind. He gazed across the valley over high rolling hills. The air was very clear. Beyond the hills rose the Maritime Alps, and the highest peaks had snow on them.

He took her arm—he wanted her to feel, he told himself, that she was again a prisoner—and as they started toward the house he recited the legal formula. She was to assist in the search. Any attempt to hide potential evidence, or to divert, interrupt or delay the administration of justice was punishable to the full extent of the law.

She unlocked the door and pushed it open. "You won't find anything," she said, adding on a descending note, "I already looked."

Jacqueline had got over her strong emotion of the day before. She felt in control of herself, and to some extent therefore of her situation. She was resolved to stay out of jail at almost any price. Her husband needed her, for one thing, and the disgrace if she were imprisoned would be insurmountable. She would have to sell the shop.

Since Bellarmine held her freedom if not her life in his hands, she had begun to study him. She had noted his courtesy toward her. She noted too the hunger with which, for brief moments, he sometimes eyed her. Her situation was perhaps not as weak as it appeared.

231

Upon entering the farmhouse, she had glanced quickly around, weighing the appearance of the place since her last visit. She had no idea what her husband might have been up to, but to find a sack of gold or money in the middle of the living-room floor would not have surprised her greatly. Bellarmine—events—had shaken her faith, never very strong, in Lambert. She believed him entirely capable of tunneling into that bank, or at least of harboring the sewer gang, if they were his friends. He was a man who would do almost anything for excitement, and he was careless.

Although there was no sack of gold anywhere, she saw at once that Lambert had been there in her absence, for there were ashes in the fireplace—she had left it clean.

To Bellarmine, who had followed her, she said brightly: "It's cold up here, isn't it." She gave him a smile and a mock shiver. "I'll make a fire."

Bellarmine appeared to appraise her briefly. "I can't allow that," he said.

So he had already noted the fireplace, and considered the ashes important.

"Why not?"

But her newfound confidence had evaporated at once, and she twisted her fingers together. Together they moved quickly out of that room and into the bedroom where, on the floor beside the armoire, there was a pile of Lambert's laundry.

"We'll start the search in here," he said, and called to his men.

It made Jacqueline worry about the laundry at her feet. It too could be incriminating, and she wanted to check it out before Bellarmine did. For this she needed a reason for wanting to be alone in her bedroom, and one came to mind.

"I'd like to put on fresh clothes first."

"I'm sorry." He tried heavy charm. "You look lovely as you are."

She pouted: "It's not nice to wear the same things you had on yesterday."

"After we've searched the room," he told her.

She watched them unfold and examine every hanging garment, every blouse, every sweater. They even went through her underwear drawer, and she flinched to see them do it. Lambert's laundry did not interest them. They moved it with toes, and left it there. Immediately she scooped it up and threw it in on the floor of the armoire.

They tapped and sounded every centimeter of wall, floor and ceiling. They examined the mattress for unsewn seams, or resewn seams. They lifted it, shook it. When they put it back in place, she began to remake the bed, choking down her indignation.

As the search moved out of the bedroom, Jacqueline said to Bellarmine: "And now if you don't mind, I'd like to change." He nodded, and she locked the door on him.

The shutters had been thrown open to admit enough light by which to search, and she decided not to close them. As she began to unbutton her dress, she gazed out at the sun-dappled forest behind the house. She guessed what would happen, and soon noted out of the corner of her eye that it did.

Bellarmine had gone outside, and walked around the house. He had remembered that the shutters were open, and his purpose, he told himself, was only to make certain she did not escape into the woods. As he came to the rear of the house, he saw that the woods began about twenty meters from the bedroom window, and he took up position there half hidden by bushes. He could see into the room. Jacqueline still wore the navy-blue wool dress, though it was half unbuttoned. He saw her select fresh underwear and carry it into the bathroom. He heard water running. She was gone about ten minutes— for him, ten minutes of intensely erotic anticipation. When she came out she had brushed her hair, put on fresh lipstick apparently, and she was wearing only a bra and panties. Bellarmine turned around and gazed steadily straight ahead into the trees.

Peering through the slats of the bathroom shutters, Jacqueline had seen that he was still there, still watching her open window, and as she walked out into the bedroom carrying her dress in her hands, she told herself she was more dressed than in a bikini on the beach. She did not feel immodest. In any case, he was some distance away. Without looking in his direction, she busied herself arranging and hanging her dress. Taking her time, she lifted out her two other dresses and studied them, as if considering which to put on. She gave him what she hoped would pass for an eyeful, but when from the corner of her eye she caught a glimpse of him, she noted that he faced now into the forest, and she felt strangely touched. It had never occurred to her that his consideration for her extended to any depth. That he had refused to overstep the strict line of what he perceived to be her privacy surprised her, and the only conclusion she could come to was that he must care for her more than she had supposed. It made her feel suddenly tender toward him, so that she had almost to shake herself back into a state of reality. This was the man who held her husband captive—herself too. It was her job to manipulate him. If he fell in love with her, fine. But she must keep her own feelings strongly in check.

Dressed again, wearing one of her husband's cardigan sweaters against the bright chill of the day, she went outside into the yard. He stood on the cobbles, hands in his pockets, and she went and stood near him.

A van had drawn up on the cobbles and detectives were unloading gear.

"It's a beautiful day, isn't it?"

"It's good to breathe mountain air," he said. "The sea air down in Nice is so damp."

"Yes, it is."

The mood that enveloped them was almost one of courtship, and she was astonished. Be careful, she told herself. He wants something from you and you would be unwise to trust anything about him.

Bellarmine led two of the new men inside, giving them instructions in a low voice, and when she looked into the main room later, she saw them on their knees with their heads in the fireplace, picking out bits of charred paper with tweezers.

Outside, two of the detectives had begun quartering the ground with war-surplus mine detectors. Behind them moved two more with picks and shovels, and each time a hit was signaled they levered up cobblestones and they dug. Jacqueline stood beside Bellarmine while a good deal of farmyard junk was unearthed—horseshoes, barrel hoops, steel wheels off plows.

"He didn't bury anything," Jacqueline said. It pained her to watch her courtyard, her land violated. "I would have noticed anything freshly dug."

A little later the men who had come in the van departed. Only the men searching the house were left, and when Jacqueline offered to prepare lunch, Bellarmine sent his car to the village for fresh bread, eggs, cheese, a bottle of wine. She cooked omelets, laid out plates and glasses, then sat with four strange men around the table in the kitchen. They finished the wine the detectives had brought and she opened a bottle from the carton under the sink. They finished that bottle too and part of another. It was as if they were all members of the same family. The three young detectives were very polite. She rather liked them, and when lunch was over they thanked her profusely before going back to work. While she washed dishes Bellarmine stood near her in the kitchen. Although her husband, being American, dried for her all the time, she had never known a Frenchman to do so, not in her family or any other. But they chatted amiably as she worked. She was in a good mood. His search had turned up nothing so far, she believed.

That afternoon the search moved to the shed. A great deal of lumber, a ladder and stacks of tiles had to be carried outside first. Bellarmine and Jacqueline, both wearing coats, stood in the doorway watching.

"You said you searched the house yourself a short time ago," he said to her.

"I was looking for something I had mislaid."

"Did you look in here?"

It was hard to meet his eyes.

"No."

Methodically the detectives began to test and tap the floorboards. They found the hollow place at once, and one of them went out to the car and came back carrying a tire iron. With it they pried up the boards. Underneath, lined with roofing tiles, was a space about the size of a duffel bag full of stolen papers. A duffel bag lay down in there too, but it appeared deflated and empty.

"What does he usually keep in there?" inquired Bellarmine, peering into the hole.

Jacqueline, genuinely surprised by this find, was afraid he would think she was lying. "I don't know. I didn't know there was a space there."

A detective, having lifted the sack out, was rummaging inside it. "Look what I've found, *patron*."

It was a U.S. Army carbine wrapped in a piece of oily blanket. Bellarmine looked from the weapon to Jacqueline.

"Whose is that?"

Jacqueline was not sure the question was innocent. Nonetheless, she answered: "My husband's."

It brought a half smile to Bellarmine's face. She did not understand this smile. "What are you grinning about?"

He only shook his head, but his grin had vanished. Since it was against the law in France for a civilian to possess a weapon of this

235

type, he now had a charge on which he could hold Lambert indefinitely. But Jacqueline didn't know this, and he didn't tell her. He could hold her too, if he wished, while waiting for additional evidence to turn up. Which he also didn't tell her. Of course the gun represented a political problem also. Most likely it had helped liberate France. Maybe no one would want to use it as evidence. A political decision would have to be made. Sapodin would have to make it.

An attic, a chicken coup, and a root cellar remained to be searched. It would take time. Jacqueline, knowing nothing of the gun laws, was feeling increasingly confident. "Do you want to go for a walk?" she asked.

She walked beside him out to the road, and they began hiking uphill. The road was narrow, its surface crumbling in places. They came out above the forest and the road crossed an open plateau. As they walked they could see the village off across the valley, about two kilometers away.

"You're not going to put me in jail after all, are you?" inquired Jacqueline.

Her confidence showed in her voice.

He hesitated so long that she stopped walking and faced him. "I don't think so, no," he said.

"Can I count on that? I mean, it's sure?"

She waited until he had solemnly nodded his head.

"You had me worried there for a second." She began to laugh with pleasure. "Well, that's a relief," she said, and reaching up, she kissed him on the cheek.

His hand went to his face as if he had been stung, and he walked along with his eyes fixed on the road.

"You're a nice man," she said. She grinned at him. "I mean you try not to admit it to yourself, but you are."

He continued to walk along head down.

"Hasn't anybody ever told you that before?"

It brought a half smile to his face. "Not too many people, no."

"Well, I think you are, anyway."

At the entrance to the village they turned around and started back. To avoid talking of Jacqueline's husband and Bellarmine's investigation they talked of France's disastrous war in Indochina—Dien Bien Phu was surrounded and might fall. There was also a terrorist war against French rule in Morocco, and a second terrorist war about to break out in Algeria. "France has lost her way," Bellarmine told her.

She was surprised that the concept of France meant so much to him, and said so.

"A man has to believe in something," he replied.

She put her arm through his. It was partly a calculated gesture, but more than that she was moved that he would share such sentiments with her. She no longer doubted his genuineness.

They stopped to admire the view across the valley. Bellarmine sucked on a blade of grass, and for a while both were silent.

"Are you acquainted with a man named Roy LeRoy?" he asked her.

She nodded soberly. "His name is Leroy Billings," she said, and told him what little she knew, adding: "Maybe he's the man you're looking for. Maybe he's The Brain."

"Maybe."

They walked on. At length he said: "If your husband goes to jail for a long time, what will you do?"

She looked at him sharply. "I don't know."

"Will you divorce him?" he asked doggedly.

"Do you care?"

He gave no answer to her question, nor she to his. Instead, feeling annoyed, she moved off down the road some paces ahead of him.

When they got back to the farm the detectives were finished and waiting out front. One held the carbine by the barrel in his hand.

"Anything?" Bellarmine asked them.

"Nothing else, *patron*."

"Put that in the trunk of the car."

He turned to Jacqueline. "I'll take a look at that play now, if I may."

Without a word, she led him to Lambert's desk and drew forth the dossier she had examined herself only a few days before. He sat down and scanned the various versions, shaking his head briefly, as if perplexed. "I don't see any completed play here."

"No," she said.

Apparently it was the cable signed "Alexander Levy" that made him decide to carry off the entire dossier. "You'll be given a receipt for it."

"What will you do?"

"Make contact with this Monsieur Levy and find out the truth of the matter."

She studied the floor. "I see."

237

"You'll have to spend the night in the hotel again," he told her in the car going down to Nice. "I'm sorry, but I have to do it that way."

This was a disappointment. She was in custody still. Nonetheless she managed a smile. "That's fine with me." It wasn't, and she began to wonder again how far she could trust him.

In Nice he left her at the hotel—and left a guard downstairs— saying he had things to do. She imagined he would be back promptly and so took her time getting ready for him. She lingered in her bath, then lay on the bed in a towel thumbing through magazines he had let her buy earlier. She dressed and made up with care. As the hours passed she became irritated with him. In her impatience she contemplated the possible fate of her husband for almost the first time that day. Realizing this, she felt ashamed. Guilt took possession of her. But to be any help to him she had had to save herself first, had she not? Which had taken all her concentration. But such excuses failed to sooth her conscience, and to torment herself, she began enumerating her husband's virtues. He did not covet other people's possessions. He did not covet possessions at all, and there was no malice, she believed, in him. Whatever he did could not have been done with criminal intent.

Bellarmine did not come back, and she dined alone in the hotel's small restaurant, an interior dining room without windows, and containing only six tables. A policeman in uniform lounged beside the front desk with his coat undone, smoking.

After dinner she went to bed. The policeman, who had accompanied her upstairs, sat now on a chair in the hall reading the newspaper. She could hear him turning pages through the door.

He was relieved at 2 A.M. The low voices in the hallway woke her. She heard one guard clomp down the hall, followed by a soft thump as the relief tipped his chair back against the wall. For a while she listened to the same rustling newspaper, or perhaps another, and lay unable to sleep. Loyalty to her husband came on strong. She was consumed by guilt again, by outrage at being still a prisoner herself, and by other emotions too complex for her to sort out. She wanted to hurt Bellarmine if she could. She began to pace the room. At length she became conscious of the silence outside her door. No pages rustled, no chair creaked. She opened the door a crack—the guard seemed asleep in his chair, which was tilted back at a forty-five-degree angle. The newspaper was spread over his lap like an automobile rug from the unheated cars of her childhood.

She dressed, packed her small grip, left her magazines in a pile on the bed, and stole out past him into the hall. Backing down the hall, she watched him all the way. Only when she was in the stairwell, when his head and kepi had disappeared above the landing, did she begin to hurry. She almost sprinted down the next two flights, bursting forth into the tiny front hall where the night concierge slept in his chair also. The front door was locked from the inside. She opened it and stepped out onto the sidewalk. No cars passed, no people. She peered up and down the street. Silence. Empty pools of streetlights. She felt joyous, free. Crossing to her shop, she let herself in, relocked the door, stepped back into the stock room and climbed into her own bed. She lay awake in the dark contemplating what she had done. She was so exultant it was a long time before she fell asleep.

# CHAPTER 23

The same headlines and photos had appeared that day on the front pages of newspapers all over the world. In Washington Saul Avery saw them. He was at breakfast with his wife in his town house in Georgetown. He was eating a grapefruit, and when he recognized Lambert's picture, it was as if he had been kicked in the chest. All the air went out of him. The segment of grapefruit in his mouth flew ten feet across the room, where it struck a windowpane and fell on the floor. His wife in her bathrobe thought he was having a heart attack.

But he recovered quickly. "They caught the sonuvabitch who looted my lockbox," he said. His next thought was that he had best get to Nice fast, for he could not depend on Adjunct Mayor Picpoul, in his absence, to make the decisions that would have to be made. He saw Picpoul as a perfect symbol of the French nation: charm, flair and no backbone. In a crisis the French looked to America for help. It was invariable. They put themselves under the protection of the money and the power.

He caught a State Department plane to London, a four-engine

239

DC-4, that afternoon. In addition to the crew only two other people were aboard, himself and, at the last minute, a courier. For most of the twelve-hour flight he paced up and down the luxuriously appointed fuselage. That the stolen documents were about to surface seemed certain. He remembered every word of Lambert's remarks to him in the Ruhl bar—cryptic words then, not now. In London he would catch the Nice plane; his office had booked him on it. Various contingency plans worked their way through his mind. He flinched from none of them. Lambert might still have the papers. The police might already have them. There would be a price to be paid. If it was reasonable, he would pay it. If not, if someone tried to trifle with him, he was prepared to deal with that too.

The corrupt *notaire*, Jacques Verini, was in the first-class section of an Air France Viscount leaving Karachi when the latest newspapers were brought to him. He was two days out en route to Australia, ostensibly to visit his daughter. He intended to stay there until this thing blew over—six months if necessary. He read of the capture of Lambert, the presumed Brain, with great interest. The name and face meant nothing to him, but he congratulated himself for being where he was. He was safe. He had got out of Nice—out of France—in time.

Eugène Henri Baldasaro, sometimes known as Henry the Welder or Henry the Torch, read the papers over the steering wheel of a car parked in a Brussels street outside the main branch of the Banque de Bruxelles. His liquid profits from the Nice job were in a lockbox in the vault of this bank, and he was trying to read between the lines. How had the *flics* got on to them all, even the American, The Brain? How much did the police know? Did he dare go in and make a withdrawal?

He had been parked here some time already, and had become convinced that the bank was not being watched from the street. If staked out at all, it was from the inside. He was safe at least until he went in there, an insane risk. But he was on the run. He had to have money.

After getting out of the car, The Torch stood on the sidewalk and glanced nervously around. He wore dark glasses and a checkered sports jacket which he tugged down over his hips. He tugged it down several times. Then he strode into the bank.

He looked for the Bureau de Change sign, and found it. He was in luck—there was a line. Taking French money out of his pocket, he joined it. He had his false identity card ready. If a stakeout team was in here, he would have a minute or two to find it.

He spotted the *flics* at once. There were at least two of them. One, wearing a brown suit, was at a desk beside the door examining every face that went past him. He had not recognized The Torch coming in. Would he going out? The second *flic* was downstairs in the vault itself. The Torch saw him come to the top of the stairs. He also wore a brown suit. He stretched, yawned, and threw a grin at his colleague. Then he went back down again.

Having reached the head of the line, Henry the Torch pushed his ten-thousand-franc note through the grille.

"Gimme Belgian francs." The cashier was a quite lovely young woman. He didn't notice her. Grabbing up the money he stepped to one side and tried to catch his breath.

As he went out past the *flic* at the door, he pretended to be counting and folding the Belgian notes in his hand. It was as if this took all his concentration. He walked head down, eyes on the money, chin practically on his chest. He waited to feel the hand on his shoulder, but this did not happen.

Back in his car his heart was pounding, and he was soaked in sweat. For about five seconds he cursed violently, silently. All his assets were frozen—his apartments unrentable, his gold gone—his lockbox was no doubt already empty. *Merde.* Five seconds was all he could afford. Wrenching the borrowed car into a U-turn, he started back to the frontier. His only chance was to get back to Marseille, find a *mec* who would hide him or, better still, a woman, and make contact with Faletta. Of course Faletta's help would not come cheap. Sooner or later the The Torch would be asked to pay a heavy price. But he could not worry about that now.

After leaving Lambert, Bellarmine had gone straight to the American Consulate to see O'Hara. The FBI agent, he found, had the use of an office there.

"Cigarette?" He had taken the package out of his pocket. O'Hara refused, and took out his own pack of Gauloises. Both men lit up.

"I've got new names for you," said Bellarmine. "Try LeRoy Billings, U.S. Army, deserted in Italy in 1944 or '45. Also Alexander Levy, theater producer." He showed Lambert's telegram.

They went upstairs and he watched while O'Hara tapped the new information out on the machine.

"Any news on why Hoover is interested in the case?"

"I haven't been able to find out a thing."

Bellarmine gestured at the teleprinter with his chin. "I'll be at the *commissariat* when you get a reply."

But he went first to the Customs Building. It was on the Quai Lunel, the street that ran along one side of the horseshoe-shaped Nice port. One of the white ship ferries was just in from Corsica. Cars and trucks were driving out of its entrails. The Customs Building formed one side of the street, and the smooth white wall of the ship formed the other.

It was just dusk and the air was balmy. People were sitting outside the cafés all along the Quai Lunel. Bellarmine went into the building, up to the second floor and along the corridor. The chief here exercised customs jurisdiction over all the smaller ports at this end of the Riviera. Earlier he had agreed to send telegrams to Toulon, Marseille and Sète, which controlled traffic in the ports to the west, requesting information on LeRoy's PT boat. He had sent telegrams also to French customs headquarters both in Algeria, an integral department of the French Republic, and in Morocco, a French protectorate, as well as to French customs agents in Tangier.

"And nothing has come back?"

"Not yet. The boat in question may be at sea."

"Well, you'll keep me informed, monsieur."

"It goes without saying, monsieur."

The customs chief was impatient and anxious to get rid of Bellarmine. Bellarmine saw this and did not know why. He put it down to simple rudeness, but in fact a major customs operation was scheduled for that night, and the chief had work to do. Certain information had been purchased, and cutters were being deployed up and down the coast. The customs chief had no reason to suppose this operation involved LeRoy, and he might not have informed Bellarmine in any case. Law-enforcement personnel dealt in secrets every day. Indeed, their business relied on secrets almost exclusively. Which was not to say they were very good at keeping them. Juicy tidbits were revealed to girl friends, to barmen and to the press almost as a matter of habit. Secrets were kept habitually—and with an almost religious fervor—only from each other.

The customs chief gave Bellarmine a perfunctory handshake, told him nothing, and sent him out into the night.

Back at the *commissariat* Bellarmine called Lussac out of the interrogation room.

The interrogation was now about thirty-six hours old. The regulation number of meals had been put down in front of Lambert, two each day. Of course he had almost instantly been made to jump up and answer questions, and the dishes, which were sometimes still steaming, had been taken away. Lussac or one of the other interrogators had made all the appropriate notations in the log, and he showed them to Bellarmine now. Each entry was succinct, the exact time plus the comment: *Refused to eat*. Attached to the log were the bills from the restaurant across the street that had delivered the food. The log according to law was faultless. Lussac also showed entries regarding rest periods. Several were noted both last night and today. What was not noted was that Lambert, once having been allowed to fall asleep, was jerked immediately to his feet again each time. But Lussac did not have to explain this to Bellarmine.

In any case, the prisoner had not cracked so far, he said.

"A few smacks in the head with the telephone book might make all the difference," said Lussac.

"No."

"One could be careful. With a foreigner I understand how careful we have to be."

"No."

"The bicycle wheel?" suggested Lussac hopefully.

"No."

Bellarmine was with Sapodin when the report came in from the lab in Marseille. Seven bits of charred paper could be identified as legal stock; most were old, and of a type and manufacture that had been current before the war; they had not been produced since.

It was Sapodin who had taken this call, and he had invited Bellarmine to listen in on the extra earpiece. Furthermore, one of the bits, measuring seven centimeters by four, part of a will apparently, contained handwritten words and could perhaps be identified by its owner.

They were still digesting this information when O'Hara again knocked on the doorjamb. They looked up to see his cheery smile already poked halfway into the room. He said he had information that he would impart over dinner.

Bellarmine had been contemplating dinner with Jacqueline—not because of his feelings for her, he had convinced himself, but because she might drop information that would advance the case.

"Let's go to a restaurant," said O'Hara.

"I'll signal my driver," said Sapodin, and lifted the phone.

Bellarmine would not now dine with Jacqueline.

The black police Traction Avant deposited them in front of the Restaurant Raynaud on the Quai des États-Unis facing the sea. It was one of five or six restaurants side by side. People, mostly tourists, were sitting outside in the warm night sipping apéritifs.

Raynaud's, halfway along the row, had been chosen by Sapodin because its owner owed him a favor and would not present a bill. They sat down on the terrace and the waiter came for their order. Bellarmine and Sapodin asked for Pernod. The FBI agent ordered Scotch on the rocks.

"All these waiters speak English," he told his companions. "I don't know how they do it. Our waiters back in the States don't speak French, I can tell you that."

"So what do you have for us?" inquired Bellarmine.

But O'Hara's attention had been caught by the fishing boats working offshore. Some were close in, working almost in the glow of the restaurants. Putt-putting along on one-cylinder motors, they were putting down nets. Others were about half a mile out and were represented only by running lights. As the boats moved up and down on the swell, the points of light seemed to wink on and off like stars.

"What do they catch?" O'Hara demanded.

"They make a poor living," said Bellarmine.

"Small things," said Sapodin. "Squid, *petite friture, rougets*—I don't know how such fishes call themselves in English."

"Did you get an answer from Washington?" said Bellarmine.

"First from New York," said O'Hara. "Alexander Levy died before Christmas. So he didn't buy our friend's play in February, or send the telegram."

"His organization, perhaps?"

"He worked out of his hat."

"His hat?" said Sapodin.

"He had no organization."

"So in addition to charred fragments of papers from his fireplace," mused Sapodin, "he must explain to the court his sudden wealth also."

"Explain to the court?" said O'Hara.

Bellarmine described how, in the course of his trial, Lambert would be obliged to take the stand, where he would be interrogated by the president of the court who would endeavor to make him, in effect, testify against himself—to convict himself with his own unsatisfactory answers. Later the three judges and nine jurors would retire to deliberate together, and the jurists would heavily influence the verdict.

Sapodin, grinning, raised his glass in a toast: "To the late Monsieur Alexander Levy," he said.

"What else do you have for us?" said Bellarmine.

O'Hara dragged folded papers out of an inside pocket. "Interpol had nothing on this Roy LeRoy Billings," he said. "I checked."

"Interpol will not touch political or military crimes," said Sapodin.

"The U.S. Army had plenty, however."

A tablecloth was laid, and dinner was ordered. While waiting they studied the telex pages, which gave a capsule version of the army career of LeRoy Billings. Born Pampa, Tex., May 2, 1920—this, Bellarmine calculated, made him thirty-four years old. Drafted Apr. 11, 1942. Promoted sergeant Sept. 2, 1942, Fort Sill, Okla. Charged with stealing U.S. Army stores, Cefalù, Sicily, Aug. 8, 1943. Court-martial, Palermo, Sicily, Aug. 10. Convicted. Reduced to private; ordered to forfeit two-thirds pay; returned to combat. Appointed sergeant Salerno, Italy, Sept. 30, 1943. Charged with diverting U.S. Army stores to the civilian black market, Naples, Italy, Nov. 10, 1943. Court-martial. Reduced to private; returned to combat. Charged with murder of military policeman in street brawl Jan. 18, 1944, Naples. Escaped from stockade. Deserted. The U.S. Army had no record of him after that nor was there any State Department record of a passport issued in the name of LeRoy Billings.

"So he's using a false passport," said Sapodin.

"A sweet fellow," noted O'Hara.

"Maybe he's The Brain," suggested Sapodin.

Customs had recorded each of LeRoy's arrivals and departures from Villefranche harbor. LeRoy, Bellarmine remembered, was parked there for most of three months just before the break-in. Otherwise he appeared to spend most of his time elsewhere—at sea or in Tangier. It didn't seem possible that he could have planned and put into operation a job as big as this one in only three months, most of which must have been spent digging. He had no base in Nice, whereas Lambert did.

By the time they had finished their hors d'oeuvres they were well into their second bottle of wine and in an excellent mood. The case seemed in better shape than any of them had thought.

The waiters came, set up a serving table next to theirs, lit some burners, and began to prepare and serve the specialties they had ordered: a bouillabaisse for Sapodin, frogs' legs provençale for Bellarmine, steak and fried potatoes for O'Hara. The FBI agent refused to share their salad on the grounds that he could not be sure of the purity of the water in which it had been washed. This amused the other two. They were all cops together, and under the influence of all this new information plus the wine, they had begun to enjoy each other's company. At the end, Sapodin and Bellarmine shared a chocolate soufflé; O'Hara, slightly drunk, ordered flaming crepes Suzette.

It was well past midnight when the three policemen strolled across the Promenade and stood looking out at the sea, enjoying the fresh breeze on their faces. The sea was dark, except for the lights of the fishing boats, which seemed to have congregated. They occurred now not as individual stars but in clusters, like galaxies.

"In the morning they'll sell their catch out of barrels in the open marketplace," commented Sapodin.

"Don't you Frenchmen ever stop thinking about eating?" said O'Hara.

"They'll spread their nets to dry right about where we're standing," said Bellarmine, "and go to bed. The women will squat here in the sun mending the nets."

The chauffeur was asleep in the car. Sapodin banged his signet ring against the glass to wake him up. O'Hara was driven back to the consulate, the others to the *commissariat*, where, as they came in the door, Sapodin was handed a message asking him to phone customs. They went up to his office where he placed the call.

"They've got Roy LeRoy," he said when he had hung up. He took out his handkerchief and wiped his bald pate. "I don't know what kind of shape he's in. There's been some shooting."

# CHAPTER
## 24

LeRoy, approaching the French coast, was four days out from Tangier. He had crossed the Mediterranean slowly, running on only one engine at a time, his hold empty: to bring over a load of cigarettes this trip was not, he had judged, worth the extra risk. The other cargo paid too much more. He had with him a great deal of cash money from the sale of Lambert's gold—enough to finance tonight's transaction, and then some.

Crossing slowly, LeRoy was only being careful. He was conserving his engines and, since he would not be able to top up before starting back, conserving fuel. Below decks the PT boat carried ten thousand liters of high-octane gasoline. These tanks were still full. On deck in flat aluminum wing tanks out of war-surplus bombers lay most of ten thousand liters more. The wing tanks had been Lambert's idea, and he had ordered them installed just after he and LeRoy bought the boat. By doubling the boat's range, they had put the entire Mediterranean cigarette trade within their reach.

But the game was no longer cigarettes. To avoid being sighted, LeRoy had stayed well out from the various coastlines, and with only the Arab as crew he had had to lay up nights off dark islands to sleep. LeRoy did not trust the Arab. He trusted almost no one, which, he believed, was why he was still alive and still in business. The first night he had anchored off Tabarca, south of Alicante, and the second in the lee of Conejera, which lies off the southeast corner of Majorca. Rocks with nobody on them. He knew every such island in the western Mediterranean and had used most of them. Whether his hold was full of contraband or empty—as now—he did not like people to know where he was. It gave them an edge over him—if they knew where he was they could perhaps deduce where he was heading. He had stood each day at the helm, crossing the placid sea at about nine knots, watching his compass, watching the charts, and at dusk gliding into the shade of an empty island. He and the Arab ate out of cans. The weather stayed fine and he had slept on deck, being careful to keep the ignition key in his pocket and a revolver in the sleeping bag beside his leg. Each time he woke up, he listened carefully to the darkness all around him, to the lapping wavelets, to the movement of the boat as it rocked and creaked. He woke up several times each night, for he had learned to sleep lightly.

A four-day crossing. Contraband could be run with relative safety only once each month. A careful man approached the heavily patrolled southern coast of France only in the dark phase of the moon, and tonight's shipment of arms had been scheduled for precisely twenty-eight days after the last one. To Roy LeRoy, moonlight was for lovers and werewolves. It was bad for business. He was not a romantic man.

Four days at sea. Four days out of touch with the news. LeRoy had felt he could afford such a crossing, but now, as he pointed the PT boat between the two beacons, as he closed on the dark shore of France, he knew nothing of the arrests in Marseille, of the arrest of Lambert. He expected to be talking to Lambert ten minutes from now—the Arab was crouched up on the prow waiting to throw Lambert a line.

The beacons had fallen well behind him. He was inside the curve of the bay. Far to the left flickered the dim lights of Cavalaire. Ahead was the out-of-season hotel whose bulk he had begun to discern, and whose dock he could not see at all.

Cool black water bathed the bottom of the boat. Cool black air bathed LeRoy's face. With one engine barely turning over he glided toward shore. Now the beach appeared. It had an almost phosphorescent glow. The disused hotel loomed up, then the line of low trees behind it. He still could not see the dock—nor Lambert on the end of it waiting for him.

The sea was close to flat calm, the best kind of sea for him since it permitted maximum speed in case of an emergency. With the open horizon behind him he ought to be visible by now to Lambert, meaning that there ought to be a signal, the few quick blinks of a flashlight, as they had agreed.

However, no signal came. This did not alarm LeRoy. He was still some way out. He still had room to maneuver. But it made him cautious. He reduced speed still further, and lifted Zeiss night binoculars to his eyes. He had stripped them from the neck of a German corpse in Italy in 1943. He fanned them around, scrutinizing the beach itself, the dark hotel. The beach was empty. The hotel was still shuttered. He could see no one on the terrace. He could not see the dock at all. It was too low, too close to the sea. It was in the shadow of the hotel as well as the shadow of the night. Nor could he see any figure that might be standing on it. After a moment he raked the row of trees behind the beach and thought he saw a flash of light—perhaps a cigarette being lit. That would be the truck waiting hidden in the trees. Good.

Roy LeRoy was a predator, and had a predator's instincts. He was physically more attuned than most people to the emanations of the world around him—at least to those dangerous to him. He had stayed alive a long time, and now, three hundred yards from the hotel and closing, he felt the hairs begin to stand up on the back of his neck. He was certain he was close enough for Lambert to perceive the loom of the approaching boat, but still there was no signal. He throttled down still further, and listened intently. The breeze was coming off the land. It brought with it the scent of pine cones, but no noise at all. LeRoy realized that, under the circumstances, such intense silence was not normal. And where was Lambert? His head became filled with possible explanations. Lambert could be back in the trees with the truck, or taking a pee against the wall of the hotel. Nonetheless, something was wrong.

LeRoy turned to port, pushed the throttle gently forward, and glided slowly away from shore. He wanted a moment to think this over. The Arab, surprised, started back toward the wheelhouse. LeRoy was conscious of this, but only barely.

When the boat had gained another hundred meters of sea room LeRoy's glasses again raked the trees, the hotel, the terrace. Nothing. He sought but could not delineate the shadowy shelf that was the dock. He then made a mistake, a bad one. He shut down his engine completely, and listened hard.

The Arab was halfway to the wheelhouse. "Why we stop?" he called. But there was no time for an answer.

Five hundred meters astern and slightly to starboard a searchlight came on. It was not pointed directly at him. It was pointed toward shore. It bounced crazily—off trees, off the shuttered hotel, off the smooth surface of the sea. It veered and bounced across the water like a stone skipping. It was like a drunk who keeps falling but picks himself up and goes on. Within three seconds LeRoy's PT boat was caught full in its glare, and its movement stopped.

He had already reacted. He had hit the starter button on number one engine, the one he had just shut off. The engine did not immediately start. He heard it churn and grind. He hit number two. To be caught close inshore with all three engines shut down—he could not believe the extent of his bad luck. He could not believe he had been such a fool.

*"Halte, douane française,"*

It was some jerk bellowing into a megaphone. The voice bounded across the water at him. It was not a loudspeaker. French custom launches did not have loudspeakers.

Number two engine had started. LeRoy hit number three. It too started. He pushed the two throttles all the way forward and spun the wheel. At the same time he leaned on number one starter button. But the engine only continued to grind.

The megaphone voice again boomed across the water. *"Halte, douane française."*

On two engines the PT boat had leaped ahead. It left a wake curved like a sickle and shot out toward the open sea. On two engines the PT boat had a top speed of about twenty-two knots, about the same as a cutter. The third engine had still not caught. Flooded probably. LeRoy's only chance was to give it a few minutes rest. His only chance was to run. Run. Run. Run.

Up front, knocked down by the violence of the boat's surge, the Arab clung to a cleat. For the moment he could only hang on.

LeRoy had reacted faster than the cutter, had already gained sea room. Once he had gained a bit more, he would throw the PT boat into some saucered turns, shake off the searchlight beam, and disappear into the darkness. Even on two engines, he believed he could escape.

Then a second searchlight came on ahead of him. It too bounced like a skipping stone before locking onto him in its turn. There were two cutters, not one, and to get away he would have to pass between them, which was impossible. If they fired shots they would blow him out of the water.

He believed he had been sold out. Cursing, he blamed Lambert, though it was not Lambert's fault. Yesterday an informant had come forward in the north. He knew little more than the license number and approximate route of the truck heading south. That, and the cargo. The cargo was what excited the policemen. Roadblocks had gone up. At one of them near Aix at 4 P.M. this afternoon gendarmes had stopped the truck. Under interrogation the truckers had been faced with two choices. They could keep their mouths shut, thus assuming responsibility for running arms to North Africa; or they could claim ignorance of their cargo, in which case they would be obliged to reveal their intended destination. This decision had proved easy for them to make. They had not hesitated. It was a different pair of truckers from the first time. They did not have Lambert's name, nor LeRoy's. All they had was the name and address of the disused hotel on the beach at Cavalaire. They were to deliver their load there, they said. They had believed themselves to be transporting crockery for the hotel, they said.

Every customs launch east of Marseille had been ordered to sea at dusk. They had taken up position in the night off either end of the beach at Cavalaire, and also off many other likely beaches for twenty or more miles to either side—no *flic* wanted to risk missing whoever came to pay for and pick up an arms shipment as big as this one.

Now, bracketed by the two searchlights, and with his number one engine still refusing to fire, LeRoy began slaloming across the smooth skin of the sea, trying to escape the glare that soaked him in terror, bathed him in an icy sweat. He was exactly between the two cutters, only about a hundred meters ahead of them, and they were trying to converge on him without losing too much ground. His slaloming enabled them to do this, and it did not shake off those icy white lights.

He might have stopped and let them board him. He was clean. There was nothing of an incriminating nature aboard, and by approaching inshore he had committed no crime. But he was guilty of so many past crimes that he was unable to see his present situation clearly. He had feared this moment during more than six years of contraband running, and now that it was upon him he reacted as he had programmed himself to react so long before.

Both cutters were closer now, and again the voice came booming across the water.

"*Halte, douane française.*"

With two engines running out of three, with his hull slapping the water, LeRoy heard only the noise, not the words themselves. Again and again he punched at the button of number one, and at last, miracle of miracles, the engine fired. He gave it a moment, during which it sputtered and choked, then very gently, fearing to flood the cylinders again, he eased the throttle forward. The sputtering ceased.

The engine came on full, and the PT boat almost leaped out from under him.

He felt a glorious surge of pleasure, pride, power. "Let's see them catch me now," he screamed aloud.

He heard the bullets before he heard the noise of the guns. He heard them in the air over his head and he heard them whack into his hull. The cutter to starboard was firing at him. A glance that way revealed the muzzle blast behind the glare, spurts of fire in the night. Immediately he began to slalom again. He was gaining on them rapidly. In a moment he'd have more room, he'd be clear. He'd simply run away from them.

Now the cutter to port opened fire also. The two cutters were firing tracers at him, lacing his bow, making stitches along the waterline. He saw the Arab, caught in the cross fire in the open, trying to crawl to the safety of the wheelhouse, for the wheelhouse was armor-plated. Although the torpedo tubes and machine guns had been removed before the boat went on the war-surplus market, the armor plating around the wheelhouse had not been. LeRoy had left it in place for just such a night as this one. He heard bullets ping off this plating now. This was followed by a ragged hole that appeared in the Plexiglas in front of his face. "Jesus," he muttered.

Forward, the Arab suddenly jerked to his feet clutching himself. Then he fell down again. He lay writhing near the edge of the deck. The searchlights showed LeRoy his face. He could hear him screaming over all the other noise, or thought he could. Swerving to port, to starboard and back again, LeRoy realized the man was going to roll over the side. He saw it happen, and flinched. It couldn't be helped. He was trying to save himself and the boat, and had no time to worry about anyone else. He looked back and saw the brown face bobbing a moment in the brightly lit wake. The cutters didn't stop for him either. Then he was gone.

About then LeRoy realized he was standing ankle deep in water. Bullet holes along the waterline, he imagined. Sea water must have got into the wheelhouse. The boat would not sink from a few bullet holes in its plywood hide, not right away, and he was gaining on them. He was making it, the bullets were not striking the armor anymore though he still had not escaped the cursed searchlights.

Their white light showed him what he was standing in. It wasn't water. He could see holes in those aluminum deck tanks. One was ripped completely apart, and its contents had slopped down into the

252

wheelhouse. He looked down at his feet. He was standing in hundred-octane aviation fuel, which must also be leaking through the floorboards on to red-hot engines. At any second the PT boat would explode, and he threw the switch that shut down all three engines instantly. The sudden loss of way threw his head against the wheel and nearly knocked him out. It was as if the boat had struck a wall of water. As it wallowed heavily, LeRoy jumped up onto the deck and ran as far forward as he could get. He did not want to die, and was running away from the imminent explosion. He watched the searchlight beams shorten as the cutters came up to him out of the gloom.

# CHAPTER 25

It was well past midnight as Bellarmine entered the interrogation room.

Four detectives in shirt sleeves were questioning Lambert, whose mouth still contained a cigar. They looked as exhausted as he, and their voices were hoarse. Lambert, squinting around the projectors, gave Bellarmine a grin. "Glad to have you back," he said, but his face looked made out of stone, and the grin might have been cut into place with a chisel. There was no mirth left in it or him.

He had been awake more than forty-one hours. During the next seven—the legal limit—he would either crack or not crack. By now, in addition to crushing fatigue, in addition to feeling dirty, used, he would be very hungry also, which was why Bellarmine was carrying half a dozen chocolate éclairs.

He was freshly shaven and had just sprayed himself with eau de cologne. He had thrust a fresh handkerchief into his breast pocket. Now, having entered the cone of light, he approached Lambert, who lifted himself from the desk and stood defiantly upright. They were about the same height. They stood face-to-face two feet apart. The odor of stale cigar smoke confronted the aura of Bellarmine's perfume.

"You smell like a whore," said Lambert, and tried another grin. This one showed all his teeth. Abruptly Bellarmine reached into it

253

and plucked out the soggy cigar. He threw the butt across the room at a metal basket.

"Take the cigars away from him," he told his detectives.

Exhaustion such as Lambert's reduced a man to the most primitive of his emotions. Stripping him of his cigars was like ripping a pacifier from the mouth of a baby. He looked as if he was going to cry.

Bellarmine's intimidation, having begun now in earnest, would continue by every possible means. The éclairs came next. He undid the cake box and passed one around to each detective. The sixth éclair he placed on the edge of the table where, despite the projectors, he believed Lambert could see it. With that, all five detectives stepped into the light. Munching their éclairs, licking their fingers, they launched a new barrage of questions.

"Hungry, are you?"

"Where is the gold?"

"The documents."

"Admit it."

"Then you can sleep. And eat."

Bellarmine decided to send his detectives out of the room. "Have a nice dinner," he advised them. "Have a nap. Then come back. The prisoner will still be here."

Once alone with the prisoner, he picked up the final éclair, waved it, put it down intact. Lambert's eyes remained fixed on the pastry, and he swallowed hard.

"I spend the day with your wife."

Lambert's eyes sharpened. "She knows nothing about any of this."

Having noted this reaction, Bellarmine thought: In some way he is sensitive about his wife.

"She told me you speak French perfectly well."

This time Lambert's grin looked genuine. "*Et alors?*" he said. He looked doubly proud. Proud to have mastered his tormentors' language. Proud his charade had held them off so long.

But to Bellarmine this seemed an important breakthrough, his first. "Your wife—" He shook his head as if with regret. "Such a lovely woman." His voice hardened. "But she did not want to go to jail and so she told us all about you." And he began to enumerate the subjects Jacqueline had supposedly covered. "The trip to Switzerland, the play you did not write, the name Alexander Levy, the name Roy LeRoy Billings. Oh, yes, she helped us search your house also."

Lambert looked up sharply. "You searched my house? What did you find?"

"Everything," said Bellarmine with what he hoped was smug self-satisfaction.

Lambert, watching him closely, said nothing, and Bellarmine was obliged to continue. "We found your illegal carbine under the floor. We found the remnants of the papers you burned, and which our lab has been able to identify."

"That's not much," said Lambert, and to Bellarmine's surprise, he began a defense of his wife. This most loyal of women would never betray him, unless Bellarmine had tricked her. But the defense became impassioned, almost hysterical. She knew nothing about his activities, was totally innocent, he shouted.

To Bellarmine, all signs showed Lambert was coming to the end of his strength.

From his notebook he withdrew the blue telegraph form, and Lambert seemed to flinch to see it. "You've made many mistakes, and Alexander Levy, who happens to be dead, is one of them."

"My wife has nothing to do with this."

Walking over to the table, Bellarmine picked up the final éclair and began to eat it. Afterward, slowly, voluptuously, he licked his fingers. And watched the movement of Lambert's Adam's apple, the hard, dry swallow.

"You leave my wife alone."

Lambert was on his feet.

"My wife is guilty of no crime."

"Unfortunately," Bellarmine answered, "under French law she will go to jail." He paused. "Unless you wish to admit your part in this sad affair. My superiors ask only that I give them The Brain. They are not really interested in causing trouble for your wife. Are you The Brain, Monsieur Lambert?"

Lambert's head seemed to draw down into his shoulders. He was like a man cringing from a blow that had not yet been struck. His eyes were blinking rapidly.

You've got him, thought Bellarmine, who felt like a winning boxer. Two or three more punches and his opponent would go down. "Tell me about Roy LeRoy Billings," he purred.

The door opened and in came Sapodin with fresh detectives.

"Customs took Billings into custody tonight," purred Bellarmine.

After a pause, Lambert said: "He's a friend."

"Who else was with you in the vault?"

"You locked up the wrong guys," Lambert muttered. "Most of them I never saw before in my life."

Bellarmine nodded. "Which ones are wrong?" He added, "You can help them. One word from you and they're back on the street."

When Lambert did not answer, Bellarmine turned and walked out of the light. It was important to force Lambert to keep focusing and refocusing his gritty eyes.

"Whether or not you admit to being The Brain is almost immaterial to us," he said. "We have enough to indict you, and in France that means detention. You'll spend the next two years in jail even if, at the end, you are acquitted at trial. So why not admit you're the Brain? Think about it. You'll be famous. Headlines, all over the world." He added in a hard voice: "And it will save your wife from going to jail with you."

From out of the darkness came Sapodin's voice. "He's not The Brain. He's too small a personality to be The Brain. The Brain, believe me, is Roy LeRoy."

"Roy?" said Lambert.

Sapodin stepped forward into the light. "When I speak to the press tomorrow, that's what I'll tell them. Roy LeRoy."

"Roy?" Lambert tried to laugh, but made only a series of choked sobs. "A joke. Tell me it's a joke. The Brain conceived a plan of genius." He was almost pleading, and so groggy he scarcely knew what he was saying. "Don't you see?"

"Why don't you tell me how you did it?" said Bellarmine gently. If Lambert confessed, the court would treat him lightly, he added. He was a war hero and had helped liberate France. He had even performed a public service, for as a result of his crime the police had been able to dismantle the Faletta clan in Marseille. The Brain should really take credit for all that. The true Brain should get the headlines, not a false one. Admit it, Bellarmine coaxed him, and save your wife from prison in the bargain. She doesn't deserve jail. Save her, and save yourself. Admit you are The Brain.

Lambert seemed clearly about to topple. He was wetting and rewetting his lips. One more punch should do it, Bellarmine thought. Just a push. Bellarmine was supremely confident and Sapodin, he saw, watched him almost with awe. This is how an interrogation is supposed to be conducted, he told himself, and his voice oozed kindness.

"You don't want your wife to go to jail."

"No."

"You can save her."

There came a knock on the door, and the mood was broken. A

256

detective stuck his head in and said in formal French: "One demands the Commissaire Bellarmine."

This was not the moment to break off the interrogation. "Later," said Bellarmine.

"With all urgence," insisted the detective.

What could it be? thought Bellarmine. In a case like this it could be anything, and he glanced at Sapodin, who nodded. After hesitating briefly, Bellarmine left the room. Behind him he heard the questioning resumed.

"Is Roy the one who spread shit all over everything?" It was Sapodin's voice and the tone was accusatory. Wrong tone, wrong question. It made Bellarmine wince.

"Shit on you, pal," replied Lambert's voice through the door. A detective guffawed.

In the hall waited the uniformed *flic* who had been on guard at Jacqueline's hotel. His prisoner had escaped, he blurted. What should he do? If Sapodin found out it would mean his job.

It could mean Bellarmine's job too, and he took the *flic*, a man of about fifty-five, into an office.

"Were you asleep?"

"Absolutely not, monsieur." The *flic* attempted to appear indignant. He had been in the toilet at the end of the hall, he said. A man had to relieve himself after all. A man could not be blamed. Obviously lying, he was near tears. He saw himself before the council of discipline, the police of the police, men who were merciless, men who hated *flics*—hated what they themselves were. He saw his job gone, pension gone.

"You were asleep," said Bellarmine curtly.

Admitting it, the *flic* began to blubber. "Give me a break, monsieur—please, I beg you."

"Go home," Bellarmine ordered. "I'll see if I can save you." The blubbering turned to sounds of gratitude, and the man wrung Bellarmine's hand. But Bellarmine cut him off—shook him off. "Out. Fast. Breathe a word to anyone and you're finished."

Standing in the corridor he heard the *flic* clomp down the stairs and out of the building, and he brooded about Jacqueline. She would go to jail now for sure if anyone found out. Crazy woman. He would not be able to save her. No one would. Why had she done this? What possible reason? He knew the answer Sapodin would come to—the answer anyone would come to—that she was herself involved in the crime and had gone underground. Troubled, he opened the door to the interrogation room.

In his absence Sapodin's line of questioning had evidently not changed.

"Did you spread the shit yourself?"

"That's quite a toilet fixation you got, pal. Did you ever think about seeing a shrink?"

It made Sapodin angry. "Who killed the derelict?"

This question horrified Bellarmine. It no doubt horrified Lambert too. Although he might have been ready to confess to the bank, he was not likely to admit to murder too.

"What derelict?"

"The drowned derelict."

"Oh, *that* derelict." Lambert, grinning again, seemed to have regained all his strength, and with it the will to outlast them. "The Brain might know—when you catch him."

The interrogation went downhill from there, until finally Sapodin stalked out of the room. Left alone, Bellarmine attempted to re-establish the old mood, but he failed. Forget the derelict, he said. The derelict was in no way connected to Lambert or to the break-in. Lambert should be thinking about saving his wife from jail, about the world headlines that were his if he wanted them. He should be thinking about eating, about sleeping. His ordeal would all be over in five minutes if only he would admit he was The Brain.

But Lambert's grin was back in place. He had stopped blinking, stopped wetting his lips. "I can outlast you," he growled. "I can outlast the whole pack of you."

Toward dawn Bellarmine brought in a detective who sat at the table in front of an upright typewriter. He was there to pound out the *procès-verbal* that would be Lambert's confession. This confession was dictated by Bellarmine, and to give it credibility he included certain details not printed in the papers, such as the make and type of the acetylene tanks. Lambert grinned broadly all the time his "confession" was being written.

"Sign that."

Sapodin had come back into the room. "Have Shithead there sign it," suggested Lambert.

Sapodin began shouting at him. "You're The Brain. Admit it."

"I admit nothing," said Lambert and he never did. He had beaten them.

258

At 8 A.M. they took him over to the Palace of Justice where he was indicted by Juge d'Instruction Fayot and remanded to the men's house of arrest. The charges were qualified theft in connection with the Banque de Nice and illegal detention of arms. The second charge, though in some respects a technicality, would stand up a good long time, even if the first did not.

Sapodin wanted to indict Jacqueline on the same charges and Fayot was willing, but Bellarmine succeeded in arguing them out of it. Not only was he convinced of her innocence, he said, but he believed she could be of great help to the continuing investigation. If they put her in jail she would be of no help at all.

Fayot shrugged: "Release her, then."

Only Bellarmine knew she had already released herself.

The last of these discussions took place over café au lait and hot croissants in the café across the street.

Juge Fayot then departed. Sapodin and Bellarmine lingered over their empty cups, the empty croissant basket while Sapodin tried out his replies to questions he would be asked at his impending news conference. "Our position is that Lambert is The Brain, and we've got him," he told Bellarmine.

"What's our evidence against him?"

"We have important evidence against him," responded Sapodin. He nodded his head sagely. "I won't give them many details."

"Will you mention LeRoy?"

"We'd best hold him in reserve."

"What about the loot?"

"We expect to put our hands on that momentarily."

"And the documents?"

"Our position is that Lambert burned them all. They're gone."

"Why did he steal them in the first place?"

"Blackmail. Obviously there was nothing juicy in them."

"Are more arrests imminent?"

"More arrests are imminent." Sapodin both looked and sounded confident. "After that," he said, "I'll congratulate the various detectives. You too, of course."

"Would you like me to stay for the press conference?"

"That won't be necessary," said Sapodin stiffly.

Bellarmine could see the headlines already: "Sapodin Breaks Heist of Century." But he was too tired to care.

"A good night's work, Bellarmine. I congratulate you."

259

"It was your leadership, *patron*."

Sapodin went back to the *commissariat* and the waiting mob of reporters, while Bellarmine walked home alone along streets that were still in shadow. The sunlight had dropped down from the roofs of the buildings opposite. On the walls it brought out all the faded pastel colors, the pinks, the pale yellows and greens. It seemed to bring out all the food odors too, the odors of France, for the doors to the shops were open. He passed bakeries, wineshops, dairy stores. He sniffed aromas that were so normal to him he scarcely noticed them.

He was brooding. The case troubled him. It was still not over. He felt no elation, only fatigue and emptiness.

His feet led him, despite himself, toward Jacqueline Lambert's perfumery. To his surprise he saw that her door was open also. As he came up she was sweeping out her shop. She stopped stock-still when she saw him. For a moment neither spoke. She stared at him with defiance.

"I ought to lock you up."

"Do it then." She stood with a truculent expression on her face, arms folded, embracing the broom.

"Your husband has been indicted."

Her eyes closed as if involuntarily. She opened them again. "When can I see him?"

"Tomorrow probably."

She looked so miserable that he was moved to add: "Look, I'm sorry."

But she shook her head. "It's not your fault."

"Why did you run off last night?"

"Because I wasn't guilty of anything. And I didn't want to stay a prisoner. Don't you see?"

"No, I don't see. You risked all sorts of terrible things for yourself, not to mention me."

She gazed down at the pavement. "You've never been a prisoner. You don't know what it's like."

She looked lovely to him this morning. He felt an almost overpowering response to her. He wanted to embrace her. But he was also furious with her. His emotions were so strong and so conflicting that they baffled him. No woman had ever made him feel this way before, and he did not know what to do.

He put his hand out. "Will you shake hands with me?" he said.

It sounded idiotic to him even as he said it, but his hand was out there and she was staring down at it.

For a moment nothing happened, but then her eyes rose, and a half smile came onto her face. He felt her smaller hand in his. They focused half smiles on each other. The handshake signified either a beginning or an ending, Bellarmine did not know which. He let go of her, went up to his flat and fell asleep.

# PART IV

## CHAPTER 26

Marcel Faletta had problems, and knew it. He sat now in Marseille at a table at the rear of the Café de l'Amitié on the Rue de Récollettes. He owned or controlled approximately seventy-five bars and nightclubs between Marseille and Nice, but this one, being the first of them, was still the only one he thought of as "his" bar. It was where he spent most of each day. The afternoon newspaper lay spread open on the table. He and two of his brothers were looking at it. For Faletta—for his brothers too—the news it carried, though replete with errors and imbecilities of every kind, could not have been worse. "The Brain Indicted." "Faletta Clan Dismantled." "Sixteen Gangsters Still Held."

Faletta inhabited a volatile world. Struggles for power and for turf were constant, and one could not apply to the courts to enforce one's claims. Headlines like this invited his rivals to move against him, and he would have to fight back. The police and the journalists had brought a gang war down upon Marseille. This was going to be costly, both in money and in lives, and Faletta, as he read and reread, could not be sure his clan would survive it, or that he personally would survive it. He was a man who, like the pope, ruled through faith. His position was invulnerable only as long as people believed. But, as today's papers pointed out, he had entrusted the so-called Heist of the Century to an outsider, not only a non-Corsican but non-French, who had bungled it, which seemed to prove failing powers of judgment on Faletta's part. And he was poorer by sixteen men. He was also sixty-one years old.

It was at this juncture that news of Henry the Torch was brought to him by the same Besse who had driven Henry and a certain late bicycle mechanic up to the quarry in the hills. It was both good news and bad. Faletta received it with no show of emotion. The Torch was holed up in the room of the prostitute known as The Duchess, meaning that for as long as he was there she could not work. She was demanding immediate action from Faletta. So was Henry, who was afraid that in her annoyance, inadvertently or not, she would give him away. The Torch had no money and was asking to be smuggled out of the country. North Africa? South America? He didn't care. He was asking Faletta for help.

Faletta nodded curtly. It took Besse a moment to realize he had been dismissed. He went up to the bar and ordered a glass of red wine. Behind him, Faletta turned away from his brothers also. Needing time to think, he went into his office and closed the door. What to do with The Torch was a problem, but his reappearance now was also comforting. To know that The Torch was there, that Faletta might use him at any time, would cause his rivals to take a step backward. The Torch was the most redoubtable killer in Marseille and an absolutely reliable workman and everyone knew it, and to have him on hand made Faletta feel almost safe.

Faletta had come to Marseille at thirteen from Calenzana, a village high up in the steep, pine-shrouded mountains of northwest Corsica. All around Calenzana the terraces dropped downhill like staircases built for giants. They supported olive groves, orchards, vineyards. Within these small concentric circles, man over the centuries had mastered nature, but elsewhere the maquis reigned. The maquis undergrowth was as tangled as hair. It was composed of juniper, buckthorn, heath, myrtle, rosemary, lavender, aromatic plants that perfumed the mountain air. Below the village tumbled a mountain torrent that contained trout, and above it rose a beech and chestnut forest. Higher still were stony alpine pastures in which sheep grazed, and small lakes cradled in stony basins, and peaks that were white with snow from November to May. Faletta's boyhood was a time when few visitors came to Corsica. The later generations of tourists would discover and be thrilled by villages like Calenzana. They would fish for the trout, hunt the wild boar and migrating game birds, tramp through the forests, breath the invigorating air. They would go back to their cities and rave about Corsica's unspoiled beauty.

But for Faletta, who was the son of a woodcutter and maker of charcoal, his own village—all of Corsica—was suffocating. At ten he was already at work tending sheep on the high plateaus and the biggest city he had ever seen was Calvi, population three thousand, capital of the province. But from Calvi the ship ferries left for Nice and Marseille—to Corsicans these places were known as "The Continent" and many Corsicans before him had gone there to seek their fortunes. Faletta himself arrived in Marseille on a summer day in 1906 with all his belongings in a paper parcel under his arm and less than twenty-five francs in his pocket. He found work in a bar run by a countryman from Calenzana, and he watched and he learned. In his spare time he went to a gym and lifted weights. He stood only five feet eight inches tall, but by the time he was twenty he weighed 210 pounds, none of it fat, and he owned a piece of the sidewalk on the Rue de Récollettes and had two girls working it for him. The terrain was not ceded to him, he simply took it, and after that defended it, first with his fists, then with guns.

World War I interrupted Faletta's rise. In 1916 he took a machine-gun bullet through the ankle—he would limp ever after—and was invalided out. He was among the first of the young toughs to return to Marseille. He put together a small gang. There were more robberies. With his profits he acquired additional girls, additional meters of sidewalk, and then his first bar. By the mid 1920s he had many bars, and enough money to begin bringing over his brothers one by one. He took over protection and shylocking rackets, and increased his investment in prostitution. He came to control the traffic in girls between Marseille and North Africa, and between Marseille and South America. He had a legitimate empire and a criminal one, but the two were mixed together, in fact inseparable. Both had to be defended with guns. This meant the establishment of a small army.

Faletta became known to the police and to France in general as one of the caids of the Milieu. The word "caid" is Arabic in origin, and can best be translated as chieftain. There were more than two dozen Milieu clans in Marseille at this time, but only the most

265

prominent among their leaders were known as caids. Caids were men who had acquired political power in addition to power over the streets, and Faletta's dated from the election of 1935.

Marseille was a difficult, sometimes impossible, city to govern. It had about as many political parties as Milieu clans, making it also a difficult city in which to get elected. Candidates actively sought the support of certain caids, because caids could supply muscle, and a candidate with muscle could control any political rally, either break it up or start it cheering. The result during the mayoral elections that year was a kind of civil war in the streets. The rival clans began shooting at slight provocations, or none, and the corpses of the pimps, the shylocks, and the so-called gun bearers began to pile up in the dark alleys near the Gare St. Charles and in the narrow streets adjacent to the Opéra. Faletta had backed the Socialist candidate, who was elected. During the next two years, a later investigation showed, Faletta had managed to place large numbers of his friends and compatriots in municipal jobs, almost a hundred of whom turned out to be not only unqualified but ex-convicts.

World War II split the Marseille Milieu cleanly in two. Most of the other caids decided to collaborate with the enemy. Faletta opted for a posture of resistance. However, he was prudent about it. His various bars and nightclubs were open to all.

After the American invasion of southern France, the Germans abandoned Marseille, and the city went through a period of nearly total anarchy. The Communist Party was almost the only organized group left, and it governed, more or less, for the next two and half years. Prior to the municipal elections of 1947, it was judged necessary by Paris, and by the American CIA, to destabilize the city as much as possible—if the Communists could be proved incapable of governing, it might cost them the election—and for this Faletta's help was needed. Marseille became a city of constant strikes instigated by Faletta, and of rioting in the streets, with the result that the Communist's lost. Next Faletta organized "spontaneous" demonstrations against the unions. Bands of armed hoodlums "liberated" certain industries from the strikers, particularly the docks, where the first shipment of Marshall Plan aid to France was waiting to be unloaded.

About a year later an official form was placed in his judicial dossier: subject totally inactive; seems to present no danger to public order.

Faletta had built a sumptuous villa on the Corniche d'Or overlooking the Mediterranean east of the city. He called it the Villa Calenzana, and all the ceilings were decorated with the Corsican coat of arms. He went back to Calenzana briefly to have himself elected mayor of the village, and to preside over a party that lasted seven days. He built another luxurious villa there, to which he promised he and his wife would one day retire.

It was in Corsica that Faletta first saw Lambert. He was at Calenzana on vacation, and one morning one of the gun bearers on duty at the gate came up to the villa to tell him a "foreigner" was there and had asked to see him.

"Foreigner?" inquired Faletta sharply. To Corsicans like the gun bearer, foreigner meant anyone, including Frenchmen, who was not a Corsican. "Foreigner from where?" But the gun bearer didn't know.

It was noon. Faletta was dressed to go into Calenzana where he would sit in the café and hold court. This was his habit every day when in residence in Corsica. The villagers would troop in and pay homage and some would ask for favors.

Lambert was brought up to the villa and into the living room through the French doors. There was a guard to either side of him, and he glanced around at the garish, expensive appointments.

"Did you search him?" said Faletta.

The guards had not.

Faletta gave an annoyed jerk of his chin. "Search him."

Lambert grinning, his eyes never leaving Faletta's, stood docilely while they patted him down.

"He's not carrying, *patron*."

With another jerk of the chin, Faletta dismissed the two men. "You've got five minutes," he told Lambert. "What do you want?"

But he was already impressed with this man who was American or English and who might easily have spoken to him in the village later, or in his café or his nightclub back in Marseille, but who instead had sought him out here where he lived.

He listened attentively as his visitor outlined his plan for looting the Banque de Nice. Lambert had already reconnoitered the sewers and the inside of the vault itself. He presented specifications that proved the job feasible. He knew how many safes and lockboxes had to be cut open. He had investigated the possibility of burglar alarms— there were none inside the vault.

Faletta had not invited him to sit down and did not intend to do so. "Why come to me?"

Because he needed equipment and expertise he could not procure himself, especially acetylene torches and men to run them. He offered half the proceeds.

"Who are you?" Faletta interrupted curtly. He was amazed at how coolly this foreigner could discuss committing a major crime in France.

"You tried to buy me out a year or so ago. I refused to sell."

"You're the cigarette runner." These were unpleasant memories on both sides. Faletta had sent emissaries to Tangier. He had not negotiated with Lambert personally. The emissaries had got beaten up by Lambert's crew. In retaliation some of Faletta's men had burned one of Lambert's boats.

"What's your name?"

"Call me The Brain."

"Do you think I can't find out?"

"Find out then. But don't expect me to tell you."

No one talked back to Faletta. He found that he was amused and even pleased by Lambert's impertinence, though of course he did not show this. He was pleased by the man's imagination too, because in Milieu circles imagination was rare.

"How'd you find me here?"

"You think you're the only one who's ever been to Corsica?" Lambert snorted. "My unit was here five months in 1944 training for the invasion of southern France."

"You know Corsica?"

"We lived in tents behind the beach at Calvi. The girls practically wore veils. They wouldn't have anything to do with us." He gave an engaging grin. "I've hitchhiked all over this island. Every time I got a day off I went exploring. When did you build this villa? The last time I was in Calenzana there was only a stone barn on this spot."

Faletta was extremely impressed.

By the time they met again a week later in the Café de l'Amitié in Marseille, Faletta had solicited the advice of his brothers and of his sister Restitude, and had decided to go along with Lambert's scheme, and he told him so: he would assign men to the project. Of course by then he knew Lambert's name.

His principal reason was perhaps not what Lambert supposed. He had a great many men at his orders, and these had to be kept busy. To work on something of the size of the Banque de Nice was good for their morale. If it succeeded it would be something they could be proud of. If it failed, no harm done. Or so it seemed.

Afterward he had been as stupefied as the rest of the world at the grandeur of Lambert's success, his own success. In the days following the coup, rival caids had filed through his bar, congratulating him, shaking his hand, giving him the accolade on both cheeks.

Now, however, his success had exploded in his face. His empire was suddenly vulnerable to take-overs. He himself had become vulnerable to assassination—more so than at any time since before the war. It was a feeling he did not like.

His immediate problem was to find a safe house in which to stash Henry the Torch. He would allow the news to circulate that The Torch was back, and this would worry everybody. It was the best protection he could have.

Where to put him?

Faletta, like most Frenchmen of peasant origin, believed in owning land, the more the better. In an unstable world it was all a man could truly count on. Therefore over the years he had invested heavily in parcels of land, principally dilapidated or abandoned farms. He owned ten or a dozen—he wasn't sure exactly how many. One was near Brignoles, about sixty kilometers northeast of Marseille, not far off the road to Nice. On it he grazed sheep, and he had installed there an aged uncle from Calenzana to look after them.

An old stone farmhouse. No electricity or telephone, and water came from a well. The farm was at the end of a dirt road more than two kilometers long. No one ever went in there, why should they? On this farm The Torch would be safe until Faletta needed him. He would not like it, but he would sit there and wait. He would do what he was told.

Faletta's other problem was Lambert—a problem, he realized, of his own making. In sponsoring the assault on the Banque de Nice by a man who was not a Corsican, who was not even French, he had committed the worst type of mistake in judgment—he had committed an act of impropriety. He had not seen this until the crime had failed. He had done something improper. In moving against him now, the other clans moved with the approval of tradition.

Faletta was not an idiot. Thoughts of Lambert enraged him. He took his continued existence almost as a personal insult. It was as if Lambert had burglarized his house, or laid hands on his wife. But his problem was not one of revenge. It was not sufficient simply to have Lambert killed, which would have been easy enough, even in jail. His problem was the previous impropriety. He had somehow to reverse it, and this might prove extremely difficult to do. He was trying to think it out.

# CHAPTER
## 27

Bellarmine was in the grip of two obsessions. One was Lambert, the other Lambert's wife. Hoping to strengthen the case against the presumed Brain, he had ten detectives probing his past life, and another ten reinterviewing witnesses.

But it was Bellarmine's sexual obsession that dominated him. He was like an adolescent boy. Jacqueline Lambert was part of his every waking thought, but he could not tell if it was only a night with her he wanted or much, much more.

He had warned all his detectives away from her. They were not to question her he told them during a briefing at the *commissariat*. She was his personal property. As he said this he saw the leers start, and so gave a leer of his own, adding the boast that he would "work her like a strip mine." The line earned him an easy laugh, but if it ever got back to her, it would cut off their relationship instantly, like the blade of a guillotine.

Bellarmine had one advantage over most courting males—he always knew where the object of his desire could be found. She had a shop to run. She could not, so to speak, cross the street to avoid him. Which was perhaps what she wished to do—he could not tell. Each time he came in, she seemed to flinch. After that she concentrated her attention on whichever sale she was trying to make. She extolled perfume to someone, though usually in a voice that seemed to have gone off slightly. His appearance seemed to have moved her in some way. But perhaps she was only afraid of him.

Business, she told him one afternoon, had never been better. "Everybody wants to come in and have a look at the scarlet woman, I believe." She gave a brittle smile. Immediately afterward she turned her back on him, replacing unsold boxes on the shelves behind her, while he tried to smile in a friendly way, a smile she did not see.

She turned abruptly and faced him. "I can use the extra money to pay my husband's lawyer."

Adolescent passion was no match for this. Advantage over a woman, he reflected, was usually momentary and almost always they made you pay heavily for it.

He offered to take her to dinner. He had a car, he said.

"A police car? That's nice."

But her gaze remained locked in his. In some way she was reaching out to him, as if asking his understanding, his help. Perhaps she was asking him to find some diplomatic device by which she could accept his invitation. Or perhaps he was only imagining all this. The signals men and women sent out to each other were often more subtle than those employed by governments. He had never known how to read them very well, and so perhaps now was mistaken.

"It's parked right out front."

She refused to climb into a police car where her neighbors might see. And she wished he wouldn't come into the shop either, she said.

He had the impression that he had played a scene like this with her before. They were starting over again, but they were different people now and playing by new rules.

He offered to wait for her in front of the Ruhl Hotel. It was a way of promising anonymity. She could climb in unobserved by anyone she knew. The Ruhl was less than two blocks away, but belonged to a different orbit. It was like a bauble on a shirtfront. A flamboyant stickpin in a tie. A tourist hotel that in no way touched the real life of the city.

Urgency, more than he would have liked, crept into his voice. "Surely you don't want to dine alone tonight," he said.

Her eyes had dropped to her glass countertop. After what seemed to him an extremely long wait, she said:

"In front of the Ruhl."

They drove east along the sea, crossed behind the port of Nice, climbed the hill and came out on the lower Corniche on its ledge on the cliff that overhung the sea. As they rounded the headland, the great horseshoe-shaped Rade de Villefranche came into view. On its flat black surface, illuminated by strings of bulbs like outdoor Christmas trees, rode four American warships. The village of Villefranche, as they moved through it, was full of American sailors. They stood at bus stops, on corners. They sat on the terraces of the cafés. They negotiated with the prostitutes who patrolled the top of the dark streets that led down to the port.

Then Villefranche was behind them, and the road was dark again,

271

and he turned out on to the Cap Ferrat. The long, ragged cape had a narrow neck, then widened. Out here were the opulent villas of the very rich, most surrounded by high stone walls, but also the untidy farms of peasants—men and women who had worked this arid stony land since before the rich ever came, and who worked it still. The village of St. Jean, when they came to it, amounted to a few small shops and several restaurants and hotels. Its marina was filled with poor fishing boats moored among magnificent yachts. The Voile d'Or Hotel stood on the bluff above this port, and there the policeman and the shop owner dined by candlelight in the garden. They faced back toward the high, steep coastline. They could see the tiny lights of cars moving along the Corniche roads. There was moonlight on the water close by, and to the east was Italy.

The hotel was owned by an expatriate English couple. There was a guest book on a pedestal just inside the front door. Bellarmine and Jacqueline, had they perused it, would have noted the names of dozens of celebrated people who had stopped here. Nearly all the names were foreign. Those written in faded ink were predominantly English. The newer names were often American. The Riviera was the most famous playground in the world, and the most expensive, too expensive for the local French, whose culture could not compete with what was only a subculture, but one which, having been laid on top of their own, had submerged it, had drowned it under the incredible weight of its jewels and its yachts, its sophistication and its chic.

Some of this Bellarmine was aware of as they dined, but he did not speak of it. For long periods he did not speak at all, and neither did Jacqueline. Both were too nervous to make real conversation, for the one subject they had in common stood between them. His prisoner, her husband. Perhaps each was interested in the other only as a source of information.

Jacqueline was desperately in need of a friend—she had thought out her relationship to this man no further than that—especially one who knew the workings of the legal bureaucracies, as she did not. But to admit to him even this much might give the appearance that she was using him. It might scare him away.

As for Bellarmine, there were details about Lambert's existence—and about Jacqueline's—that he wished to know. With a few words, especially indiscreet words, she could save his detectives weeks of work. But although Bellarmine the detective might have asked her direct questions, Bellarmine the aspiring lover could not appear to be interested in the answers.

He was a man torn between duty and desire. He told himself tonight he was pursuing both ends simultaneously, but this was not the case. He told himself he was working her slowly, carefully, aiming her to the bed and to the witness box at the same time. But he wasn't. He studied her profile by candlelight, and otherwise made no progress in any direction at all.

These thoughts came to him—clearly and with a certain degree of pain—only at the end of their meal, as they watched their desserts being prepared: crepes Suzette—what could be more fitting than to dine outdoors at night in a garden overlooking the Mediterranean while something elaborate went up in smoke?

"Some lawyers came by my shop during the day," Jacqueline commented. "They all wanted to represent my husband."

Bellarmine said: "It's a case any lawyer would like to have."

"They left their cards." She had torn them all up, she said, and had contacted a lawyer recommended by the woman who had the leather goods shop next door.

"It's like being a divorced woman." She gave a wry laugh. "Men come flocking from all over, or so I'm told. With me it's lawyers."

Bellarmine only watched her, and tried to disguise the yearning he was afraid must show in his eyes. Desire like this was not normal, not for a man of his age. He did not understand it, could not have begun to explain it to anyone, much less to himself.

"You're not divorced," he said, a remark that seemed to him so stupid that it silenced him at once. Divorce was still another subject they could not discuss.

There was no way of knowing what another person felt, never had been. Ninety-nine percent of one's thoughts, loves, hates, fears could not be communicated. Every man—or woman—in the world was locked inside himself—herself—from day of birth to day of death. In a sense no true communication between man and woman was possible except by touch.

Jacqueline drew a line on the tablecloth with the edge of her spoon. "No, I'm not divorced."

After dinner he drove her back around the Rade. They again glanced down on the garish floating warships. When he drew to a stop in front of her dark shop, she shook hands with him and started to get out of the car.

He knew he ought to let her go; furthermore, she should not be approached again for several days, and then only casually. These were the tactics dictated by duty. The skilled policeman should bow and withdraw, because the alternative was to risk compromising the investigation—the subject would be alerted, possibly even alarmed. But to wait several days before seeing this woman again was an idea he could not bear.

"Tomorrow is Sunday," he said. "We could—" He stopped, not knowing how to phrase what he wanted to say.

There was a long silence. Then Jacqueline said: "This Sunday I have to take the bus up to Vence to see my mother."

It was less than an outright rejection, though less than acceptance also.

"I could drive you up there."

"I'll have to spend a couple of hours with my mother," she cautioned.

"I have friends I can call on. I can wait to bring you down again." The friends were an invention, and he was a man who hated to wait. But for her he wanted to do it.

"Why are you doing this?" she asked bluntly.

She had him off balance at all times, and he could not imagine what answer to give.

"It's Sunday for me too," he said. "I don't want to spend it alone. Is that so wrong?"

"Come in the afternoon," she said. "I have to see the lawyer in the morning."

# CHAPTER
## 28

Again the airliner taxied to a stop at Nice–Côte d'Azur airport. Again Congressman Saul Avery, who must have been waiting impatiently at the door, bounded down the stairs. Again Charlie O'Hara, parked a short distance from the nosewheel, waited in one of the consulate's Cadillacs.

The scenes in one's life keep repeating themselves, O'Hara thought.

"Let me take those bags for you, Congressman," he said, coming around the car.

Avery handed them over. "Why do I keep running into you down here, Charlie? What phony excuse are you going to give me this time?"

"Excuse me, Congressman?" said O'Hara, doing his best to look bewildered.

Both got in the car. The doors slammed. Avery had a right to be suspicious, but O'Hara was ready for him. The FBI agent was fifty-two years old. There were a great many subjects about which he was ignorant. But he had spent his entire professional lifetime in the study of certain other subjects, particularly what he believed to be the two principal forces directing human events: greed and fear. These were the wind and sea on which floated the boat of mankind. The successful man—the successful cop in any case—was the one able to gauge their power most accurately most of the time. O'Hara believed himself such a man. Greed and fear cast a reflection on a man's face like a mirror held under his chin, and he believed he saw this reflection on Avery's face now.

"Actually," said O'Hara, "I happened to be here on something else and got word you were coming."

Avery gave a grunt of disbelief and looked out of the window.

On the seat between them, as the car moved beside the sea toward the city, lay a manila envelope. O'Hara pushed it across. "I've been able to find out a few things for you," he said. "It's all in there." Information was the most powerful force of all, more powerful than wind or sea, and a skilled agent gave up as little of it as possible at all times. This was almost the first thing O'Hara—every agent—had been taught at the FBI Academy.

Avery, as he reached into the envelope and pulled out papers, was almost purring. "Why thank you, Charlie." The envelope contained only press clippings from French newspapers, plus a copy of the Army's background report on Lambert. Enough, O'Hara hoped, to calm Avery's suspicions and to start him talking.

When he had finished reading, Avery removed his glasses, closed the lid of his glasses case on them, and for a time sat in silence. "Not very much in there, Charlie," he said at last.

He is desperate, O'Hara thought.

Avery was not desperate, merely tired and irritable. O'Hara had misread him.

"I'm having trouble getting information out of the French," said O'Hara apologetically. What is he guilty of? he asked himself. What's he done? "I'm beginning to win them over, though." Avery possesses, is possessed by, guilty secrets, O'Hara reasoned. He owns them and they own him. He fears that Lambert may be in possession of these secrets, whatever they are. That is why he is here.

O'Hara kept his voice casual. "What's your interest in all this, Congressman?" he inquired pleasantly.

"I had some important papers in my lockbox, Charlie."

Avery's face was averted. He stared out at the sea. It was a windy day. There were many whitecaps. He's like a block of ice with stress lines in it, O'Hara thought. Tap him in the right place and he'll shatter.

Avery himself felt no such stress. He wanted a meal and a few hours sleep.

"I'd sure like to get them back. That's why I'm here, Charlie." He turned to face O'Hara. "I don't suppose any papers have turned up yet?"

"Not yet, Congressman."

As they passed inside the city limits of Nice, the sea was being blown up onto the stony beaches. A permanent mist hung above the deck chairs on the Promenade. No one was sitting in them today, O'Hara noted. "The police say he burned them all," he said. "They found fragments in his fireplace."

"So I read, Charlie. What else do they say? You got any friends over there? What can you find out for me?"

O'Hara at the wheel watched Avery carefully. He may hand me this whole case, he thought. "The chances are," he replied, "that the papers you're interested in got burned."

"Not these papers, Charlie," said Avery firmly. "I sense that these didn't get burned."

"What kind of papers were they?"

Avery eyed him sharply. "Business papers, Charlie."

O'Hara pulled up in front of the Ruhl Hotel. The doormen, dressed like pashas, lifted Avery's bags out of the trunk, and O'Hara slammed the lid down.

"I landed in southern France on D-day plus two, did you know that, Charlie?" Avery said. "The rank was brigadier general." Once again he exuded power and O'Hara was surprised.

"I knew you had been a general, of course," he said.

"I took Nice on the fifteenth day. Set up my headquarters here in the Ruhl." He pointed upward. "Right up there on the sixth floor, same suite." The soft Louisiana accent got suddenly harsh. "I'm used

276

to giving orders, Charlie, and I'm giving you some now. You find out what the police know, and you come and tell me, okay?"

"Right, Congressman, or should I call you General?"

"Just get me that information."

"I'll help in any way I can, Congressman."

Two grooms had come out of the hotel to take Avery's bags. The two pashas stood nearby, fake turbans in hand, waiting for their tips.

"I'm not a rich man, Charlie," Avery said, and his manner seemed confident and assured. There was no hint that he was about to offer O'Hara a bribe. "My congressional salary is seventeen thousand five hundred dollars a year, as you know. I make a few thousand above that with my speaking engagements." He paused once more. "I want those papers back, Charlie. You have friends on the force, you talk to them. You want to hire somebody to help, I could pay a few hundred for that. I could pay, maybe, five hundred for that."

So it wasn't really a bribe. You could take it either way. Smart. He wrung O'Hara's hand and stepped into the hotel.

O'Hara, thinking about Avery's lost documents, slid into his seat and started the engine. What could they be? O'Hara was sick of France and the French, and he had begun to see this case as one that would catapult him back to Washington and into the highest echelons of the Bureau. His target was not Lambert—what did he care about Lambert? It was Congressman Avery. When this was over he would either nail him or own him.

Shops along the Rue Masséna were all closed. The corrugated-iron grilles were down, locked tight the length of the street. The street had that empty Sunday-morning look to it.

Bellarmine rapped on the glass door, then cupped his eyes with both hands and peered into the perfumery. After a moment he saw Jacqueline come out of the corridor that led to the stock room. She crossed behind the counter and knelt to unlock the door. She was wearing a broad-brimmed white hat and white gloves.

As they drove along the Promenade des Anglais they too noted how windy the day was, the flags and palm trees blowing, the whitecaps on the sea, the constantly replenished mist that hung above the rows of deck chairs.

Both seemed to be seeking something to talk about, some neutral subject, and at last they settled on one—Nice during the war. What was it like? he asked her.

The first troops to occupy the city were Italians, she told him—Alpini, the elite mountain troops. They wore feathers in their hats. All they wanted was to eat in the restaurants and flirt with the girls. The Niçois didn't mind them. Most Niçois were of Italian origin anyway, for Nice had been French only about a hundred years.

But once the Germans came, life got very hard very quickly. There wasn't enough to eat. The Riviera, being basically mountainous, could not feed itself; nothing much grew except flowers. There was no petrol for the many small fishing boats. The fishermen were still allowed to put to sea but could go out only as far as they could row. The food trains came down from the north, stopping frequently along the way, and by the time they reached Nice, tucked into the southeast corner of the country, there was often nothing left on them. For five years the world's playground was forgotten by the world. Worse, it was forgotten by France. It was as if the rest of the country had decided to punish it for its long collaboration with foreigners. The punishment was starvation. People lined up outside butcher shops at two o'clock in the morning. They rode the tramway out to the Var River, the end of the line, and walked across toward the few peasant farms on the other side, where they negotiated with the peasants for vegetables. The peasants were very arrogant, and charged outrageous prices. They made the people go through the fields picking their own vegetables, which they weighed with roots and dirt still attached. The peasants made money during the war. The horse butchers made money too. People learned to eat what they could get.

"You didn't see any pigeons in the parks anymore," said Jacqueline with a smile. "Pretty soon you didn't see any cats in the street either. And the sea gulls learned not to come in too close to the Promenade."

One of the casinos stood on a jetty a hundred yards out into the sea. In 1943 German sappers blew it up. They said it interfered with possible fields of fire, but according to rumor the other casinos paid to have it demolished. When peace came there would be one less.

"Casino scandals are no new thing in Nice, I see," said Bellarmine.

"Excuse me?"

His comment had gone over her head. "Never mind."

There was a blackout, of course. A curfew was imposed. Now from 10 P.M. until dawn the streets were empty of Frenchmen and French-women, every house was blacked out, and it was as if the city had

278

been abandoned to the forces of darkness. It belonged, symbolically at least, to the German patrols who occupied that darkness.

Jacqueline and her parents had lived in a big, bright apartment overlooking the port. The Germans emptied these buildings and boarded them up. Jacqueline and her mother moved into the back of the perfume shop.

"We were lucky. We had a place to go. Lots of families didn't."

Later the Germans demolished many of the buildings around the port, theirs included.

At eighteen she passed her bac and was accepted into the university at Aix-en-Provence, but a telegram came: her father had died in a prison camp in Bavaria.

She went to work in the shop beside her mother, but there were too few customers. Although some perfume was manufactured during the war few people could afford to buy it.

"It was all right once the Americans came. There were so many of them and they had so much money." She smiled. She had got a job in the PX, and her mother's shop had prospered too. "The Americans all wanted to send perfume home to their mothers."

"Not their girl friends?"

"Mostly their mothers."

But one of them wished to marry this young woman, Bellarmine thought, and did.

Jacqueline's recital had lapsed. He did not want to hear about her marriage, and presumably she did not care to speak of it.

Instead she watched the scenery while he stole glances at her profile. Carnations grew on terraces to both sides of the road. Higher up the slopes stood isolated farmhouses, and their orange tile roofs were brilliant in the sun.

"And you?" said Jacqueline. "What would have become of you if there had been no war?"

The most frequently asked question of and by young people all over Europe during those years: What if there had been no war?

He might have become a lawyer, Bellarmine told her. But by the time the war ended he was too old to go back to the university, could not have endured it. But what was he trained for? The Army seemed the only life he had ever known. "So I went into a different army, the Sûreté Nationale." It was a proud time to be a policeman, and he explained why. During the war a French Gestapo had been formed in Paris, with headquarters at 93 Rue Lauriston. A few renegade policemen headed it, and its ranks were filled out by hardened inmates liberated from French prisons. They were given uniforms and guns by their German masters. Overnight the criminals became the police. Granted rights of search and seizure under the "law," plus all the cars and petrol coupons they asked for, this deadly gang began a reign of terror that lasted four years. They broke into the houses of prominent people, arrested the occupants on trumped-up charges, and "confiscated" whatever valuables they found there—paintings, tapestries, jewels. Back at the Rue Lauriston, "suspects" were tortured into revealing where other valuables were hidden, and into signing over ownership of lockboxes and bank accounts. The gang committed also a great many outright stickups of banks, post offices and trains, and when ordinary police agencies tried to move against them, the German Gestapo took over the cases and shelved them. The Rue Lauriston gang had access, naturally, to existing police archives, from which their own dossiers disappeared completely, even as they culled other dossiers for the names of informants and secret witnesses, numbers of whom were then murdered.

After the liberation of Paris, with the German Army in full retreat, most leaders of this French Gestapo, including nearly all the renegade policemen, were rounded up and shot. The policemen apparently were prisoners of their own bourgeois mentality, and were easy enough to find. But most of the former convicts ran. They went underground. They sought help from their prewar cohorts, and in most cases got it: false identity cards, hiding places, money, arms. It took years to root them out one by one, and in the meantime they had gone back to their former trade, principally armed robbery. Anyone who resisted them was shot down in cold blood. These were men who faced execution if caught—most had already been condemned to death in absentia—and they had nothing to lose.

To be part of the hunt for such men had seemed to Bellarmine as noble a crusade as the one just ended.

At this point in his narrative he fell silent, remembering. He had felt just as much a patriot as before, for he was again fighting for France, the ideal of France, a purified France. A man had to have an ideal or he couldn't live. But he did not say any of this to Jacqueline, because he feared he would sound silly.

The postwar crime wave was the most vicious France had ever known, and a new group was formed in Paris called the Office for the Repression of Grand Banditisme. Bellarmine was an *inspecteur prin-*

*cipal* by then, and when asked to join this elite group, he accepted. He worked out of Sûreté headquarters. Detectives never called it headquarters. They called it La Grande Maison, or else La Boîte. But he was almost never in Paris. He was sent on missions to Lille, in the north, where the slag heaps from the mines rose up into man-made mountains, beyond which the flat plain stretched away toward the Low Countries. He spent two years in Lyon, and another two in Bordeaux. He was in on a number of famous cases—he began to name for Jacqueline several of the notorious criminals he had arrested.

However, these names meant nothing to her, and she looked at him blankly.

"Did you ever hear of The Angel of Death?"

"No."

He gave a rueful smile.

"I arrested him. He was the last of the Rue Lauriston gang." His voice trailed off. A man reaches all his life for recognition, he reflected, each one working within his own orbit. But every orbit is minuscule, and two steps outside it no one is aware of it or him. The most brilliant acts a man can perform, the most courageous, are no better than most local wines—they do not travel.

"I'm sorry," she said. "I should know those names."

The emotion that took possession of him could only be called gratitude—that she had perceived his disappointment and been moved to apologize.

A year ago, he told her, he had been promoted to *commissaire* and had been transferred to Nice. The Brigade Criminelle here was his first command.

From Jacqueline's expression he saw that this detail astonished her. She was having difficulty restructuring her image of him—so he had not been a *commissaire* all of his life after all. One's own life is a progression of steps up a ladder. Any normal man is always aware of how tenuous his rise has been. Each rung is unsteady. He can never lose sight of the one below, nor be sure of attaining the one above. But outsiders never perceive that a man is standing on a ladder at all. Instead they accept him as whatever he appears to be at the moment.

They drove into the village of Vence. Cobbled streets. Moss-covered fountain with water overflowing its sides. The café tables were out on the main square.

Jacqueline's mother lived in a small hotel on the Avenue Henri

281

Matisse. But when Bellarmine pulled to a stop, Jacqueline did not immediately get out of the car.

"Are you sure you have friends you can pass the time with?" she asked uncertainly. Seeing him hesitate, she said: "You don't, do you?"

The name of even one fictitious friend would be enough, Bellarmine thought. Instead he laughed and said only: "Don't worry about me."

Jacqueline looked out the window at the hotel. "Would you like to come in and meet my mother?"

Bellarmine switched off the ignition. "All right."

And so he met her mother, an immaculately groomed woman with gray hair, thin to the point of frailty, who watched him carefully, and her daughter carefully, and who said very little. He took them to a tea room upstairs over a narrow street. The conversation ran on tracks designed to skirt the subject of Lambert. Mother and daughter were not at ease with each other and neither was at ease with Bellarmine. Madame called him "monsieur" and refilled his cup several times as if he were the man of the family and had to be cosseted. Back at the hotel all three went into the game room and played three-handed belote on a felt-topped table for an hour, and the conversation fixed itself exclusively on the cards. At last Jacqueline murmured that it was late, they had best get back to Nice, and she stood up.

"I've been reading the papers all week," her mother said. Here it comes, Bellarmine thought, the subject we've avoided all afternoon. "You might have telephoned."

"It's so difficult to telephone, *maman*." Jacqueline had begun twisting her fingers together.

Bellarmine said: "Perhaps I should wait outside."

But Jacqueline asked him to stay, for his presence imposed brevity, even silence on her mother. "We've been all over this before, *maman*."

"We just didn't know how bad the situation was until now."

"*Maman*, please."

Mother embraced daughter. "I'm on your side, little one," she said. "Divorce—I don't think you should wait, do you?"

"*Maman*—"

"Promise you'll think about it."

"I'll think about it, *maman*."

On the steep, winding road down toward the coast and Nice, Jacqueline said: "I'm sorry you had to see that."

Bellarmine said only: "I liked your mother very much."

Jacqueline gave a smile. "She liked you, too. Under the circumstances that's to be expected, I suppose. You're not a foreigner, and you're not in jail."

There were cars on the road now, all winding downhill to the cities on the coast. The sun was very low, so that it struck the buildings, trees, and roadside flowers on their sides, producing long shadows and violent colors.

"You said you could get me in to see my husband."

The beauty of the moment and his yearning for the woman beside him produced in Bellarmine a kind of physical pain. "You might see him now, if you like," he said, making the pain worse. "I'll take you there."

The men's house of arrest was up beside the Paillon at the rear of the city. After escorting Jacqueline inside and making the arrangements for her, Bellarmine went out and sat in the parked car and waited for her for an hour and brooded. He was as miserable as a jealous husband who had trailed the lovers to a hotel. There was nothing to do now but wait for the woman to come downstairs again with her cheeks roughened and the odor of the other man still on her.

# CHAPTER
## 29

Lambert sat up on his cot and stared stupidly around. He realized a hand had been shaking him but did not know where he was. He was like a man who had been hit on the head. Exhaustion had addled his brain like a concussion. He could not remember the sequence of blows that had put him here—wherever he was—and so sought to read the clues. A sink. A toilet with no lid and no tank—a porcelain funnel into the floor. Beside it a bucket. Bars on the window. Not a hotel then. Although he remembered nothing of coming to this place, he recognized it for what it was.

A prison, and he was in it.

The shaking hand belonged to a guard. "Someone to see you."

He sucked in his first conscious chestful of prison air. A noseful of odors: part hospital, part locker room, part latrine. Disinfectant plus human wastes.

He followed the guard out past the thick wooden door and down corridors, past other wooden doors, all with square spy holes cut into them. The doors were all closed and latched, the spy holes closed. Behind those doors—what? Other prisoners? Prisoners he knew perhaps. Colleagues. Friends from the sewers. At the end of the corridor a barred window, and he saw that outside it was night.

He glanced at his watch. Nine P.M. He began to remember his interrogation, and a ride in a van. He must have slept about twelve hours.

Downstairs the guard led him into what looked like a dining room or small banquet hall. Polished parquet floors. Oil portraits on the walls. A big polished wood table. High-back chairs. At this table sat a man of about sixty with a briefcase open before him. Lambert sat down opposite, and the guard took up position in the doorway at the end of the room.

"Your wife asked me to drop in and say hello to you," said the man. He pushed across an envelope. "From your wife."

Without taking his eyes off him, Lambert accepted the envelope and rammed it into his back pocket.

"I am Maître Maurel—an advocate. Your wife has asked me to represent you. I suppose the first question to settle is this: Do you have funds to pay for a defense?"

"You don't beat around the bush, do you," said Lambert in English.

"I beg your pardon," said the lawyer in French.

Lambert gave him a grin and switched to French. "If I knocked over the Banque de Nice, I'm rich. If I didn't, I can't afford you. Is that what you're trying to tell me?"

"I beg your pardon," said the lawyer again.

"Why don't you come right out and say it?" said Lambert. "Am I The Brain or not?"

The lawyer began nervously stacking the papers in front of him.

"Let's put it another way," said Lambert. "If I'm The Brain, you're dying to represent me. If I'm not, it's a bore."

Beside the lawyer's briefcase rested a small paper parcel. He pushed it toward Lambert. "I always like to bring my clients shaving material and a toothbrush first thing. They are usually pretty grubby by the time I see them." He attempted a convivial grin.

284

Lambert grabbed the package and opened it. Toothbrush. Small tube of Kolynos toothpaste. An American safety razor, a box of Gillette Blue Blades. It made him rub the two-and-a-half-day stubble on his face. His cheeks were rough and his teeth felt covered with nap. "How much do I owe you for this?"

The lawyer attempted a second convivial grin. "Don't worry about it. I'll put in on the bill."

"No, I want to pay you now," insisted Lambert. "You see, there's not going to be any bill. Not from you."

The grin vanished. "I beg your pardon."

"Look at it from my point of view. Are you good enough to defend me? Have you defended any famous criminals in the past?"

The lawyer frowned. "Young man, I was defending criminals before the bar before you were born."

"Famous criminals, I said. Criminals like I'm supposed to be."

"I didn't come in here to discuss with you my past clientele."

"Gimme a couple of names. Big-time criminals. Guys you got off."

The lawyer stood up, closed his briefcase, and snapped the catches. He pushed a business card across the table at Lambert. He looked quite angry, and Lambert grinned at him. As he bowed stiffly and left the room, Lambert began to laugh. He laughed so hard that tears came to his eyes. He picked up the business card and tore it in two. He felt extraordinarily pleased with himself. Then he took the package of toilet gear and started back to his cell.

"I'm hungry," he told the guard, who was behind him.

"You want to send for food, you can," said the guard. "You got money, don't you?"

Lambert felt his back pocket for his wallet. To his surprise it was there, where it was supposed to be. They must have given it back to him.

"I'll let you have the menu," said the guard. "They bring the dishes to you. You tip the waiter, and you tip us."

This surprised Lambert. He was in preventive detention, awaiting trial, and the other rules would surprise him also. He could wear his own clothes, smoke all he wanted, send out for reading material as well as meals, and visiting rules were flexible. Once convicted he would be transferred to Les Baumettes or one of the other fortress-type prisons, and life there would not be the same.

By the time he had finished shaving, his dinner had arrived: fresh bread, a fresh salad, a not bad *boeuf bourguignon*, a slice of apple tart for dessert, and a bottle of rosé de Provence. When he had finished all this he went back to bed and slept until morning. The letter from Jacqueline lay unopened on the shelf that hung from the opposite wall. He was not interested at the moment in anything she might have to say to him.

His next visitor came the following noon, another lawyer. Lambert was standing at his window, staring out, when the guard came to get him. It was a sunny morning, and a breeze blew through the bars onto his face. A railroad train went by about level with his window, though on the other side of the wall, of course. He was watching people who hung out of the train windows staring across at the tops of the prison buildings. They were on their way to Italy, or wherever they wanted to go, in any case more free than he was.

He followed the guard downstairs where he met a new lawyer, a bald, burly man of about forty-five. He was sitting in the same chair as that white-haired goof last night. Who was he and who had sent him? Jacqueline again? This thought irritated Lambert.

"Maître Cresci, monsieur," the lawyer said, and shook hands. It was a partial handshake on the lawyer's part, about two and a half limp fingers.

Lambert recognized the name at once. "Who's paying you?" he demanded.

But Cresci only smiled. Lambert should relax in the confidence that the best possible defense would be provided him.

"Who sent you?"

Cresci launched into another speech. He had been sent by a prominent Marseille businessman and philanthropist, who was one of Lambert's closest friends, apparently. M. Marcel Faletta, for such was the close friend's name, had spoken warmly of his friendship for Lambert, and of his desire to be of help to him now in his time of need.

"Who?" said Lambert. "Faletta?" He shook his head. "*Connais pas.*" Don't know him.

If Cresci was surprised, he concealed this. However, he studied his manicured fingernails before he spoke. "My fee has been taken care of, and I can assure you that you could not be in better hands."

"I've seen your name in the paper," Lambert said. "Every time some Corsican gangster gets caught bombing a nightclub, you're the lawyer. Hit men are another of your specialties. You've represented just about every hit man in Marseille at one time or another, wouldn't you say?"

The lawyer's face had darkened and he tapped his fingernails on the tabletop.

"Maybe we should discuss the details of your case."

"I can't afford to be represented by you," Lambert interrupted, and he grinned.

The lawyer's drumming fingernails became like hoofbeats on a wooden bridge, and this made Lambert laugh outright. "I'm innocent, you see. It's all a big misunderstanding."

"Faletta wants to help," said Cresci.

"I can't accept help from a perfect stranger. I have my pride." It pleased Lambert to twit Cresci, and through him Faletta. Everybody in Marseille was terrified of Faletta, but Lambert was not.

"Monsieur Faletta is particularly worried about certain missing documents that weren't supposed to be missing."

So this wasn't a joke after all, thought Lambert. Faletta thinks he's been double-crossed and he thinks I did it. To Cresci he said: "There are about sixteen of his men locked up. Have him ask them."

"He has done so—through me, of course, and is satisfied they are not involved."

"I can't help you, pal."

"One other thing Monsieur Faletta would like to know. Can he depend on your—friendship?"

"On my silence, you mean." Lambert stood up and gazed in the direction of the guard in the doorway. "I have to get back to my cell. Thanks for coming." He stuck his hand out, and when the lawyer extended the same two and a half fingers as before, Lambert grasped them and squeezed until he heard the knuckles crack. Cresci's entire body seemed to flinch from the pain. This made Lambert laugh again.

He had barely lain back on his cot when he was taken downstairs yet again. This time the visitor was O'Hara, who introduced himself as the consular representative. Was Lambert in good health? he asked. Had he been beaten or tortured? What were his needs? In what way could the consulate help him?

Lambert said: "Didn't I see you in the room when they were interrogating me?"

"Me?"

"A big crew-cut guy. I think it was you."

"Do you want the consulate to get you a lawyer?" said O'Hara.

"I've got one, thanks." He didn't, but he knew whom he wanted.

"What else do you need?" said O'Hara.

The two men eyed each other.

"Maybe we can help you at the consulate," said O'Hara. "Do you want to tell me anything?"

Lambert said nothing.

"Otherwise, it looks pretty bad for you."

Lambert shrugged. "I'm innocent." He gave a broad grin. "What more can I say?"

"I hear they found fragments of the missing documents in your fireplace."

"You hear a lot, pal. What are you, FBI? CIA, maybe?"

"There are people worried about those documents. If they could get them back, maybe they could get you out of here."

"But I like it here," protested Lambert, grinning again. "It's a chance to catch up on my sleep. And for the next couple of weeks I don't have to deal with too many jerks." And he strolled past the guard out of the room.

"You're an arrogant son of a bitch," said O'Hara to his back.

In the corridor Lambert felt like a beautiful girl fighting off suitors from all directions. He had what a lot of men wanted, and they were sniffing around him like dogs in heat. It was so obvious it was comical.

The lawyer he sent for, an American named Sharkey, arrived a few hours later.

Sharkey was another of the conquering army washed up on the Riviera after the war, though different in type from Lambert. Now approaching middle age, he was a foppish, soft man who kept an office on the Rue du Congrès opposite the U.S. Consulate and paid regular bribes to the consulate's mostly French clerks. He lived off those Americans in difficulty whom these clerks steered to him, and he lived well. Since he was not licensed to practice in France, he dispensed his legal advice illegally. But he always hired French lawyers to represent his clients if the case went to court, billing the clients for bigger fees than any Frenchman would have dared, and so the authorities left him alone. He liked to wear silk smoking jackets when receiving clients, a voluminous foulard around his throat, his matched police dogs crouched to either side of his desk. In the street he affected the same foulards tucked into double-breasted blue blazers. To Lambert he always smelled as though he wore perfume. He had met him at the time of his marriage. Sharkey had provided the necessary documents—for a stiff price. Sharkey, to Lambert, was basically a thief, he ate and drank too much, and he was a joke as a lawyer.

They sat opposite each other in the prison *parloir*, and Lambert felt the need to twit Sharkey also.

"I'm handing you the case of your life, Sharkey. I'm going to make you famous. Headlines all over the world. The Shark defends The Brain."

Sharkey protested in his mild middle-aged monotone. "I can't plead before the bar here," he said. His complexion was entirely smooth. No beard showed. He seemed as asexual as a priest. Also he had evidently eaten a hearty Sunday dinner, and drunk much wine, and these odors warred with the perfume that wafted off him.

"I'll have to hire a French lawyer as my associate," he said. "His fee may be quite steep."

"You're good, Shark," said Lambert expansively. "You're really good. It isn't the Shark who overcharges these poor fools. It's that *salaud* of a French lawyer they never even see."

Sharkey was exactly the lawyer Lambert believed he needed at the moment, and after sending him away, he spent the rest of the afternoon lying on his bunk with his hands behind his head, staring out through the bars at the Mediterranean sky, calculating. Sharkey's presence on the case would keep all the other lawyers away—his wife's lawyer, and particularly Faletta's lawyer. If he wished to retain his debonair image as The Brain, Lambert reasoned, he had to separate himself definitively from Faletta. Beside which, he guessed he had caused Faletta to look pretty bad lately. To retain Sharkey put a safe distance between himself and Faletta. Between himself and the local law-enforcement establishment also. It gave him time to plan.

His cot bore no pillow, only a bolster so old it seemed to be filled with unshelled hazelnuts. Throughout the afternoon Lambert punched at it with his fists, seeking and failing to punch it into a shape conforming to his head. No matter—the discomfort kept him alert, his mind boiling. If The Brain could bust into the Banque de Nice et de la Côte d'Azur, he could certainly bust out of such a poor excuse for a jail as this one. All it would take was several weeks while he learned the routine. Sharkey was another poor excuse, and would lull to sleep the men who watched him. They would cease to believe he was The Brain at all. They would believe him as dim-witted as his

289

lawyer. They would learn their mistake only when he had departed. The Brain strikes again.

He lay on his bunk smirking while the day passed. His barred patch of sky turned from blue to gray to black, and then the thick wooden door opened behind his head and a voice told him his wife was waiting for him downstairs.

He glanced at her letter, still unopened on the shelf opposite his cot. There was no time to read it now.

In the *parloir* she stood beside the table, looking distraught. He walked over and kissed her briefly. Her agitation showed especially in her hands. She played with her wedding ring, twisted her fingers together.

"I stopped off and got you some clothes," she said, and directed his attention to the small bag that stood on the table.

"That's nice." He quieted her hands by taking them in his. "How are you?"

She was so obviously upset that Lambert sought to soothe her. The best way to do this, he decided, was to convince her of his innocence. The police had made a terrible mistake, he protested. They needed a scapegoat, and an American scapegoat made them look especially good. They could blame the crime on the hated Americans, did she not see this?

He saw her face brighten. He was concerned for her, wished to please her, and so continued along the same line. He had no idea why the police had picked on him. "I just happened to be there, I guess." It would all work out in a few days, he promised her. In a few weeks at most he would be exonerated. The police would be obliged to make a public apology to him in the newspaper.

But Jacqueline, at the end of this impassioned declaration, seemed skeptical, unable to meet his eyes.

"Jacqueline, I swear to you I'm not guilty." Such was the sincerity in his voice that he believed this himself for the moment, and so, he saw, did his wife. But her belief faded before his eyes. "Don't you trust me?" he asked.

"You lied to me once," she said, after hesitating. "You told me you sold your play."

"Oh that," he protested, and in the manner of a small boy, he was almost pouting. "I only wanted to make you happy. It had been so long since I'd seen you happy. I did it for you."

Disengaging her hands, she sat down at the table.

290

"I did finish the play," Lambert declared. "I did send it to New York. It's making the rounds of the agents." He had himself convinced, and he began nodding his head up and down. "It may get taken any day. You never know," he finished vaguely.

Jacqueline said: "The new car, our trip to Switzerland—where did the money come from?"

Lambert frowned. "Cigarettes."

"But you swore to me you had got out of the cigarette business."

"Except for one last shipment. That's where the money came from. You do believe me."

"I don't know."

Lambert had begun pacing, and he knew he had her attention because she watched him so closely. Her head moved back and forth like a spectator at a tennis match. "The police asked about the money too, but I couldn't tell them. Because running cigarettes is also a crime." He saw how much she wanted to believe him. "Not a very bad crime, you understand. Everybody in France buys contraband cigarettes, the cops and judges included."

After a pause Jacqueline said: "I wrote you a letter. Perhaps I shouldn't have."

Lambert waited.

"I said some things in it."

"I know you did." She felt guilty about the letter and Lambert wondered what she had written.

"I'll stand by you while you're in trouble. After that—"

"I don't deserve even that much," said Lambert humbly. He took her hands again, and his voice was again full of concern. "Tell me how you are."

It made a torrent of words spill out. Jacqueline began to describe how she had been held in custody herself, and then forced to watch search parties ransack her shop, the farm, their hands going through her closets, her dresser drawers.

"You poor kid," said Lambert solicitously, though his mind was elsewhere. She was like an acquaintance met on a street corner, who failed to recognize that her concerns were small compared to his. "Did they look in the bathroom?" he asked solicitously. "And the kitchen?"

"Of course."

The kitchen was the important place. The photos and documents in the manila envelope were under the sink at the bottom of an open

carton of wine, with twelve unopened bottles and the cardboard sepa-
rators standing on top of them. "But they didn't find anything?" said
Lambert.

His wife studied him a moment. "Should they have?"

"You never know," said Lambert coolly. "They might have planted
something."

Jacqueline resumed her description of the search, the hands even
going through her underwear, violating things never worn by anyone
but her, a kind of rape. "It wasn't pleasant," she said.

"And it was my fault. You can't imagine how sorry I am." In fact
he was scarcely listening to her. He was thinking about the wine. It
took his wife an entire weekend to finish a single bottle, and some
weekends she didn't even go up there. The documents were safe for
twelve weeks' minimum.

Jacqueline was still talking. The *commissaire* in charge had hung
around her neck the entire time, she said—was still hanging around
her neck.

"His name is Bellarmine," said Lambert.

"Is it?" said Jacqueline.

Lambert began to brood about the policeman. "This could prove
very useful," he said, and he began to encourage Jacqueline to spend
time with the man, to make up to him, to find out every detail of
this phony case against her husband. "Then come and tell me."

"You think that would help?" She looked off into the distance. "To
make up to him?"

Lambert assured her that it would. It was the best help she could
give him.

"I sent you a lawyer," she said after a moment.

"He was a very expensive lawyer. Since I don't have any money to
pay him, he refused to take my case."

"He said you sent him away."

"Not true," Lambert insisted.

"What will you do?"

"I've had to hire Sharkey."

"He's a silly man."

"Well, he's the most we can afford."

"But with him as your lawyer you'll never get out of here," she
cried.

"Of course I will. I'm innocent."

"You need a better lawyer than Sharkey."

"But how would we pay him, unless—"

"Unless what?"

"Could you mortgage your shop?"

When his wife did not answer, Lambert walked over behind her chair, put his hands on her shoulders, then slid them down to cup both her breasts. At this point two things happened simultaneously. The guard in the doorway turned away, and Jacqueline, embarrassed, lifted his hands and stood up abruptly.

Outside the jail Jacqueline climbed into the Citroën beside Bellarmine. By then she was more distraught than ever. Her husband was innocent, she said. His request that she mortgage her shop proved it. "He never robbed any bank," she blurted out. "He doesn't even have enough money to pay a lawyer."

"*Le salaud,*" muttered Bellarmine.

"He wouldn't ask me such a thing otherwise. He isn't that diabolical."

"Yes, he is," said Bellarmine. Driving, his lips were compressed into a thin line.

But Jacqueline clung to the promise—the ideal—with which her marriage had started. To do otherwise was to throw away every minute of it here and now, the good times and the bad—the ideal of it as well. It was too much to ask.

Wanting only to be alone, she asked Bellarmine to drive her back to her shop, and he complied.

For a few minutes they sat outside the shop in the dark car. "Will I see you tomorrow?" asked Jacqueline. There was no energy, no emotion left in her, and she was not sure why she wanted to see him—was it just to be with him, or to probe for information that might help her husband?

"Jacqueline, please let me help you," he said, and something— perhaps the tone of his voice or the concern in his eyes, or perhaps the words themselves—so touched her that she burst into tears.

Bellarmine leaned across and took her in his arms. Now she wept into the side of his neck, and breathed the scent of his skin, the odor of his suit, of the cigarettes he smoked all day. She had wanted to be held tight by someone ever since this terrible thing happened, and to her surprise she did not even feel guilty—her husband had given her permission to make up to this policeman, had he not?

"Thank you for being so nice to me," she murmured. Then she disengaged herself, got out of the car and went into the shop without looking back.

293

# CHAPTER
## 30

Faletta had expected attacks on his empire, and they came.

Unauthorized by him, four unknown girls began to patrol portions of the Rue Thubaneau, encroaching on the terrain of his own girls already there. Receipts fell for everybody. The newcomers were said to be under the protection of Urbain Zampa, caid of an expanding new clan. While Faletta waited to learn more, a black Peugeot drew up outside one of his bars near the Gare St. Charles. Guns leapt up from the floorboards, and about thirty shots were fired into the bar, killing the woman at the cash desk, who was a former mistress of Faletta's, and wounding two patrons at a table in the rear. These gunmen may or may not have been sent by Zampa—Faletta could not be certain. Nor could he afford to wait to find out. Zampa's headquarters was a bar on the Vieux Port. It was destroyed the following night by a plastic explosive that went off in the toilet, killing a waiter sitting there, and setting fire to the entire building.

About an hour later one of the four new whores on the Rue Thubaneau took a client upstairs to the room she used. As soon as she had undressed, two other men rushed in. While these two held her down, the third gouged a cross into the right side of her face—the so-called *croix de la vache*—with a piece of broken beer bottle. All three men then raped her and left. That girl was never seen again on the Rue Thubaneau, and neither were the other three; Faletta was satisfied.

For some days the incipient gang war lapsed, and he believed he had stopped it. Then Besse was assassinated on the sidewalk as he strolled out of the Versailles, Faletta's nightclub. It was still daylight. Two men on a motor scooter—a favorite method of execution in Marseille—drove up onto the sidewalk. The passenger riding pillion fired five times. They were upon Besse before he had time to draw his own piece, or to react. The first bullet struck him in the face and killed him instantly. The other four as he was going down missed. Three dug stone chips out of walls. The fourth killed a North African street peddler. The Arab in his fez fell down and lay half buried under the rugs, deflated hassocks, cheap wallets, and even cheaper silver trinkets he had been hawking through the streets.

The location of this crime—Faletta was meant to be seen as unable to protect even his own stretch of sidewalk—made it a personal insult, and he ordered immediate reprisals. But Zampa then struck back and the score rose, murders and plastic bombings both, and among the many corpses figured some of his own top men as well as Zampa's.

Now Faletta was obliged to lay on extra security precautions, which he did not like doing since it made him feel cowardly, and he ordered his brothers to do likewise. He became the prisoner of his bodyguards, all his movements constricted, unable to move without them, and each day was a fight not only for his empire but to keep from getting killed.

All this he blamed on Lambert.

Roy LeRoy sat in a cell in Toulon, Marseille's satellite. He had not been brought to Nice after all, for no evidence had been developed to link him to the Banque de Nice case. The same lawyer who had represented him during his cigarette-running years represented him now, and this man had appealed to the court for restitution of LeRoy's money, his boat and his freedom. The gunrunning case against him was extremely weak, the lawyer pleaded. LeRoy had been arrested at sea—in effect before any crime took place, and so he was innocent of that charge, leaving only his refusal to stop and be boarded by customs. His defense was that he had thought them not customs men at all, but pirates. Since he was carrying a great deal of money, none of it bearing serial numbers from the Banque de Nice, quite naturally he had run—or attempted to run. Anyone else would have done the same. At the very least, the lawyer wanted LeRoy granted "provisional liberty under caution." The "caution" could amount to the approximately half a million dollars confiscated from his PT boat, plus the boat itself, which was moored in the customs portion of the Toulon naval base. But so far the *juge d'instruction* who had the case had rejected the lawyer's arguments.

The lawyer assured LeRoy he had a good chance of winning his case when it came to trial a year or more from now, though he might have to wait in jail till then. In the meantime customs was lovingly repairing the riddled PT boat, for it was believed that the courts would soon award the captured prize to the service, whereupon it would become the scourge of the coast, and so the ruined deck tanks had been removed and the mixture of gas and water pumped out of the bilge. The multiple holes in the plywood hull had been plugged and the exterior was even being repainted.

Henry the Torch was a prisoner also, having been condemned to the silence and isolation of Faletta's farm, where he had developed a strange routine—he attacked the edge of the encroaching forest each day with an ax. Swinging with vicious energy he felled tree after tree, left each one lying there, and moved on to the next. He hated the trees as he hated the soundless plowed fields, the barren meadows. He hated the dogs, the sheep, the birds, and all growing things. He longed for a woman. He longed for the cacophony of the streets of Marseille. He hated most of all the aged Corsican peasant, Faletta's retainer or relative or whatever he was, who ran the farm and who drove the rusted old pickup into Brignoles once a week to replenish their stores. The old man came back each time with an armload of fresh crusty breads, upon which The Torch threw himself avidly. But after the first day the remaining loaves were less crusty and no longer fresh; day by day they became increasingly hard until by the end of the week they were like stone, and to chew bread was to risk breaking teeth. The old man didn't care, he had no teeth anyway and soaked the bread in his soup. They conversed in Corsican, the only dialect the old fool spoke. But he had nothing to say. He kept repeating the same stories, laughing over and over in the same places, until The Torch thought he would go mad. Each week he sent him into town with a message for Faletta: get me out of here. But the old man never delivered these messages, or if he did, no reply came back.

Each day, after having knocked down six or seven trees, The Torch retreated into the old stone farmhouse. Soaked in sweat he drank beer and stared at the walls. Television had not yet come to this part of France, and the farm had no electricity anyway. The Torch did have a portable radio. It was domed like a church and heavier than a case of wine, and he listened to it constantly, his only companion. He did not care what it played. The radio was noise. He liked it. If asked what he missed most about Marseille, he might have replied: "The noise." Sometimes he wished he were in jail. It was, arguably, a better place than here. If a man felt the need to knock something down, he could knock down another man, see the blood flow, wait to match himself against whatever would happen next.

The days passed and The Torch continued to wait for word from Faletta.

• • •

Congressman Avery was still in Europe. He expected any day to learn who had his documents, and therefore could not leave. So in a sense he was as much a prisoner as the others. From time to time he inspected U.S. military installations in France and West Germany. He went to Berlin and was photographed shaking hands with the mayor. Across the ocean, in Washington, his office put out reports about all the work he was doing, principally on Marshall Plan expenditures. He was busy cutting them down.

He was not worried about how long his constituents, and especially the New Orleans power brokers who had put him in office, would continue to tolerate his too-long absence. They would tolerate it for however long he chose.

Meanwhile, Nice's sole remaining casino filled up every night. Business was extremely good. The big spenders were Greek shipping magnates, Arab oil sheiks, Italian industrialists—people who had not yet heard of Las Vegas. Most of the gamblers, however, were American. Hundreds came as part of organized tours, but there were many high rollers, including film executives like Jack Warner and Darryl F. Zanuck, both of whom bet always with pretty young things at their sides—starlets perhaps, or secretaries. Who knew? Or cared? Avery watched all this. He watched as profits were routinely skimmed off the top, but made sure he got his share. Sums of money, he noted, were allocated each month as bribes for the Games Police, with the result that no skimming was noticed by them. Protection money was paid to a man named Gaetan Guiaume, representing the Faletta interests in Nice, and this guaranteed an absence of "incidents." There were no fights in the gambling rooms. No big winners were stuck up on their way back to their hotels. Checkrooms and lavatories did not catch fire.

Avery's profits were as good as he had hoped for, and they flowed into his numbered account in Switzerland. The IRS could link him to this money only if he spent it, and that was one of his problems. With the threat of Lambert hanging over him, he could not spend it. He was a rich man obliged to behave as a poor one. This was galling. The other problem was the orgy photos.

Adjunct Mayor Picpoul began to insist that the incriminating documents and photos must have been burned by Lambert, as the police claimed. But Picpoul had not stood at a bar rail with Lambert. Avery, who had, knew otherwise.

"Wishful thinking," he snorted. He had contempt for most Europeans, Picpoul in particular. He had reviewed his one meeting with Lambert a hundred times. He had considered and reconsidered Lambert's every line of dialogue.

*"Some people don't resemble their pictures too much. But you do. Exactly."*

The blackmail threat was coming, but when? What was Lambert waiting for?

Lambert was the only one of these prisoners whose spirit roamed free, or so he believed. He ordered fine meals twice a day. In French jails, it seemed to him, you could eat better than in most American restaurants. He was allowed a shower twice a week. He was allowed almost anytime he wanted to walk in the courtyard, where he sometimes conversed with other men awaiting trial. He was a celebrity to them. They were fascinated by him. So were the guards.

He decided to work on a new play, setting himself further apart from the other inmates. He would romanticize jail. The plot came to him almost without thought. It would be about an American being held in a French jail, and would be autobiographical in most respects, except that the hero would not know why he was in this jail, whereas Lambert did. In the first act the hero would gradually become aware of what the charges against him must be. In the second act, he would escape from his cell, and in the third act would rejoin his loving wife and flee the country.

Now that he was famous around the world as The Brain the play would certainly be produced. He spent many hours visualizing the eventual production—the scenery, the way the actors would speak the lines. But he did not write any of these lines. Any producer would consider him big box office and would put the play on. His notoriety would attract ticket buyers. The play would run forever. All he had to do was write it, and he sent for a typewriter, which was brought to him. He rolled paper into it, then got up and looked out of the window.

But he had not actually tried to write anything in several years, and it proved impossible for him to make himself start now.

In the meantime he was busy seeing people—either they visited him or he visited them. Sharkey came three or four times a week, sometimes more. The Shark had nothing else to do, and striding in and out of the prison seemed to make him feel like a real lawyer.

Twice a week his wife came.

She came in the evening at the close of business hours, and once was allowed to bring in a complete meal bought in a *traiteur* shop: stuffed baby lamb *en croûte*. She brought and laid out a tablecloth, wine and glasses, cutlery. They dined in the *parloir* and she told him what she had learned. Most of the men held in Marseille were being released for lack of evidence. It had proved impossible to connect Roy LeRoy with the Banque de Nice case and the dossier on him had been closed. The search for Eugène Henri Baldasaro—Henry the Torch—was continuing. Most of his share of the gold had been found in a bank in Brussels. All this, Jacqueline said, she had managed to pry out of Bellarmine. She was still prying.

Everything she had told Lambert so far he already knew from the newspapers. He told her to stop straining herself. The *flic* was evidently still around her neck. She did not seem to mind too much.

And twice a week Lambert was driven through the streets to the Palace of Justice to be interrogated according to law by Fayot, the *juge d'instruction*. Handcuffs and leg-irons were removed and he took a chair across the desk from Fayot. Two guards stood with their backs to the ornate double doors. Fayot's *greffier* sat down at his machine. Sharkey was always present. His French associate was sometimes there. Fayot cross-examined Lambert, while the *greffier* noted down each response. Lambert always enjoyed himself. It made him proud to match wits with the French magistrate in French. Fayot never smiled at any of Lambert's answers, but certain of them convulsed Sharkey, which was fun, even though Sharkey, who usually came from a heavy meal, and much wine, was somewhat easy to convulse.

At least once during each interrogation, while the guards stiffened behind him, Lambert got up and strolled to the windows. He heard the creaking of the leather as their hands went to their guns. The French windows looked down on the Rue de la Préfecture three stories below. High-ceilinged stories. About thirty-five feet to the street. More, maybe. Too high. Impossibly high. If he jumped he'd be killed. But the possibility was intriguing. It was the biggest gap in their security that he had noted so far.

Between the Palace of Justice and the prison he rode inside a locked van wearing the handcuffs and leg-irons. Any attempted escape en route, if he could get out of the van, would leave him clanking through the streets of Nice in chains. It had to be before the chains went on or after they came off. Fayot's window then, but how?

It was Fayot's job to prepare the so-called "instruction," to examine in depth all the defendants, evidence, and witnesses, then turn his dossier over to the court for trial. But the outcome of the trial depended on the findings in the dossier and would be almost foreordained. It behooved most defendants therefore to cooperate. Lambert, however, was not "most" defendants. He kidded Fayot, frustrated him, told jokes at which Fayot did not laugh. Usually Fayot got mad and ordered him chained up and taken away.

Bellarmine came to see him. They strolled in the courtyard and worked each other for information. But Lambert only received, he didn't give. Roy LeRoy in jail, Bellarmine told him, was suing France for the return of his boat and money. This made Lambert laugh. "Roy LeRoy versus La Republique Française," he chortled. "A landmark case."

The cop said: "There were some Englishmen in that vault too. What can you tell me about them?"

"Englishmen?"

"English-speaking."

Lambert tried to look puzzled. "You don't say."

"About half a dozen."

Lambert felt a grin spreading, but closed it off. "I'd like to help you."

"Who were the others?"

"Because you seem like a real nice guy."

"Roy LeRoy was one, no?"

Bellarmine, walking beside the tall, thin crew-cut American, was getting exactly the silly, arrogant replies he had expected. He was not there to quiz Lambert about possible English accomplices, but to study him. To try to observe him through Jacqueline's eyes. To understand, if he could, what kind of a marriage it had been, might still be.

Lambert said: "You keep me segregated from the Banque de Nice prisoners here. Why? They're famous guys. I'd like to meet them." And he showed all his teeth, pleased with himself.

Lambert, when he spoke idiocies like this, sounded to Bellarmine more like Jacqueline's son than her husband, making any sexual relations they may have had almost like incest.

He did not like to think of sexual relations between them.

The courtyard was small and private. They came to the end of it and turned around.

300

"There's a gang war in Marseille," Bellarmine said. "The Falettas are finished. It's a struggle for succession."

"Who's responsible for that?"

He studied him briefly. "You are, I expect."

"I'm an innocent man," said Lambert, smirking. "I'm a playwright."

The American seemed to enjoy annoying people. One side of Bellarmine's mustache lifted in scorn. "You talk about writing," he said cruelly. "You just don't do it."

Stung, Lambert replied: "How's my wife?"

"Your wife says hello."

But the question had shocked Bellarmine. He knows I'm in love with his wife, he thought, guiltily. But how could he know? He's a prisoner in jail. There's no way he could find out.

Unless she told him.

If she told him, he thought, I wish she'd tell me.

*"Your wife says hello."*

The briefest possible hesitation had preceded this reply. One he hoped Lambert had not noticed. But why the guilt? he asked himself. There is nothing to be guilty about. Nothing has yet happened between us, and may never.

"Something I do not understand," he said. "A man like you, he is better off unmarried. So why you marry?"

He got exactly the flip answer he expected. "The war was over. I didn't want to go home."

"That is no reason to marry."

"She had a store. She could support me while I wrote my play. In Europe they take artists seriously."

Bellarmine said nothing.

"And she was certainly a beautiful girl." Lambert, remembering, was shaking his head in admiration.

"She is a beautiful woman."

"It was the only way I could get her into the sack," Lambert said, and eyed him.

Bellarmine remained silent.

"Maybe you don't understand that word."

"I understand it."

"She wouldn't," Lambert explained, "take her clothes off otherwise. Play games with me."

"I said I understand it." Again he felt Lambert eye him.

The American, hands in his pockets, resumed walking, resumed

301

remembering. "She was some lucious piece. She really loved it at first. Afterward not so much."

"You grew apart," said Bellarmine stolidly.

"I grew. She didn't. But those first few weeks—was she hot for it!"

"A man should not talk like this about his wife."

"Why not?" said Lambert, and he grinned. "She's my wife, not yours."

They stared at each other. Neither spoke and Lambert's grin faded.

"I'm thinking of breaking out of this jail," he said.

"Go ahead," said Bellarmine. "You're the one man everyone wants to kill. You stirred up the wrong hornet's nest. On the street you would not last a minute."

"I'm a hero," protested Lambert jovially.

"Go back to your cell and write a play instead. It is safer."

"Well, I warned you."

After leaving him, Bellarmine went and stood on the beach and gazed out to sea. It was about noon—a cool, overcast day. The sea was gray and the sky was gray. Far out there was no horizon. Sea and sky were indistinguishable one from the other. He was very conscious of the air around his face. It had rained earlier and probably would rain again in the afternoon.

He was trying to come to terms with Lambert, with Jacqueline, with himself. When he shifted his weight the stones shifted beneath his shoes.

"I thought I'd find you here," said Jacqueline's voice.

He turned and gave her a smile. She carried a blanket and a picnic basket. They spread the blanket and sat down. As he began to uncork the wine, he told her he had just visited her husband.

"I asked him why he ever wanted to get married."

Jacqueline would not meet his eyes. "What did he say?"

"He talked about how beautiful you were."

Jacqueline, reaching into the basket, frowned.

"He said he wanted to stay in Europe and write plays."

The surface of the blanket was not smooth. She set down glasses and balanced them.

"Other than that," said Bellarmine apologetically, "he didn't make much sense." He waited.

She gazed straight out to sea. "It's true he wanted to write plays," she said presently. "At least he said he did. He had such beautiful ideas. I was going to support him while he wrote."

"Yes."

"I didn't mind. There were a lot of young Americans here at the time. They were all going to be great writers. He was the only one married. They used to have these terribly profound literary discussions."

"They talked about Paris in the Twenties," guessed Bellarmine.

"They said they were doing the same thing here on the coast." She turned an earnest glance his way. "When you're that age you believe things like that."

"Yes."

"When he got successful we were going to move to America."

"I see. And then?"

"One by one the others all went home. But he didn't."

"Because he had you."

"Because he had me." she was peeling a hard-boiled egg. "I suppose that was why."

"Why did you marry him?"

"Because I was in love with him." The words made Bellarmine flinch. "Oh, yes, was I in love."

She handed him the peeled egg and he studied it.

"I was in love with him because—you don't know what it was like here. When the Americans came. When Nice was liberated there was shooting in the streets for several days. We couldn't go out. We had nothing to eat but a sack of cornmeal. My mother prepared corn cereal for breakfast, a corn cake for lunch and corn pudding for dinner. Then the shooting stopped and what seemed like the entire American Army was there, driving around and around the Place Masséna, and the whole town was out and everyone was cheering and crying."

Bellarmine poured out wine.

"When I worked in the PX, one of the girls was fired for stealing—trying to steal—five bars of chocolate. We had to wear these uniforms—sickly yellow blouse with a sickly green apron. I was so ashamed I used to come to work with a coat on over my uniform, even in summer."

"I understand," said Bellarmine.

"And then *he* was there. To me he was a creature from another world. He seemed so mysterious. He drank milk. He walked with his hands in his pockets. He didn't sit down in a chair, he sprawled. His hand was at his hair all the time. His table manners were different, he even held a cigarette differently. He knew how to repair cars, to throw a ball. Oh, yes, I was in love with him. Was I ever in love."

She's talking about sex, Bellarmine thought. The American turned her on sexually. They responded to each other. To Bellarmine came a too-vivid image of Jacqueline wearing only a sheen of sweat, wrestling on a bed—on many beds—with someone—with anyone who was not himself. That Lambert was her husband made no difference.

"I know what you're thinking." She watched him.

"No, you don't," he said. The jealousy of it was the worst of his experience, and he stared out at the opaque sea.

She gave an odd laugh. "In a sense I married him for his wealth. He didn't have a sou. Legally he couldn't even work in France. He was still the richest man I could even imagine. Because he was American, you see. He owned the future. And he promised to give it to me."

"But he didn't," said Bellarmine.

"Nobody ever married more for wealth than I did."

"And now you feel guilty about it."

"Yes."

"Everybody feels guilty. Eat your lunch."

A little later, after they had repacked the basket, refolded the blanket and had turned their backs on the sea, Jacqueline said: "If he did it—what you say he did"—they were trudging across the stones toward the staircase up to the Promenade—"it was because he woke up one day and said to himself: 'Let's do something that's exciting and interesting and fun.' "

"Don't get romantic about it," said Bellarmine harshly. "He looted a bank. He caused untold pain to hundreds of people. He deserves whatever he gets for it."

His meeting with Bellarmine had left Lambert in a bad mood, and he did not know why. Returning to his cell he picked up the manuscript of his work in progress. In three weeks he had managed four and a half pages. Not quite one full scene. He did not now read this scene. He knew well enough what was in it. He tore the manuscript to bits and dropped it into the dry toilet bowl in the corner of his cell. Then he dumped the bucket of water in on top of it, and that particular play vanished forever.

His next decision followed closely. He was tired of jail. It was time to leave, and he saw, or thought he saw, two possible ways to do it. But he would need help, and so he ordered Sharkey during a regularly scheduled visit the next afternoon to contact Congressman Saul Avery wherever he might be: "Tell him I want to see him. Tell him to get his ass over here."

"That's preposterous," responded Sharkey. "He won't come."

"He'll come."

# CHAPTER 31

Avery in his suite at the Rhul contemplated Sharkey with distaste. The blazer, the pretentious foulard. Florid face and white hair. Pompous, offensive man. Americans who had gone native were no different from the English colonial types of the past. Their exalted sense of position was based on race alone. They could be seen as an early-warning system—the first manifestation of the onset of national decadence. Proof that the hard cutting edge that had formed the empire in the first place was already dulled by the sybaritic pleasures that the natives, as a last-ditch defense, had thrown into the conquerors' path. Conquest had been stopped in its tracks, not by juggernauts but by forbidden games. This man Sharkey was a perfect example of it. In France he had struck a pose, and found it mesmerizing. Life to Sharkey was contemplating himself in the mirror. He had brought the blackmailer's message and didn't even know it.

France—the French—had tried to do the same thing to Avery himself, of course, but he had ignored them and got his business set up. Profits were accruing. He had turned their weaknesses back on to themselves. He had cashed in.

Except that a problem had arisen, a blackmailer who threatened to ruin him, and who must be dealt with.

After ushering Sharkey from the room, Avery stood on his balcony looking out. The Mediterranean was across the street. There must have been rain last night in the mountains, washing down mud, for a greenish-brown stain extended out from shore about a half mile. Then the sea was blue again.

Avery pondered. At home a public figure, realizing the possibility of blackmail, took steps to protect himself. With normal care the risks could be reduced to a minimum. Abroad, imagining himself safe, one was more willing to take chances. In his own case too willing. Obviously he had made a mistake. Now it would have to be rectified. He saw a number of ways to do this.

Far out to sea, emerging from the white haze, Avery spied one of the liners from Corsica. A white liner on a white day. A ghost ship. Its lines were indistinct, but heavy. Like the threat that hung over his life. He was a retired brigadier general and a four-term congressman, one of the most powerful in Washington; the threat could be removed.

Sharkey preceded him into the house of arrest. Avery allowed it, and Sharkey seemed proud to serve as guide. To show the way down jailhouse corridors seemed to make him strut—how ridiculous. Avery sniffed the jailhouse aroma. Lysol mixed with pea soup mixed with stale urine, almost like schoolrooms.

The administration building was a kind of Provençal mansion with an orange tile roof; it certainly did not resemble any American prison Avery had seen. In the *parloir* they waited for Lambert. It was like a room in one of those empty châteaux in the north. This building might have been a palace once. The notion did not surprise Avery. The French liked palaces and continued to find new uses for them. As a people they were unable to shed their love for material things. They guillotined the owners, then turned their houses into ministries, into post offices, into museums, into public buildings of all kinds. Functionaries moved desks into drawing rooms. The brass door handles remained, the wedding-cake ceilings, so in a sense the aristocrats had the last laugh after all. Nothing much changed. Electricity was invented, indoor plumbing came in. The French fixed pipes into corners and ran wires up walls. They painted these places about once a century. Every public building was a visual exposition of the history of the nation.

Lambert strode into the *parloir*.

"You may go," said Avery to Sharkey.

It made Sharkey sputter. "But I represent the accused—"

"I said you may go," said Avery, and Sharkey went.

"You're not too impressed with my lawyer," suggested Lambert, and he grinned.

Avery only stared back, until the half smile disappeared from Lambert's face.

"Get on with it," the congressman said. "What do you want?"

There was enormous tension in the room, both men felt it, and Lambert began to giggle.

The giggle became an ugly laugh. "But I just don't understand how you could have posed for those pictures, Saul. May I call you Saul?"

Avery at this moment did not understand how either. Although he had no intention of trying to explain it to Lambert, he had tried for the past several weeks to explain it to himself. But sexual arousal, he believed, confused a man's judgment—women's judgment too. In the heat of passion, men and women—not just himself—will take part in acts that, in broad daylight, might seem to them improper or revolting, compromising or even dangerous. There had been other incidents back in Washington. Avery considered himself an expert on the subject. In the confusion of sexual games one forgot normal caution. And over here in France one's recklessness was abetted by an emotion that was almost hilarity. *We own this place. I can do anything I like here.*

"We own this place," murmured Lambert, as if reading his thoughts. "I know that feeling."

Avery supposed he did. It was probably what had made him rob the bank. Back home the idea probably never would have occurred to him. Over here different standards seemed to apply. One behaved—differently. As if nobody was looking, as if foreigners—Americans at least—could get away with anything they pleased. Virtually all tourists felt this. They had been released from the strictures placed on them inside their own societies. Their personalities seemed to change. Some merely became boorish and loud. Some committed acts formerly unthinkable.

"You are The Brain," said Avery. The blackmailer he had feared for so long. But now that Lambert sat across the table from him he felt no fear, only a kind of kinship.

Lambert gave a slight inclination of his head, as if acknowledging a tribute. But he said only: "I have some things you want."

"What is your price?"

"Get me out of here and I give them back."

"How am I supposed to do that?"

"You're an important man. Your friend the adjunct mayor is an important man. Go convince the *juge d'instruction* to release me."

"I have no influence here," Avery stated. "Name some other price." The French judicial system, he knew, was independent of the other branches of government. Theoretically, pressure could not be brought

307

upon it by the police or local politicians, and supposedly it was immune even to influence from Paris. "There is nothing I can do for you."

"Then I make certain photos, certain documents public." Lambert stood up and started out of the *parloir.* The interview was over. But at the door he turned. "Why don't you talk to the adjunct mayor about it and get back to me?" He walked out. For about five minutes Avery only sat there, considering options. Then he too walked out, though by the other door.

He found Picpoul in his garden. It was not the type of garden Avery was used to. There was no sprinkler system, no lawn. Grass did not seem to grow in this soil and climate. Gardens around the villas above Nice consisted of alleys of fruit trees—orange trees, lemon trees, pear trees—plus alleys of semitropical flowers, particularly geraniums. Bougainvillea, purple in the sun, climbed the walls of Picpoul's villa, and most others. It entwined itself in his balconies. Grapevines shrouded his fences, and served as an impenetrable hedge around the property.

Two of Picpoul's goons stood guard at the head of the driveway. A third polished his official car.

"*Et alors?*" said Picpoul.

"Calm down," Avery said. "I have some ideas."

They evolved a number of possible plans, and Avery went back to Lambert and presented the first of them. Picpoul, he said, was contacting other important men who had held boxes in the Banque de Nice. They wanted their documents back also. Pressure would be applied on the Minister of the Interior. The minister would put pressure on the *juge d'instruction,* and the *juge* would accord Lambert what was called "provisional liberty under caution."

"No good," said Lambert. "What you're talking about will take weeks."

"First we get you out of jail," said Avery stolidly, "then we find a way to get you out of the country."

"In five more days I make public what I have."

"You'll sit here until we get ready to get you out," snapped Avery, and he left the jail. But he found Picpoul and told him to hurry. Lambert's threats had become explicit.

Picpoul put together a group that included Marcel Doussac, supposedly the richest man in France, and they called on the minister in Paris. All of them then flew back to Nice and were received in

Fayot's office where the minister acted as spokesman. If Lambert were released, these men would get their documents back. Lambert could then be rearrested and—

"Would then flee the country, you mean," said Fayot. The young magistrate believed his entire career rode on this one case, which was by now famous all over the world. He categorically rejected any step the world might see as improper. He refused these powerful men, and showed them out.

The powerful men, finding themselves in the hallway, realized they had made a mistake. They had brought maximum pressure to bear all at once and now had no fallback position. Pressure should have been applied over a period of days. It should have seemed to Fayot vaguer, more threatening. Nonetheless, they were astonished that he had refused them. They could not believe it. All agreed that in France such a man would not go far, and they started to leave the Palace of Justice.

By the time they had reached the bottom of the great marble staircase, they had decided to offer Fayot a bribe.

That same evening they sent a man to his apartment. Fayot made no attempt to raise the sum in question. He simply closed the door in the man's face.

Avery had been waiting for news in the Ruhl bar. In America he would have handled this alone. There would have been no need to use these idiot Frenchmen as intermediaries. He stared darkly into successive glasses of Scotch whiskey. Each refill came with a single tiny ice cube floating in it. French penury with regard to ice infuriated Avery. Goddamn country couldn't even afford to put ice in the drinks. Each time he had to demand more ice. Each time supplementary ice was grudgingly brought him. You'd think the stupid barman would learn, but he never did. Avery waited in the bar until news of the failure of the bribe attempt had been communicated to him, after which he had one more drink, then went to bed.

By morning he had decided to send O'Hara to visit the *juge d'instruction*. The FBI man was to suggest to Fayot that Lambert was an American secret agent, whom the American government wanted released at once. The American government would be "displeased" if he weren't. American displeasure could take many forms and would have grim results for France.

"I don't know if I can say such things, Congressman."

309

"Shut up and listen, Charlie." O'Hara was to describe him as one of the most powerful men in Congress. He was to suggest that Avery himself might deign to meet with Fayot, if necessary, to settle final details.

"I'm just a cop," said O'Hara. "You're the congressman. Why don't you go?"

Because Fayot must be made to see Avery's power—a powerful man was one who sent representatives to do his dirty work. But Avery did not explain this to O'Hara.

"There are national-security aspects to this you may not know about," he said.

"I'm sure," muttered O'Hara.

"I don't have to take lip from you, Charlie. Just do what I tell you, okay?"

While waiting for O'Hara's return, Avery strolled the Promenade des Anglais, from time to time pausing to look down on the stony beach, which was crowded with bathers. It was hot, a day of blinding sunshine, and he felt confident. This was the United States of America speaking now, or so Fayot would perceive. Let's see the young man stand up under that kind of weight. The fringes of the umbrellas blew in the sea breeze. Fayot would fold. The pallets were laid out in neat rows from seawall almost to the water's edge. Most had bodies lying on them. He peered down on rows of backs being fried in oil—tiny bikini bottoms and undone bra strings, and he waited, hoping a girl might lift up, giving him a glimpse of something. He was certain that this time Fayot would see reason. America spoke to the French nation as if from a pulpit—from a position not only of political and economic superiority, but of moral superiority as well. Therefore America's wishes—or the wishes of one of her senior representatives—would be obeyed.

"He was unresponsive, Congressman."

O'Hara had materialized beside him. Avery frowned.

A path of duckboards covered with coco matting parted the rows of pallets, extending from the seawall down to the edge of the gentle surf. Avery watched as two girls in bikinis passed each other, the one sleek with oil, the other beaded with sea water. It was like simultaneous front and back views of the same girl.

"It's shocking, how the girls show themselves here," said Avery.

"If I ever saw my daughter wearing one of those things," answered O'Hara, "I'd paddle her bottom for her."

"Did he suggest that I come and see him?"

"He said there was no point to it."

"These Frenchwomen don't seem to have any modesty at all, do they?"

"Lambert is a criminal," said O'Hara cautiously. "I don't see how you can justify getting any further involved in a criminal case."

"Let's drop it, shall we, Charlie?"

Back to the jail went Avery. "We're still trying things." He gave Lambert a smile and a sock in the arm.

Lambert rubbed his fingers together in the universal symbol of money. "You go to the *juge d'instruction*," he said, "and you get your checkbook out. You buy me out of here, and I give you what you want." He sounded like a man explaining something obvious to a child. "He's a Frenchman. The French are all corrupt."

Avery believed this too. However, Fayot seemed to have proved otherwise.

"We already tried it. I'm not an idiot, you know."

Lambert, bitterly disappointed, retorted: "You must be an idiot, to pose for those pictures."

Like most men Avery had daydreamed since puberty of one day taking part in an orgy—he would fuck three or four gorgeous broads in a single night, while watching other men do likewise. Suddenly here in Nice as a general in the liberating army, he had met people of power and the daydream had become reality. Or rather, he had met people interested in re-establishing their power, and they had used him as a means to this end. He was there as a liberator, but they treated him as a conqueror, and he had not corrected them. He had behaved as one. He had put together the syndicate to buy the casino. Picpoul or Maître Verini had supplied him with women each time he came here, and not streetwalkers. They were more like show girls, or else people's wives. He had enjoyed himself, and his ego had expanded along with his member. He had won a star on his shoulder and then a war. He had won four straight elections. He came to believe he was only getting his due.

He had been invited to his first orgy in 1947, and his last, the one that had been photographed, had taken place two years ago, during the casino negotiations. Only five orgies over a space of seven years. None of them sinister, until the final one. The photographer had been one of the women. This was what had so disarmed him. For this reason it had not seemed dangerous. They all wore masks for the camera; they were all in this together. What harm could it do? He had posed willingly, and so had his partner, a really luscious woman, the busty young wife of one of the other adjunct mayors. He had wanted a photograph of himself fucking her.

It never occurred to him that Verini meant to hold the photos hostage, hold him hostage. That was bad luck. And then Lambert had wound up with them, which was incredibly bad luck.

"Your time is nearly up," said Lambert coldly.

"A jailbreak," mused Avery. "Suppose we broke you out." He had been mulling over this idea for several days. They would go to the Milieu, who would arrange it.

"What are your relations with the Corsicans in Marseille?" asked Avery.

"You can't trust those guys. They're gangsters."

"They can get you out of here."

"Maybe. But I'm afraid they may not like me anymore." He was not joking now. "First they break me out and then they put me to death in some picturesque way. As a lesson to others." Lambert gave a grim laugh. "It would be a lesson to you, too, I'm afraid. The stuff I have on you would automatically be made public."

Avery was silent.

"I have a better idea," said Lambert. "You bring in the CIA."

Avery studied him.

The CIA guys were experts at arranging jailbreaks, Lambert told him. They had done it numerous times in numerous countries since the war. Of course most of the men rescued were their own agents. Avery should pass Lambert off as a U.S. agent of some kind, and the jailbreak could be arranged.

"You're not a secret agent," Avery muttered, "you're a thief."

"Don't get sanctimonious with me, pal. I didn't pose for those pictures."

"No," said Avery coolly. "You're the one who robbed the bank."

"Your constituents are going to love those photos. And wait till the IRS learns of all those casino profits you haven't paid taxes on."

They glared at each other.

"You better go lean on the CIA."

Avery began to nod his head up and down. "It's a possibility," he conceded. His Louisiana drawl had become slower, its tone ever more menacing. But Lambert never noticed.

312

Lambert seemed to swell up with cockiness. "I need a motorcycle and one good man. Tell them that. The rest I can take care of myself."

Avery's head again nodded up and down. "These things of mine you have—who else knows about them?"

"No one."

"How can I be sure?"

Lambert gave an ugly laugh. "The Heist of the Century is more than three months in the past," he explained. "Nobody's bothered you in that time. No one has bothered the adjunct mayor either. There are ten or fifteen other guys in jail, but none of them have spoken of it."

"That's true."

"What more proof do you need? And as soon as I'm on the street you get them back."

After a pause Avery said: "You may have made copies. This thing could go on and on."

"Too dangerous," said Lambert. "As dangerous for me as for you. And why should I bother? I don't need money, and once out of here I won't need you anymore. Satisfied?"

"It sounds logical," said Avery.

"So get the CIA moving, okay? You don't have much time." And he turned and left the room. The guard followed, closing the door behind him. For a moment Avery sat alone, thinking. As he rose to leave he noted that the conference table was polished to such a high gloss that he could almost see his reflection.

# CHAPTER
## 32

The Blue Train, the crack Paris-Riviera express, left Nice every night at 8 P.M. That night Avery was on it. He slept badly. Half the night he lay with the shade up watching the Rhône Valley pass by his bed. This thing was getting really bad. The worst of it was that he had to do everything himself. The French were no help to him at all. At the U.S. Embassy on the Place de la Concorde he paid a courtesy call on the ambassador and several other officials, then slipped into the office of a man named Tuttle, whom he knew to be the CIA station chief in France. As quickly as possible Avery brought the conversation around to Lambert, whom he identified as a man falsely accused of a grave crime.

"You're not serious, Congressman."

Avery had decided to devote two or more hours to this talk with Tuttle. "Certain proofs have come into my hands that firmly establish his innocence," he began. Avery didn't care if Tuttle believed this or not. Just so long as he felt Avery's power, and eventually acceded to it. "The man is being railroaded to prison by foreigners," he continued. "He's a fellow American, and he's a constituent of mine as well." For the next ten minutes Avery discoursed on Lambert's qualities—his war record, his career as an author, his "grieving little wife." He himself was under great pressure from "back home," he said.

Tuttle evidently decided he had best match Avery in patriotic fervor, for he began to denounce the press, whose reports had certainly made Lambert sound guilty.

This subject was good for another twenty minutes, not all of it about Lambert. Both men discoursed on French journalism—underpaid reporters, inaccurate stories, scandalous headlines. They recounted anecdotes, made each other laugh. They became friends. Avery's Louisiana accent became broader. He called Tuttle a "good ol' boy." He was working hard, but it didn't especially show. This was a technique he was very good at. He was like a salesman putting a customer in the mood to buy.

"Suppose this man was one of your own agents," Avery interrupted. He made the question sound almost an idle one. "Lambert, I mean. Could you arrange his escape?"

He watched Tuttle's eyes narrow. "It's an interesting idea," said Tuttle.

"How would you go about it?" asked Avery idly.

"We have operatives in the field to handle such things for us."

"Local people. Specialists."

"That's right, Congressman."

"A lot of people want that man out of jail. They want us to get him out."

"Us?"

Satisfied that Tuttle understood him, Avery began to tell anecdotes about his career in Washington, about Congress, about the White House. The purpose of this was to drop names, to awe—to overawe—the CIA man. Avery was careful not to overdo it. It was a job he had performed often. He had learned to perform it with great skill. The anecdotes concerned the President, the speaker of the House, the Senate minority leader. They were interesting anecdotes, some were amusing, they led one into the other, and not all showed Avery in a heroic light. "I was on Ike's staff in North Africa, but now I call him Mr. President, just like everybody else."

"He campaigned for you, didn't he?" remembered Tuttle.

Whether deliberate or not, it was a form of encouragement. Avery began to talk of high French officials who now came to him for help. The French were totally dependent upon American aid and American friendship, and Lambert as an American was an embarrassment to them, he said. They did not want a highly publicized trial.

"What's your interest in this, Congressman?" asked Tuttle bluntly.

In addition, explained Avery, documents were missing from the bank vault, and if Lambert went on trial, or even remained in jail, such documents might come to light.

"But you said the man was innocent," said Tuttle.

Avery told some more anecdotes. These involved the military defense complex. He himself was vice-chairman of the Armed Services committee. Defense contractors came to him for candidates for executive jobs. He had recommended a lot of men in recent years, men who now earned good money—more than congressmen earned, Avery added with a chuckle. Tuttle himself was the type of man they wanted, he said. A man of proven patriotism, with service abroad. "Look me up if you're ever interested."

"That's very interesting, Congressman."

Avery switched to talk of the Indochina war. The present French government was about to bug out, hand Indochina over to the Communists. He said this had to be averted, and Tuttle agreed with him. "Here's the twist," said Avery. "All these French governments are wobbly. If Lambert escapes, this one will fall and the peace talks will collapse."

Tuttle kept silent.

"We certainly don't want Indochina to go Communist, do we?" said Avery.

"No sirree," said Tuttle.

"Good," said Avery. "That's what we're all trying to prevent."

The Indochina argument seemed to interest Tuttle more than anything so far. Perhaps he saw himself single-handedly ending the peace talks. To keep the French bogged down in Indochina was in America's interest. For as long as French boys died there, American boys wouldn't have to. Or perhaps he had begun to think of a job with Lockheed or Chance-Vought.

They decided to have lunch together, and so were seen getting into an enormous embassy car and being driven out through the gates, something the congressman had wanted to avoid. It did a man's reputation no good to be observed frequenting these CIA spooks.

They dined in the Bois de Boulogne at a restaurant situated among the trees near a waterfall. The tables were set outdoors on the terrace in the sun, and the noise of the waterfall punctuated their haggling, for the only detail left to settle was the amount of money required.

"If I spend money," said Tuttle, "I have to inform Washington."

"I have access to some private money. How much would you need?"

A sum was mentioned. "It shouldn't cost so much," said Avery promptly.

"It may cost even more than that," contradicted the CIA man. "The talent I'll have to line up is pretty high priced."

"It can be done with one man and one motorcycle," stated Avery.

"A jailbreak? Don't make me laugh."

"That's what he says."

"Jesus, is the prisoner arranging this himself?"

"One other thing. It's got to be done fast." Avery pushed a thick envelope across the table.

"Fast? You don't want much, do you?" But Tuttle put the envelope in his pocket. The CIA had decided to take on Avery's case.

The two men were aboard the Blue Train when it pulled out of the Gare de Lyon that night. Neither knew the other was aboard, and when Tuttle got down in Marseille at 6 A.M., Avery in his compartment was still asleep. While the train continued on to Nice, Tuttle caught a taxi to the American Consulate, where he bathed, shaved, and then went out to begin calling on contacts. In France, as in all countries, the CIA was involved in activities that were often criminal in nature. To perform specific acts—break-ins, assassinations, whatever—the CIA hired experts—local gangsters. Tuttle therefore had a strong working relationship with elements of the Marseille Milieu, and that morning he visited two caids he had used in the recent past. But both refused any assignment involving Lambert on the grounds that Faletta had done so, and look what had happened to him.

Tuttle had not planned to call on Faletta. But now he changed his mind.

At noon he stood at the zinc bar in the Café de l'Amitié, and while waiting, he sipped like any honest French workman a glass of red wine. Faletta, as was his habit, came in about five minutes later. Flanked by two bodyguards, he moved down the bar shaking hands, calling some patrons by name, though not Tuttle. Tuttle saw him go into his office in the back and close the door. The two bodyguards sat at a table just outside and the barman brought them a bottle of red wine. After about five minutes, Tuttle stepped toward the rear as if toward the toilet, veering at the last moment through Faletta's door, which he opened without knocking. The bodyguards made no move to stop him. Faletta, who was seated behind the desk, looked up with a quizzical expression on his face.

Tuttle, who spoke good French, asked after the health of Faletta's wife, his brothers, his children, his sister Restitude. The CIA was unique among American organizations operating abroad—it sometimes employed people who spoke the language of the country.

"I've got a job for you," said Tuttle at last, and he said what it was. One man on a motorcycle might be sufficient—this remained to be seen. Details would be provided through a contact. He pushed half the contents of Avery's envelope across the desk, holding back the other half in reserve.

Faletta put the envelope in a drawer. "And the contact?"

"Our man Sharkey," said Tuttle. He knew that Sharkey, one of his part-time agents, was also Lambert's lawyer, and this was still another reason he had taken on the case. If the escape succeeded, or even if it failed, no CIA connection would show.

Tuttle's final reason, though as strong or stronger than the others, was purely visceral. To flaunt another country's laws, to destabilize governments, to mix with criminals, to break the law with impunity—these were satisfactions in themselves. Most of all, Tuttle simply loved plots. Conspiracy delighted him, and from now on he would be able to follow this one in the papers like a baseball game. And if the plot did fail, no harm done.

He went back to the train station and continued on to Nice, where he gave Sharkey his instructions and distributed a bit more of Avery's money. He also saw Avery, telling him that arrangements had been made, all systems were go. Tuttle felt so pleased with himself that he even agreed to a celebratory drink with Avery in the Ruhl bar, a mistake, for it happened that they were observed there by O'Hara.

Recognizing Tuttle, O'Hara asked himself why the CIA man was in Nice and also why he and Avery were drinking champagne. Since he couldn't tail both men away from the Ruhl, he chose to tail Tuttle, who led him to a subsequent meeting with Sharkey and then to the train station, where the CIA man boarded the Blue Train back to Paris.

It was enough to convince O'Hara that some kind of plot was in motion, but he didn't know what, and he was unsure what his next move should be.

Avery settled this matter for him by summoning him that same night to the Ruhl.

"I won't be needing you anymore, Charlie. You might as well go back to Paris."

O'Hara, who wanted more than ever to stay in Nice, began to suggest several ways that his services might still prove useful.

"Piss off, Charlie," interrupted Avery curtly.

O'Hara was not used to being talked to like this.

"I'll phone the embassy and tell them you're on your way," said Avery. "How soon shall I tell them you'll be back in your office?"

It made O'Hara furious. He had no intention of leaving Nice now, and the next morning he went around to see Bellarmine.

They sat outside a café on the Place Masséna and the early sun slanted in under the arcade. Bellarmine ordered coffee. O'Hara ordered orange juice, but as soon as it was served he realized his mistake. Although the south of France teemed with orange trees, nonetheless orange juice here was undrinkable because of the way it was served—an inch of juice and two spoonfuls of sugar in the bottom of the glass. One filled the glass from the carafe of water served with it, and one stirred. The result, to O'Hara, was a weak, flat, orange soda.

"Take this away," he told the waiter. To Bellarmine he said: "The French haven't caught on to orange juice yet. Why is that?"

Bellarmine sipped and said nothing.

"It might be a good idea to put a tail on the guy's lawyer," suggested O'Hara, and he waited for a response.

"It's unwise to tail lawyers," muttered the Frenchman. "The other lawyers don't like it."

"The judicial establishment, you mean. Well fuck 'em, I say."

Bellarmine only grunted.

"There's pressure from Washington to get your prisoner out of jail," said O'Hara.

Bellarmine nodded. "I'll take some precautions." Money went down on the table. Both men stood up. O'Hara watched Bellarmine cross the street and go into the *commissariat*. He had told him as much as he could, and he walked back to the consulate.

Sharkey was waiting when Lambert was brought down to the *parloir* that afternoon. Lambert as he entered the room looked highly amused. "Well, if it isn't the Shark," he said. Avery had already come and gone. "So you're a CIA guy, eh, Shark? I never suspected."

They sat down opposite each other.

"You should spread word around the Riviera," Lambert suggested. "It would help your image. Sharkey the Spook. You'd get invited to all the best places."

But Sharkey could read new respect in Lambert's eyes, and he was pleased.

Lambert said: "Have you been with them long?"

"No, not long." If the news now spread, Sharkey wondered, would it help his practice? His image? Although he had been accepting money for several years, this would be the first significant thing he had done to earn it.

"What do you do for them? What's the job like?"

Mostly he provided Tuttle with gossip about the Côte d'Azur's foreign colony. Sexual stuff often enough. "I can't talk about it," he said, adopting a pose of secrecy. It would not in the retelling sound very brave.

"How'd you get mixed up with those guys, Shark? That's what I should have done. How'd it happen?"

"You can't apply," said Sharkey. "They have to come to you—if they think you occupy a position in society that could prove—useful."

He had stayed behind on the Riviera after the war, and had gradually established a clientele, but this clientele did not grow and lately had begun to diminish. He did not want to be forced to leave Nice, which was so beautiful, so slow-moving, so removed

319

from pressure. He was *someone* here. And so, when Tuttle had first approached him, he had been receptive. It had seemed easy money. Until now.

Now he found himself mixed up in a jailbreak.

"What's your plan?" Sharkey nervously asked his client.

"You don't need to know."

"I'm the guy who's going to set it up."

"You're going to set up one part of it. I'll set up the other part myself."

"I'm taking risks just as big as yours."

"You are taking risks, Shark, I'll grant you that." There was admiration in Lambert's voice, and Sharkey was pleased by it. Nonetheless, Lambert told little. Tomorrow afternoon he wanted a man on a motorcycle stationed in the Rue de la Préfecture near the front corner of the Palace of Justice. At 4:10 precisely the man was to start the engine of his motorcycle. Five minutes after that, if all went according to plan, Lambert would bestride the pillion seat behind the driver, and off they both would go.

"Go where?"

"Not far. Who's going to be driving the motorcycle, an American?"

"I don't know. Go where?"

Lambert laughed. "You should know such things, Shark, a lawyer as important as you."

"What do you care who's driving? You speak the language here, don't you? Go where? And how do you get out of the building?"

Sharkey believed he needed to know more details, that his employers would demand them. In their absence he might not get paid. Yet he was not certain of this. Indeed he had not been certain of much for years. He was an American pretending to live like a Frenchman. Unlike Lambert, he tried to blend in. As a result he was often unsure what his conduct should be. Lambert, who had chosen to remain obviously, arrogantly American, had an easier role to play.

"The Palace of Justice is swarming with cops," Sharkey said. "You make a break for it there, they shoot you down."

"No, they won't."

"I need to know how you expect to get out of the building. And where does the motorcycle take you?"

"You don't need to know anything of the kind."

"How do you get out of the country?"

320

"Good question," said Lambert, and he grinned and said no more.

Sharkey owned a tiny 4-horse Renault. From the house of arrest he drove doggedly to Marseille, a trip that took three hours. He was tailed there by two detectives driving a black Traction Avant, but did not know this. O'Hara had spread the alarm, and detectives now watched Sharkey's every move.

In Marseille he parked in front of the Café de l'Amitié and went inside. He knew Faletta's reputation. They shook hands. Touching Faletta, even though the caid was smiling and cordial, made the hairs stand up on Sharkey's forearms. After relaying Lambert's "instructions"—there was no other word for it—he began to apologize. He had been unable to find out even where the motorcycle driver was to take him.

But Faletta cut him off. Doubtless Lambert intended to switch almost at once to another vehicle, or perhaps a boat. "Never mind, *mon vieux*," he said cordially, and offered Sharkey a drink. "The ride will be short. Very short." It sounded so ominous that again the hairs rose up on Sharkey's arms.

Faletta said he would confirm the operation that evening, and asked Sharkey to come back then. They left the bar together—preceded by one bodyguard and followed by another—which frightened Sharkey. He was now involved in a business whose outcome he could not calculate.

While waiting, he sat in a café over a single tiny cup of black coffee. Perhaps it was fear that caused his mind to dwell on prostitutes. He knew the Rue Longue. His feet took him there after a time—solely to appraise them, he told himself. Finally, after glancing furtively up and down the street, he selected one. Walking several paces behind so that no one could connect him to her, he followed her into a hotel. One of the things Sharkey liked about life in France was what he thought of as "easy sex." But he would never have dared pick up a whore in Nice. Marseille was different, he thought, as he took his pants off. No one knew him here; no one could carry the news back to Nice.

The bored detective waited in the doorway across the street for him to come down.

When Jacqueline came to the prison that night, she brought with her an elaborate dinner. Such privileges were not usually accorded prisoners and their wives, but she was not aware of this. Throughout the meal she asked her husband the same questions as always. Was he comfortable? Was he satisfied with the legal defense being prepared for him? Was he sleeping all right? She did not know what else to talk to him about.

Was there anything she could do?

"Yes, there is," Lambert told her, and spoke of the small jetty where the Paillon emptied into the Mediterranean. He had promised someone he'd have a boat waiting there tomorrow afternoon from four o'clock to five. He gave Jacqueline an embarrassed shrug. "Obviously I can't make the arrangements myself." He eyed her almost beseechingly.

She did not like the sound of this. "What's it about?"

"Cigarettes."

"No," Jacqueline told him.

But he took both her hands, pleading in a low, earnest voice. "You've got to do this thing for me." If the boat was not there, then he would not be paid his share, he said—and he desperately needed money for his legal defense. She had not yet, after all, mortgaged her store for him. This accusation was entirely unfair. Nonetheless, it provoked feelings in her of terrible guilt—as he knew it would. "There's no way you can get in trouble over this," he assured her.

So she hesitated, which must have seemed encouragement enough to Lambert. The person to contact, he said urgently, was the Englishman named Thompson. Thompson had driven one of Lambert's PT boats during the years when he had had two—the good years. Once Lambert had spent a fortune to get Thompson out of jail in Spain. Later Thompson had got married to a girl from Nice and had dropped out of the cigarette trade. Jacqueline had met him once. He had bought a speedboat and in the summer made his living towing water skiers—mostly tourists—up and down in front of the Ruhl. He had towed Jacqueline a year or so ago and had refused to take payment for it. She had not seen him since.

Her husband handed her an American hundred-dollar bill. "Give Thompson this much. He gets the same when the job is completed."

"I didn't say I'd do it," said Jacqueline.

"You're turning into a woman I don't know."

"Am I?"

"You're changing before my eyes these last several weeks. I don't understand it." It was as if he were watching her in a film from which every other scene had been cut, he told her.

"That's a line from one of your plays," she retorted. "And not one of your better lines either."

When she got up to go Lambert tried to extract a promise from her. Would she make the arrangements with Thompson?

"I'll have to think about it."

"I have to know your answer."

"I'll get a message to you."

"Don't send any messages in here. Are you crazy?" In a milder voice he said: "If I don't hear from you, that means you'll do it, okay?"

She inclined her head, took his kiss upon her cheek and walked from the room. Under her arm she carried the restaurateur's dirty dishes wrapped in the paper they had come in, and she left behind her a *parloir* that still smelled of *pigeon aux lentilles*, and a husband who snuffed the pungent air once, twice, then stepped through the door behind his guard.

Bellarmine was waiting for her in the black police Citroën outside the prison. She slid into the seat beside him and for a time did not speak. He did not speak either, though for a reason she would have found incredible. He was in the grip of the same sexual jealousy as before. It was very intense, and it made no sense at all—it happened to him every time she went in there to see her husband, as if it were a hotel and she was in there making love to him. With French logic he had examined his emotion from every side. Its absurdity was clear. Nonetheless, he felt it, and each night had difficulty speaking to her when she at last came out.

He took her to a café in the old town. The tables and chairs were pushed out on to the small square. There was a fountain. One side of the square was the centuries-old cathedral.

They waited in silence until the waiter had set down their order— chamomile tea for Jacqueline, Calvados for Bellarmine. Lighting a cigarette, he watched her stir her tea.

"Anything new with him?"

"No, nothing new."

But she could not meet his eyes, and as she considered her husband's strange request—the speedboat—she wondered if he knew she was lying. Nor did she know whether she should carry the message to Thompson, and she wished she could ask Bellarmine's advice.

"Is there anything new in the investigation?" she said instead.

"No," answered Bellarmine, also a lie. He was meeting with his detectives in an hour to plan a raid that might break this case wide open. To avoid staring hungrily at her profile, he watched his smoke rise, and mulled over the decisions to be made.

Presently he paid the check and they stood up.

"I'll take you home."

Jacqueline frowned. Home? "Yes, back to the shop," she said, and got into the black car and sat beside him as he drove. The two of them, she reflected, were certainly alike in one respect. They were alone in the world. They had no one but each other. He had held her in his arms only once, the night she cried into his neck. Apart from that he had scarcely touched her. Perhaps he had no interest in her except as a tap into her husband.

Bellarmine, driving, had similar thoughts. Perhaps she agrees to see me only to be forewarned of any steps against her husband—or against herself.

It was possible they were equally in love with each other—both at times hoped this was true—but neither trusted the other at all, and so their relationship did not advance. They remained what might be called intimate acquaintances. They had shared now several candle-light dinners, but at each one Lambert had seemed to be standing on the table between them, and in the end he had snuffed out all the flames, leaving them in darkness.

When Bellarmine pulled up in front of the shop, Jacqueline murmured something about the lateness of the hour—it was then about ten-thirty. She was really very tired and would go right to sleep, she said, and she stifled a yawn that seemed fictitious to both of them.

Bellarmine said he felt the same. Five minutes from now he would be snoring.

He watched her safely inside her shop. She smiled at him through the glass. Both waved. Immediately afterward they began deceiving each other.

Jacqueline waited only until certain Bellarmine's car was gone, then walked rapidly down the sidewalk toward the Ruhl Hotel where there were taxicabs. She had decided to deliver her husband's message and money to Thompson. She never imagined that Thompson's passenger tomorrow was to be her husband. It would be some man they had done business with, she guessed, probably a smuggler trying to sneak himself and/or merchandise out of France and into Italy. The frontier was about thirty-five kilometers down the coast. Well, if Thompson wished to do it, this was no concern of hers, and she felt certain that she could not be held legally involved, whatever it was.

Bellarmine in the car had turned toward his flat, but once out of sight of the shop he drove straight to the *commissariat* where nine detectives were waiting for him, one of whom this afternoon had tailed Faletta to the Brignoles farmhouse. The detective had stayed so far back that at times, he bragged, he had been guided only by the dust that Faletta's car raised far ahead above the road. He was sure he had not been spotted. Faletta had stayed only ten minutes in the farmhouse. The detective had watched his car leave. He had watched from a hilltop two kilometers away.

Bellarmine looked around him. Ten detectives in all, including himself; two carloads. They would come up on the farmhouse at dawn and go in with guns drawn, he told them. He believed Faletta was harboring a fugitive there, probably someone from the Banque de Nice gang. They would find out who it was, he said, and went over the reasoning in his mind: Lambert sees Sharkey, Sharkey sees Faletta, Faletta goes to the farmhouse—it had to be connected. At dawn they would grab the fugitive and after that they would grab Faletta for harboring him. Let's see Faletta's political connections get him out of that!

He ordered his men to rendezvous at the *commissariat* at 3 A.M., then sent them home to get what rest they could.

He unlocked the door to his flat just as Jacqueline a block away let herself back into her shop. An hour had passed since they left each other. They lay in their separate beds trying to fall asleep.

# PART V

## CHAPTER 33

It was beginning to be light. The road leading up to the farmhouse was dirt, potholed and almost two kilometers long. Although they rolled slowly and with headlights extinguished, Bellarmine knew that they advertised their presence from a long way off. The cars, in low gear, bounced and swayed, creating what sounded to him like a storm of noise and moving so slowly they breathed their own dust. According to the maps he had studied there were no roads leading out in other directions. Theoretically there was no risk their quarry could get away. The risk was that they would get shot at as they got out of the cars. He wished they could properly have surrounded the farmhouse. Instead both cars were approaching by the same dirt road, one behind the other, and as it came into view, the sun popped suddenly above the distant low mountains, blinding them.

One car slid to a stop in front of the farmhouse; the other drove around behind, as planned. The men sprang forth holding guns.

The old peasant had come out of the house and stood watching them arrive. He stood in the farmyard, his leather face closed against them. He was dressed in filthy overalls and high rubber boots that were clotted with mud. In his hands he carried a shovel, which he held like a weapon.

While his men fanned out around the house, Bellarmine attempted to question the old man, who muttered incomprehensible responses in Corsican. The men had entered the farmhouse now. They searched it room by room, but it was empty, and as they moved toward the outbuildings the sun threw long shadows behind them. Using the flat of his hand as a sun visor, Bellarmine began to scan the distant fields, and at last was able to discern the small moving cloud of dust far off to the east. He could barely see it beneath the glare, but he was sure it was moving, diminishing in size even as he watched, and he guessed, rightly, that it was made by a man on a motorcycle. Now he knew that every outbuilding would prove empty too. A few minutes later he was proved right.

It was not difficult to imagine what had happened. The old Corsican was one of those peasant farmers who rose each day in the dark. Today he had been already out tending to chores in the dark when he had heard in the distance the noise of the approaching cars. Probably the motorcyclist, the fugitive, his clock attuned to a big-city cadence, had been still in the farmhouse snoring. But the old man woke him, and he leaped on the motorcycle and was gone. It was no good trying to chase the cloud of dust across country, across stony meadows, and plowed fields. To chase it by car was out of the question.

Lacking radio communication, for neither car was radio equipped, there was nothing Bellarmine could do about calling for help.

As soon as the farmhouse and its outbuildings had been thoroughly searched, he sent one of his cars into Brignoles to telephone the Bishopric in Marseille. He wanted judicial identity technicians sent out here. He wanted the motorcyclist identified by fingerprints or any other means if possible. He wanted to know also who else had been frequenting this place, and the drinking glasses and the sides of the empty bottles in particular might be able to tell him.

Henry the Torch, meanwhile, had come out of the fields and down onto N-7, the principal coast road, and he drove toward Nice and his rendezvous with Lambert. He was hours ahead of schedule, and so would have to hole up somewhere. He did not equate this morning's raid with a leak in Nice. He was worried only about what he would do with so much time to kill. Nor was he particularly worried about being recognized, for he was wearing a helmet and goggles. He was dressed in his habitual leather Windbreaker, in olive-green slacks, and in black crocodile shoes already covered with mud and dust thrown up by the motorcycle. Later he would stop for breakfast, at which time he would use the napkin to clean off his shoes, and he knew he would feel much better afterward—he hated looking down at his shoes, the mess they were in right now. He was making perhaps fifty miles an hour, the engine throbbing between his thighs, the wind beating at him. He carried a .25 caliber automatic under his Windbreaker, and he could feel the outline of the gun as the wind flattened it against his chest. It was not much of a weapon. It fired very small bullets. But it was big enough for the job required of it today, and afterward he would be on his way to Senegal—so Faletta had promised. Faletta had contacts who would set him up there, where everybody, even the niggers, spoke French.

Bellarmine sent one car and all the detectives who could crowd into it back to Nice. Keeping the other men and car, he followed the technicians back to the Bishopric, for the only way to get them to work quickly was to wait for their report outside the laboratory door.

He had known in advance that his presence in the building would provoke a response of the *divisionnaire* who headed the Marseille detachment of judiciary police, and he was not disappointed, being summoned to this man's office within ten minutes of his arrival.

"What are you doing in my jurisdiction? Why wasn't I informed?"

Bellarmine was ready for him. "But I thought you had been informed, *Monsieur le Divisionnaire*," he lied. "Monsieur Sapodin told me he would take care of it."

At the mention of Sapodin's name, the *divisionnaire* seemed to take half a step backward. "Sapodin knew about this?"

"But of course." Bellarmine had phoned Sapodin last night, an elementary precaution. It was Sapodin who had decided not to alert Marseille, because Faletta was involved, and the Bishopric, therefore, could not be trusted.

The *divisionnaire* lit his pipe. He took his time about it. "Well, that's another story," he said at last. "Got time for a chat? Why don't you sit down?"

Within an hour fingerprints from the farmhouse had been matched to Eugène Henri Baldasaro, known as Henry the Torch, to the old Corsican peasant of course, and to one of Faletta's known bodyguards, but not to Faletta himself.

Bellarmine walked across to the Palace of Justice where he argued for most of an hour with a *juge d'instruction* named Danton. He wanted a warrant issued for Faletta's arrest, but Danton refused him. Although certain evidence did seem to link Faletta to the Banque de Nice, and to the fugitive welder, this evidence, legally speaking, was defective and insufficient.

"If you had his fingerprints at the farmhouse, maybe," Danton said. "But you don't have them, *mon cher.*"

Bellarmine understood that Faletta's political connections were too strong. Danton was afraid to indict him on such a weak case.

"You see my point of view, *mon cher?*"

Coldly, silently furious, Bellarmine loaded his detectives into the car and began the long drive back to Nice. It was nearly 6 P.M. before they got there. The long, frustrating day was nearing its end, or so he thought. But as he drove up to the *commissariat* he saw that there was a commotion out front, a mob of people pushing and shoving. They seemed to be trying to force their way into the *commissariat*, and this amazed him. Then he saw that they were reporters and photographers, and he knew what this meant—something sensational must have happened, some new and especially heinous crime perhaps. As he began to force his way through the mob to the door, he was recognized, and the reporters began crying his name, clutching at his clothing. Everyone was shouting and he could not make out what had happened.

At last he had fought his way through them. He was inside the building. But the commotion inside was incredible also. Phones were ringing. People were shouting. Uniformed men and detectives were running in all directions. Now he distinguished the name Lambert for the first time, and from the isolated phrases that reached his ear he understood that Lambert had tried to escape, had jumped out of Fayot's window.

Then he's killed himself, Bellarmine thought.

He was trying to get a straight story from two detectives and a uniformed *flic.* He knew Fayot's window. It was too high. It was suicide.

Bellarmine ran up the steps. He found Fayot in the third-floor hallway surrounded by detectives who were trying to calm him down. The young magistrate seemed incoherent.

Bellarmine took him into an empty office, closed the door and sat him down. "Just tell me the story," he said. "Tell it step by step. How did this awful thing happen?"

# CHAPTER
## 34

That morning Lambert had awakened feeling not only confident but eager. He lay snug and cozy in his cot and projected the triumphs that the day would bring. He saw himself already on the street, strolling into a shop, buying new clothes, sitting down in a fine restaurant and asking for the wine list. For Lambert a triumph imagined was a triumph achieved. He experienced it as vividly as if it already existed. He heard the applause. He was an American, and no French jail could hold him.

As he got out of bed and dressed, he said goodbye to this cell, projecting as far as tomorrow morning—he would order breakfast on the terrace of a hotel somewhere and send the waiter for a newspaper. "THE BRAIN STRIKES AGAIN"—he would read the headlines over and over, probably while trying to control his laughter. Perhaps it was the imagining of these headlines that spread his smile widest. Perhaps the idea of publicity was to him more precious than freedom, more to be cherished. Radio bulletins, newsboys hawking extras, whole cities agog. He was a man who took sustenance in imagining that he occupied space in other people's lives—the lives of strangers, the lives of countries. He was like a medieval mystic—he experienced states of exaltation that were self-caused.

His confidence was so real to him that it showed on his face, and even the guard who let him out into the courtyard for exercise remarked on it: "What are you grinning about?"

"I feel good today," Lambert told him. He marched around and around the courtyard, squaring each corner, breathing deeply, grinning at nothing. He grinned the forenoon away. He was grinning when he sat down to the sumptuous lunch he had ordered, and he grinned as he ate.

Each Thursday so far he had met with the *juge d'instruction* in the Palace of Justice beginning about 4 P.M. They had come to get him precisely at three, different men each week, but the time the same. Today's escape plan was timed to the minute, but suddenly he realized how late it had become. Three P.M. was well past, the half hour was coming up, and the hallway was silent outside his wooden door. Fayot, for unknown reasons, must have canceled today's interrogation. There would be no trip through the streets, no cheers from bystanders as he was led into the Palace of Justice, no possibility of escape. This was his first and only attack of nerves that day.

Behind him the cell door was thrown back.

He was handcuffed. His ankles were manacled also. He clanked across the yard and climbed into the prison van where he was locked into an individual cell about the size of a telephone booth. Inside was a rough bench. He sat down and tried to still the pounding of his heart. The engine started up, and the van began to move. Lambert in his box began to hyperventilate, his eyes tightly closed. He felt the van turn each corner.

Presently it stopped and he waited. After about ten minutes, he heard the back doors thrown open, footsteps approached his telephone booth, a key turned in his lock.

He walked to the back of the van and two uniformed officers helped him alight. Between his ankles was a foot and a half of clanking chain. Beside him bulked the side of the Palace of Justice. Across the street stood shopkeepers and pedestrians. When he grinned and waved, some of them called out to him.

The CIA's motorcycle, he noted, was exactly where it was supposed to be, about fifty feet ahead, engine off, resting on its kickstand. A man in a white helmet seemed to be working on it. Lambert peered up at Fayot's window. Its location had not changed. It was still about thirty-five feet up—a third-floor window. A man who jumped from that window would be lucky not to be killed. Almost certainly he would break an ankle or a leg. But he did not believe this would happen to him. He could jump and survive. No one else could. Only an American could. The Brain could, and he visualized himself in a few minutes, coming down, the wind in his hair.

As men with machine guns crowded around him, he verified the one other essential detail of his plan. Normally the curb along the Rue de la Préfecture was parked solid with judges' cars and prison vans. This was the case today too. Good.

He was herded into the building and up the stairs. Grinning and clanking, he allowed himself to be moved down a marble corridor to the door marked with Fayot's name.

Fayot came forward all smiles, hand outstretched even before Lambert's chains and handcuffs had been removed. "*Ça va, Monsieur Lambert?*"

Lambert shook hands with him, why not?

Fayot ushered him toward the chair beside the desk. The *greffier* took up his position at his machine. There were only the two armed officers left in the room. The rest of the guards were outside.

"Well, Monsieur Lambert," said Fayot cheerfully, "what shall we talk about today?" And he offered cigarettes across the desk. Fayot was always cordial, as if he did not care how many years his "instruction" lasted. Why should he care? No trial could begin until he turned the dossier over to the prosecutor, and he was not the one who had to wait out this time in jail.

Lambert glanced around at the guards. "Would you mind if the two gorillas waited outside, Judge?"

He had made the same request the week before and Fayot had quickly waved them out. From Fayot's point of view there was no risk. Lambert was not a violent criminal and the hall was full of men with machine guns. Now Lambert waited to see if this would happen again.

When Fayot seemed to hesitate, Lambert beamed him a bright false smile. "Whatever I might want to say to you today," he suggested, "I wouldn't want them to hear."

Fayot frowned.

Is he going to do it or not? Lambert asked himself.

But he maintained the fixed smile as he watched Fayot square up the pile of dossiers on the desk.

"I can't talk with them in here, Judge."

He saw Fayot take this bait. The prisoner had perhaps decided to cooperate at last, and tell all. With a jerk of his head, Fayot sent the two guards out of the room. As soon as the door had closed behind them, he leaned forward conspiratorially: "If you want to be cooperative," he purred, "you'll find that I can be cooperative too."

Lambert had begun smirking. He could not help it. He was already out of that window. He was as good as gone.

In the street a motorcycle engine came on. To Lambert all motorcycles sounded alike, and this one might have belonged to anyone. Down there in the street the normal life of the city went on. People entered and left shops, all of them ignorant of the drama about to take place up here. Under these windows, vehicles moved along on two wheels or four. But Lambert had no doubt that the engine that had just erupted into life was the CIA guy's engine. The CIA guy had just given him the agreed-upon signal. It was time to leave this place, and he stood up and began pacing. "Give me a minute to think this out, Judge," he said, and the orbit of his pacing widened. "I've made my decision you understand."

Fayot was beaming. "Take your time, *mon vieux*," he murmured.

Lambert was ten feet from the window. "I just want to run it back and forth in my head a moment longer, Judge." He was eight feet from the window—was he going to do it or not? Did he dare?

"We have all afternoon, *mon vieux*," encouraged Fayot.

With a sudden lunge, Lambert was at the window. He grasped the window handle, twisted it open, pulled the two windows inward. The sill, like the walls of the building, was a foot thick, and Lambert leaped on top of it, already teetering outward. Behind him he heard Fayot cry: "Oh, no!" The idiot probably thought he was watching a man commit suicide, and perhaps he was right.

About twelve feet below the window was the wide cornice above the high ornate palace doorway. This cornice, a kind of Grecian overhang, was clotted with pigeon feathers, Lambert saw now. Caked with pigeon shit. It was perhaps terribly slippery, something that hadn't occurred to him in advance. It was also much farther down than it had seemed to him looking up. Furthermore, it was still twenty or more feet above the sidewalk, even if he managed to stabilize himself upon it. Superman himself would have hesitated, but The Brain did not. His concentration now was total. He was acutely aware of all of his muscles, of the placement of his feet and hands, and this gave him confidence. He believed himself an exceptional American, one in total control of his body and of his balance, and he jumped.

He landed on the cornice with knees flexed, crouching for equilibrium. For a fraction of a second he managed to steady himself—long enough. From the cornice he leaped outward so as to crash down on the roof of a parked car—a judge's car most likely, Fayot's car if there was any justice in the world. He landed on the roof flat-footed, knees flexed, and felt it cave in under him. It was almost as good as landing in dough. The roof caved in ten inches or more. He felt the shock up through his body, but there was no pain, he had not broken or sprained anything, and he leaped out of the vast dent he had made, leap number three, down on to the street, already running. He ran forward ten steps and forked the motorcycle. The engine came up like the roar of an airplane, and the machine hurtled forward with such sudden power that it almost left him sitting on the sidewalk. Then he and it and the CIA guy were speeding down the street. Lambert, his arm locked around the driver's midsection, glanced over his shoulder and up. He saw Fayot there framed in the window, a small, almost tragic figure rapidly diminishing in size and importance, and he let go with one hand and gave him the finger, at the same time shouting back at the top of his lungs: "*Au revoir, mon vieux.*" Then he began giggling almost hysterically.

At the corner the driver turned left and swept diagonally across the Place du Palais, cutting a swath through the knot of chauffeurs smoking there. They jumped back to save their lives, but clearly their dull minds failed to grasp the revelation that flashed before their eyes. Ahead was the opera house—on gala nights its sidewalk was crowded with swells in evening dress. There ought to be a crowd right now to witness his passage, the greatest gala of the year or century. But alas the building was as blind as the chauffeurs.

The driver veered left, speeding down the narrow street beside the old rococo building, passing the locked stage door, then bursting out into the brilliant glare of the Promenade des Anglais, and racing along next to the sea, speeding west in the direction of the late sun itself down a broad boulevard with palm trees down the center.

Three blocks ahead the Paillon debouched into the Mediterranean. By standing in the stirrups Lambert caught a glimpse of the jetty there—an instant later he could see the tail of Thompson's speedboat, then Thompson himself standing on the jetty beside it. Good old Thompson. He could already hear Thompson's cry of welcome as he sprang on board: "I knew it was you." Thirty minutes later both of them would be safe in Italy. That Thompson, who had a wife and children, would then be unable to return to France had not yet occurred to Lambert, and never would.

Lambert's elation was immense, not only because total freedom seemed so close, but also because the presence of Thompson and his speedboat proved the extraordinary loyalty Lambert was able to command over old comrades, over his own wife—Jacqueline had made the contact after all.

It was time to inform the CIA guy that their ride together was to be a short one. In ten seconds he would be safe aboard the speedboat, and he shouted into the CIA guy's ear: "Stop here. Stop."

But the motorcycle showed no signs of slowing down, and Lambert began banging the man frantically in the back, shouting: "Stop. Stop here. Stop."

Now they were abreast of the jetty. An instant later it was behind them, a block to the rear, two, three. Lambert was still banging on the driver, who only hunched farther forward, ignoring commands and blows both, until at length Lambert ceased hitting him.

Slowly the driver straightened up again. The helmet turned until the grinning profile showed, one Lambert recognized.

"Change of plans," The Torch shouted back.

He's had all his teeth changed, Lambert thought irrelevantly.

Once past the Ruhl the Promenade des Anglais widened still farther. Hundreds of strollers on the boardwalk but almost no traffic in the street. Almost no parked cars either, and Henry the Torch opened his throttle wide. Lambert could do nothing now but hang on as their speed went up and up. They were moving so fast he couldn't even see—he was obliged to close his eyes against the wind, to duck his head down into the protection of The Torch's neck.

He was obliged to think this through, also. But he could not think. He had gone almost immediately into intense anger. His triumph was being taken away from him. He was being kidnapped. The speed of the machine was so great he could not even glance back over his shoulder toward the jetty where the gallant Thompson must still be waiting.

Instead, knees clenched tight against the heartbeat of the machine, he clung to The Torch and gave in to his frustration. Someone would pay for this. He did not at first see The Torch as a threat to him. He was simply furious. The Brain had been thwarted. His escape plan would have to be changed.

Gradually he forced himself to reason more clearly. Because of its topography, Nice was a difficult city from which to escape. The cliffs and mountains crowd downhill until they almost touch the sea. To the west the city ends at the Var River. Only two bridges cross the Var, and Lambert thought they had best get across one of them fast, and into the more open country beyond, before the police threw up roadblocks.

But Henry the Torch had other ideas. With a screech of brakes and a *vroom*, *vroom* from the throttle, with a wrenching movement of his powerful arms, the motorcycle veered right, plunged inland between buildings, and in a moment began to climb. A few seconds after that it was above the orange rooftops of the city, climbing a series of switchbacks. Reaching the crest of this first precipitous hill, the road

336

ran along between carnation farms. The flowers filled narrow terraces that dropped downhill in staircases of color to both sides. The road up here was narrow and not straight, sometimes running between houses. The Torch evidently knew where he was going for at the next fork he veered left without slowing. The motorcycle plunged down into an interior valley, then climbed again. Riding pillion, still blinded by the onrushing wind, Lambert attempted to peer into the future. He needed a course of action, and did not have one. Nor did he know where he was being taken.

The carnation farms disappeared. The road as it climbed deteriorated also, and the motorcycle struck a rut that threw him eight inches off the seat. He came down clutching The Torch tighter than ever, his hands were claws, and it was then that his fingers came in contact with the gun. The man was wearing it in some kind of shoulder holster that had swung around in front and hung now just to the left of his breastbone. With great care Lambert's fingertips caressed the leather Windbreaker. He delineated through clothing the gun's exact shape, exact location, an act that, at another time and place, might have seemed to him terribly personal, almost sexual in nature, like groping the sweater of a girl in a movie. The difference was that the girl, however fixedly she might stare straight ahead—The Torch continued to stare straight ahead also—was always entirely aware of his fingers. Whereas The Torch presumably was not. There was another difference also. Lambert was motivated now not by sexual arousal but by the first faint spasms of fear.

The motorcycle had reached another fork. To veer right was to continue up into the high mountains, and if The Torch took this direction it would prove Lambert's alarm unfounded. He knew these roads, more or less. Escape over the mountains was possible. The frontier with Italy lay just beyond the ski stations. He and The Torch, both fugitives, could escape from France together.

"Go right," he shouted in The Torch's ear, for the motorcycle had begun to slow, and he did not want to believe himself sentenced to death. In the high mountains, at the very least, he could hole up indefinitely, for it was wild, impenetrable country.

But The Torch aimed the motorcycle into the left fork and opened his throttle again. The left fork led down. Suspicions confirmed. It was not the CIA that had rescued him but the Milieu. He was still a prisoner. His execution had been ordered, a verdict that allowed no appeal.

In a series of sweeping turns the motorcycle began to descend toward the valley of the Var. At a certain moment the forest beside the road fell away, and the Var itself came into sight far below—it had an enormously wide bed, most of which was being used for truck farms, for like a thin strip of aluminum the river itself ran only down the center. At times the river flashed back like light from glass, and as Lambert watched it approach he went through a number of emotional states very quickly, including various types of fear, followed by an accurate calculation of his chances and lastly by a kind of murderous petulance. That he was in the clutches of the Milieu, rather than the CIA, meant he had been lied to, by Avery, by Sharkey. The injustice of it outraged him. The Brain had been betrayed. It was intolerable. He would not tolerate it. Lambert too had been taught violence at an early age, making him in his present mood a far more dangerous man than Henry the Torch.

Henry, meanwhile, had a problem, and it was a serious one. He was lost.

Outsiders usually imagined that the Milieu ran a loose operation. Crime, it seemed, was anarchy, and regulated therefore by no one. But nothing could be more false. In fact crime was a business like any other, but because it was vulnerable in the extreme to certain pressures unknown to legitimate professions, its hierarchy in France as elsewhere enforced the most intense discipline imaginable. In a business where a single errant step could start a civil war—which was bad for profits, not to mention health—rigid discipline was absolutely essential. Turf and tariffs were strictly regulated, free-lance decision-making was not tolerated, and any employee who dared disobey specific instructions was dealt with summarily.

And specific instructions were precisely what The Torch had been given—he was to take Lambert to a specific place within a specific time and there perform specific acts. That these instructions had come from the mouth of Faletta himself only reinforced their sanctity. It was Faletta himself who had handed over the map marked in red crayon now in The Torch's pocket, and he had studied it for an hour last night, and for another hour in a roadside café near Fréjus this morning. It was Faletta who had decided on his destination, the musician's villa near Aspremont where he and the others had lived during the digging of the tunnel. It was also Faletta who had handed over the satchel containing Henry's usual tools, his handcuffs and blowtorch, and this satchel now rode strapped to the rack behind Lambert. Once at the villa, Lambert was to be handcuffed to a post in the cellar and asked to divulge information about the missing documents. Since The Torch's methods were infallible in such cases, it was assumed that Lambert would divulge plenty. The Torch would then depart on a Vespa motor scooter he would find in the garage. As if to emphasize the importance of the plan, Faletta had taken the trouble to explain it more fully, including even those parts of it—the larger picture—that did not concern The Torch. As soon as he had made his way back to Marseille, the police would receive an anonymous call telling them where to find the remains of Lambert. Simultaneously, a description of Lambert's corpse would be given out on the street, news for rival caids to consider and digest. The Torch understood what was being told him. Faletta's name would regain its ability to evoke terror. Attacks on his organization might diminish or even cease. As for any information concerning the documents that The Torch would also bring back, Faletta would decide what to do with this when he knew what it was.

All this Faletta had painstakingly explained to him. He had been made to repeat it several times before the caid, satisfied, had left the farm. The Torch had then sat down to study the map, and he had committed his route, he thought, to memory.

Nonetheless, he was lost. He had missed a turn somewhere. He was unable to find the villa.

So far he had not been worried about Lambert, whose impotence at such high speed was total. Lambert was like a comet, or an artillery shell—committed to a trajectory not of his own choosing. His possible actions or reactions did not even have to be considered until the villa was reached—until the motorcycle came to a complete stop. Once there The Torch would simply yank his gun out and point it at him, and march him docilely down into the cellar.

Ahead was another fork in the road, another choice to be made. Already he guessed this ride had occupied ten to fifteen minutes longer than planned, meaning that he risked a roadblock or a patrol of gendarmes at any moment. As he approached the fork he made his decision—he would have to stop and consult the map. Briefly he considered Lambert behind him. Obviously he couldn't hold a gun on him and then expect him to remount. Was Lambert a threat to him or not? The Torch decided not. The man could not possibly suspect the fate that was in store for him. He was sure to trust The Torch a while longer, trust the Faletta organization to conclude this escape attempt, which was certainly working well enough so far. In any case, The Torch had no choice. He had to stop. And so, approaching the fork, he applied the brakes hard. The machine lurched and shuddered, at the end sliding almost sideways to a stop, with his feet skittering along to hold it upright. Letting the engine idle, he reached into his Windbreaker pocket for the map. He had by then considered most possibilities, not all. He had not reckoned that Lambert would strike without warning.

Forearms snaked around his throat. From one second to the next The Torch found his wind cut off. He was unable to breathe. He was a very strong man. He was thirty-eight years old and had lived by violence all his life. But Lambert was only thirty-one, in a state of transport, and he had struck both unexpectedly and from behind, for he knew what every soldier had been taught—that speed and surprise are more disruptive than firepower by far.

Lambert knew nothing about Henry's blowtorch in the satchel behind him, and therefore had nothing personal against him. He had a hammerlock on The Torch's throat. To him The Torch was just a workman obeying orders. He did not mean to kill him. What was essential was to dump him and steal the bike.

Attempting at first only to break Lambert's grip, The Torch must have been close to blacking out before he thought to go for his gun. Lambert could not see this movement, but he sensed it. Flinging him violently down to the ground, he dove on top of him. The motorcycle, its engine and tail pipe searing hot, tumbled over onto both of them as they rolled, searing only The Torch, who screamed. Lambert tried to find another hammerlock even as they twisted out from under the bike. But Henry's head jerked out of his grasp, and as it did so his helmet popped off. It struck the road like a melon, making a ringing thud, but did not roll. It was a German parachutist's helmet, war surplus of course, or perhaps a war souvenir. It was leather-padded steel with ear holes so that the parachutist would hear the command to jump. This one had been painted white with house paint, for it was so close to Lambert's face that he could see the brush strokes. He was on his back, still trying to strangle Henry, who lay on top of him.

The Torch's gun came clear. Lambert needed a weapon, and fast. The helmet was there beside him. His right arm was still wrapped around The Torch's neck. His left sought the helmet, and he employed it.

He smashed Henry in the face. It was a heavy helmet, much heavier than it looked. Lambert had his thumb through one ear hole, as if inside a bowling ball. He swung the helmet like a bowling ball. Over and over again, and The Torch's face turned to blood.

Lambert scrambled out from underneath him. The gun hand lay outstretched on the pavement, and Lambert stood on the wrist and kept swinging the helmet. He beat The Torch to death with it.

It was some time before he realized this. Henry's nose had disappeared, his lips had been sliced open by his teeth and by the edge of the helmet, and he was smiling a smile that would last forever. There was more blood than Lambert had seen since the war.

Lambert, who had been bent over the corpse, stood up. He was breathing hard. He peered up the road the way they had come, and then down both forks. He could see no one in any direction, and when he listened he heard no traffic coming. The road here was high on the ridgeline with trees along both sides.

In France Lambert's face had become more famous than any film star's, and he knew this, and so he wiped the helmet clean on Henry's clothes and put it on, his first official act so to speak. He snapped the chin strap into place. His second act was to drag The Torch to the edge of the road and drop him into the ditch beside it. Next he walked along uprooting small bushes, which he brought back and tossed on top of the body, covering it more or less. It was the best he could do. He looked around for The Torch's goggles and found them some yards away, smashed. He kicked them off the road toward the ditch. After a moment's thought he went back to the body and searched it, disarranging the bushes—in times of stress a man's thoughts and therefore the jobs he assigns himself rarely assume logical order.

He found money, a pair of sunglasses, a map, papers for the motorcycle, The Torch's false identity card. He put on the sunglasses and put the other things in his pocket. He spread the bushes back on top of the corpse.

The motorcycle lay on its handlebar and stirrup, the engine still turning over. He righted it and climbed astride. For a moment he practiced with the throttle, the brakes, the gearshift. With one foot out for balance, he made several slow circles in the road, almost like a circling shark. Then he threw the machine into low gear, opened the throttle wide, and with a jerk took off up the right fork. He knew more or less where he was. He was too far from the sea to attempt to get back there, too far from the Var to attempt to get across. There was only one escape route open to him that he could see: the mountains. He would ride the motorcycle up into the mountains and then

341

across into Italy, where he would be safe. He thought of the former smugglers' tracks that were said to lead across. He would have to find one. There were many such tracks, some of them signposted for hikers by the Alpine Club, and if one proved too precipitous for a motorcycle, he had only to find another. In an hour or so he would be hungry, and he would get hungry at regular intervals after that for however long his flight lasted, and so he decided to stop first at his farm—it was on the way—and collect whatever food was there. He would pick up other supplies too: extra clothes, a ground cloth, a blanket, matches, a compass. His farm would be his salvation. The police would stake out the place as soon as they thought of it, but they had many other jobs to do first. There was time, he believed, to get in there and out again before they came. And he would leave the photos and documents where they were. For the time being they seemed safer at the bottom of their wine carton than on his person.

Tonight he would get as high up into the mountains as he could, and as close to the frontier as he dared. Tomorrow he would begin looking for one of those tracks across.

# CHAPTER 35

Bellarmine, accompanied by two uniformed policemen, went to the perfume shop. Jacqueline must have been expecting him, for she stepped outside onto the sidewalk. Her eyes went from him to the flanking uniforms and back again. Her mouth hung slightly open. It was the face of a woman who thought she was about to be arrested.

"Your husband has escaped," he told her, and tried to read her expression, her mind. Obviously she knew this much already. Much time had passed. The news was on the radio, had spread throughout the town.

Like Fayot, Jacqueline began to babble. He could not make much sense of it, except that she seemed to think Lambert safe in Italy already.

"By sea it's so close." she blurted out.

"By sea?"

"Didn't you say he went by sea? You said—I thought—"

He had said nothing of the kind, and his eyes narrowed.

"But—"

She had gone speechless, and seemed terrified. His heart sank to recognize these signs. She knew about this escape in advance, he told himself. She helped set it up. "Why did you say by sea?" Don't make me arrest you, he pleaded silently.

"Automatically I thought by sea," Jacqueline said. She was stuttering. "Italy is so close. It was a natural thought."

The escape must have been set up for sea, but the motorcycle, according to reports, had turned inland. Why? "He didn't go by sea," Bellarmine growled. "They went up into the mountains."

Jacqueline's expression changed, but he could not read it clearly. She looked puzzled and then relieved—as if now he might not arrest her after all. "I'll leave these two men here," he told her coldly. "Your husband may try to contact you."

"He won't hurt me. I don't need protection."

"If he does contact you," Bellarmine told her harshly, "I want to know about it." There, it was said. He had given expression to the one unforgivable emotion in a relationship of this kind, the belief that she would betray him. A kind of adultery divided them. It had already taken place or soon would take place, making impossible the existence of any state of love.

In addition, he had just made Jacqueline a prisoner again. He saw her mouth harden as she realized this. But there was nothing else he could do. Giving a slight bow, he got back into his car.

The phone was ringing even as he re-entered the *commissariat*.

"Paris on the line."

Previously there had been two calls from Sapodin and one from an extremely agitated Minister of the Interior. Each time Bellarmine had reported on the dispositions taken so far. The borders were closed, the airport was closed, the Riviera marinas were all closed. He had detectives moving through outgoing trains. He had posted roadblocks at all the various bridges, even those well upriver. He had sent two men to stake out Lambert's farm.

It was Sapodin again. Paris was in a turmoil, he said. In the National Assembly a deputy had even made a speech about the risibility of the French police, of the French race.

343

"The pressure on my office is tremendous," Sapodin said, and he paused, as if to let the weight of this pressure come down on Bellarmine too. For a moment both contemplated what was for them the central fact of life at this time. France was a defeated country struggling to get back on its feet. Unfortunately it was trying to do this while at the same time losing three more wars—in Indochina, Morocco, and Algeria—simultaneously. Each Paris government was a fragile coalition, and some were so weak they failed to last out a single month. If Lambert now should escape abroad, he could be expected to call a press conference at which he would, in effect, give the finger to France. This absolutely must not happen. "If it does happen, the government will fall," Sapodin said, and paused again.

And others will fall with it, Bellarmine thought. Probably Sapodin, possibly me.

"From such a humiliation, the national psyche would not be able to recover," Sapodin said.

This was true, Bellarmine believed, and was reason enough to mount the most intensive manhunt imaginable.

Sapodin was too shrewd to come down to Nice and assume personal command of a search that might fail. "I've arranged for extraordinary powers to devolve upon you, Bellarmine," he said. Though a mere *commissaire*, Bellarmine was to assume de facto command of units of the customs service and the gendarmerie. In addition a hundred CRS troops—the national riot police—were being sent in and put at his disposal. "It's up to you, Bellarmine," Sapodin said. "Lambert must not get out of France," and he hung up.

In a matter of hours Bellarmine had more men than he could easily deploy. He sent them out in pairs to scour all the surrounding roads, to knock on every door of every isolated villa. He was trying to pick up the scent—any scent at all, no matter how faint.

About 10 P.M. a CRS patrol reached the intersection where The Torch's body lay in the ditch. Something glittered in their headlights, and when they got out and bent over the road, they saw it was glass from broken goggles. The goggles themselves were in the grass on the verge and had evidently been run over a number of times. In any case, they had been crushed flat. But the metal borders showed no rust, meaning they had not been there long, and so the two policemen shone their flashlights all around, eventually shining them on to the contents of the left-hand ditch.

By the time Bellarmine had reached the spot the police photographer was already at work. The body still lay in the ditch. Bellarmine peered down on it. It was illuminated only by car headlights and by a succession of grotesque explosions of light by the photographer.

The corpse, Bellarmine was told, had no identification. Though the face was ruined, of course, there was no sign of any other wound, and he was perhaps the victim of a hit-and-run driver—who could say?

Bellarmine did not think so. He did not believe in coincidences of that kind. Any corpses found tonight would be related to Lambert's escape. "Have his prints been rolled?"

"*Oui, monsieur.*"

There was nothing more to do. He went back to the *commissariat* to await the fingerprint identification.

An hour later the technician phoned with his report. Having missed The Torch at Brignoles this morning, Bellarmine had found him here tonight. He gave a long, low whistle as he hung up the phone, for he understood, he believed, most of what had happened in between. That Lambert had killed The Torch and was now alone on the motorcycle seemed obvious. Furthermore, he was almost certainly still on this side of the Var, and the roadblocks would keep him there.

The press still clamored at the front door of the *commissariat.* Bellarmine did not believe in the public's right to know, but now he decided to use the press for his own purposes, and he went downstairs and stepped out into the noisy jostling crowd. He told them that Eugène Henri Baldasaro, known as Henry the Welder and Henry the Torch, one of the suspects being sought in the Banque de Nice case, and believed to be the driver of the escape motorcycle, had been found murdered in a roadside ditch some forty kilometers north of Nice, presumably by the so-called Brain, Lambert, who was believed to be holed up in the mountains thereabouts. He was armed and must be considered extremely dangerous.

As soon as he had made these brief, sensational statements, refusing to answer any further questions, Bellarmine stepped back inside. The press did not need to know more, and in any case could be relied upon to invent and embroider better details than he was able to give them. But tomorrow morning's headlines, he believed, would reduce pressure from Paris, would give him breathing space. And pressure on Lambert would be greatly increased, for Bellarmine had changed, he hoped, the public's attitude toward him. This was no longer a joke. The Brain had become a murderer. No one would root for his escape now. Lambert would learn of his changed status if he had a radio. If he went near any villages, he would read it in the headlines in the racks of the newspaper kiosks. He would begin to feel the hot police breath all around him. He would begin to make mistakes.

At dawn the patrols Bellarmine had arranged during the night departed from in front of the *commissariat*. Bleary-eyed after two hours' sleep, he went with them. But so did a dozen or more cars full of journalists. It made for a caravan of vehicles resembling the Tour de France bike race, and when it had reached the high mountains, it advertised its presence for miles around by the noise it made and the dust clouds it raised. The next day the same thing happened, and the next. And Lambert, if he was in there, was not sighted. The long, frustrating search at first produced no results at all. Only toward the end of the week did the first vague reports begin to come in. A grocer in Lucéram telephoned to say that Lambert had entered his shop the night before. He thought he had. The man, if it was Lambert, bought a dozen oranges and two long sausages. He seemed to be on foot, for he walked off down the street carrying his purchases. He was wearing a black beret. Though the sun was below the peaks by then, and it was nearly dark, he was wearing sunglasses. The next night a woman in St. Sauveur who tended the town's only gas pump in front of her house was brought downstairs before midnight by a man pounding on her door. It was a traveler whose motorcycle was nearly out of fuel. As she pumped the lever by hand she tried to make conversation, but the stranger did not answer. He wore a black beret and sunglasses.

Bellarmine had never been to either of these villages before. Lucéram proved to be set on the flank of a mountain. Most of the village streets were in steps. In St. Sauveur some of the streets were in steps also. The streams and melting snows above the village had been channeled to run downhill in an open storm gutter beside the main street. This imparted a delightfully cool, fresh note to the mountain air. It gave the feeling that the entire village was air-conditioned. Bellarmine noted that the two villages were thirty-five kilometers apart, meaning Lambert, if it was Lambert, was moving around a lot. He also noted that there were no telephones in either village except for the public phones inside the post offices, and these at the hour of Lambert's visits, if it was Lambert, had been closed for the night. Lacking access to telephones, both witnesses had been obliged to wait for morning before calling in their news. So the trail was already cold each time Bellarmine got there. Although there was no way to check the witnesses' stories, he tended to believe both of them. He was more convinced than ever that he had Lambert trapped in these mountains, and that it was only a question of time.

Avery too had read the news stories about Lambert's escape. If they were true, then Lambert had managed to escape only from jail, not from France, and the threat to Avery's name and career was twice or three times what it had been. Once back in custody Lambert could—probably would—accuse Avery of complicity in his escape, and he was so famous, the crime and its aftermath was so bizarre, that he would be heard and might be believed all over the world. Although Avery realized he had now committed jail offenses on both sides of the Atlantic, he told himself he was not worried about prosecution. No one would dare—he was too powerful a man. He was also a man unused to failure. This whole business had to be ended, and fast.

He flew to Paris to see Tuttle. In the embassy he threw the morning newspapers on to Tuttle's desk.

"These things happen," said Tuttle soothingly.

"You bungled it."

Tuttle gave the hands down sign, such as baseball umpires use to signal that the runner is safe. "It's over as far as I'm concerned," he said, "I'm out of it."

Although Avery railed at him, he could not alter this decision, and he flew back to Nice where he summoned Adjunct Mayor Picpoul to his suite at the Ruhl.

"Lambert must be killed," shouted Picpoul. "Once and for all this has to end."

The man seemed close to hysteria, and this to Avery was the real danger—that one of the Frenchmen, Picpoul or one of the others, would crack, go to the prosecutors, and attempt to trade an American congressman for immunity for themselves. He saw himself as a bigger fish than any of them, than all of them put together. Any prosecutor would be interested. The decision would have to be made in Paris at the highest level—it was a bad situation to contemplate.

Lambert could not be killed if he could not be found, snorted Avery. He did not want to hear talk like this from Picpoul or any of their other associates. It was inflammatory. It was talk that would be repeated and embroidered upon. It was the kind of talk that flew about on wings. Ultimately it would reach the ears of the wrong people, at which point it became dangerous—incredibly dangerous—to all of them.

There are ways out of this, he told Picpoul. He projected confi-

347

dence. He was a big man in an expensive suit inhabiting an expensive suite, and he calmed Picpoul down. What they needed to do, he began, was to find Lambert and talk to him. Although on the face of it, this might sound impossible—since the police couldn't find him—perhaps there was a way. He had a plan, he said, and they began to discuss it. Avery brought the details out slowly, and in so doing brought Picpoul into the plan. He made him feel himself a contributor to it by planting ideas in Picpoul's head that the adjunct mayor then brought forth as his own. There was a reason for such tactics. The plan required Picpoul's active participation in a way that would put his career even more in jeopardy than it was right now. He had to be made ready to accept such risks, and this would take time. He was hours away from being prepared for it. Avery had the time, and he had the heavy patience of the skilled political negotiator as well.

"The question is, how to find Lambert," he said.

Here Avery stopped and sought suggestions from Picpoul, but none came.

Well, continued Avery, if we can't go to Lambert, perhaps we can make Lambert come to us.

"How?" said Picpoul.

"Suppose," said Avery cautiously, "we put out bait that would bring Lambert down from the hills."

"What bait?"

"Bait that would seem beautiful to him," said Avery. "Bait he could not resist. Then we could talk to him, recover the papers and photos, and get him out of France."

"Cut off his head," said Picpoul.

Avery shrugged.

"And what is this irresistible bait?" Picpoul's tone was sarcastic, yet he seemed calmer. He was beginning to approach the problem rationally. In a moment he would come up with suggestions, and Avery would steer him as subtly as possible toward the only valid solution.

"When you go fishing," mused Avery, "you put out bait suitable to the particular fish you're after—catfish, trout, whatever." He watched Picpoul's reaction carefully.

They began to discuss the various baits that had always lured men: power, sex, money.

"He's already got all the money in the world," said Picpoul. "Stashed in Switzerland probably."

"Right."

"Money won't work."

"He's on the run and probably scared," mused Avery. "A woman wouldn't interest him under those conditions."

"Probably not."

More discussion. They discussed the meaning of the word "bait" and the meaning of the word "irresistible," and Avery waited for Picpoul to perceive and suggest the solution Avery had settled on long ago, the one that exposed Picpoul himself to so much risk. But this did not happen, and Avery was obliged to suggest it himself.

To a man in Lambert's predicament, he said carefully, the only irresistible bait would be safe passage out of France, and this meant a boat.

At first Picpoul didn't see it. "Which boat?" he asked.

Well, said Avery, it would have to be a pretty special boat, one able to take him all the way to Africa. Which meant speed, range, size— and a captain Lambert trusted.

"There's no such boat," said Picpoul.

"I've got it," said Avery "The PT boat. Roy LeRoy."

Avery had brought Picpoul this far step by step. But the rest would be up to Picpoul. Avery was not going to be able to implement the plan alone and he brought forth its most vital element. Both men knew that Roy was in jail in Toulon, his boat impounded. But suppose he could be got out of jail and his boat returned to him?

Picpoul could see only the difficulties. "Impossible," he said.

"On the face of it, yes." said Avery, "but what if—"

What if Roy and that PT boat were waiting offshore? This was certain to bring Lambert down out of the mountains, if it could be arranged. Arranging it might be troublesome, but perhaps it could be done. Did Picpoul see a way it could be done?

The adjunct mayor did not.

Suppose Picpoul pulled some strings with the *juge d'instruction* in Toulon who had the case, argued Avery, or even paid him. Picpoul was a powerful man. More powerful than he knew, perhaps.

This suggestion stopped Picpoul in his tracks. "And then?" he said. "Do we just let Lambert sail away? After all the trouble he's caused us?"

To have to depend on others, particularly non-Americans, was repugnant to Avery. One thing at a time, he told the Frenchman. The first job was to get Roy released and his boat released. Could Picpoul do it?

The adjunct mayor did not want even to consider it, but Avery cautiously applied more and more pressure, under which Picpoul began to bend. He said he did not know. For a man in his position even to try was dangerous. He would have to think about it.

LeRoy had not been convicted of any crime, Avery reminded him. In America he would be out on bail by now. But he was implicated in several crimes, responded Picpoul. To the French the difference between implicated and convicted was semantic only.

Avery began to remind him of the threats that hung over them both. The casino documents, the obscene photos. Those photos, Avery reminded him, showed Picpoul waving his erect *bitte* in the air, all seventeen centimeters of it.

"In France such photos cannot hurt me," said the adjunct mayor. "I could still win elections." He attempted a smile. "The men would vote for me out of envy, the woman out of love." That the casino documents should come to light was what worried him, not the photos.

"Our constituencies," said Avery, "are different. With me it is the other way around."

"I'll think about it," said Picpoul.

"Think hard."

And the two men parted.

The death of Henry the Torch, his strong right arm so to speak, was the most humiliating event of Faletta's career—and one of the most dangerous, for it exposed his vulnerability for all his rivals to see. The most notorious killer in the Marseille underworld was no longer a presence, and therefore Faletta himself was no longer to be feared, or at least less to be feared. Half the clans in Marseille would come for him, he believed.

And he was right, for two men who worked for him were assassinated near the Gare St. Charles only two nights later. They were shot down from a doorway. They had not even had time to draw their own weapons. Others of his men promptly made themselves scarce. When he sent for them, they made excuses or could not be found. They had stepped back from him, as if stepping out of the cross fire. On the third night a plastic charge exploded in the coatroom of his nightclub, the Versailles. It killed the hatcheck girl and tore the left arm off the barman. Several patrons were wounded by fragments, and Faletta might well have been killed himself—his usual table was nearby—except that he had begun varying his movements. He had reached the nightclub two hours later than was his habit, only to find the front door blown out, pools of blood on the floor, and a horde of policemen asking questions. The *flics* took statements from everyone, Faletta included. He told them he had no idea who might have planted the bomb, or why.

Faletta knew it would be wise if he went into hiding. His wife, sister, and brothers advised him to do this, but he refused. To hide would be to abdicate. Rival caids would like nothing better. In his absence they would parcel out his empire among themselves.

So he decided not to hide. Instead he would continue his normal routine. He would move by different streets at different times than in the past, but he would continue to meet friends and customers in his bar by day and in his hastily repaired nightclub by night.

The weakness of his position was so obvious that there were many who expected him to be gunned down any day. He half expected it himself. However, he continued to sit in his customary chairs, and to play his customary role as host, and when strangers came through his doors he did not flinch. No one ever said he was not a brave man.

More than ever he saw Lambert as the cause of his trouble, and he concluded that the only quick way to reverse the balance was to get to him before the police did, and bring him forward. Show him off. It was a matter of propriety again. What happened to Lambert afterward was not particularly important. He would decide once he had him.

But how was Lambert to be found?

Faletta's first idea was that Sharkey might be in contact with him. In any case, Sharkey had been part of the escape plan, and therefore part of The Torch's death, meaning that Sharkey needed to be punished.

Faletta sent men to Nice to pick Sharkey up and to bring him to Marseille for "questioning."

This was done. Sharkey, who was wearing a blue-and-purple foulard tucked into his blue blazer, was taken down into a cellar underneath one of Faletta's outlying bars. The bar was closed for the occasion. Sharkey was questioned about Lambert's possible whereabouts for more than four hours, after which he died. He was questioned principally with electric cattle prods. His penis was burned off, and his testicles roasted to the size of a walnut. Finally he was strangled with the blue-and-purple foulard. When night came his body was thrown into the Vieux Port from the back of a slow-moving car. It plunged in headfirst between the sterns of two moored pleasure boats and was found floating in the center of the harbor the following day.

Ten detectives from the Marseille Criminelle were put on the case immediately, though there were no leads to run down, not one. At Bellarmine's urging, the news was given out to the press immediately. "LAMBERT LAWYER ASSASSINATED," the headlines read, besmirching The Brain's image still further, and Bellarmine was pleased.

Sharkey's interrogators, meanwhile, had confessed their failure to Faletta—apparently the *mec* hadn't known anything, they reported, for he had certainly seemed eager to answer all their questions. The interrogators then suggested an alternative plan: that they pick up Lambert's wife and try much the same technique on her.

"What we do is, we cut off her left tit," one of them said. "If she wants to save the other one, she tells us where her husband is."

The idea sounded good to Faletta, and he sent men to Nice. But they found a pair of white batons outside the door of Jacqueline Lambert's shop, and when they telephoned with this information, Faletta told them to remain in place, waiting until the police guard was withdrawn.

Meanwhile, he turned his thoughts to Roy LeRoy.

Faletta, being in the cigarette trade also, had known LeRoy by reputation for a number of years. About a year ago he had tried to buy him out, for he wanted that PT boat, the last one remaining in the Mediterranean. This time the negotiations had taken place in Marseille, where LeRoy had come for repairs to an engine. But LeRoy had shown a considerable amount of spunk. He had laughed in the faces of Faletta's negotiators. When it had proved impossible to intimidate him by subtle means, Faletta had sent goons to work him over. They had waylaid him at night outside a bar that faced the quay where his boat was moored. He had come out of the bar seeming tipsy, if not drunk, but when they leaped on him he had fought back. A sap had appeared as if by magic in one hand and a gun in the other. He clubbed one goon senseless. After breaking the jaw of the second, he had kicked him off the quay into the water. He had then driven his boat out of Marseille and had never returned there. It was a kind of truce between him and Faletta. He was not selling his boat or giving up his business. However, he would no longer compete with Faletta and the other caids in Marseille proper. In return Faletta had decided to leave him alone. A single free-lance smuggler could not hurt him very much, and to stop him he judged to be more trouble than it was worth.

This was the man who now occupied most of Faletta's thoughts. He sat in his bar while two of his men stood guard forward. He knew Lambert and LeRoy had been partners at the time when there were two PT boats, not one, and then partners again in the vault of the Banque de Nice. He believed LeRoy would know how to bring Lambert down out of the mountains. Faletta also knew the *juge d'instruction* in Toulon who had the LeRoy case, a man named Bordat. He knew him very well indeed, and he filled an envelope and had his lawyer, Cresci, carry it to Bordat's office by hand that afternoon.

Avery and Picpoul were driven to Toulon in the adjunct mayor's official car. It had been arranged that Avery, posing as LeRoy's congressman, would visit him in jail, sounding him out. Picpoul, meanwhile, would drop in on Bordat, the *juge d'instruction*.

LeRoy came into the *parloir* wearing a short-sleeved polo shirt, so that most of his tattoos showed, and as he grinned in response to Avery's greeting, the two gold teeth in the front of his mouth seemed to light up the room.

Avery explained who he was, seeking to appear to LeRoy as a figure of authority. In any case, it was no use trying to conceal his identity now. From then on he told a series of lies. Whether or not they convinced LeRoy he could not tell, and did not really care. He explained that the CIA, for national-security reasons, had arranged Lambert's escape from prison. However, the escape had backfired, and the poor man was now at large in the Maritime Alps with the combined police forces of France searching for him. It was in the national interest of the United States that Lambert be smuggled out of the country. The CIA would like to enlist the services of LeRoy, as a loyal American, to aid in this work.

"How does it sound so far?" inquired Avery.

LeRoy's gold teeth flashed. "Tell me more, pal."

Pal? Avery swallowed his annoyance. Though a United States congressman, he had need of this man.

"Then you are agreed in principle?"

LeRoy nodded.

"Do you think you could make contact with Lambert?"

"No problem."

Avery appraised him briefly. "How would you do that?"

But LeRoy gave his irritating gold-toothed grin and only shook his head. "Leave that to me, pal. The important question is, can you get me out of here?"

"Suppose I could get you out and your boat out. Do you think you could get Lambert aboard it and out of France?"

"Now you're talking," said LeRoy.

Again Avery silently appraised him. There was another stage to Avery's plan, and he believed that LeRoy would agree to it. But it would not do to bring it up now. One stage at a time. "Good," he said presently, "I'll get back to you," and he stood up and started out of the *parloir*.

LeRoy said: "You forgot something, pal."

Avery turned and gave him a haughty look.

"What do I get out of it?"

"You get your boat back, my good man. And you get out of jail."

"They confiscated my money."

After a brief pause, Avery said: "I'll see you get it back."

At the Palace of Justice, meanwhile, Picpoul had pushed an envelope across the desk of Juge d'Instruction Bordat, who slipped it into a drawer without opening it. The terms had been arranged through intermediaries in advance. Bordat signed the two release documents—for the man and for the boat—in Picpoul's presence, called in an underling and sent them on their way.

"The fellow won't go far," Picpoul said, much relieved. "Considering how much of his money you're holding."

"And we've saved the state the cost of feeding him too," commented Bordat piously.

"Giving him his boat back is a good idea too. He'll be able to make a living while awaiting trial. He won't be a public charge."

"My thoughts exactly," said Bordat. He had been about to sign the documents anyway, and there were now two fat envelopes in the same drawer. But he was careful to conceal this from Picpoul. He made it seem that he was glad to do a favor for such an important politician as the adjunct mayor of Nice—not to mention for his powerful American friend. Nonetheless, as he showed his visitor to the door he wondered briefly what exactly was going on, why this sudden interest in Roy LeRoy. He decided it was best that he did not know.

Men were waiting for LeRoy outside the jail; he was taken immediately to the Café de l'Amitié in Marseille, where he was almost pushed into a chair across the table from Faletta.

"You've caused me a lot of trouble," Faletta said.

LeRoy, having refused to sell him his PT boat, having beat up two of his goons, believed himself about to be murdered.

"I have a job for you," Faletta said.

LeRoy watched him with small ferret eyes. He was sweating and knew Faletta could see it.

"I want you to find Lambert." It was not a suggestion, it was an order.

"What's in it for me?" said LeRoy with false bravado.

"Your boat."

"You want me to do more than just find him, don't you?" said LeRoy. He felt a surge of hope.

Faletta said nothing.

"They took all my money," said LeRoy testing it. "I'm broke."

Faletta pulled out a roll of bills, counted off 100,000 francs and handed this to LeRoy. "That's a week's expenses," he said. "You do this job for me, and I'll see you get your money." LeRoy began to believe that Faletta's job offer was legitimate; if he was careful, he could leave this bar alive.

"What proof do I have that you can do it?" he said.

"I got you out of jail, didn't I?"

LeRoy wasn't sure who exactly had got him out of jail. But he kept this thought to himself, and continued to study the table top, while Faletta gave him his instructions.

At Faletta's side sat a man whose name had not been given, a man who spoke English. The entire transaction was being conducted through this interpreter. It made for slow, heavy going. On the other hand LeRoy and Faletta sometimes seemed able to understand each other perfectly well via signs, gestures, silences, without the intervention of words at all. LeRoy, for instance, understood perfectly well what Faletta was asking him to do.

"You have no objections?" inquired Faletta.

LeRoy said: "The guy is nothing to me." An exaggeration. He spoke out of fear. He liked Lambert well enough, though he had never approved of him. Lambert, like most Americans, was open and trusting, and this would make LeRoy's job easy. Lambert believed in glory, the biggest whore in the world and one that had never seduced LeRoy. A whore who would get a man killed. Lambert believed also in other classic American virtues, which LeRoy saw as dangerous and therefore stupid. He had rejected them long ago. He considered himself now more European in outlook. One watched in others for base motives to predominate. One protected oneself at all times.

One did not double cross a man like Faletta.

"My associate here will arrange details," said Faletta and he stood up from the table. Preceded by bodyguards, he went out of the bar into the sunlight outside.

LeRoy, as he returned to Toulon to claim his boat, was thinking that he now had two employers. He wondered if they knew about each other. All he himself wanted now was for the *juge d'instruction* to give him his money back, and after that to escape Faletta. He was worried about Avery as well, but not as much. Under the circumstances he did not care much about his former partner one way or the other, except to recognize that today was not Lambert's lucky day.

# CHAPTER
## 36

The name in the headlines every day was Jacqueline's name too, and business in her shop had never been better. People came in off the street and waited in line to be served, often five or six customers at once, though the city was full of other perfume shops. People came from the other side of the city, they came in pairs and groups, and waited silently as if in church. Most she had never seen before. Many were rough types, as unused to perfume shops as to museums, and the majority were men. Waiting, they stared. They watched her hands wrap packages or brush back her hair. They watched for her to smile, which she had extreme difficulty doing. They waited to hear the sound of her voice. This satisfied many of them, who then left without buying. But others bought. They bought sizes and quantities they did not need or want. They satisfied their curiosity, but it cost them money. This sideshow had an entry charge, and they paid it—paid for the privilege of being in the presence of a celebrity. If she had been a singer or an actress, they would have cadged an autograph, and thus got away free. But she was not, and their fleeting contact with the famous became therefore expensive. Jacqueline was becoming, in a manner of speaking, rich.

She hated it.

At least one uniformed policeman stood outside her door all day. He did not interfere with trade. He was merely there, a ticket taker who took no tickets, a circus barker who did not bark.

There was sometimes a detective across the street as well, and her mail was being watched. Each morning the postman went by without stopping. Ten minutes later a detective brought in her small stack of letters, principally bills from the perfume houses that supplied her. Presumably the detectives were looking for a letter or telegram from Lambert, an attempt to contact her. If they found one, they never told her. Her phone was not tapped because she had none. She was lucky there. She imagined going to bed at night and sensing police hands even on the instrument on the table beside her pillow.

Twice her photo had appeared in the *Nice Matin*. She had avoided reading the Paris papers, but perhaps it had appeared there too; she did not know or want to know.

A man named Alberti, who owned the perfume shop farther down the street, came in each day ostensibly to borrow some item for which he had a customer. Such borrowing was common among the shops, but Alberti, Jacqueline perceived, was nerving himself up for a different proposition and at last he came out with it. He invited her to spend the weekend with him; there was no reason, he said, why his wife should know.

Jacqueline was affronted to the point of tears, but could not weep because there were customers in the shop—foreign tourists, as it happened, people who understood neither the import of Alberti's offer nor how dirty it made her feel.

Another customer, a man she had never seen before, made a similar offer later the same day.

And one of the detectives who brought the mail had ceased addressing her as "madame." Now he eyed her up and down and called her "*mon petit chou*"—my little cabbage. He turned their brief conversations whenever he could toward sexual innuendo. Finally he offered his services in any way she might name, at the same time brushing his clothing back so as to display his pistol. It seemed to Jacqueline a phallic gesture, as obscene and offensive as if he had opened his fly.

Her shop, only a long block inland from the Ruhl Hotel and the sea, drew tourists too, foreigners who did not ogle her, did not know

357

who she was. There was no way they could be aware of the depth of the nightmare through which she stumbled every day. Nonetheless, she found it difficult to smile at them too.

There was no contact from her husband, and Bellarmine never came near her. These were the two men in her life, and she had been abandoned by them both. They were like schoolboys playing hide-and-seek in the nearby hills, neither of them interested in her, interested only in each other, and the game. The chase was everything.

At night she locked herself in her stock room alone. She prepared food for herself that she did not eat, then sat on the bed holding open a book that her eyes refused to read. She had a small radio that played all evening, and to which she did not listen. Across the street in a doorway stood a detective. Probably he was there all night. In any case he was always there whenever she went down into the dark shop and stood behind the counter and stared out at him through the intervening glass.

Evenings after closing up she usually went shopping for food. She went out with a string bag and the detective following along behind. The sidewalks were still crowded and people nudged each other, pointing with their chins, as she walked by, as the detective walked by. There was always a crowd inside the *boulangerie* at that hour. People were buying the long, hot fresh breads for supper. This crowd, and the crowds in other stores as well, always fell silent, fell back, when Jacqueline entered, and when she reached into her purse for change, people seemed to become fearful, as if expecting her to bring forth a gun, or perhaps a curse. Or so she imagined.

When the string bag was full, the detective trailed her back to the perfume shop. She locked herself in and him out, and he took up his post across the street again.

Sunday came. She shopped for food, then bought a paper at the kiosk on the Place Grimaldi next to the bus stop. She pretended to stand reading it. The detective stood about twenty feet away gazing off in the opposite direction—some of them were really quite polite, or tried to be. When the next bus screeched to a stop, his head jerked around. However, Jacqueline appeared to ignore both the bus and him, her head being buried in her newspaper.

But just as the bus started up again she leaped aboard the rear platform, and the bus pulled off down the street. The detective ran after it. As it gained speed he was sprinting hard. But the conductor, who was making change for her, never noticed, and up front the

358

driver was busy driving. She saw that the detective had stopped running. He looked very small. He was shaking his fist at the bus.

Numbly Jacqueline took a seat.

Now he will look for a phone, she told herself. But on a Sunday he would have difficulty finding one. The post offices were closed and there were no outdoor phone booths. He would have to find a bar. It would take time. She would not be arrested right away.

On the outskirts of the city she got down from the bus and waited for another that would take her up to the farm. She expected a police car to come along first. Men would jump out and grab her. But her bus pulled to a stop and she got on it. It took her out of the city and up into hills that soon became mountains, and after a while the terrible weight on her chest went away and she began to breathe normally.

She got down from the bus and, carrying her string bag, walked up the road toward the farm. There was a black police car parked on the cobbles in front of the house. The two detectives were playing cards. They were dealing the cards out across the top of the hood. It gave her a start to see them there: perhaps she had eluded one detective only to be arrested by two others. But they had been on post since dawn, they told her. She saw there was no radio in their car. There was no way they could know that she too had become the object of an active police search. They were extremely polite to her. They offered to pull their car up to the top of the road. They understood that she might like some privacy. Although nothing explicit was said, they seemed to understand what her life had become, how much a fugitive's relatives could suffer in a case like this.

"If you need us, madame," one of them said, "just call out."

The foliage was so thick at the head of the road that she could not even see them. She gave a broken laugh—their kindness made her want to cry—then unlocked the front door and went into her house.

She saw at once that Lambert had been there. Either that or the detectives had stolen his field glasses and some of his underwear. She went quickly through the house. There were other things missing too: a blanket, his raincoat, a flashlight, some food. In the kitchen she found that wooden matches had been laid out across the table. They spelled: "I love you."

Now she did begin to cry, not because she was touched by her husband's sentiment, or because she believed in his love, but because all this was so totally bewildering. What had she done to get herself into a mess like this? And when and where would it end?

She changed into a summer sun dress and gathered up some fashion magazines: *Elle, Modes de France.* She went outside onto the cobblestones, got a beach chair out of the shed, extended it, together with its foot rest, and sat down in the sun and began to thumb through the magazines. It was hard to concentrate on them. She saw that the style in shoes had changed. Her own were now out of date, and she glanced down at them. The rounded toe was out. The pointed toe was in. The heels were still high and stiletto thin, though. Pleated skirts with cinched waists were in, and blouses in pale colors. Shoulder pads were less prominent.

The sun was on her face, on her forearms, on her calves. When she looked up she could see across the valley, high hills with mountains behind them. The sun was warm on her skin, and she unbuttoned the lower part of her skirt to expose a portion of her thighs. After a moment she undid the top buttons of her blouse, offering her throat and upper chest to the sun also.

She fell asleep. It was the first deep, dreamless sleep she had known since the day her husband was arrested—since this terrible thing happened, and she sank down into it, she embraced it like a lover, devoured it the way a starving person devours food.

The shadow of a man had fallen across her. She could feel this shadow like a weight. At first she thought she was dreaming. Then she knew she wasn't, and her eyes snapped open. Although she did not otherwise move, she was instantly on guard. A pair of legs beside her head. She followed them upward.

"Oh," she said, "it's you."

It was Bellarmine. He wore a dark summer suit and the same gray fedora he had worn all winter—no doubt the only hat he owned.

Realizing how much of her was exposed, she became embarrassed and jumped up. She buttoned her blouse first, then stooped to button the bottom of her skirt. It was late afternoon, and she peered across at the sun, now low in the sky.

"I'm sorry if I woke you."

"I've had a nice nap," she said. "How are you?"

She saw that the other two detectives stood a short distance behind him and that both cars, his and theirs, had been driven into the yard.

Also a breeze had sprung up. It blew through her hair, across the goose bumps on her arms, and she hugged herself, feeling suddenly cold. "Would you like to come into the house?" she said to him.

As he followed her inside, she saw him glance carefully around, practically sniffing the air. Remembering the message spelled out with matchsticks, she thrust her arm into the kitchen and erased it. They stood in the main room. "Would you like to sit down?"

Bellarmine, still peering about, said: "I can only stay a minute." He added almost apologetically: "There are a few more posts I have to check yet." So he hadn't come to arrest her. Or at least he was pretending he hadn't.

She didn't trust him, yet she didn't want him to go. He frightened her, and yet she felt secure when with him.

She walked him to the doorway, where he turned with his hand on the knob. "You haven't heard from—from your husband—by any chance?"

Perhaps she should tell him that Lambert had been here, had taken things. But if she did she would have to tell him about the matchsticks. Love was such an easy word to spell, and in Lambert's case it had no more value than the matches he had used.

"No," she said, "I haven't heard from him."

In the doorway, Bellarmine nodded. Jacqueline, watching him, didn't know what she felt about him. She knew she didn't want him to leave.

"Will you come back later?"

"If you like," he said.

She turned away from him, afraid he might see how much his reply pleased her.

"I'll see you later, then."

He went out. The door slammed.

When she heard his car go off, she went out into the yard. The other two detectives stood some distance off, talking to each other in low voices. She dragged the beach chair back into the shed. The magazines lay on the cobbles, glossy pages blowing in the wind. She gathered them up and carried them back into the house.

It was dark when Bellarmine returned. He came into the house and took off his hat. Its sweatband had left an imprint high on his forehead. "It's getting chilly out," he said. "The nights are very brisk up here, aren't they?"

It made her think of the two detectives waiting outside in the cold. Good manners demanded that she invite them in. She was a well-brought-up young woman, and good manners exerted on her an enormously strong pull. But she looked across at Bellarmine, who cared about her, or at least she believed he did, and realized she

361

wanted to be alone with him, at least for a little while. And so she would not invite the other two inside just yet.

"Is there any news?" she asked. But even this banal question upset her, and she was wringing her hands together as she waited for him to speak.

"He was sighted over near Sospel this morning. Maybe he was. One never knows how reliable these reports are."

"Sospel?"

"It's quite close to the Italian frontier."

"Maybe he got across."

"There really isn't much chance of that."

She felt her chin begin to quiver. "This is so hard," she said. "So hard." She was staring fixedly at the floor, trying to hold the tears back. The next she knew Bellarmine's arms were around her, and he was pressing her head against his chest.

"*Pauvre petite*," he said. "I'd give anything if you didn't have to go through this."

Straightening up, she drew away from him. From across the room she said: "It's pretty late."

"We could have dinner. A restaurant in one of the villages around here, perhaps."

Jacqueline said: "I can't bear people staring at me."

When Bellarmine did not answer, she said brightly: "I could fix something here. Would you like that?"

He followed her into the kitchen where she emptied the contents of the string bag on top of the messed-up matches. "Let's see, we could have lamb chops, a salad, bread, cheese."

Bellarmine produced a half smile. "There's wine, I trust."

There was the carton under the sink. "Oh, yes, there's plenty of wine."

He reached under and withdrew a bottle, opened it and filled two glasses. Jacqueline prepared the dinner with her glass beside her hand. Bellarmine sat at the table and watched her work. While the chops sizzled, she sat beside him, and they filled their glasses a second time. She drank the wine without tasting it, hoping to become relaxed. Instead she felt only guilt, and told herself she did not know why. Her mind became focused on the two detectives outside in the night. That was part of the guilt. Her conduct was rude. Was this all that was bothering her? If so, she could invite them inside. But she knew that she did not want them inside. She did not want them out there either. She did not want them nearby at all, witnesses to whatever would happen next.

She said: "Your men must be hungry."

"They have food with them, I think."

"I suppose I should invite them in," she suggested. Let him make the decision.

Bellarmine stood up from the table. "Why don't I send them away?" It was not so much a statement as a request for permission, and Jacqueline realized this.

"All right," she said, though once they were gone then anything might happen. Anything? Like what? she asked herself. She did not know, and refused to think about it. Whatever it would be, she did not want two detectives out there able to report on her, able to spread her shame still further.

She heard the front door open and close again. Then Bellarmine came back into the kitchen and sat down. "I've sent them down," he said.

She did not know what this meant. Sent them where? And for how long? An hour? Several hours? All night?

Bellarmine may have been as embarrassed as she. "It's silly of me to keep this place staked out anyway," he said, as if trying to fill the silence that had fallen between them. "He—" Was he unable to refer to her husband by name? "He won't come here."

"No," Jacqueline said.

"He must know we'd be watching this place."

Jacqueline said: "I don't want to talk about him. Please."

After dinner they went into the main room and discussed building a fire. They discussed nights like this, which were really quite chilly. A fire would really take the chill off the room. To build a fire was really a fine idea.

They built the fire, but once it was blazing the room grew so hot they had to open the windows. This made them laugh. After moving back from the hearth they finished the first bottle of wine and started on another. Jacqueline put the radio on, and the room filled up with music. For a time both stared silently into the flames, but presently Jacqueline got up and began to move in time to the music. She thought Bellarmine might ask her to dance, but he only watched her over the rim of his glass, a half smile lifting one side of his mustache.

She was obliged to say: "Dance with me."

"Sure." He put the glass down and stood up.

363

He danced badly. Still, it was nice to feel a man's arms around her. This man's arms. It was nice after so long to be held tight by a man. She kicked her shoes off, becoming suddenly shorter. Her forehead now pressed against his chin, and they swayed to the beat of the tunes.

"Your men will be coming back soon," she suggested.

"They won't come back tonight."

She rubbed her forehead against the bristles along the line of his jaw.

"You told them not to?"

"Yes."

"Why did you do that?" she said, and was appalled at how arch she sounded. She was immediately ashamed. She hated coy women. But how else to jolt him into action of some kind? So far he seemed content only to hold her close, which was satisfying in a way, but not satisfying enough. She wanted to know where he wished to take her, and when and how. Though only one destination seemed possible tonight under such circumstances as these, still she had not admitted this even to herself, much less to him. But her life had been so empty for so long, and it seemed now on the verge of being filled again, if only momentarily, and she wanted it to happen. In some mysterious way she seemed unable or unwilling to wish for anything else.

His response was to kiss her. His mustache raked her nose, her lips, her eyes. Her husband had never worn a mustache, and before him she had known only beardless boys. Her only previous experience kissing mustaches consisted of other people's husbands at New Year's Eve parties.

But serious kissing had now begun. His tongue was in her mouth, and his hands moved up and down her body. Her cheeks were burning, and her knees seemed to have liquefied so that she was afraid she might fall down.

She clung to him. "Are you sure your men won't come back?"

For an answer, he picked her up and carried her into the bedroom. She was breathing into his ear. Yes, she thought, this is what I want. It was what she had wanted for hours, or for weeks, though she admitted it to herself only now for the first time. She wanted not to be alone anymore. She wanted to offer herself to this honest, honorable man. She wanted to be employed by him, to feel him expand inside her being until she was not herself anymore, but had become part of another.

364

In the bedroom he set her upon her stocking feet, but she felt so dizzy that she sat down on the bed while he undressed her. He started with her nylons, his fingers fumbling with the snaps of her garter belt high up under her skirt, just as her husband had done the first time.

That job accomplished, he covered her face with kisses, but there was too much light in the room and she was embarrassed in advance about nakedness. Her knees were too bony for one thing—he had never even seen her knees before. In addition, the door to the other room was wide open, and she could hear the crackling of the logs in the hearth: normal privacy had not been secured. She began to worry about fire. They had forgotten to put the screen in front of the fireplace, she believed.

All this time, she noted, Bellarmine remained single-minded, for she could feel air upon her breasts. Her husband had always been the same, single-minded once he started, perhaps all men were, and if this was true then there could be nothing sublime about this moment as she experienced it, nor about any subsequent moment either. Her husband had been a very good lover, or so she had imagined at the time, though what did she know then? In a few moments, presumably, she would have something to compare him against. She remembered that she had never loved her husband so much as when he held her tight afterward, not making love anymore, not breathing hard anymore, just holding each other tight.

She sat naked and alone on the edge of the bed, waiting for Bellarmine, who had abandoned her momentarily and was throwing off his own clothes as fast as he could, a series of grotesque movements that at another time might have made her laugh. But she did not find them a bit funny now. He was hurrying, as if afraid she might change her mind, which in fact she was in the process of doing. If he really wanted her, he was right to hurry, though why should he want her? Why should anyone? As he pushed her down onto the pillow, she noted that the shutters were ajar. Since the lights were still on in the room, whatever they did on this bed would be visible to anyone outside there in the darkness. Most likely there was no one, for it must be midnight or later, and the nearest habitation was two kilometers away. No one would be strolling about in the forest at this hour—except possibly his detectives. Or her husband. His detectives were unlikely—he had sent them away, and she believed him a man whom no subordinate would disobey. But her husband seemed to her a distinct possibility. He had an almost mystic ability to turn up whenever his own interests were at stake. As they were right now. Or perhaps he came here every night. He was a man in desperate trouble. Perhaps he came here every night looking for her, needing help from the only human being in the world he could trust. The wife who had pledged to him her troth. The wife who had taken the vow seriously at the time, and still did. The wife who was about to commit adultery. He would crawl through the forest to the lighted window. He would peer inside, and that is what he would see.

But there was no longer anything she could do about it. Bellarmine was in bed with her, had pulled the covers over them both. Again her face was being covered by kisses, and her body searched by his hands. It was too late now.

He could feel the whole length of her against him. The sheets, he noted, were cool, and her flesh was as hot as fresh bread. He was no cynical policeman now, just a man in love with a woman and in bed with her for the first time. To accord and be accorded this ultimate intimacy seemed to him at this moment the holiest of human acts, and as he approached it his chest felt bursting with emotion. It was as if he had expanded his lungs to the maximum. He could take in no more air. He knew that part of what he felt was pride—pride to have reached this far, to have conquered all of the multitudinous female defenses, women threw up so many, new ones every day, every year—but most of it was love for this woman, the purest love he had ever known. He was where he wanted to be at last, and believed she was too, the heat of her proved it, and then he was astonished to realize that she had stiffened, was no longer making any response.

He stopped caressing her, and only held her close. "What's the matter?"

"I don't know."

He believed she knew very well, and he waited for her to tell him.

"It's just—I—that—"

She began to sob into his chest, and he accepted her tears for what they were: woman's oldest known method of apologizing. Their oldest known method of saying no, also. The tears washed away his pride, removed all his hopes, until only his great love for her was left.

"I can't," she sobbed. "Please don't hate me."

"You're still in love with your husband."

"I'm not in love with my husband. I'm in love with you. I think I am. But I'm still married to him, don't you see?"

366

He did not see. It was nice to be told that she loved him, he supposed, but he was not sure he believed her. Her verbal declaration in no way matched the physical declaration she had shied away from.

She got out of bed and padded naked to the armoire—he watched her buttocks move—where she found and put on a bathrobe. Then she went to the shutters, pulled them in and latched them closed.

Bellarmine sat with his back against the headboard watching her. "Come back to bed," he suggested gently.

She was wiping her eyes with a handkerchief. She shook her head. "It's as if I know he's out there, watching. Please don't hate me. Try to understand."

"He's not out there. He's many, many kilometers away, according to our information."

But he could not budge her. He recognized that special obstinacy that women sometimes apply to sexual matters, and so gave up trying. She was obdurate enough already. He did not wish to risk hardening her further against him.

As soon as she saw she had convinced him, she came forward and took his hands. She sat on the edge of the bed and thanked him for being so understanding. She kissed him gently—on the forehead, on the nose, on the lips.

He offered to drive her down to Nice at once, for it was very late, and tomorrow, Monday, she would have to open her shop at the usual hour. But she rejected this suggestion. "I need a little time to think," she told him. She would take the bus down in the morning, she said. For tonight she wanted to stay on at the farm, to be alone, wanted time to confront her thoughts. She caressed his cheek. "Maybe next time," she said in a soft voice. It was not exactly a promise, though he wished to take it as one.

"I'll come and fetch you in the morning," Bellarmine said. "How about that?"

It brought a bright smile to her face, and she agreed. He should come up somewhat early. She would fix breakfast for him, after which they would ride down together.

She walked him out to the car. It was so dark out there on the cobbles that he could no longer see her face, but he kissed her briefly and held her tight, then drove out of the yard and up on to the main road. When he had reached the other side of the valley he stopped the car and gazed across at the lights that were the farmhouse. He decided to wait there until all the lights had gone out. Watching

367

across the void he felt almost married to her. Although he had not consummated his love for her this night, he felt joined to her by sex nonetheless. They had shared a sexual experience, had they not? They had lain naked in bed together, and if they had stopped short of their goal, this was not really significant. These were the same thoughts, he realized, that a teen-age boy might have felt in his place—but then love reduces every man to the level of a teen-age boy, does it not? The desire to expand into someone else is the same, one is all yearning and no knowledge.

Across the valley all the lights had suddenly gone out. Restarting the engine, he drove down out of the dark mountains toward the sea. It occurred to him that he should send detectives back here at once. There ought to be someone watching the farm all night. But to order the old detectives back, or to find new ones, would require explanations. Why had they been sent away in the first place? What had he hoped for? Ribald jokes would be made. It would become known that she had sent him packing.

A police presence here tonight was not really necessary, he decided. The farm could survive without it. He would send a team of detectives back in the morning, which would be soon enough.

Bellarmine was scarcely gone before Lambert came in through the front door. He seemed completely at ease. It was his house. "I thought he'd never leave," he said.

Jacqueline was astonished to see him suddenly standing there—and also terrified. She was speechless, and for a moment only stared. Then she rushed about the house pulling the rest of the shutters closed, turning out lights.

"I've been sitting out there in the bushes for hours, waiting for him to go," Lambert explained conversationally. He gave a cheerful laugh. "I'd begun to think he planned to spend the night."

"No," Jacqueline said.

"No, what?"

"He didn't plan to spend the night." She had begun almost imperceptibly to tremble.

"You're trembling," Lambert said. He came over and put his arms around her. "What's the matter, did I frighten you? I'm sorry." He kissed her. The kiss lasted a long time, though she stood like a stone. He began trying to force his tongue into her mouth. How long was he out there? she asked herself. His lips were pressed against hers.

368

Where was he watching the house from? How close was he? As close as the bedroom window? Had he been staring in the bedroom window at them?

Her husband had never had leanings toward perverted sex—not in her presence, in any case. He was not a voyeur. She could not imagine him calmly watching his wife make love to another man. To him sex was always straightforward and romantic. Very American—not European at all. But perhaps he had changed. She could not have imagined him as a wanted criminal either, and the events of the last few weeks had proved to her only that she did not know him at all.

"You've stopped trembling," he said, and released her. "Did you get my message with the matches?" he asked proudly.

"Where were you out there?" she said, gesturing toward the forest behind the house. This was one detail that had to be cleared up immediately. How much had he seen?

He had been up above the road, Lambert explained. He had been afraid to get too close. He had been in position before dark, but at the time there had been two police cars in the yard. He had seen one leave and had waited for the other to follow.

"I knew I'd find you here tonight," he told her. He was embracing her again, stroking her. She was as rigid under his hands as she had been under Bellarmine's. More so.

"I was about to come down close to the house and peer in the window," Lambert said cheerfully. "See if I could figure out how much longer before he was going to leave."

If Bellarmine had stayed—if Lambert had found her in bed with him—another five minutes and she would have been caught in the act, dishonoring all three of them, dishonoring the sanctity of the marriage bond as well. Lambert's reaction would have been—what? Something had saved her, whether God or her guardian angel or luck, she did not know, but she was weak with gratitude.

Lambert, however, was exuberant. He wanted a shower. He hadn't bathed in a week, he said—and a hot meal, and after that to sleep in a bed with his wife. He wanted to make love to his wife.

He went into the bathroom and she heard the water run.

"The police say you killed that man," she said. She stood in the doorway looking at him.

"I never touched him. He ran the motorcycle off the road. I was lucky I wasn't killed myself. Look at this." He showed her the scratches

369

and bruises, most of them nearly healed, on his arms and legs. "I had to leave him there."

She wanted to believe him. She was half convinced. He had never been a violent man, and always totally gentle toward her.

There was food left over from the meal she had prepared for Bellarmine. She had not been hungry then, and still wasn't. She cooked the remaining lamb chop, and Lambert, when he came out of the shower, wolfed it down. He wolfed down everything she put in front of him. His hair was wet and combed, and he was wearing clean pajamas and a bathrobe. When finished, he took her by the hand and tried to lead her into the bedroom.

"You should leave."

"No."

"It's dangerous for you here."

"I don't care." He was peeling the bathrobe off her, weighing her breasts in each hand.

"He could come back at any moment."

"He won't come back."

But he might, and the idea stiffened her.

She saw that Lambert was giddy with excitement, only part of it, she realized, sexual in nature. He was aroused by her body. He was aroused by the danger as well. Every minute that he spent here increased his risk, and he knew this, and did not care, or perhaps even sought the risk, enjoyed it above all else. As he led her to the bed and pushed her down on it, all she could think was that the man who might come through the window now would be Bellarmine; she risked being caught in the act for the second time in one night, but this time by the man she loved, and whom she would lose as a result. It was all too much for her. She was so distraught, almost destroyed by the situation in which she found herself, that she made no protest as she felt her husband's hands, as his body came down on top of hers. She permitted herself to be used. Let him do with her whatever he liked.

It was only later that she was betrayed by her nerve endings, or her loneliness or her despair. Despite her efforts to ignore Lambert's attentions, her traitorous body began to respond to him. She was horrified but unable to help herself as she began to match him thrust for thrust, slowly at first, then with more energy and hope than she believed was left in her. The bedclothes were on the floor before they stopped, and she had to remake the bed so that they could sleep.

The result was that she dozed fitfully the rest of the night, her body sore, coming awake to brood about love, and about betrayal, and about the relationship between the two, for both words had legal, emotional and sexual meanings, and if indeed she loved at all, then whom had she betrayed and how much?

At daylight she woke with a start. She listened to the healthy breathing of her husband, who still slept beside her, then threw a frantic look at the clock. Bellarmine, if true to his promise, would be here at any moment for breakfast, and she shook Lambert violently awake, made him dress hurriedly and thrust a package of food into his hands even as she forced him out of the door.

"I love you," he said, and was gone.

The words brought tears to Jacqueline's eyes, not for sentimental reasons, but because they constituted a new burden, and she was already carrying so many that the idea of one more nearly broke her. Why did he say that? she asked herself. She did not believe it for a moment. Her husband loved only his own extravagant emotions. But she would never be entirely able to disbelieve it either.

Lambert, halfway across the yard, came loping back. "Get a message to Roy LeRoy," he told her. He knew that LeRoy and his boat had been released. He had heard it on the radio or read it in a newspaper—it was not clear to her which. "Tell him I'll meet him anywhere he says. Then come back and tell me where." He would watch the house, he said. She should leave lights on to show the coast was clear; he would come in to receive whatever news she brought him. With her help and LeRoy's help, he would be safe in Tangier very soon. Once there he would send for her.

He loped away again. In two seconds he was out of sight.

It was a performance that stunned Jacqueline, made her realize how much her conduct in bed last night had cost her. The word "spouse" meant "accomplice." She was still her husband's accomplice. She was as guilty as he was, as bound by the marriage vow as ever.

She heard the bark of Lambert's motorcycle, a noise that flowed uphill. Half a minute later she heard a car coming across the valley: Bellarmine, most likely. On time. Full of hope. Full of a belief in her virtue, though in her own eyes she had no virtue left. Rushing back into the house, she cleaned up after her husband, hung his pajamas on the deepest hook in the armoire, hid the laundry he had left behind, replaced his shaving brush and razor in the medicine

371

chest, banged the dried clots of mud from his shoes and brushed the dust with her hand into the cracks in the tiles on the floor. She was trying to conceal two things, that her husband had used the house last night and that he had used her as well. She was trying to hide evidence of legal guilt and sexual guilt both. She did not want Bellarmine to know to what extent she had been unfaithful to him. Had she overlooked anything? She could not be sure. There was no time to look further, for she heard the police car roll in over the cobbles, and she went outside to meet him.

"Did you sleep well?" he asked solicitously. He had got out of the car.

"Not very." He looked haggard too, but his eyes trusted her, and she reached up and stroked his cheek, and believed that never in her life had she felt this ashamed.

"It's late," she said. "Let's not have breakfast here. Let's stop at a café."

He nodded and got back into the car. He threw the door open on her side.

He had decided to end the stakeout on her farm, he told her as he drove. "If you want to use the place, you can anytime. You won't be bothered."

She was surprised. "Thank you." It was a kindness that could cost him his career. I don't deserve it, she thought. Don't risk your career over me, she wanted to tell him.

He gave a mock leer. "Of course I reserve the right to visit you here."

It was a way of telling her he would wait for her until she was ready. They would not have to go to some hot-bed hotel together, sneak into her stock room or his grim flat. Whatever would happen between them would happen quite normally, in due time, in her own house. There would be no detectives to send away first.

"So invite me."

"You'll always be welcome here," she said in a broken voice.

# CHAPTER
## 37

In the American Embassy in Paris O'Hara stormed down the hall, brushed past the secretary who tried to stop him and burst into Tuttle's office. He slapped that day's *France-Soir* down on the desk in front of Tuttle.

"A friend of yours was found floating in the harbor in Marseille yesterday, I see."

Tuttle glanced down the paper. Showing was part of the "LAMBERT LAWYER ASSASSINATED" headline, and a photo of the late Mr. Sharkey. Tuttle again gave his palms-down sign. "I can't help that."

"I think maybe I ought to look into a few things around here."

"Is that a threat?"

"Things that wouldn't stand up under a little investigation."

"Who is Sharkey to you?"

"He was a harmless, nice kind of guy," said O'Hara. Some years ago he had asked Sharkey's help in identifying some women an assistant secretary of state was seeing in Nice.

"And maybe I should investigate you," said Tuttle.

O'Hara nodded grimly, spun on his heel and left the office.

That afternoon he caught a Viscount down to Nice, and an hour after he got there he was with Avery in the Ruhl bar having a drink and probing for information, but he got none. He did not know exactly what he was looking for, but this whole case stunk so much that he ought to be able to dig up something.

From the Ruhl he went to the *commissariat* on the Rue Gioffredo, where he found Bellarmine. He wanted to know how Sharkey died, the grisly details, and Bellarmine told him. It was a story of the type that most policemen generally recounted only to each other, as if other human beings would be incapable of understanding it. Only cops lived lives in which such obscene detail as this was commonplace—to the point where certain human beings came to seem obscene. Sometimes even life itself.

"They burned his cock off," repeated O'Hara. "Jesus." He was more moved than he had expected to be—moved enough to wish to share what he knew with Bellarmine.

O'Hara believed he had lost control of Avery. In any case, he had lost whatever influence over Avery he had once had. Also he felt every policeman's bitterness at losing an informant. He had liked Sharkey more or less. He had certainly not disliked him. A policeman's existence was focused around his fight against evil. This was true even of corrupt policemen, and O'Hara was by no means corrupt. In the case of Sharkey the forces of darkness had triumphed. It left O'Hara feeling that his own role in life had been diminished—he himself was a lesser man than he had been a few hours before.

"Listen," he said urgently to Bellarmine, "there's an American congressman here named Avery. He's in this up to his balls."

"I know the name. He had a box at the Banque de Nice. One of those looted, I believe."

"I think he arranged Lambert's escape from jail," O'Hara said, and he saw the momentary surprise in Bellarmine's eyes. "I think he's trying to contact Lambert even now. I think you should put a twenty-four-hour tail on him."

Overcome by the passion of the moment, O'Hara had reverted to the man he had been at the beginning, the idealistic young agent who cared only about his own personal war against the evil in the world. Avery was evil, and O'Hara no longer cared who put him away, himself or another—this French policeman here, for example.

"I want to be of help if I can," he said.

"Thank you," said Bellarmine.

O'Hara had felt himself so totally American that crimes against Frenchmen and French law—the rape of the Banque de Nice, for instance—had not really touched him. He had had no strong reaction one way or the other. Such crimes did not stick in his craw. He had not felt what was to him the strongest of a policeman's emotions: aversion. But now he did. The murder of Sharkey, who was an American, an informant, almost a friend, had touched him to that extent.

He stood by while Bellarmine called in two detectives and ordered them to begin what was to be a twenty-four-hour tail on Avery. When the two detectives had gone out, Bellarmine extended a package of

American cigarettes across the desk. They lit up, and for a moment smoked quietly, colleagues at last. This realization brought with it certain embarrassment, so that Bellarmine felt constrained to add a typically banal police remark: "Let's see what the tail turns up."

But Roy LeRoy had sailed into Nice an hour before, and Avery was in a taxi en route to the port to give him final, specific instructions. The detectives sent to the Ruhl were about five minutes too late. The tail would begin only when Avery had returned. They settled down to wait.

As soon as Avery's taxi had disappeared around the Monument aux Morts, LeRoy jumped on to the quay, walked up to the street and waited for a Number 17 bus, which, about ten minutes later, deposited him a block from Jacqueline Lambert's shop. LeRoy's mind normally contained only one fixed idea at a time. The way to contact Lambert, he believed, was through his wife. That Jacqueline was already in contact with him seemed to LeRoy a certainty. Or if he wasn't, contact would be made soon. A man holed up in those mountains needed help to get away. Where would he go for it? LeRoy knew Lambert; he would go to his wife.

When he came to the shop LeRoy paused to gaze in through the glass. The place was empty of customers at the moment, and Jacqueline stood behind the counter, her eyes downcast, her thoughts he knew not where. As he watched her, he considered his idea one more time. It still seemed sound to him, and he went inside. The bell tinkled and Jacqueline looked up sharply.

Recognizing him, she demanded in English: "What you want?"

"To get a message to your husband," LeRoy answered. And he favored her with the same gold-toothed grin he had flashed earlier at Avery and Faletta.

Jacqueline knew this grin. It had chilled her often enough in the past and it chilled her now. It seemed to her the grin of a man who was different from other men. She could imagine him perpetrating some terrible outrage while grinning like that.

"Your husband's in a mess, isn't he?"

Jacqueline did not answer.

"And I'm the guy who can get him out of it. So have you seen him?"

He watched her closely.

375

"Look, I know you don't like me," he said. "But this is serious. Your husband needs me."

"You're the last person he needs."

"I can get him out of France."

Jacqueline may have wished to ignore this remark too, but she could not do so. "How?"

Again the grin. LeRoy considered it his best and most winning expression. Unfortunately he had a habit of grinning in the wrong places, or holding the grin too long. It was this that people found frightening. He did not understand it, but he was used to it, and he saw that Jacqueline was frightened now.

His grin at last waned. "I got my boat back," he told her. "I got it parked right here in Nice."

Jacqueline nodded, but did not speak, so LeRoy continued. "It's his only chance," he said. "First stop, Tangier." As he waited for a reaction, he watched her through narrowed eyes.

"I—I have no way of getting a message to him."

"If those frog cops catch him," said LeRoy conversationally, "it's the guillotine for sure." He added: "He did kill that guy, didn't he?"

"It was an accident. The bike crashed."

"Sure." LeRoy gave a brief bark of a laugh. "His head will bounce into the basket just the same. Anyway, you did see him, didn't you? You just told me you saw him."

Jacqueline seemed unable to meet his glance.

"You and I together can save him, baby."

To herself Jacqueline conceded this. She bowed her head, conceding it to LeRoy too.

"Alone he's got no chance."

Just then the bell over the door tinkled, and a customer came in. It was the girl from the tailor shop across the street; she had broken a nail and wished to buy a file. Jacqueline was grateful for the interruption. In her profession, the girl commented with a smile, a snagged fingernail could ruin an hour's work. Her "profession" was to manipulate a fine electric needle to repair runs in used nylon stockings. She worked at a table in the shop's front window and passersby sometimes stopped to watch her. Nylons were so rare that girls like this sat in tailors' windows all over France repairing them.

Jacqueline watched her recross the street, then turned back to LeRoy. "What's your message."

The gold-toothed grin reappeared. "Tell him I want to take him on a cruise." The notion caused LeRoy to give a brief laugh. Then he leaned forward intently. "There's a dock he knows about. Tell him I'll be offshore each night for the next three nights waiting for his signal. Same signal as last time. Got that?"

Nodding, Jacqueline peered down at her hands.

It was nearly dark. She got off the bus and started down the dirt access road toward the farm. The bus was the last one of the day, and she heard it grind on up and around the back of the hill, its noise diminishing till all she could hear was the surrounding silence. She came into the yard and crossed the cobblestones. She was wearing flat heels, having changed into them on the bus. As far as she knew she had not been tailed to the bus stop. She had slipped away from her shop in high heels carrying a string bag, as if going out for food. She had noted no police presence around the shop these last few days. Bellarmine must have pulled the stakeout back there too.

Nor, this time, was there any police car parked in her yard. There were no detectives nearby that she could discern, though she stopped and listened for voices, for movement. Nonetheless, she had the impression she was being watched—her husband presumably, and she hoped he would come forward quickly, pick up his message and leave. She wanted to get this over with as fast as possible. She wanted him out of France, and out of her life, the sooner the better. She owed him this one last act, however dangerous for her, this one last crime she would commit for him. Then it would be over.

She unlocked the door, went into the house and put on all the lights, every one, the signal Lambert had chosen. Pacing the main room, she lit a cigarette, but after a moment stubbed it out and went through all the rooms, checking to see that no bulbs had burned out, that all shutters were flung back. She wanted the lights visible to Lambert from however far away he might be watching.

Much time passed. She grew hungry, but decided against preparing herself a meal lest her husband appear in the middle of it, meaning she would have to prepare food for him too, share a final meal with him. She forbore even opening a bottle of wine. She didn't want to share anything at all with him ever again, merely to fulfill what she perceived as her final duty, and turn her back on him forever. But still he did not come.

She sat with a book in front of the fireplace in which no fire burned. The book was *Tant Qu'il y Aura des Hommes—From Here to Eternity*. The famous American best seller had just been translated into French. It was about men in the Army in Hawaii on the eve of World War II. It seemed to her to describe perfectly all that was base about men. She believed she would never remotely understand them. They were given to coarse drives and coarser behavior, and everything about them was incomprehensible to a woman. She put the book down and began glancing through fashion magazines again, each glossy page designed to soothe her with dreams of fine clothes she would never be able to afford.

She waited.

She must have been dozing, for the knock on the front door made her jump. She was on her feet instantly. She moved her fingers through her hair and went to open the door, believing she must have locked the door by mistake. Lambert had had to knock to be admitted to his own house. But the door was not locked at all, and she was struggling to understand what this meant even as she pulled it open.

Standing in the doorway was Bellarmine.

The sight of him made her gasp, and for a moment she could only stare.

"May I come in?"

She stepped back. "What are you doing here?" she said, and noted the tremor in her voice. Perhaps he would put this tremor down to surprise, but it was caused by bewilderment and by fear. She began marching through the house turning off lights, and scarcely heard Bellarmine's answer.

"I was in the neighborhood," he said, "and saw that you were here." It sounded like a lie to her, the police were still watching her after all, and in fact this was the truth. One of Bellarmine's detectives had tailed her to the bus stop, and Bellarmine had hurried up here as soon as the report reached him. During the long, hard drive he had feared walking in on a rendezvous between her and her husband, which would have meant the end of all of his illusions about her and about himself. But this had not happened: she was alone. He was immensely relieved and for the moment blind to any contradictory evidence—Jacqueline's strange deportment, all these lights.

In her terror Jacqueline moved from lamp to lamp, turning certain ones off, then on again. She would have to leave something lit for as long as Bellarmine stayed, but she was too shaken to decide which. She would have to pull shutters closed, and quickly, for who knew how near her husband might be? "I didn't hear your car," she babbled.

378

And for good reason. He had rolled down the dirt road as slowly and noiselessly as possible, engine extinguished. He had stopped at the edge of the yard and come across the cobbles almost on tiptoes.

"You must have been asleep," he assured her. But he was beginning to be perplexed by her manner, by all this turning on and off of lamps.

Jacqueline doused the kitchen lights. She reached into the bathroom and hit the switch there. She strode into the bedroom with Bellarmine a step behind and found that its lights were out already. She switched them on again.

And found herself face-to-face with her husband.

Lambert gestured over his shoulder at the window. "I came in through there." He had a gun in his hand, and he gave a brief apologetic laugh. "I've made a mistake, I guess. Or you have—" He waved the gun at Bellarmine. "One of us has, anyway."

Watching from across the valley, Lambert had observed no police activity in or around the dilapidated stone buildings that constituted his farm. Deep inside the forest behind him his motorcycle was propped against a tree. He lay across a boulder with field glasses at his eyes, peering out through foliage. He was waiting now for the last bus. If she was not aboard, then he would move away from the area at once—to be noticed around here would no doubt cause renewed police surveillance of the farm, cutting him off from Jacqueline, and by projection from Roy LeRoy.

He was confident Jacqueline would contact LeRoy for him, but it might take a few days. If she failed him, then he would have to come down out of the mountains to the coast and try to steal a boat. But she would not fail. With her help he would sail away from here in style. Once out of the country he was safe, he believed. He could not be extradited back to France. There had been no trial. He was not a convicted felon. Evidence against him was relatively scant.

As he raised his binoculars and studied the road still again, the bus came into view across the valley. He was sure Jacqueline was on it and with that the lenses seemed to fog over and he imagined himself back home in America. He would thumb his nose at the French, provoking the grandest headlines yet. Extremely famous now, he would finish his play, and producers would fight one another for a chance to put it on.

The bus screeched to a stop at the bend in the road close to the

379

farm. He watched a woman step down, and his heart leaped up like a lover's—Jacqueline. He lost sight of her as she walked into the access road, glimpsed her again crossing the cobblestones, then saw all the lights come on in the house.

The signal.

He was very pleased, and believed he had never loved her so much as at that moment. He had only to pick up the message she had brought him and be off.

But he stayed where he was, glassing the house from time to time, making sure. The building seemed ablaze. As the night darkened, the forest seemed to catch fire from its reflected glow.

Waiting, he wondered what to do with the documents and photos safe in their carton under the sink. Assuming Jacqueline had brought him the message from Roy, he wouldn't need them anymore. But if he dug them out of there, burned them, say, over the stove, Jacqueline would take this as proof of his guilt—at present she thought him innocent, he believed. He did not want her disillusioned. Her approval was important to him. Once upon a time she had worshiped him, had looked at him with awe, had trembled every time he touched her. Such adoration was harder to evoke in her now, but he believed he could do it. So maybe he would just leave the stuff where it was. Walk away from it and take her with him. They would walk away from it together. He was sure she would come. He had only to ask her.

After a while he walked up the floor of the forest and threw a leg over his bike. Without starting the engine he rolled it silently down through the trees and bounded out onto the road. The house was about a kilometer away. He rolled slowly, silently downhill, from time to time losing sight of the farm. Coasting like this took patience. He had been coasting at least half the time for days now. It conserved gasoline, and it was quiet. But the road leveled off and it was necessary to kick the engine alive. At low revs he continued on, making little noise. At the point where the road came nearly abreast of the farm house, he dismounted and rolled the bike down into the trees below the road. The underbrush was quite thick and at first he could not see the house. He moved toward the halo of light. Then he could see it, and he stopped once again to listen. All the lights were on, and there was no noise or movement he could detect, but he was in no hurry. He was being careful, and in addition it gave him pleasure to imagine Jacqueline's anxiety as she waited for him. She would be really nervous by now. The longer she waited, the happier she would be to see him.

At last, satisfied, he sat astride the bike and rolled even closer to the house. He was making some noise, not very much, crushing twigs and dead leaves, the occasional low branches brushing against his clothes. When he was still about fifty feet away he leaned the bike against a tree and listened hard. A while ago he had heard a car, but there was no sound of it now. He could hear nothing at all except the breeze moving through the trees above his head. Below him was the rear of the house, their bedroom, his and Jacqueline's. He remembered that he had approached the building much like this on the morning after the heist, and had spied on his wife through the bathroom window. He remembered how erotic this had seemed. It would be nice to do it again right now. Crouching, he crept silently up to the wall and peered through the bathroom window. But the room was empty. The bedroom was empty too. He put his fingers against the French windows and pushed, and the two windows folded open into the room. He threw his leg over the sill and climbed in. Then, to his alarm, he heard voices, the sound of people's feet. Stepping to the switch he threw the room into darkness. But the voices and footsteps continued to come straight toward him.

Jacqueline stared at the gun. Its single eye was focused on the middle of her breastbone. Lambert wagged the barrel. He seemed to her both shocked and scared. He had not expected to run into a policeman, and where there was one there might be others.

He said: "Get out from in front of him."

"No," cried Jacqueline, and instead of stepping to one side, she stepped backward into Bellarmine, shielding him with her body.

The import of this gesture was not lost on Lambert. His eyes widened. "Oh," he said, "I see."

"You see nothing," said Jacqueline.

"Nothing," said Bellarmine in a choked voice. He was in a rage at his own stupidity. He was also frightened, for Lambert's situation was so precarious that his mental stability could not be relied upon.

"Search him," Lambert ordered his wife, and when she hesitated he added almost in a shout: "Do it or I'll shoot him right between the eyes."

"Do what he says, Jacqueline."

She began to pat Bellarmine down. She patted his chest, his waist.

"He doesn't have a gun."

"Try his ankles," Lambert ordered, "his legs."

She snaked her hands from his ankles on up.

"I'm not armed," said Bellarmine tightly.

"Why not?" Suddenly Lambert seemed quite relaxed, as if there were time now for conversation, as if he wanted to learn more about his wife's feelings for this man.

"I left it at the *commissariat*."

"Why?"

But the reasons were not clear even to Bellarmine. Because he had feared finding Jacqueline and Lambert together and wished to avoid being forced to shoot at her husband. Of course his main hope had been to find her alone, in which case his mission would be magically transformed into one of courtship. One could not court a woman while wearing a gun, or at least he could not. To carry a gun into a love affair seemed to him obscene. To walk about armed seemed in itself an aggressive act. Of course love was an aggressive act also. A man tried to force a woman to respond to him alone. But it was at least a different type of aggression. Bellarmine's thoughts on the subject were entirely confused. In any case, he had chosen to leave his gun behind.

"Empty out his pockets," Lambert ordered.

So she reached into pockets that lay against the inside of Bellarmine's leg, fishing coins out, finding and removing his badge also. It seemed a far more sexual act to her than anything that had transpired when she was in bed with him.

From his back pocket, she removed his handcuffs.

"Handcuff him to the bedstead." When she did not rush to obey him, Lambert pulled the hammer back, cocking the gun.

"Do it," said Bellarmine tightly, and she did. The ratchets clicked home around the brass bar, around his rather thin wrist.

"How come you obey him, and not me?" said Lambert.

"Go away from here," Jacqueline said. "Far away. Go."

He lowered the gun. "We'll go together."

Her lips were compressed, and she shook her head. "Never. No."

"Come on outside with me, I want to talk to you." He pulled her out of the bedroom, down the short hall, out through the main room and out the door.

On the cobbles he withdrew a flashlight from his pocket, pointing its beam around the yard until he had located Bellarmine's car. He dragged Jacqueline toward the car, where he opened a jackknife and began slicing the valves off the tires. The air went out of all four, and the car subsided to its rims. A grinning Lambert reappeared beside her.

"You have a message for me, don't you?"

"LeRoy will wait for you the next three nights," Jacqueline told him in a tight voice. "He says you know the dock. The same signal as last time."

"Thank you," said Lambert. He was nodding his head up and down, still grinning. "Neat." But after a moment's thought he jerked his chin toward the house. "Did you tell him?"

"No." Then she added fiercely: "But if you harm him, I'll tell the world. You'll never get away."

"What do I want to harm him for? Listen"—he put his arms around her—"there's room for you on board. By this time tomorrow we can be in Tangier. And after that, the good old U.S. of A. You've always wanted to see America, haven't you?"

"I'm staying here." She was surprised how calm she felt, and also how sure of herself. "Now go. Get out of France. Get out of my life."

"You know you don't mean that."

She saw that Lambert, having received the news he came for, wanted to be off—safety must have seemed to him so close—but at the same time he wanted his wife to come with him. He was pulled two ways at once. Either he required her presence to enhance his own image, or else he really did love her in his way, a possibility Jacqueline was unwilling to consider.

Pouting almost like a small boy, Lambert said: "Not even one last kiss?" She tried to shake herself loose from his embrace.

"Just one," he said, still holding her.

She permitted herself to be kissed—it seemed a small price to pay to get rid of him. Then he was loping across the courtyard, rounding the end of the building, and crashing through the woods toward where his motorcycle must be parked. After a moment she heard the engine come on and thought she had seen the last of him, but instead he and it came crashing out of the forest again. He skidded to a halt at her feet, and the kickstand went down. "I better say goodbye to your boy friend before I go," he announced, and ran into the house.

Shouting: "No, no, no," Jacqueline ran in behind him and threw herself in front of Bellarmine, again protecting him with her body.

But Lambert's gun was still stuffed in his belt, and the expression on his face was one of amazement. His glance went from one of them to the other, as if he could not quite believe what he had seen.

He reached around behind his wife's body, testing the security of the handcuffs. Satisfied, he straightened up. "You'll be here a while, I expect," he told Bellarmine. "Sorry I had to do it. I've had to immobilize your car too."

For a moment, looking preoccupied, he seemed to gaze toward the kitchen, as if he meant to go in there, and this mystified Jacqueline. But then he stepped back from the bed. Vigorously he nodded his head at Bellarmine. "I just want you to know that it's been a pleasure meeting you," he said. "You were a worthy opponent in every way. I'm only sorry we couldn't both come out winners."

Bellarmine's mouth, Jacqueline noted, had dropped open at this speech, but she herself only shook her head and wanted to cry. This was her legal husband, to whom she had devoted irrecoverable years. He turned and dashed enthusiastically out into the night, and she had never seen him look more like a small boy. The motorcycle was idling. They heard it come on with a roar, and then they listened to its sound diminishing until it could be heard no more.

Bellarmine's eyes sought Jacqueline's. She was aware of this, but her own eyes sought only the floor.

"Go out to my car," he told her gently. "In the glove box you'll find some keys."

She ran out and did this. When she had unlocked the handcuffs, he stood flexing his wrist beside the bed. He seemed to be trying to decide what to say.

"I think he came here to receive a message from you," Bellarmine told her. "I think you gave him that message. You must tell me what it was. You must tell me where he's going."

But Jacqueline was unable to speak. Without lifting her eyes from the floor, she only shook her head.

She felt Bellarmine take her hands. "Try to understand," he said in the same soft voice, "he's an embarrassment to everybody: to the Milieu, to certain highly placed politicians, even to the police. We have reason to believe there are hit contracts out on him. Whoever finds him will kill him. The average *flic* who finds him will probably kill him. You're the only one who can save him. You must tell me where to look."

So Jacqueline was battered by new emotions. Loyalty to this decent man here. Loyalty to herself. Loyalty to her husband, who might be shot down more easily if she told what she knew than if she kept silent. Her deepest hope was that Lambert would escape from France, and that all this would at last be over; she could start again. Or perhaps she wanted him killed as punishment for all the suffering he had caused her. It was impossible to make sense of her own muddled thoughts. A certain dock—she believed she knew which one, but if she was mistaken and sent the police to the wrong place, then surely they would arrest her.

She could not meet Bellarmine's eyes. "But I don't know where he's going," she said. "I wasn't told."

He strode from the house, and she followed behind. He got a flashlight from the car, and shone it briefly on his ruined tires. The car could not be used. With all four tires flat its bottom rested on the hump in the lane. He could not get it up onto the main road. There was no phone in the house and no radio in the car.

"I'll send someone to fetch you," Bellarmine said, and he began striding across the cobbles toward the road.

"Where are you going?"

He intended to walk until he found a phone, he called back over his shoulder.

Both knew that finding a phone up in the mountains might require a ten-kilometer walk, perhaps more, and use up hours. Whatever villages he passed through would be locked up tight. People were not going to open to a strange man who knocked on their door in the night, and few had phones anyway.

"Wait," Jacqueline said. "There's a bicycle in the shed."

She watched him wheel it across the cobbles toward the dark, rutted access road. He was trotting alongside it, in a hurry now, but unwilling to mount until he had reached the surfaced road above. He disappeared from sight, and then the sound of him vanished also. If he pedaled hard he might get down to Le Chaudan in—how long? She had no idea. He could knock on the door of the gendarmerie there. Lambert would have a considerable head start. Too much? Too little? Jacqueline felt abandoned by both men, and full of fear for each of them as well.

# CHAPTER
## 38

Lambert started down out of the mountains. He had long since thrown away The Torch's white helmet, for helmets only attracted attention. Motorcyclists would not begin wearing them for a number of years yet. It wasn't popular. Most still wore flowing scarves instead, and their skulls most times cracked on impact. As for Lambert, in his ultimate dash for freedom, he wore a black beret pulled down low over his brow, and sunglasses to protect his eyes against the wind that he breasted as he ran. The sunglasses darkened the night too, but he did not mind that. He defied anyone to stop him now. He defied the wind itself. Moonlight buttered the trees, and the stars were like roses.

The few roads this high up were narrow and steep, with many switchbacks. He rode without lights, freewheeling down every precipitous slope, coasting as far as possible up the opposite side, then listened hard before restarting. At this time of night these dark, desolate roads were empty. What traffic there was, he avoided. Whenever distant headlights approached, whether from in front or behind, he pulled off the road. He hid behind bushes, a tree, a farm building. He extinguished his engine, crouched and waited. He watched the glow get nearer, brighter. He hid behind the hot, ticking bike, and watched profiles move past him through the night. He listened to the diminishing noise, for engines that might fluctuate in cadence, that might slow or stop, as if to come back. But this did not happen, and when they were out of hearing he remounted. When he came to villages he was equally cautious. Some, being on the downslope, he coasted all the way through, totally silent except for the soft whine of spokes, of tires. Others he motored through at low revs, making relatively little noise, waking, he hoped, no one.

All these techniques he had evolved for moving by night. It took time, but time was not a problem. He had thrown the police off his

386

track, he believed. In the past week he had allowed himself to be observed several times in villages close to the Italian frontier. Police patrols would be looking for him there, not here, and Bellarmine, chained to the bed, would not advise them otherwise. He had a whole nightful of time, far more than he needed.

But by then Bellarmine, who did not stop at all, was only a short distance behind him, and gaining. The bicycle was in surprisingly good shape, better shape than he was. The tires were pumped up hard. The thing was rusty, but the sprockets and chain apparently had been kept greased. He was pedaling hard, and the road ran mostly downhill. Moonlight showed him the way. He had decided not to approach the isolated houses, not to stop in the dark, shuttered villages. To pound on doors would take too much time, and his chances of finding a telephone were small. Besides which, he realized grimly, he did not really want help. This was between himself and Lambert, or at least between the police and Lambert. It did not concern outsiders. Let them sleep. He and a few others would protect them while they did. This was the police function. It always had been, since the days when towns first put watchmen on the walls, and it always would be. He would make directly for the gendarmerie at Le Chaudan, and this was fitting. It was their case too, and had been from the beginning. Only then would he stop and ask for help.

Like a Tour de France racer coming down out of the Alps, he knifed across the apexes of switchback curves, saving distance and time. He leaned out over the road. On the uphill grades he stood on the pedals. He was soaked in sweat, and his thighs were like licorice. He must be nearly down now, he hoped he was. He had begun gasping for air. The gendarmerie could not be much farther.

Lambert came down out of the mountains and passed through Le Chaudan. He crossed in front of the gendarmerie. He was in the valley of the Var. If patrols were out in the mountains he had slipped past them all, and yet the most dangerous part of his run came now. He had reached the Var itself and had to get across, but how? This high upriver, bridges were rare. Since a master criminal was loose—himself—the police no doubt watched them all. The place where the PT boat was waiting offshore was still more than a hundred kilometers away. How to get across the Var? An easy question. He already knew the answer.

387

The Var sometimes carried much water, though not now. Whenever rains were heavy, and in spring as the snows melted in the Maritime Alps, the Var filled up from bank nearly to bank, and so levees had been built across it every kilometer or so to spread it out and control it. Lambert had decided to drive across the river on top of one of these levees, and he drove on to the major road that ran beside the river and motored along looking for an access ramp down to the riverbed. He found one within a few hundred yards and scooted down it. Then he shut down a moment to listen. Had he been seen? But he could hear nothing except water sluicing over a levee about a hundred yards away.

He put his headlight on so that he could see what he was doing, and found the levee and started across the river. The levee was like the riser of a great concrete step. It was about two feet wide. The river spilling across it was about six inches deep, and he dismounted and walked the motorcycle through the water. The footing was slippery, and there was not much room. On one side was a ten-foot drop, on the other a churning mass of water mixed with stones. He was walking in wet, slippery shoes. Water poured over his feet, through the spokes of his wheels. Then he was through. The levee was dry again. He wheeled the bike the rest of the way across—he was afraid to try to restart on such a narrow ledge.

When Bellarmine got off the bicycle his thighs would not support him and he nearly fell. He staggered to the gendarmerie using the bike as a support. The door was locked. He began banging on it. Some minutes passed before the duty gendarme, rubbing sleep from his eyes, opened it. It was the boy who had driven Bellarmine and Chef Duclos to the pianist's villa so many weeks before.

He pushed in past him. "Wake up everybody," he cried. "Get them down here. Then get the cars out."

Striding to the telephone, he rang through to Nice, but the duty officer must have been asleep there too. While the phone rang, Bellarmine again considered the possibilities open to him. Obviously Lambert was making a run for the coast, but where? Assuming he had reached the Var, he had two choices, to head down to the coast immediately or go straight west across the country. Believing instinctively that Lambert would go west, Bellarmine decided to leave the coastal roadblocks and patrols to be organized in Nice. He himself would head west too on the road he believed Lambert had taken.

Lambert would not risk bringing a boat in at this end of the Riviera. He would head for the other.

When the duty officer at last picked up the phone, Bellarmine began giving orders. It was complicated. He was trying to mobilize a great many men in the middle of the night, and the man at the other end of the line was half asleep. He made him repeat every word.

As he hung up, Chef Duclos, buttoning his tunic, came down the stairs. Duclos seemed half asleep also.

"In the car, *chef*," Bellarmine told him. "I'll explain as we drive."

On the other side of the river Lambert had picked up the road to Gilette and had begun climbing. Gilette was an old walled city, and the road narrowed to go through it. A streetlight hung from a building at the entrance to the village, and another at the other side. Then he was through.

The mountains here were lower than those through which he had come. He kept driving west. The roads were still very narrow. They climbed, then came down again, and when he began to pick up signs to Draguignan he turned south, driving along the high tilted plateau, the country beginning to fall away toward the sea. At Draguignan he came to the American military cemetery, and there he stopped, still believing he had all the time in the world, and peered through a wrought-iron fence at rows and rows of crosses that seemed to glow in the moonlight. He had been thinking about this cemetery for the last hour or more. Buried here were those who had fallen in the invasion of southern France. Some of the crosses marked the graves of men—boys really—who had been his friends. By rights he ought to be lying there himself, and he stood brooding about this, his bike stilled and crackling beside him. He clutched the bars of the fence with both hands, bars that incarcerated all those young souls in there. He himself was not inside this jail or any other. He was outside, and very much alive, but he remembered moments in which life had hung by a strand. This place here he had somehow avoided, which had made everything else possible, all these years in France, and tonight's odyssey or pilgrimage or whatever it was as well. For he was quite aware as he made this run that he was not so much escaping from France as saying goodbye to it.

Duclos drove. Bellarmine in the passenger seat had a road map on his knees. He held a flashlight on it. The trouble was that as the

389

country opened up there were more and more roads, more and more choices to be made. They had started out with the three gendarmerie Juvaquatres running in convoy. He had since sent the two others off exploring important secondary roads. Now he came to still another fork. The sign said five kilometers to Draguignan. "Take a left here," he shouted to Duclos.

Lambert let go of the iron fence and turned away from the rows of crosses. Remounting, he pointed his motorcycle south toward the sea.

He was not afraid of police patrols now, nor of getting lost, and did not have to consult any maps. He knew these roads intimately, for he had fought over many of them, and had moved truckloads of cigarettes over the rest. He plunged into the Maures, rugged low mountains covered with forests of chestnut trees and maritime pines. The trees locked arms over the narrow road. It was as dark as if he were driving in a tunnel, and in all the time he was in the Maures he passed no other vehicle. When he came out into the open, he could see the sea ahead with an orange moon hanging over it. The moon was as fat as a hamburger roll, the kind on sale in America.

He rolled on toward the sea. He was almost safe now and was very happy. He came to the coast road, which seemed lit up in the moonlight and which was possibly watched by patrols searching for The Brain. Then he was across it and hidden in the trees behind the same beach on which he had landed in France for the first time as a boy, and from which now he would leave France forever, and he began to miss Jacqueline, for she was France to him. In France he had lived, it seemed to him, an entire lifetime. No, even more. Measured by other people's experiences, he had lived two or three lifetimes, and he congratulated himself on all he had seen and felt and loved in France—all that France had given him. Beginning to feel somewhat maudlin now, he told himself that he owed the man he had become to France, and he realized that he had learned to love France as Frenchmen did, like a woman he had made love to, and he hated to have to say goodbye to her tonight for the last time. But perhaps when he was in America, Jacqueline would come to him.

Bellarmine too had turned south. Duclos pushed the Juvaquatre as fast as it would go but no motorcycle showed in the headlight beams. The road ahead remained dark and empty. Then the car topped a rise and he could see the sea ahead, and he sensed with a feeling of terrific disappointment that he had lost. If they had not caught Lambert inland, they would not catch him now. The coastline was too rugged, too indented, there were too many places where he could be taken off.

"Drive along the coast road," Bellarmine told Duclos. "It's all we can do." God help Lambert now, he thought.

Stepping to the edge of the trees, Lambert peered through the night at the hotel whose dock would soon see him safely away. When last visited the building's shutters had been closed against the winter emptiness inside. Of course those same shutters were closed now too, for the French always closed their shutters at night, but dim lights glowed behind some of them. These were the stairwells and hallways presumably, and behind all the others, Lambert sensed, people slept. There was a light burning over the front door, and most likely, a night concierge dozed behind the front desk.

He peered out to sea under the path of the moon but could discern no shape or movement beyond the rippling of the sea itself. He certainly could discern no PT boat. Nonetheless, he was certain it was there, would have bet his life on it, was in fact doing so. He had no doubts at all, not one. His luck was about to carry him all the way home. He had only to shine his flashlight to receive answering blinks from Roy LeRoy, after which the PT boat would glide forward and take him off. He was so certain of this, and so in love with his certitude and with the moment, that he delayed signaling to savor its flavor a bit longer.

He stepped forward out of the trees, pointed his flashlight to sea, and gave five rapid blinks in succession, the signal.

Exactly as prearranged, the reply came: four rapid blinks, then a pause, then one long one.

Lambert walked confidently back to his motorcycle. As he climbed astride it, hiking it with his feet slowly forward through the trees, he began to laugh. He came to the edge of the beach and waited. He was atop a low dune with the last row of trees overhead, and he watched the ladder of moonbeams on the water until such moment as the PT boat should glide across it. Thirty seconds later this event happened. For a moment the great gray speedboat shone as if in a spotlight. Then it disappeared, and about a minute passed before its shape began to emerge again from the night. It was approaching shore at a very slow speed, as if moved only by the onshore breeze, and Lambert watched it come and was absolutely tense with excitement and pleasure.

Now the PT boat was a hundred yards from the end of the dock, now fifty. Lambert kick-started his engine and nosed down the face of the dune. The steering went soggy as the front wheel furrowed the sand. He crossed the beach toward the hotel. He might have abandoned the motorcycle at any point and continued on foot, but he wanted this ride to stand as his final gesture, and gestures have to be perfect, especially insolent ones. And so he steered up onto the hotel's terrace, and from there onto the dock and out to the very end of it. He shut down the engine, planted the kickstand, and almost in the same motion leaped off the motorcycle and out toward the PT boat's pointed prow. He was like a man jumping overboard, but the timing was perfect. He was a man saved.

Immediately LeRoy threw the boat into reverse, and the boat backed slowly, quietly away from shore, making less noise than the motorcycle had made, backing away in a sweeping sickle-shaped arc. Lambert came running across the foredeck even as the boat changed directions, beginning now to surge powerfully out to sea.

"Don't I know you from somewhere?" he asked as he jumped down into the cockpit. "Aren't you a friend from somewhere?" Feeling giddy with delight, almost hysterical again, he threw out his hand. "Shake, friend."

LeRoy at the helm gave a thin answering grin, and the two men shook hands.

"We'll take it slow till we get some sea room," LeRoy explained. "We don't want to wake everybody up."

"Let 'em wake up. What do we care? Next stop Tangier."

"Tangier," said LeRoy after a moment. "Yeah."

As the engines came on full and LeRoy headed straight out from the coast, Lambert glanced at his watch. It was 4:25 in the morning. In about fifteen minutes it would begin to be light. But by then they would be fifteen miles out—well outside French coastal waters. He would be totally safe. Hell, he was totally safe already. Holding his beret in one hand he stuck his head out into the slipstream. Spray slapped his face, individual drops stung his cheeks like lead pellets. When he yanked his head back inboard, his hair was soaked, water was dripping off his eyebrows, and he was grinning the hugest grin of his life.

"How about some coffee?" he said to LeRoy. "Would you like me to make us some?"

LeRoy at the helm looked thoughtful. "Sure. You do that."

Left behind at the helm, LeRoy studied both his dials and the situation in which he now found himself. For one thing, Lambert was armed. The papers had reported him armed, and a moment ago in the binnacle light LeRoy had looked for and found the bulge at his belt that could only be a gun. This was a complication and had to be pondered. In addition a great many questions had occurred to LeRoy during the last several days. He wanted to present these questions to Lambert and hear what answers came back.

"Coffee's on," said Lambert. He had come up from below. He was wearing the beret again.

"Who stole all them documents?" LeRoy yelled over the engines' noise, "out of the bank?"

"Who do you think?"

"I thought we agreed not to."

"I changed my mind. Good thing, too. Or the CIA wouldn't have helped me escape."

Jesus, thought Roy LeRoy, the CIA is involved in this too, another complication. "I thought it was The Torch who helped you escape."

They were shouting to each other over the noise. "The CIA put him up to it."

"And the documents?"

"I burned them."

"All of them?"

The binnacle light shone upward on Lambert's face, and he was grinning. He nodded disarmingly. "Right."

LeRoy felt increasingly puzzled. "There's a congressman named Avery running around Nice," he shouted. Of his two employers, he understood Faletta's motives perfectly. But Avery's were a mystery to him. He wanted this mystery cleared up before he took any steps that would be irrevocable.

"What about Avery? Where does he fit in?"

Lambert laughed. LeRoy decided that never in his life had he seen a man as pleased with himself as Lambert seemed to be. It was extremely irritating.

"Some of the stuff was about Avery," Lambert explained. "He could have got in a lot of trouble. That's why he got the CIA to help me."

"And Avery's documents are the ones you kept," yelled LeRoy. These repeated references to the CIA made him uneasy.

Again Lambert laughed. "For a while. Then I burned them too."

"I don't get it."

"I wanted to see if you could blackmail a man with stuff that doesn't exist," said Lambert. "And you want to know something? You can."

It was getting light fast now, and they surged across the placid sea.

"I still don't get it."

"It was more fun that way."

"I see," said Roy LeRoy. But he didn't. However, he did believe Lambert had burned the missing papers. It seemed to him the sort of crazy thing Lambert would do.

The coffee was perking and Lambert went below. When he reappeared, he handed across a mug so hot it almost burned LeRoy's hand. He put it down on top of the chart table. "So you stole all that stuff, causing a lot of extra heat put on the rest of us, and then you simply destroyed it all."

"That's right." Lambert smirked. "What do we care about those Corsicans? None of our guys are in jail. So what's the harm?"

LeRoy's eyes sought his dials, and he nodded grimly. The harm was that LeRoy was still under indictment in Toulon, and the *juge d'instruction* there was still holding a great deal of his money. The harm was that the whole country was in an uproar. The harm was that Faletta and Avery saw their very existence threatened—and saw Lambert at the root of it. The harm was that he, Roy LeRoy, had accepted contracts from both of them. Lambert had been right the first time. Those documents would have been better left in the vault.

"Avery's documents," said LeRoy. "What were they?"

But Lambert refused to tell him. He had no intention of telling anyone, he said, adding: "I don't want anyone else bothering the poor jerk."

"Jerk?"

"Yeah. He's just a jerk. I don't bear him any grudge."

They fell silent, as if yelling over the noise had tired them. The PT boat was now about thirty miles offshore. The sun had popped up red as a gumdrop on the eastern horizon. When LeRoy glanced behind him, nothing could be seen of the coast except the pink snow-covered tops of the Maritime Alps far inland. The coastal cities had vanished. It was no longer possible for Lambert to orient the boat's position relative to one city or another, even if he was suspicious, which he did not seem to be, and LeRoy permitted their course to fall off toward the east. He was heading back toward Nice. The sea was empty all around them. There was a little time left, but not much.

In response to Bellarmine's general alarm every customs launch between Marseille and Nice had put to sea, and near Cavalaire, less than an hour after first light, one of them spotted a motorcycle parked on the end of a dock beside a hotel. This seemed odd, and the launch approached shore for a closer look. In France that year transport of any kind was somewhat rare and very expensive. One did not abandon valuable motorcycles on the ends of docks. Especially one did not leave a bike unlocked, the key in the ignition, as was the case here. The launch, having tied up to the dock, radioed for help and gendarmes came out from the nearest barracks to investigate. They woke up every guest in the hotel, but no one claimed the motorcycle, nor knew how it had got there. They went into the camping grounds in the trees behind the beach and shook people awake in every sleeping bag, every tent. But no one owned the motorcycle.

Bellarmine arrived at the hotel with two carloads of detectives, and he attempted to set up a command post in the game room. Unfortunately the hotel's single telephone line was not in service. It branched through the village post office, which did not open until 8 A.M. In a rage Bellarmine sent his detectives through the hotel interviewing patrons a second time. It was obvious to him that the driver of the motorcycle had been taken off the dock by a boat. Someone must have seen something, especially if the boat in question was, as he suspected, as huge as a PT boat.

But no one had. People stood around in bathrobes. Some of the women had curlers in their hair. They waited to be told what was going on, but Bellarmine told them nothing.

A camper was found farther down the beach. He had seen the PT boat, or something that may have been the PT boat—he had been out of his tent urinating against a tree. He had seen it in the moonlight—a big boat.

The telephone came on. Bellarmine ordered every cutter at sea to converge on the Cavalaire area. How much time did he have? He ordered light planes belonging to the gendarmerie to scour the sea for the PT boat, or any other big or suspicious launch. Lastly he read the numbers off the motorcycle into the phone.

Presently vehicle registration called back. The license plate was false; no such numbers had ever been issued. So almost certainly the bike on the dock was Lambert's. There was nothing he could do now but wait.

A little later customs rang up from Nice. LeRoy's PT boat had just come back into port after a night's fishing. A customs agent had already gone aboard and had found no contraband of any kind.

"Hold LeRoy," Bellarmine shouted into the phone. But it was too late for that; LeRoy was already ashore.

Two hours later, after a wild ride down the coast, Bellarmine spoke to the Nice customs chief in person. LeRoy had come into port flying the yellow *libre pratique* flag, the signal that he had nothing to declare. He had tied up and waited for a customs agent to come aboard.

The agent, when summoned into Bellarmine's presence, insisted that he had searched the PT boat thoroughly. He had noted nothing suspicious, and had jumped ashore. LeRoy had followed. He had seen LeRoy climb into a taxi, which drove off in the direction of the Monument aux Morts—toward the Promenade des Anglais.

Bellarmine sent judicial identity technicians swarming aboard the empty PT boat. They were carrying Lambert's fingerprint card and within minutes found his left thumbprint on a coffee mug.

After leaving two detectives at the boat with orders to pick up Roy LeRoy whenever he should return, Bellarmine went back to the *commissariat* to wait for reports to come in. The search planes might discover some other suspicious launch on the high seas—perhaps Lambert had transferred to it. He had ordered customs launches to make a thorough search of the Riviera's many outlying islands, especially those off Hyères and off Cannes—perhaps Lambert was hiding on one of them. He could think of no other steps to take, and in any case would be taking them much too late. He was quite certain that it was too late already.

LeRoy had gone to the Ruhl and had rung Avery's suite. Ten minutes later they had sat down together at a table in the breakfast room. Both had ordered coffee. "Make that American coffee, hear?" said Avery to the waiter.

"Good," said LeRoy, "I can't drink the local mud either."

"*Oui, monsieur*," said the waiter. "American" coffee meant powdered Nescafé mixed with boiling water, and it amazed the waiter that anyone, American or not, could drink such stuff. However, nearly all tourists, after one cup of "French" coffee, were quite specific about the coffee they required.

"Mission accomplished," LeRoy said when the waiter had left their table.

"Was it—difficult?"

"Nothing to it."

Avery did not know what this meant, nor did he want to know. Presently he said: "Did you find anything? Papers? Anything like that?"

"Whatever you were worried about," LeRoy told him, "he burned it."

"Let me give you a warning."

"I don't care whether you believe me or not."

The waiter wheeled over a trolley bearing their breakfasts. The Nescafé had already been mixed, and he poured it steaming out of a silver coffeepot with a long, thin spout. Both men inhaled the aroma. "Smells just like home, don't it?" said Roy LeRoy. But it made him remember the mug Lambert had brought up to him on the bridge, the one so hot he had had to set it down on the chart table. The heat had not bothered Lambert, who had emptied his own mug right away.

"Good to the last drop." Lambert had put the mug down and smacked his lips.

"What's good to the last drop?"

"What you're drinking." Lambert pointed. "Maxwell House. It's their slogan. You see it in all the magazine ads."

"I never noticed."

Lambert gave LeRoy a friendly sock in the arm. "That's because you only read the love stories."

"Where'd you get that gun you're packing?"

"This?" Lambert dug it out of his belt. "I took it off The Torch." It lay in the palm of his hand and he studied it a moment. LeRoy watched him, and calculated.

"I guess I won't need it anymore," Lambert commented, and he reared back as if to throw it overboard.

But LeRoy stopped him. "Let me see that."

Lambert handed it over. "It's better to get rid of it," he advised. "No telling what crime it might have been involved in."

"So what if it has?"

397

"The cops can trace guns, stupid. Haven't you ever heard of the science of ballistics?"

Roy saw that the gun was loaded. He weighed it in his hand and came to his decision.

Avery said coolly: "What proof have you of—of mission accomplished."

LeRoy took a folded handkerchief out of his pocket, and placed it on the tablecloth between them. Pushing the coffee cups out of the way, he began laying back its various folds until the object it contained was exposed. One glimpse was enough for Avery.

"Put that thing away," he hissed. "Are you crazy?"

The congressman sat with his eyes focused on the far wall of the room. His breathing was audible.

The object in the handkerchief was Lambert's left ear.

"I don't know if you remember his ears," said Roy LeRoy, fingering this one. "He had very funny ears. They were flat on top." His finger traced the line in question.

LeRoy thought Avery's reactions somewhat humorous but he forbore laughing, for he had a message to get across. He was folding up the handkerchief. "You wanted proof," he said.

Lambert had gone below. When he came up he was carrying a baseball cap he had found down there, and as LeRoy watched, he ripped the black beret off his head and in almost the same motion clapped the baseball cap on in its place. "*Voilà*," he cried, "I'm an American again." Crouching in a batter's stance he posed for LeRoy. "Casey at the bat," he shouted. He was absolutely gleeful. "Home, sweet home," he shouted, "here I come." Turning, he scaled the beret out into the wind. "Goodbye France," he shouted.

Believing he had never heard so much joy in the human voice, LeRoy raised The Torch's gun and pulled the trigger. He heard the detonations over the engines' noise and this surprised him. The boat did not falter on its course. This surprised him also, though why? He felt the grin come onto his face, the one that frightened people.

Shot four times in the back, Lambert folded at the waist and would have fallen overboard, except that LeRoy, rushing forward, grabbed him by the belt. He laid him out almost tenderly on the deck, thinking, I've done you a service, pal, you never knew what hit you, and you died with all your illusions intact. You died happier than any man I ever saw.

He went through Lambert's pockets, keeping the money, jettisoning everything else. He found no documents from the bank vault— nothing Avery or anyone else would pay money for, unfortunately.

He went below and found a disused flywheel and some wire. He also picked up a rusty knife he sometimes used to clean fish. When he came up on deck again, Lambert still lay there looking happy, and LeRoy stood for a moment looking down on him. It amazed him that men would order another man killed for paper, and he thought it ironic that in this case the paper didn't even exist. He put the flywheel aside and grasped the fish knife, then he bent down over Lambert's head.

Drinking his Nescafé, LeRoy watched Avery, who would not meet his eyes. After refolding the handkerchief and slipping it back into his pocket, he said conversationally, "I wired a flywheel to his leg and put him over. He went down very fast, arms over his head. He was still grinning. Not many guys go down grinning." After a moment, LeRoy remembered, he had heaved the gun over too. Lambert had been right—no telling what crimes it might have been involved in.

"We have a deal, you and I," LeRoy told Avery. "I've done my part, now you do yours. I want my money back. You get them to give me my money back, or you'll be looking at your own ear in a handkerchief."

He waited. After a moment Avery flashed him a ghastly smile. "It'll take a couple of days," he said.

"That's how much time you've got," LeRoy told him. "A couple of days." He stood up beside the table. "I'll be gone most of today on this errand I have to do. From tomorrow on you can find me at my boat." And he strode out of the breakfast room. He was about to catch a train to Marseille to show the ear to Faletta, but he did not say this.

Behind him Avery too rose from the table and moved out of the dining room. Once in his suite he got himself under control and began to make phone calls: to the cashier downstairs requesting that his bill be prepared at once; to Pan American, reserving a seat on the afternoon Constellation to America; to the consulate, requesting that a car and driver be sent over to take him to the airport; and to his friend and confederate Adjunct Mayor Picpoul, to whom he spoke somewhat cryptically for about ten minutes. Their problems were ended, he said. Lambert would not bother anyone any further. Having taken care of the matter, Avery was obliged to return to the United States at once, and probably would not return until after the congressional elections in November—"Or until this thing blows over." Their business arrangements would continue unchanged, as in the past.

"Bon voyage, my fren'," said Picpoul, and the relief in his voice was thicker than his accent. "You have my felicitations."

It made Avery laugh. "Felicitations to you too," he said, and hung up.

When he followed his bags out of the hotel the consulate's black limousine was waiting. To his surprise, he saw that the driver was O'Hara.

"You still here?" he said, and frowned.

But as they drove along the Mediterranean toward the airport, Avery began to feel in an expansive mood. The sea breeze was blowing in against his face, and he didn't mind talking. He had decided, he said, to forget about his missing documents. It was highly possible they would never turn up. Lambert was probably dead. According to his information, he added smugly, he might be.

"How's that, Congressman?"

Avery realized he might have said too much. He had hired private investigators to look into it, he said vaguely. They had investigated the thing for him and indicated Lambert had died.

"Some time last week, maybe," Avery said vaguely. "So they tell me. Maybe he had a fall up there in the mountains. Or some goddamn thing."

As soon as Avery's plane had taken off, the disturbed O'Hara drove to the *commissariat* to see Bellarmine.

The two men sat in Bellarmine's office with the French windows open onto the courtyard. A breeze swirled around the courtyard, from time to time rattling the glass in Bellarmine's door.

"He says Lambert is dead," O'Hara said. He was probing for information and he could not be sure Bellarmine would give him any.

"I wonder how he knows."

Now both sought information, and from the most difficult source of all, each other. Bellarmine took a package of Chesterfields out of his pocket and offered them across the desk. He then gave the same version of the story that would go into his report—accurate, except that it failed to mention the presence at the farm of Jacqueline Lambert as spectator and/or witness.

"You can arrest Roy LeRoy," O'Hara said.

"If we can find him. Legally we don't have much on him. No corpse. No proof any crime was committed. No jurisdication even. The boat was of foreign registry in international waters." After a moment he added cautiously, "We know also of a meeting a few days ago between LeRoy and Congressman Avery in the jail at Toulon."

"Meaning Avery ordered it," O'Hara said and paused. "I feel debased," he said. "Can you do anything? Question him at least?"

"Since the war France has been subservient to America's slightest whim," Bellarmine noted. "I don't think my government will allow me to attempt to bring an American congressman back here for questioning, do you?"

He picked some grains of tobacco off his tongue.

O'Hara said he would go back to Washington to confer with the director. He did not add that, considering his new leverage over Congressman Avery, he stood a good chance of being promoted to the job of Bureau liaison with Congress.

"And you," O'Hara asked, "What will you do?"

"Go on looking for Lambert. Until the corpse turns up. Until proof of some kind turns up."

"It's hopeless."

"Most investigations are hopeless."

The two men contemplated each other. They contemplated the policeman's lot. To go on working when hope was gone. To hope in the face of unspeakable acts.

# CHAPTER 39

He decided to inform Jacqueline that her husband had been murdered. What he could not decide was when or how to do it. That he himself believed it was not enough—she also had to believe, because whatever future they might have together could begin only then. And so he hesitated. He waited for additional evidence. He waited for facts that he could draw around himself like a shield or an overcoat, protection against bad weather, protection against bad times. He wanted facts Jacqueline would be unable to refute, facts as proof, proof as solid as the casket that in this case would not be necessary.

Presently such proof began to emerge, and to Bellarmine it was totally convincing. It emerged in Marseille and only as a rumor at first—that Lambert's left ear wrapped in a handkerchief had begun making the rounds of Milieu-controlled bars. This rumor Bellarmine believed at once, and so did every policeman who heard it—any police organization in the world would have believed it. It satisfied the police mind principally because it was so grisly, an exact match for hard-edged police cynicism. It seemed to prove what all policemen had always suspected—or perhaps only feared—about the ugliness of the human race. It seemed also a fitting dead end for this very strange case.

But this was not to say it would convince a wife, for women's minds ran in different grooves. Women believed in trust, loyalty and related emotions, all of which are admirable in themselves, most of which were every bit as unreal and unruly as the so-called baser instincts that most often ruled the passions of men.

So Bellarmine, taking detectives with him, went to Marseille to track the rumor down. It was Faletta himself, they learned, who had begun showing the ear. He had showed it to other Milieu types, to colleagues and to rival caids in his bar, the Café de l'Amitié. He had shown it discreetly at first, then more and more openly as he realized the hero this made him in the eyes of such people. Faletta had succeeded where the police had failed. He had eliminated everybody's colossal headache, The Brain. Faletta's stature was suddenly enormous.

After that the ear had been carried from bar to bar until nearly every thug in the city had seen it. It was curious in shape, being flat on top, and it was accompanied on its travels by a newspaper photo of Lambert in profile, proving it his. When at last it had begun to stink, someone—one of Faletta's chauffeurs, supposedly—had scaled it into the Vieux Port, where presumably it was eaten by fish.

Bellarmine learned all this by arresting and questioning about thirty Milieu men over a period of about two weeks, but at the end he had no prosecutable case against anyone, for no statute had yet been written concerning dead men's ears. All he had was what the courts call hearsay evidence and what the police world calls "information," a word that carries for policemen everywhere a specific and extremely heavy power.

Having phoned Sapodin in Paris, Bellarmine told his chief what he had learned, and they discussed what to do with this "information." They would use it at once Sapodin decided. They would end this Banque de Nice case once and for all. He would call a press conference, he said, divulge as much as seemed necessary, and the newspapers would end the case for him. "It pays to have good relations with the press," said Sapodin. "Remember that, Bellarmine. They can be very useful on occasion."

So he had no time left to decide anything, and he rushed around to see Jacqueline in her shop.

"I have something to tell you," he began. But this was not the place to tell her anything momentous, for customers kept coming in to interrupt. Again the bell had tinkled just as he prepared to speak. Again he had had to step back against a display case. Of course he should take her somewhere else, but where? Her cluttered stock room—he remembered the day he had searched it—would not do, and his own grim flat was no better. He doubted she would go up there with him anyway lest someone see them—the news would spread, and her reputation would be even further compromised. He would have to speak to her in public, meaning in this shop or a café, which pointed up the curse of life in France at this time: people lived in small spaces under tawdry conditions, and were usually unwilling to invite anyone there. They met friends, they entertained, only in cafés. The cafés were their true homes.

"Please," Bellarmine said when the customer had gone out, "lock the door. I have something to tell you."

He saw from her face that she knew what it was. She seemed to cringe.

"It's about your husband."

But almost instantly she brightened, rejecting his message in advance. Whatever it was, she did not want to hear it. "I really can't talk right now. I have customers coming in, you see."

Bellarmine strode to the door and locked it.

"Don't do that," said Jacqueline. "My customers—" But she did not move from behind the counter.

He faced her, only the counter between them, plus the ghost of his former prisoner, her murdered husband, but she refused to look at him, just as for the past several days she had refused all the invitations he had tendered her, had refused to come out of her shop.

"Your husband is dead, Jacqueline."

"You're just saying that. You have no proof."

"We have—information." He frowned. Police jargon was unlikely to convince her.

"Oh?" she inquired coolly. "Have you found his body?"

"He was murdered. We know how it was done, and who did it."

"But you haven't found his body?"

"No," he conceded.

"And the murderer, have you arrested him? Has he confessed?"

"No."

"Well then—" She smiled brightly.

He saw clearly two things, that he was going to have to tell her much, much more, and that she was not going to be convinced by it. She simply did not want to believe her husband dead, because if he was dead, then she was at least in part responsible. She did not want to believe she had betrayed him that much. She was going to reject—had to reject—whatever Bellarmine might tell her.

Yet he had to try to reach her. Sapodin in Paris would start his press conference as soon as it could be arranged—he might have started already. In an hour the news would be all over the radio. It would occupy the headlines of newspapers this afternoon, tomorrow, for days to come. Jacqueline might still be able to go on disbelieving it, but would not remain ignorant of it, and he clung to the hope that if she heard the facts from him she might as a result turn to him for consolation.

"You only think he's dead," Jacqueline said brightly, "because that's what you want to think. Then you can say you've solved the case. But you're wrong. The chances are he's safe in some other country by now. He'll probably try and contact me soon."

"He won't get in contact with you ever again." snapped Bellarmine, and he was amazed at the asperity in his voice. "He's dead. Roy LeRoy not only killed him, he cut off his ear." There, it was out, from her point of view the most devastating news of all.

He saw her chin quiver, but she ignored the ear part altogether, and another bright smile came on.

"If you're so sure it was LeRoy," she asked triumphantly, "then why haven't you arrested him?"

"Because we can't find him." The PT boat tied to the wharf in Nice had been staked out for days, but LeRoy had not returned. "We think he's dead too." Informants had observed him with Faletta in Marseille, and he had not been seen since. According to the so-called word on the street Faletta had ordered him killed. He had ordered that his body not be found. Which was no loss at all, except insofar as it muddied the Lambert case.

"Jacqueline, look at me." Bellarmine sought an argument that would convince her, but there was none. "A man named Sapodin is about to give a press conference in Paris. He's an important man. He's going to announce that your husband is dead. He's going to announce that the case is over."

"But you've already announced it to me. Why should I believe him, when I don't believe you?"

"He's the Number Three man in the Sûreté, Jacqueline. When he speaks he represents the entire police establishment in France. Would he make such an announcement unless he—we—were absolutely sure?"

"Who can understand why the police do what they do?"

"Jacqueline, think about it for a minute. If there were any chance at all that your husband was still alive, that he might jump up in another country and give a press conference of his own—we'd be the laughingstock of the world. He's dead, Jacqueline. Your husband is dead."

"You can't be sure." She had begun breathing hard, chest heaving.

"We're sure." It wasn't just the ear, Bellarmine thought. There were other substantiating details. For instance, there had been no new attacks on Faletta or any part of his organization. The other clans had stepped back. He was being given the opportunity to rebuild his rackets one by one, to restructure his cadres.

"The press will be skeptical too," Bellarmine said. Though not as skeptical as this woman, he believed. "Therefore certain details will be made public during the course of the press conference. The press will be convinced, believe me."

"What details?"

His mood had become a combination of exasperation and despair. The longer this conversation lasted, the further from him she moved. He saw himself losing her forever in the space of these few lines, and so he cried out: "Jacqueline, his ear has been moving from bar to bar in Marseille like"—and he added the phrase everyone else was using— "like the relic of a medieval saint. Your husband had very funny ears, apparently. They were flat on top, apparently." He was amazed at the degree of pain he saw written on her face, and his voice softened. "I never noticed his ears myself."

Faletta and his men, instead of matching the ear with newspaper photographs for verification, should have called in his wife for verification, Bellarmine thought. She would have recognized it at once. She could have identified it for them. His ear, Bellarmine thought, or any other part of his body.

Tears had begun running down Jacqueline's cheeks.

Someone knocked on the glass door. When Bellarmine turned he saw a flock of gray-haired tourist ladies, hands cupped beside their eyes, trying to peer into the shop.

"You're talking nonsense," Jacqueline told him. "I'm not going to believe you."

Having wiped her tears away, she marched past him toward the door. "I have to wait on my customers," she said.

She unlocked the door, and the bell tinkled as the ladies stepped inside. Jacqueline served them, and other customers came in even as she finished. The little bell tinkled repeatedly, and Jacqueline, as she worked, never once looked in Bellarmine's direction. After a while he left the shop.

Sapodin's press conference went off as scheduled, and the resulting headlines were exactly what the police had hoped for: The Brain is dead, Henry the Torch is dead. Every other member of the Banque de Nice gang is in custody—an exaggeration, to say the least, though the press seemed to accept it. The trial would take place in due time. The case was over at last.

Bellarmine continued to drop by the perfume shop after that, and to invite Jacqueline to have supper with him—even an apéritif in the café at the corner. She always refused.

"I haven't heard from my husband yet," she said one evening. "I'll let you know when I do."

"You know what the truth is," he blurted. "You just refuse to believe it."

"You're looking thinner," she replied. "Have you lost weight?"

One Sunday he drove up to her farm. He found her pruning the roses beside the front door. She chatted with him for a while, and even smiled a few times, but did not invite him inside. She seemed to assume that he was in the neighborhood on some other errand, that he had merely dropped by in passing, and would soon leave.

"I've been transferred to Paris," he told her.

"That's very good for you, isn't it? Congratulations." Other bushes grew along the front of the house. She had moved off to prune them. He was talking to her back.

"I'll write and send you my address."

"If you like."

She was wearing a red sundress that showed her summery arms, and sandals, and her hair was tied back. She was so completely desirable to him, and also so unapproachable, that for a moment he considered raping her then and there, as if rape were an act not of violence but of love, capable of turning her away from another man and on to himself. He would carry her inside the house, take off that red dress, push her down, and so win her over: rape as a solution to his frustration and her resistance. It was a solution that could not work, so he drove away.

Jacqueline, as she turned back to her roses, realized in a vague way what had happened to her. She had awakened one day to the knowledge that the husband she had married was not like other women's husbands. He was a man outside the law. He was a wanted fugitive. The world saw her as the wife of a bank robber, the wife of a murderer. She saw herself as much worse—as having committed a wife's supreme act of betrayal. She might have saved her husband's life but had guessed wrong and, if the police were to be believed, had sent him instead to his death.

She was trying to understand all that had happened to her, and it was incomprehensible, and as a result she had been immobilized. She was like the victim of an accident. She was numb. If she merely forgot about it all, and got on with her life, then she would never understand it. She had to try to understand it first.

Her husband murdered? She did not want to believe it. His exploits had captivated the world, her most of all. She wanted to believe he would soon reappear, releasing her from her guilt, and the only way to believe this was to wait for him. She couldn't even divorce him unless he came back. Like the Messiah, he would come again. She would wait for this second coming.

# CHAPTER 40

Sapodin had phoned from Paris about the transfer, saying he had good news, and it was twofold. First of all, he had decided to pay him a bonus of thirty thousand francs for bringing the case to an end. There was silence on the line, and Bellarmine realized he was supposed to make a suitable expression of gratitude.

Sapodin was practically purring from the effect of his own generosity. It was as if he were giving away his own money. Bellarmine let the silence build for a moment. Bonuses for breaking an important case were a Sûreté tradition, but usually they were bigger than this one. Certainly he had hoped for more.

"*Merci, monsieur,*" he said. From Sapodin's point of view, thirty thousand francs was perhaps all he deserved. Perhaps Sapodin considered that the case was not really broken. There was no principal defendant in the dock. The Brain would never stand trial.

"I thought you'd be pleased."

"Yes, monsieur."

"What are you going to do with the money?"

It would cover the cost of a new suit—just. "I don't know," he said.

"And here is the second piece of good news, Bellarmine. I'm transferring you to Paris."

"Right away?"

"As soon as you can."

Again Sapodin waited, the better to extract gratitude. Again Bellarmine fell silent.

"It's what your career needs at this point," said Sapodin. "I have my eye on you, you know."

"It's generous of you, monsieur."

He had not lived in Paris since before the war, nor worked there since his temporary assignment during The Angel of Death case, and now he had trouble finding an apartment. There had been no new construction in or around the city, or anywhere in France for that matter, since 1939—more than fifteen years. Eventually he settled on a one-and-a-half-room flat on the fifth floor of a walk-up in the 18th Arrondissement—not far from where he had arrested The Angel. The rent was very high for a *commissaire's* salary, almost half a month's pay, and the landlord wanted key money—thirty thousand francs.

He wrote Jacqueline about his new flat, making it sound cozier than it was. The building was partway up the Butte de Montmartre, and the view was nice, he said. However, no answer came back.

At Sûreté headquarters Sapodin was always cordial to him when they met in the hall. The other *commissaires* believed he would be the first among them to receive his *principalat*, but the months began to pass, and his promotion did not happen.

He wrote Jacqueline breezy accounts of certain cases he was working on, for criminals were bizarre people and some of the things they did were downright funny. But these letters elicited no response either.

In the fall his *principalat* at last came through, making him, as he wrote Jacqueline, one of the youngest men of this rank in the entire Sûreté.

He was certain she would react to such good news, and each night when he got home from work he rapped on the door of the concierge's loge. Each night, despite his eagerness, he tried to keep emotion from showing in his voice. *"Bon soir, madame.* No letters for me, I suppose?" *"Non, monsieur."* Her answer was always the same. *"Je regrette."*

Earlier he had taken the trouble to ask questions about Odette—he was a detective, was he not?—learning she danced in the chorus line at the Lido on the Champs-Élysées. He did not go there. He had never seen a show at the Lido, one of the most famous and expensive nightclubs in Europe. In a sense, she had taken a step upward in her career, and he had been glad to hear this.

Now he went to see her. As he came in off the street it was about 11 P.M. The show was about to start, but he was intercepted near the door by the Lido's maître d'hôtel, who must have recognized him at once—not for what he was but for what he was not. He was not a rich American. Plainly he was not a tourist at all, and the Lido was not a place for Frenchmen in shiny suits.

"Monsieur?"

Bellarmine requested a table up close, and the attitude of the maître d'hôtel became, if possible, even more disdainful. But the man's sneer disappeared with satisfying promptness when he saw the police card.

"Right this way, monsieur."

The place was crowded. There were champagne bottles in buckets on nearly all the tables. He ordered a Calvados.

The orchestra started up, the lights went off. The music was very loud. Then the curtains parted, and the runway, which extended out into the tables, filled up with prancing girls. They wore sequins in their hair and on their high-heeled shoes. Their loincloths—he did not know what else to call them—were covered with sequins also. All the rest was body makeup over sleek female flesh. There were so many rosy nipples pointing out over the tables that it was difficult to tell which two belonged to which girl, and when he raised his glance a bit, he saw that the rows of smiles were all identical also.

After a brief search he separated Odette's face and body from the others. She was about ten feet from him, high kicking. She did not see him. Like all the other girls, her smile seemed directed about halfway up the dark distant wall. These girls were experts at avoiding eye contact, he noted. They looked at nobody.

Nonetheless, later in the show he found her standing directly over his table and he called out sharply: "Odette." Her glance flickered across his, but her smile did not change and a moment later she seemed as focused on the far wall as before.

When the show ended, he sat there. About ten minutes passed before he felt the chair beside him being pulled back. Odette sat down. She was dressed in a navy-blue suit. A small pillbox of a hat sat on top of her hair. Its small fluff of a veil floated forward over her eyes. She was still heavily made up, and he wondered if her body— those marvelous breasts—was still coated in makeup also.

He ordered champagne.

"Oh, Robert, you shouldn't," she protested, but she looked pleased.

He wondered how much the champagne would cost, assuming they made him pay for it. He intended to ask for the bill, though he supposed most *flics* wouldn't. And to pay it, if necessary. A matter of pride. Twice in one night he would wipe the sneer off the face of that maître d'hôtel.

The champagne came, and they drank it. "Champagne is so expensive here," Odette said. "We should have gone somewhere else."

Bellarmine lit a cigarette.

"Robert, I have to tell you something."

"No, you don't."

She had met an agent, she told him, who had promised to put her on at the Olympia.

He could well imagine the rest. "You don't have to say any more," he told her.

Odette seemed grateful, and they went out and got into a taxi together, where she whispered into his neck that she wouldn't see the agent anymore.

The taxi moved down the Champs-Élyseés, crossed the Place de la Concorde, and turned onto the quay beside the Seine. The lampposts dropped pools of light onto the moving black water. Odette lived off the Place de la Bastille. The taxi would stop there eventually—he had only to go upstairs with her and she would be content, and he knew this.

But when the taxi did stop, when Odette tried to draw him out of the cab, he could not do it—he realized how much he still hoped for something else. He was going out of Paris very early in the morning, he told her. A case he was working on. But he would come see her again soon. When he got back. If she ever needed him, the Sûreté knew how to get in touch with him.

Without a word she got out of the cab. As she crossed toward the building, she did not look back. She was fumbling in her bag for her key, movements somehow more vulnerable than any he had ever seen her make, so that he nearly got out and went after her.

The next day he took the train to Rouen.

Detectives working out of Sûreté headquarters had no jurisdiction over the city itself, for Paris had its own police force. Instead they were sent out into the provinces to give help or direction as major crimes occurred.

The case in Rouen, which involved a headless corpse on a drifting pleasure boat near the estuary of the Seine, kept him occupied five days. He got back to Paris at suppertime on a Tuesday, and again knocked at his concierge's loge. But the woman greeted him in tears. Her cat had just died, she told him. The doctors had tried everything but had been unable to save it.

"I had him seventeen years," she said, weeping copiously.

Her grief was no less real because it was for a cat, and to break into it with a request for his mail seemed to him both callous and unnecessary. After so much time he no longer expected a letter, or even hoped for one. He pressed money into her hand—"to help with expenses"—and turned toward the stairs.

But the money had made the woman's face brighten. "Monsieur, wait," she said. "A letter came."

Bellarmine gazed down at the handwriting, the postmark.

"Bad news, monsieur?"

"I don't think so, no," he said, and thrust the envelope unopened into his breast pocket. He did not want to read it. He wanted to hear Jacqueline tell him what was in it.

That night he boarded the Blue Train for Nice.